PENGUIN CLASSICS

THE MAN IN THE IRON MASK

ALEXANDRE DUMAS was born in 1802 at Villers-Cotterêts. His father, the illegitimate son of a marquis, was a general in the Revolutionary armies, but died when Dumas was only four. He was brought up in straitened circumstances and received very little education. He entered the household of the future king, Louis-Philippe, and began reading voraciously. Later he entered the *cénacle* of Charles Nodier and began to write. In 1829 the production of his play, *Henri III et sa cour*, heralded twenty years of successful playwriting. In 1839 he turned his attention to writing historical novels, often using collaborators such as Auguste Maquet to suggest plots or historical background. His most successful novel, *The Count of Monte Cristo*, appearing during 1844–5, and *The Three Musketeers* in 1844. Other novels dealt with the wars of religion and the Revolution. Dumas wrote many of these for the newspaper, often in daily instalments, marshalling his formidable energies to produce ever more in order to pay off his debts. In addition, he wrote travel books, children's stories and his *Mémoires* which describes most amusingly his early life, his entry into Parisian literary circles and the 1830 Revolution. He died in 1870.

JOACHIM NEUGROSCHEL was born in Vienna and raised in New York. The winner of three PEN Translation Prizes, he has translated some 190 books from French, German, Italian, Yiddish, and Russian, including works by Proust and Kafka, books of poetry, plays, and screenplays. His numerous awards and grants include the translation prize of the French-American society. He translated the Penguin Classics editions of Mann's *Death in Venice*, Hesse's *Siddhartha*, and Sacher-Masoch's *Venus in Furs*.

FRANCINE DU PLESSIX GRAY is the author of *Rage and Fire*, *Lovers and Tyrants*, *Soviet Women*, and most recently *At Home with the Marquis de Sade*, which was a finalist for the Pulitzer Prize (available from Penguin). She wrote the biography of Simon Weil for the Penguin Lives series. She lives in Connecticut with her husband, the painter Cleve Gray.

ALEXANDRE
DUMAS

The Man in the Iron Mask

Translated by JOACHIM NEUGROSCHEL
Introduction by FRANCINE DU PLESSIX GRAY

PENGUIN BOOKS

PENGUIN BOOKS
Published by the Penguin Group
Penguin Group (USA) Inc., 375 Hudson Street, New York, New York 10014, U.S.A.
Penguin Group (Canada), 90 Eglinton Avenue East, Suite 700, Toronto, Ontario, Canada M4P 2Y3 (a division of Pearson Penguin Canada Inc.)
Penguin Books Ltd, 80 Strand, London WC2R 0RL, England
Penguin Ireland, 25 St Stephen's Green, Dublin 2, Ireland (a division of Penguin Books Ltd)
Penguin Group (Australia), 250 Camberwell Road, Camberwell, Victoria 3124, Australia (a division of Pearson Australia Group Pty Ltd)
Penguin Books India Pvt Ltd, 11 Community Centre, Panchsheel Park, New Delhi – 110 017, India
Penguin Group (NZ), 67 Apollo Drive, Rosedale, North Shore 0632, New Zealand (a division of Pearson New Zealand Ltd)
Penguin Books (South Africa) (Pty) Ltd, 24 Sturdee Avenue, Rosebank, Johannesburg 2196, South Africa

Penguin Books Ltd, Registered Offices: 80 Strand, London WC2R 0RL, England

This translation first published in Penguin Books 2003

13 15 17 19 20 18 16 14 12

This translation is based on chapters 207-266 of *Le vicomte Bragelonne III.*

LIBRARY OF CONGRESS CATALOGING IN PUBLICATION DATA
Dumas, Alexandre, 1802–1870.
[Homme au masque de fer. English]
The man in the iron mask / Alexandre Dumas ; translated by Joachim Neugroschel ; introduction by Francine du Plessix Gray.
p. cm. — (Penguin classics)
Includes bibliographical references.
ISBN 978-0-14-043924-3
1. France—History—Louis XIV, 1643–1715—Fiction. 2. Man in the Iron Mask—Fiction.
I. Neugroschel, Joachim. II. Title. III. Series.
PQ2227 .H6813 2003
843'.7—dc21 2002193017

Printed in the United States of America
Set in Sabon

Contents

Introduction

Everything about Dumas was colossal, prodigal, oversize: his very physique, a broad-beamed six-foot-two, very tall for a nineteenth-century Frenchman; his fabled erotic appetites; the sheer volume of his literary output—fifty plays, some ninety multi-tome novels, over sixty works of journalism, biography, essays, memoirs (his collected works come to 277 volumes); and last but not least, the prodigality of his heart and his purse: in a moment of penury, he once crossed Paris to borrow five francs from a friend, forgot his gloves, and when the friend's maid came to return them, tipped her with the very coin he had borrowed from her employer earlier that day.

Born in 1802 in Villers-Cotterêts, a small market town some fifty miles northeast of Paris, Alexandre Dumas was the child of an innkeeper's daughter and of one of Napoléon's most remarkable generals, Thomas-Alexandre Davy de La Pailleterie, who passed on to his son his admiration of feats of martial valor as well as his exotic physique. Thomas-Alexandre was born in the Caribbean island of Santo Domingo. His own mother was a Negro slave, Marie-Cessette Dumas; his father, the feckless voluptuary Marquis Alexandre Davy de La Pailleterie, was descended from ancient Norman aristocracy. Brought to France as a child, Thomas-Alexandre, upon reaching maturity and being disowned by his father for insulting one of his parent's paramours, proudly took on the surname of his black mother, Dumas, and enlisted in the army. During the Revolution of 1789, Dumas's prodigious courage allowed him to rise through the ranks with extraordinary speed. Notwithstanding his distinctly half-breed features, which led adversaries to refer to him as "the black devil," at the age of thirty-one Thomas-

Alexandre Dumas was named a general in the Revolutionary armies, and became one of Napoléon's most trusted companions in arms.

But General Dumas's volatile, moody, and insubordinate character—what his son would refer to as "a typically Creole blend of nonchalance, impetuosity, and inconstancy"[1]—was ill-suited to Bonaparte's need for unswerving adulation. Their rift, begun during the Egyptian campaign, compelled General Dumas to return to France. On the way home he was captured by the Piedmontese, and after two years of imprisonment which destroyed his health, he could do nothing to diminish Bonaparte's continuing hostility. Stricken off the active list, denied any back pay or military pension, the unfortunate soldier lived in near poverty for the six remaining years of his life. He found his only solace in the affection of his wife and of the son born to them after his return, Alexandre, a child as rosy-cheeked, blue-eyed, and fair-haired as any in his village; he only developed crisp curls and darker-than-average skin upon the onset of puberty.

Left penniless by her husband's death, little Alexandre's mother moved back to her parents' home in Villers-Cotterêts, where the future writer enjoyed a frugal but carefree country boyhood. He hunted in the woods with local poachers, satisfied his endless curiosity for animal life, and pursued studies with the local village priest, from whom he acquired, if little else, solid Latin, literary ambitions, and unusually fine handwriting. The latter talent served him well when, after a few years of dismal work in the office of a local notary, he left for Paris with two francs in his pocket; he soon landed a job as copy clerk in the office of the Duc d'Orléans, brother of the monarch of France, Charles X. He became stagestruck during his first year in Paris, began to attend the theater nightly, stayed up until dawn reading Corneille, Schiller, Shakespeare, and the Greek dramatists, and began trying his hand, unsuccessfully, at his first plays. The tall, handsome, affable youth with curly brown hair, piercing blue eyes, and irresistibly charming manners also struck up an affair with a pretty seamstress, Catherine Labay. Born in 1824, their son Alexandre, later known as "Alexandre *fils*" (to distinguish him from "Alexandre *père*") would eventually become a writer as renowned as his father.

No young man with literary ambitions moving to Paris in the early 1820s, as Dumas did, could be exempted from the influence of the Romantic movement just beginning to blossom in France. To Dumas's generation, which was that of Balzac and Hugo, an interest in Romanticism was far more than a search for heightened emotion and subjectivity. It also entailed a dedication to political and social reform, a commitment particularly intensified among French liberals by the oppressive and inept reign of the pompous, ultra-reactionary Charles X (1757–1836), youngest brother of Louis XVI and Louis XVIII. Beyond defying the despotism of this monarch and of the Roman Catholic Church, the Romanticism of the 1820s evoked renewed support for the poor and the oppressed, and a particular yearning to explore earlier, more heroic, more tumultuous periods of French history.

Dumas's first successful play, *Henri III et sa cour*, which dealt audaciously with the inequity and brutal excesses of sixteenth-century court aristocracy, gave French theatergoers just the kind of Sturm und Drang they had craved. Greeted by the audience with cries of delighted horror, Dumas became famous overnight and was thrust into the forefront of the Romantic revolution. In the following years his dramatic works, as well as his political activities and his tempestuous love affairs, became the talk of Paris. In the spring of 1830, when his second hit play, *Christine*, was performed, he began an affair with the actress Belle Krelsamer, with whom he would have a daughter, Marie. That summer, he manned the barricades in the revolt that unseated Charles X and placed the fallen king's relatively liberal cousin, Louis-Philippe, on the throne. The following two years saw the apex of Dumas's fame as a playwright. His play *Antony*, which, along with Victor Hugo's *Hernani*, enjoyed the most memorable premiere in the annals of romantic drama, thrust the audience into a state of near delirium. Through Dumas's psychological legerdemain, the play's heroine, the unfaithful wife Adèle, a prototype of Tolstoy's Anna Karenina, reversed all dramatic conventions by becoming an object of compassion and pity rather than of reprobation. "It was greeted with a frenzy of applause, of weeping, of sobbing, of shouting," Théophile Gautier wrote, "the burning passion of the play had set fire to all hearts."[2] As Dumas rose from his seat, he was seized by a crowd of brawling admirers who tore off shreds of his clothing to retain as mementos of his play.

Eighteen thirty-two, the year another audacious Dumas play, *La Tour de Nesle*, was performed with equally tumultuous success, also marked the beginning of his longest-lived affair, with the actress Ida Ferrier. After a stormy two years in which he carried on simultaneously with three mistresses—Ida, Belle Krelsamer, and the possessive young matron who had preceded her, Mélanie Waldor—he took up with Ida full time, and eventually married her (in order, he explained to his friends, "to get rid of her more easily through a legal separation").[3] The ambitious, consummately narcissistic Ida, who at the beginning of their liaison was a radiant blond with facial features of singular beauty, was a skillful and accomplished hostess. And for the first time Dumas was able to run his household in the sumptuous manner he had always dreamed of. The couple held ostentatious dinner parties to which invitations were much sought, and at which the author inevitably dazzled his guests with his genial bonhomie and lavish hospitality. The culminating soiree of their eight years together was a masked ball at which some five hundred members of *le tout Paris* appeared: the aging General de La Fayette; Eugène Delacroix, who designed the wall decorations and came to the party dressed as Dante; the actresses Mlle. George and Mlle. Mars; the composer Rossini (in the costume of Figaro); the poet Alfred de Musset (dressed as a character of Molière's). After a gargantuan three A.M. meal the revelers spilled out of the apartment and onto the street, dancing a frenzied *galop*. It was an event most fitting to the jovial, fast-living Dumas, who indeed would have liked all of life to be a magnificent procession, held at a galloping rhythm. He was as flamboyant and egotistic as he was compassionate and generous, and loved every ounce of the adulation he received. Upon being bestowed the Legion of Honor in 1845 he wore it conspicuously, with a childish pleasure, alongside Spanish, Belgian,

Swedish, and other decorations, and on official occasions his chest became a clanging showcase of beribboned medals.

But Dumas's personal and literary success received mixed reviews among the Parisian elite. The long-standing view of Dumas as a happy-go-lucky, bon vivant prodigy should be replaced with a more complex image: in part because of his mulatto origins, society at large, while rewarding him amply for his talent, remained wary of his social persona. There were many racist overtones in Parisians' reactions to Dumas. Balzac referred to him as "That coon."[4] The famous actress Mlle. Mars pretended she knew he'd been in a room by its smell: "Open all the windows, it smells of Negro!"[5] she would exclaim after the playwright had visited the Comédie Française. "He's so vain," another Parisian wit commented, "that he's capable of getting up behind his own carriage to make you think he has a black footman."[6] Censoring Dumas's exuberant prolificity, the poet Louise Colet, not herself not a model of decorum, spoke for many Parisian literati when she wrote, in a letter to Victor Hugo, "What's now missing in France, in poetry and literature, is patience. In all domains one is hasty, precipitous, noisome: what an example that poor Alexandre Dumas offers! Certainly he has imagination and a kind character, but his boasting and ostentation shock and revolt."[7]

Vogues for literary genres seem to have been as fickle in the mid-nineteenth century as they are today. In the late 1830s, the popularity of Dumas's historical plays, which he was churning out at the rate of two a year, began to wane. Acutely sensitive to the demands of the marketplace, in 1838 he sensed a reawakened interest in the historical novel, which had found a huge audience in France some decades earlier through Sir Walter Scott's translated works. A few of Dumas's contemporaries had already experimented with the form: Victor Hugo's *Notre-Dame de Paris*, Balzac's *Les Chouans*, and Alfred de Vigny's *Cinq-Mars* had enjoyed a considerable *succés d'estime* but did not reach a vast public. With his habitual confidence, Dumas felt he could score a critical and commercial success by revitalizing the genre. There was another, more industrial force at play in his decision to move on to the novel: the growth of the *roman-feuilleton,* or serialized novel, was being pioneered in those years by the country's two most influential papers, *La Presse* and *Le Siècle.* In 1838 the latter publication asked him for a fictional text they could serialize. Dumas set to work reading reams from French historical chroniclers such as Joinville and Froissart looking for episodes that would particularly entice him; he carefully studied Scott's techniques, particularly his method of delineating characters in a firm, painterly way.

Realizing the vast research such books might entail, Dumas then enrolled collaborators to help him in the project. Over the years he employed scores of them, several of which he shared with popular colleagues such as George Sand and Victor Hugo. But his principal *nègre* (the common French euphemism, still in wide use today, for research assistant) was one Auguste Maquet, the erudite son of a wealthy industrialist who taught history at a prominent Paris lycée. He did not much enjoy teaching, and eagerly accepted Dumas's offer to collaborate on his historical novels, for which he was paid some 10,000 francs per manuscript, a handsome sum for a young intellectual. As generous with his name as he was with his cash, Dumas offered to have Maquet co-sign their works, but the newspapers vetoed the notion. "A page signed by Dumas is worth three francs a line," the editor of *Le Siècle* decreed, "a page signed Dumas-Maquet is worth thirty sous."[8]

So for the following decade, at the rate of two a year, the novels appeared, produced at prodigious speed like all of Dumas's works. The trilogy which begins with *La Reine Margot* tells of the struggle between Catherine de Médicis and Henri de Navarre, the future Henri IV. *Les Quarante Cinq* and *La Dame de Monsoreau* are also set in the second half of the sixteenth century, in the intrigue-laden reign of the weak, corrupt Henri III. *The Queen's Necklace* and *Le Chevalier de Maison Rouge* concern Marie-Antoinette. *Joseph Balsamo* and *Ange Pitou* take place in the Revolutionary era, the last decades of the eighteenth century. *The Count of Monte Cristo,* which, along with his Musketeers series was the most dazzlingly successful of his novels, was a tale of revenge set in the first decades of the nineteenth century. Dumas's singular ambition was to practice a kind of historical imperialism, and annex as much of French history as he could into his novels. "How shall I achieve that?" he wrote. "By working like no one has ever worked before, by suppressing all of life's details, by suppressing sleep."[9]

Never in the annals of French literature was there a fecundity comparable to that of Dumas between 1845 and 1855. Throughout that decade a score of his novels, each of them running to thousands of pages and earning him as much as 100,000 francs a piece, were serialized in Parisian newspapers. His habit was to sit at his worktable for a minimum of ten hours a day, covering his sheets of lavender-blue paper at extraordinary speed, rarely crossing anything out or revising, never using accents, commas, or any punctuation, which his numerous secretaries would insert later. He usually worked on several fictional texts simultaneously, sometimes writing narratives for several different newspaper serializations at one time. Believing that white paper ruined eyesight, he color-coded his writing sheets accordingly: lavender-blue for his novels, yellow for his plays, and pink for his magazine articles (which continued to proliferate at an unabated rate while he penned his fictions). Dumas's productivity became legendary, and deepened the literary elite's ambivalence about his work. Sainte Beuve made sly comments about Dumas's "industrial literature." Caricatures showed Dumas seated at his worktable with four separate pens between the fingers of each hand as a waiter ladled soup into his open mouth. There were rumors that he ran a literary sweatshop in his basement, keeping a dozen poor devils in line through the use of a whip, like half-caste overseers in the French colonies. A popular journalist complained that "M. Dumas, the plague of our time, infected by the industrial contagion, seems to have leagued himself body and soul to the cult of the golden calf."[10] Another pundit published a pamphlet entitled "The Novel Factory: Maison Alexandre Dumas et Cie." "Everyone has read Dumas," so the popular saying went, "but nobody could possibly read *all* of Dumas, not even Dumas himself."[11]

Despite these grumblings, the decade in which Dumas wrote

his historical novels, the 1840s, was that of his greatest popularity with the public. Audiences stood up to cheer him whenever he entered a public place. His imposing physique had not yet begun to thicken, he continued to disarm all acquaintances with his geniality, generosity, and wit. This was also the happiest period of Dumas's life: he had divorced the rambunctious Ida, who had gone on to marry an Italian nobleman. A loving father, he was finally able to draw close to his son Alexandre *fils*, now a dashing litterateur in his early twenties who had loathed his stepmother. Father and son moved in with each other and led a carefree, dissolute bachelor life, passing women from bed to bed. They also began to travel widely together, for Dumas found yet another remunerative form in the travel essay. At last he was enjoying the *modus vivendi* of independence and gaiety best suited to his temperament. His greatest happiness consisted of an isolated room; a wooden table laden with immense piles of paper at which he worked ten to twelve hours; a son and a daughter whom he could treat as comrades; undemanding young women occasionally at his beck and call; spirited friends who could regale him with scintillating conversation and help protect him from creditors and plaintive mistresses. Such were the blissful conditions he enjoyed while writing the most enduringly popular of his fictions, the vast series that begins with *The Three Musketeers* and ends with *Le Vicomte de Bragelonne* (it is the last fourth of the latter novel that comprises what we now know as *The Man in the Iron Mask*).

Dumas first conceived of *The Three Musketeers* series in the early 1840s, when he came across an apocryphal autobiography entitled *Les Mémoires de M. d'Artagnan*, by one Courtilz de Sandras. First published in 1704, it documented the dull, plodding life of a true-life officer in Louis XIII's army. Even the names Athos, Porthos, and Aramis, with small spelling changes, were found in the volume. But whereas Courtilz's three companions were unlikable adventurers, Dumas transformed them into thoroughly lovable cavaliers, some of whose traits are readily traceable to Dumas himself as well as to the virtues he most admired in his own father. The general's fabled ability to withstand one hundred enemies with the might of only his sword obviously inspired the Musketeers' own feats of Superman-like valor. Porthos's Rabelaisian hedonism, his taste for bacchanalian feasts, and easy loves are clearly attributes Dumas recognized in himself. The aristocratic melancholy of Athos might well project Dumas's idealized view of his own forebears, the Marquesses Davy de La Pailleterie. The deviousness, elegance, and devouring ambition of Aramis presents an archetype of the perpetually scheming Jesuit priest held by every liberal, anti-clerical Frenchman of Dumas's generation. As for d'Artagnan, who may be the most fictional of the four central characters, he embodies Dumas's most cherished themes: the superiority of friendship, loyalty, and fraternal bonding to any heterosexual passion; the potential triumph of agile resourcefulness over material or political power; the *débrouillardise*—street wisdom—that allows a lone individual such as d'Artagnan to outwit even the mightiest monarch on earth, his own king.

Are Dumas's historical novels true to history? Hardly. He had little interest in erudition, and no pretension whatsoever at being either a scholar or a researcher—"What's history?" he once asked. "A nail on which I hang my novels." A characteristically glaring anachronism occurs in *The Iron Mask*: Dumas states that King Louis XIV is twenty-four years old at the beginning of the narrative, which would place the story in 1666; yet in that same span of narrated days we see Louis arresting his Superintendent of Finances, Nicolas Fouquet, an historical incident that occurred in 1661, a mere few months after the king took power. Dumas could not have cared less. For a decade Dumas and his sidekick, Maquet, rampaged and pillaged through history, inventing, altering, distorting—doing whatever was needed to hold their readers spellbound. Once Maquet had provided him with a narrative skeleton, Dumas began to wield his amazing gifts of animation, which he exercised through two particular skills: one was his deftness for derring-do and melodramatic suspense: without much straining the reader's credibility, heroes spring back to power after near-fatal adventures, reappear at the door soon after they've been hurled out the window, duel their way out of any quandary.

Dumas also had a genius for flamboyant dialogues, a talent well honed, of course, by his training as a playwright. He became so famed for the ebullience of his literary repartees that in the 1840s the following parody of a Dumas exchange was published in the French press:

"Have you seen him?"
"Who?"
"Dumas."
"Father?"
"Yes."
"What a man!"
"Indeed."
"What fire!"
"Assuredly."
"And what fecundity!"
"The devil he has!"

A conversation from *The Man in the Iron Mask*:

"Tell the coachman to stop, Porthos, we're here."
"This is the place?"
"Yes."
"How can that be? We're at Les Halles . . ."
"That's right, but take a look."
"Well, I'm looking, and I see . . ."
"What?"
"That we're at Les Halles, damn it!"

It was this cinematic, rat-tat-tat vivacity of pace that Dumas strove for, rather than any historical versimilitude. And it may be his very failure of historical precision that projects Dumas's novels out of real time, and endows them with a perennial and enduring freshness.

The Man in the Iron Mask was never conceived by Dumas as an independent novel. It was in fact a smart publishing ploy, already undertaken in the mid-nineteenth century,[12] to decant the most exciting portion of the Musketeers trilogy's last chapters—approximately the last quarter of the multivolume *Vicomte de Bragelonne*—into one easily readable narrative carafe. Over the decades, different editors have dealt with the Iron Mask episodes in various ways. A highly popular 1943 Dodd Mead edition, for instance, states that it has "taken from the original novel those incidents and episodes which relate particularly to the man in the iron mask. . . . Here and there, at considerable intervals," the editor admits, "a connecting phrase or two [were] added to bridge the gap where some unrelated episode is omitted."

This Penguin Classics edition of *The Man in the Iron Mask* is one of the first which has not been submitted to any such doctoring. Beginning with the chapter of *Le Vicomte de Bragelonne* that is entitled "The Prisoner" and ending with the entire trilogy's very last chapter, "The Death of M. d'Artagnan," it reproduces Dumas's text in its original integrity. Some readers, however, might need elucidation concerning France's political situation at the time *The Man in the Iron Mask* begins.

King Louis XIII, who is omnipresent alongside his adviser Cardinal de Richelieu in *The Three Musketeers*, died when his oldest son, the future Louis XIV, was five years old. His wife, Anne of Austria, and her chief councilor, the wily Cardinal de Mazarin, ruled as co-regents until the young king's majority. When Louis XIV acceded to the throne in 1661 he was still deeply marked by the humiliations he had suffered under their tutelage. Moreover, Louis XIV's youth had been tormented by the rebellion of powerful nobles called the Fronde (1648–1653). This civil war, which pillaged and greatly destabilized national security, instilled in the young monarch a horror of any sort of political disorder, and ideally conditioned him for autocratic rule. Not endowed with exceptional gifts, he was nevertheless blessed with large measures of industriousness and discipline, phenomenal health, an astute judgment of human nature, and radiant handsomeness, qualities that would soon help him become Europe's most charismatic, imposing ruler.

The young Louis XIV portrayed in *The Man in the Iron Mask* is bent on centralizing his personal power by avoiding the possibility of another Fronde, or the ascendance of powerful figures such as Richelieu and Mazarin. He is fulfilling these goals by weakening France's more prestigious nobles and the sway of his ministerial advisers, whom he has exclusively chosen from the ranks of the bourgeoisie. A fan of the Divide and Rule principle, Louis encourages a keen sense of rivalry between all members of his entourage. The infighting between his two closest advisers, Comptroller General Jean-Baptiste Colbert and Superintendent of Finances Nicolas Fouquet, first dramatized in Chapter 6 of *The Man in the Iron Mask*, seems to delight the king. Fouquet, a former lawyer and a protégé of Mazarin's, had hoped to be made head of government upon Louis XIV's ascendance to the throne. But Louis has overlooked him in favor of Colbert, in part because of Fouquet's close association with the hated Cardinal Mazarin and in part because of the dread and suspicion aroused in the king by Fouquet's ostentatious flaunting of wealth.

This particular subplot of *The Man in the Iron Mask* comes close to being historically accurate: In fact as well as in Dumas's fiction, the great fête held by Fouquet at his superb castle Vaux-le-Vicomte, which far surpassed any yet staged by a French monarch (Chapter 15), humiliated Louis XIV by its sheer splendor, and clinched the minister's doom. A few weeks after his big bash Fouquet was arrested and sentenced to life imprisonment, a sentence he would serve until his death two decades later. This would leave the field free for the rule of the glacial, ruthlessly efficient Colbert, who would remain the King's second-in-command for the rest of his own life, and who in the last pages of the novel, hands d'Artagnan the highest honor any French officer could ever receive: a field marshal's baton.

What about Dumas's other Musketeers, whom we last encountered in that volume of their trilogy called *Twenty Years Later*? *The Man in the Iron Mask* begins a decade later still. Porthos, wealthy and retired from active duty, is now Baron de Vallon. Athos, Comte de Fère, is widowed and lives on his country estate with his beloved son, Raoul, Vicomte de Bragelonne. The supremely ambitious Aramis has become the Bishop of Vannes; and unbeknownst to most, he has also risen to be the Superior General of the Jesuits, a post that in the seventeenth century was often covertly held. As for D'Artagnan, the only one of the original four Musketeers who is still in military service, he is captain of the King's Guard and the monarch's closest confidant, subject to Louis's orders alone. In the chapters of *Vicomte de Bragelonne* that immediately precede the *Man in the Iron Mask*, Raoul has been renounced by his fiancée, Louise de la Vallière, who has recently become Louis XIV's mistress. And Athos, who has tried to plead for his son with the king, has aroused such great anger on the part of Louis XIV that he has been imprisoned for life in the Bastille, a fate from which he is about to be rescued by d'Artagnan's diplomacy and cunning.

The central plot of *The Man in the Iron Mask*, however, is as far-fetched a fiction as Dumas ever set into an historical frame, and has no factual basis whatsoever: It revolves about Aramis's attempt to replace Louis XIV, whom he considers to be already corrupted "by the license of supreme power," with his twin brother, Philippe (no chronicler has ever even suggested that Louis XIV ever had a twin). As Dumas's fictional narrative has it, Philippe has been secretly imprisoned since infancy, his parents having resolved, upon the royal twins' birth, that they wished to avoid any fratricidal struggle for the throne. In the book's opening pages, Aramis is visiting Philippe at the Bastille, and is about to apprise him of his royal birth, the nature of his fate, and Aramis's determination to put him on the throne of France. Pages later, in the chapter entitled "Crown and Tiara," another aspect of Aramis's ambition is clarified: In return for installing Philippe on the throne, he wishes for nothing less then the papacy—the pontiff was often chosen, in that century, by the supremely influential king of France. ("I will have given you the French throne," Aramis says to Philippe, "you will give me Saint Peter's throne.")[13]

Other historical high points to note throughout the narrative: Chapter 19, which displays the craftiness with which d'Artagnan handles the king's orders to imprison Fouquet, for whom the Musketeer feels a secret sympathy. Chapter 24, in which Dumas creates a brilliant, tumultuous scene in which Louis XIV and his twin brother, whom the wily Aramis has managed temporarily to spring from the Bastille, confront each other in front of the assembled court. And above all those chapters—particularly Chapter 53—in which another central theme of the entire trilogy is revealed: Playing to the king's patriotism (and also to the sentiments of Dumas's *embourgeoisé*, starved-for-heroism nineteenth-century readers), d'Artagnan manages to alter Louis XIV's stubborn will by recalling those principles of honor that prevailed in earlier, more heroic moments of French history. These ideals have been lost in the "baseness, intrigue, cowardice" that suffuse the fawning upstarts of Louis XIV's court; they are only retained, in d'Artagnan's view, by the impecunious, plain-mannered, ancient *noblesse d'épée*—the provincial gentry from which all four Musketeers have sprung, and who are now "the only models of the valor of former times. . . . Whatever remains to you of the grand nobility, guard it with a jealous eye," d'Artagnan had warned the king in one of the later chapters of *Le Vicomte de Bragelonne*, "of courtiers you will always have enough. . . . Bad kings are hated. Poor kings are driven away."[14] Eerie premonitions indeed of the following century's apocalyptic events, in which the ancient country gentry remained the monarchy's most stalwart supporters.

Even though not composed as an individual unity, *The Man in the Iron Mask* (so titled because Louis XIV eventually orders his unfortunate twin brother to be imprisoned for life with an iron mask placed over his head) may well be the most psychologically intricate of Dumas's Musketeers series: it differs from its predecessors by the great complexity of its protagonists' choices. Whereas in earlier volumes the four Musketeers acted in total accord ("All for one and one for all!"), the issue of the two contending kings poses a considerable new rift between them. Aramis easily enjoins Porthos and Athos in his plot to replace Louis with his twin brother (Athos, in particular, looks on Louis XIV as his deadly enemy because he has brought disgrace on his son), but what dreadful choices his comrades' conspiracy creates for d'Artagnan, who has been Louis's friend and protector since the monarch's earliest youth! D'Artagnan is all too painfully aware that the gentle, pacific pretender, Philippe, whose wisdom has been honed in suffering, is of character far superior to that of the vengeful, petty king. Yet an anointed monarch, in a faithful soldier's code of honor, is an anointed monarch to be protected and served. And the graying Musketeer is torn—his dilemma has the grandeur of Greek drama—between the abstract principles of virtue embodied by the pretender and the ancient standards of fidelity incarnated in Louis XIV. Moreover, how can he, Captain of the Musketeers, remain faithful to his code of honor *and* carry out Louis's orders to imprison his three beloved comrades? D'Artagnan's implacable sense of justice, and his fidelity to his friends, might well predispose him to cast his lot with the good pretender. . . . Which decision does he make, and how does he balance this conflict of conscience with his loyalty to the comrades of his youth?

As the French newspapers used to print after each installment of Dumas's novels, "*La suite au prochain numéro.*" It is the Byzantine subtlety of d'Artagnan's decisions, and the cool, resourceful wisdom with which he arrives at them, that has made him one of the most enduring and admirable characters in world literature.

Over the past eighty years, scores of film renditions of *The Man in the Iron Mask* have come to the screen. The most recent star-studded version, made in 1998, features the great Irish actor Gabriel Byrne as d'Artagnan, Jeremy Irons as Aramis, Gerard Dépardieu as Porthos, and John Malkovich as Athos; Leonardo di Caprio offers comic relief, starring in the dual roles of Louis XIV and his twin brother Philippe.

Dumas's demise was in good part caused by the most endearing of his virtues—his naïve optimism, generosity, and juvenile insouciance. ("Permit me to present to you my revered parent," Dumas *fils* used to introduce Dumas *père*, "a big child I had when I was very young.")[15] At the peak of his success, Dumas founded a playhouse—the Théatre Historique—that would be exclusively dedicated to staging his dramas. He also built himself a vast, extravagant mansion at Marly-le-Roi, in the Paris suburbs, in which a succession of plebeian stage ladies lived at his expense, often with large families in tow, helping themselves liberally to his till. Both ventures failed catastrophically in the aftermath of the Revolution of 1848, which replaced Louis-Philippe with the equally lackluster President Louis-Napoléon, Bonaparte's nephew. The French economy suffered a terrible setback, and Dumas's theater went bankrupt. The author suddenly found himself hundreds of thousands of francs in debt. The suddenness with which this multimillionaire became a pauper was in part caused by his childish irresponsibility and by the fact that he was prodigally spendthrift. Just as he would have been perfectly happy to share literary credits for all his historical novels with Auguste Maquet, so Dumas had always looked on money as something to spend immediately or give away.

In 1852, partly to flee his creditors, partly to protest the growing autocracy of President Louis-Napoléon, who that year crowned himself Emperor Napoléon III of France, Dumas fled to Belgium for a year. The only pleasure of his exile was to learn that his son, Alexandre *fils*, was now a pillar of the literary establishment and who occasionally looked askançe at his father's wild ways, had become very famous in his own right: he had scored an immense hit with his play *La Dame aux camélias*, which would remain the most popular drama of the Second Empire, and provided the libretto for Verdi's opera *La Traviata*. (Ironically, it was the sanctimonious Dumas *fils*, whose works have hardly stood the test of time, who would ultimately be taken into the Académie Française, an honor consistently denied to the enduringly cherished Dumas *père* because of his flashy, often scandalous way of life.)

The aging reprobate refused to calm down or to behave with the decorum the French expect from a venerable writer. His last fifteen years were very restless. Having found a good source of funds in publishing travel books, he began to roam throughout Europe. He traveled to England, where he remained for an entire year; to the island of Guernsey, where he visited with Victor Hugo, who had been exiled for his radical views by Emperor Napoléon III; to Greece; to Russia, which he explored for nine months. In the 1860s he rushed to Italy to lend his support to Garibaldi's uprising and spent months shipping arms to the Italian leader. Italians took warmly to the genial, rotund, exuberant old man with crisp gray curls; and while in

Naples he published a newspaper, *L'Independente*, and wrote an eight-volume history of the city's Bourbon rulers. Then Dumas suddenly turned his interest to archaeology: upon his request, Garibaldi named him superintendent of excavations of Pompeii, a task that he fulfilled with great energy and efficiency until the Naples city council turned chauvinistic, decided that a foreigner should not hold the post, and refused him the proper funds.

Throughout these years, whether in Italy or France, the corpulent sextagenarian continued to sugar-daddy his way through a new series of lovers. In 1861 one of his mistresses, Emily Cordier, bore him a daughter, Micaela, whom he doted on, and whom he legally recognized, as he had his other two children. Dumas's last major liaison was also his most scandalous. In 1868 he took up with a hustling American actress called Adah Menken, who throughout her career had arranged to be photographed with each of the famous men she had conquered. An impecunious photographer took pictures of her, barely clad, sitting on Dumas's vast lap, and published it in the newspapers. This caused a considerable ruckus, abruptly ended the romance, and incited Dumas to sue the photographer (he handily won the case). Unperturbed, Dumas consoled himself by venturing into yet another literary genre that was totally novel to him, the cookbook. He had always been a fabled chef, often concocting the principal dishes at his own dinner parties. He now set to writing his massive *Grand Dictionaire de Cuisine*, which is his last finished work, and has remained a classic among gastronomes throughout the world. Until his final months his brevity of wit, his *sens du mot juste*, never abated. The year before his death, when asked how he felt upon reaching his sixty-seventh year, he answered "*Tout passe, tout lasse, tout casse*"[16], which along with another of his phrasings, "*Cherchez la femme*," has remained a cherished euphemism of the French language.

In his last decade, the loyal Dumas, however penurious, continued to offer solace and funds to old friends more direly in need than he was. He totally supported the impoverished retired actress Mlle. George in her final years; and he was the only person to attend the deathbed of Jeanne Dorval, the greatest actress of her age who had starred in innumerable Dumas plays. But in 1870 Dumas's own health, which for decades had so triumphantly withstood the strains of overwork and high living, began to fail. When France declared war on Prussia in July he was in Marseilles on a rest cure. News of the disastrous defeats dealt to France in the first weeks of the campaign caused the patriot to suffer a mild stroke. He headed back toward Paris, but his son, fearful that the city might be besieged or pillaged, insisted that his father seek refuge in the coastal Normandy town of Dieppe, where Alexandre *fils* had moved with his wife and children. Once in his family's care, Dumas's powers deteriorated rapidly. Lying in his room within sound of the distant breakers, he began to sleep most of the day, unable to concentrate on anything more arduous than an occasional game of dominoes with his two granddaughters.

A few days before his death, which would come on December 5, 1870, at the age of sixty-eight, Dumas had a dream which perplexed him greatly. He dreamed that he was standing on the peak of a pyramid-shaped hill totally composed of his books, which were piled up, one on top of the other, like blocks of masonry. Little by little the ground shifted and gave way beneath his feet, and the mound he had been standing on became nothing more than a little heap of gray volcanic ashes. "Alexandre," he asked his son the following morning, "on your soul and conscience, do you think anything of mine will survive?"[17] Alexandre *fils* reassured his father eloquently that his oeuvre would endure, and the two men embraced.

NOTES

1. F.W.J. Hemmings, *Alexandre Dumas, the King of Romance*. New York City: Charles Scribner's & Sons, 1979, p. 15.
2. André Maurois, *Les Trois Dumas*. Paris, France: Hachette, 1957, p. 97.
3. Hemmings, p. 112.
4. Ibid., p. 135.
5. Ibid., p. 54; slightly different rendering of same citation in Maurois.

6. Hemmings, p. 135.
7. Colet to Hugo, letter of November 1854, cited in *Rage and Fire: A Life of Louise Colet*, Francine du Plessix Gray, editor. New York: Simon and Schuster, 1995.
8. Maurois, p. 174.
10. Ibid., p. 182.
11. Hemmings p. 136.
12. The first silent film version of *The Man in the Iron Mask* was made in 1913.
13. *The Man in the Iron Mask*, galley p. 157.
14. Dumas, *The Man in the Iron Mask*. New York, Dodd Mead, 1939 and 1943, with a preface by Emile van Vliet, p. 10.
    This edition, the one I read at the Spence School in the late 1940s, begins at an earlier stage in the *Vicomte de Bragelonne* narrative (three chapters earlier) than the Penguin Classics edition.
15. Hemmings, p. 111.
16. Hemmings, p. 209.
17. Ibid., p. 212.

THE MAN IN THE IRON MASK

I
The Prisoner

Ever since Aramis's bizarre transformation into the confessor of the order, Baisemeaux, the warden of the Bastille, had not been the same man.

Previously, so far as the worthy warden was concerned, Aramis had been a prelate to whom he owed respect and a friend to whom he owed gratitude. But starting with that revelation that had just thrown him for a loop, Baisemeaux was a subaltern and Aramis a superior.

The warden lit a lantern himself, summoned a jailer, and, turning back to Aramis, he said, "At your orders, monsieur."

Aramis merely nodded, as if to say "Very good!," and motioned as if to say "Lead the way!" Baisemeaux started off. Aramis followed him.

It was a beautiful starry night. The trio's footsteps echoed on the flagstones of the terraces, and the jangling of the keys swinging from the turnkey's belt rose all the way up the towers, as if to remind the prisoners that freedom was beyond their reach.

You could have thought that the change in Baisemeaux had infected the turnkey. During Aramis's earlier visit, the turnkey had been so nosy and inquisitive. This time, however, he was not only mute but also cool and calm. With his head lowered, he seemed afraid to prick up his ears.

Thus, upon arriving at the foot of the Bertaudière, they climbed its two landings, silent and a bit slow. For Baisemeaux, though obedient, was anything but eager to comply.

At last they reached the cell. The jailer didn't need to look for the key, he was already holding it. The door opened.

Baisemeaux prepared to enter the cell. But Aramis, halting at the threshold, said, "Regulations do not allow the warden to hear the prisoner's confession."

The warden bowed, making way for Aramis, who took the turnkey's lantern, stepped inside, then signaled him to close the door.

He stood there for an instant, listening hard, trying to tell whether Baisemeaux and the turnkey were leaving. Then, assured by the softening sounds that indicated they had left the tower, Aramis placed the lantern on the table and peered around.

Under ample, half-drawn curtains, the young man, whom Aramis had already visited, was resting on a green serge bed, which, aside from being newer, was completely identical to all the other beds in the Bastille. In accordance with dungeon rules, there was no light. The prisoner had had to put out his candle at the hour of curfew. You could tell he got special treatment, since he enjoyed the rare privilege of keeping his light on until the curfew bell rang.

Near his bed, remarkably fresh clothes were lying on a big leather armchair with twisted legs. A small, sadly neglected table without quills, books, paper, or ink stood next to the window. Several full plates testified that the prisoner had barely touched his meal.

Aramis gazed at the young man lying on the bed, his face half-hidden by his arms. The arrival of a visitor did not make him change his posture; he was waiting or sleeping.

Aramis lit the candle with the help of the lantern, gently pushed back the chair, and approached the bed with a visible blend of interest and respect.

The young man lifted his head. "What do you want of me?"

"Didn't you ask for a confessor?" Aramis responded.

"Yes."

"Because you're sick?"

"Yes."

"Very sick?"

The young man gave Aramis a piercing look and said, "Thank you." Then, after a moment of silence, he continued, "I've already seen you."

Aramis bowed. No doubt the prisoner's scrutiny, that revelation of a cold, sly, and domineering character imprinted on the face of the Bishop of Vannes, was quite unsettling, for the young man added, "I feel better."

"And so?"

"Well, since I'm better, I don't think I need a confessor."

"Don't you even need the hair shirt that was announced by the note in your bread?"

The young man shuddered. But before he could say yes or no, Aramis went on: "And don't you even need this priest who has something important to reveal to you?"

"If that's the case," said the young man, falling back on his pillow, "I'm listening."

Aramis stared harder at him, surprised by that air of simple and comfortable majesty, which cannot be acquired unless God places it in the blood or the heart.

"Have a seat, sir," said the prisoner.

Aramis obeyed with a bow.

"How does the Bastille agree with you?" asked the bishop.

"Very nicely."

"You're not suffering?"

"No."

"You long for nothing?"

"Nothing."

"Not even freedom?"

"What do you call freedom, sir?" the prisoner asked in a belligerent tone.

"I call freedom flowers, air, daylight, stars, the joy of running to wherever your fidgety twenty-year-old legs may carry you."

The young man smiled. In resignation or disdain—it was hard to tell which.

"Look," he said, "I've got two roses in this Japanese vase, two beautiful roses that were picked as buds yesterday evening in the warden's garden. They bloomed this morning, opening their vermilion calyxes before my gaze. With each fold in their petals they released the treasure of their fragrance. My room is filled with their perfume. Look at those two roses. They're beautiful among roses, and roses are the most beautiful flowers. So why would you want me to desire other flowers if I have the most beautiful flowers right here?"

Aramis eyed him in surprise.

"If flowers are freedom," the prisoner mournfully went on, "then I've got freedom since I have flowers."

"Yes! But air!" cried Aramis. "Air is crucial to life!"

"Fine, sir. Come over to the window. It's open. Between the sky and the earth the wind is rolling its swirls of ice, fire, warm vapors, or soft breezes. The air coming from there caresses my face when I picture myself swimming in the void while I climb on this chair, sit on its back, and pass my arm around this bar, which supports me."

Aramis's face turned gloomier as the young man spoke.

"Daylight?" he continued. "I've got something better than daylight. I've got the sun—a friend who visits me every day without the warden's permission, without the turnkey's company. My friend enters my room through the window, he draws a large, long square, which runs from the window and chews my bed drapes down to the fringes. This radiant square grows from ten A.M. till noon, and decreases from one P.M. till three, very slowly, as if, after hurrying to see me, he regrets leaving me. By the time his final ray disappears, I've enjoyed four hours of his presence. Isn't that enough? I'm told that there are poor wretches who dig in quarries, laborers who drudge in mines, and who never see the sun."

Aramis wiped his forehead.

"As for the stars, which are lovely to see," the young man went on, "they are all alike except in size and intensity. I'm favored among mortals, for if you hadn't lit that candle, you could have seen the beautiful star that I was gazing at from my bed before your arrival and that was caressing my eyes with its radiance."

Aramis lowered his head. He felt submerged in the bitter wave of this sinister philosophy, which is the religion of captivity.

"So much, then, for flowers, air, daylight, and stars," said the young man with the same tranquillity. "All that's left is my strolls. Don't I stroll all day long through the warden's garden in fair weather and in here in rainy weather, in the coolness if it's warm out, in the warmth if it's cold, thanks to my fireplace in the winter? Ah! Believe me, sir," the prisoner added, his expression not devoid of a certain bitterness, "men have done for me everything that a man can hope for, can desire."

"Men perhaps!" said Aramis, raising his head. "But you seem to be forgetting God."

"That's right, I've forgotten God," the prisoner replied, unmoved. "But why do you tell me that? Why bother talking to prisoners about God?"

Aramis stared hard at this singular young man, who combined a martyr's resignation with an atheist's smile.

"Isn't God in everything?" Aramis murmured in reproach.

"I'd say He's at the bottom of everything," the prisoner answered in a firm tone.

"Fine!" said Aramis. "But let's get back to what we were talking about."

"I couldn't ask for more," said the young man.

"I'm your confessor."

"Yes."

"Well, as my penitent, you owe me the truth."

"I ask for nothing more than to tell you the truth."

"Every prisoner has committed a crime that has landed him in prison. What crime did you commit?"

"You already asked me that the first time you saw me," said the prisoner.

"And you've eluded my question, both then and now."

"And why do you think I'll respond today?"

"Because today I'm your confessor."

"Well, then, if you want me to tell you what crime I've committed, please explain to me what a crime is. Now, if I know of nothing to reproach myself for, I say that I'm not a criminal."

"Sometimes a person can be a criminal in the eyes of the great men of the world, not only for having committed crimes but because we know that crimes have been committed."

The prisoner was extremely attentive.

"Yes," he said after a moment of silence, "I understand. Yes, you're right, sir. In that case, I could be a criminal in the eyes of great men."

"Ah, so you do know of something?" asked Aramis, who believed he had glimpsed not the defect but the joining of the cuirass.

"No, I know of nothing," replied the young man. "But sometimes I muse, and at those moments I tell myself . . ."

"What do you tell yourself?"

"That if I keep musing, I will either go crazy or unearth a number of things."

"What happens then?" Aramis asked impatiently.

"Then I stop."

"You stop?"

"Yes. My head is heavy, my thoughts grow sad. I feel boredom overcoming me. I desire . . ."

"What?"

"I don't know, I don't want to be caught desiring things that I don't have—I'm so content with what I do have."

"Are you scared of death?" Aramis asked, a bit anxious.

"Yes." The young man smiled.

Aramis felt the coldness of that smile and he shuddered. "Oh!" he cried out. "Since you're scared of death, you must know more than you're letting on."

"What about you?" the prisoner retorted. "You who had me ask to see you, you who, when I asked for you, walk in and promise me a world of revelations? How come you're now holding your tongue and I'm doing the talking? Each of us is wearing a mask. Let's both of us either keep on our masks or remove them together."

Aramis felt both the strength and the soundness of that reasoning. I'm not dealing with an ordinary man, he thought to himself. "Let's see," he then said aloud, "are you ambitious?"—without preparing the prisoner for that abrupt transition.

"Just what is ambition?" the young man asked.

"It is," Aramis replied, "a feeling that impels a man to desire more than he has."

"I said I was content, sir. But I might be mistaken. I don't know what ambition is, but I may have it. Look, open up my mind to me—that's all I'm asking for."

"An ambitious man," said Aramis, "is a man who craves things beyond his station."

"I crave nothing beyond my station," said the young man

with a self-assurance that again made the Bishop of Vannes shudder.

The prisoner fell silent. But his burning eyes, his knitted forehead, his reflective attitude clearly indicated that he was expecting something other than silence. And Aramis broke that silence.

"You lied to me the first time I saw you," he said.

"Lied?" the young man exclaimed, sitting up in his bed. His voice was so dramatic, his eyes were so ardent, that the visitor recoiled in spite of himself.

"I mean," Aramis replied with a bow, "that you have concealed from me what you know about your childhood."

"A man's secrets," said the prisoner, "belong to him, monsieur, and not to all and sundry."

"That's true," Aramis agreed, bowing lower than before. "That's true, forgive me. But am I still 'all and sundry' for you? I beg you, answer me, monseigneur."

This title vaguely disturbed the prisoner, yet he did not seem astonished.

"I do not know you, sir," he said.

"Oh! If I dared, I would take your hand and kiss it."

The young man was about to hold out his hand to Aramis, but the lightning that had flashed in his eyes vanished on the edge of his lids, and his hand drew back, cold and defiant.

"Kiss a prisoner's hand!" He shook his head. "What good would it do?"

"Why did you tell me," Aramis asked, "that you feel fine in here? Why did you tell me that you have no aspirations? Why, finally, do you prevent me from being frank?"

The young man's eyes flashed a third time. And for the third time, the lightning faded without leading to anything.

"You distrust me," said Aramis.

"In what regard, sir?"

"Oh, it's quite simple. If you know what you ought to know, you should distrust everyone."

"Well, then, don't be surprised that I'm distrustful since you suspect me of knowing things I don't know."

Aramis was struck with admiration for this energetic resistance. "Oh, monseigneur! You're driving me to distraction!" he cried out, banging his fist on the armchair.

"I don't understand you, sir."

"Well, then, try to understand me."

The prisoner peered at his visitor.

Aramis went on: "At times I feel that I am gazing at the man whom I am looking for. . . . But then . . ."

"But then that man disappears, isn't that so?" the prisoner smiled. "All the better!"

Aramis stood up. "I certainly have nothing to say to a man who distrusts me as much as you do."

"And I," said the prisoner in the same tone, "I have nothing to say to a man who refuses to understand that a prisoner must distrust everyone."

"Even his old friends?" said Aramis. "That's too much prudence, monseigneur."

"Old friends? You are one of my old friends? You?"

"Come, now," said Aramis. "Don't you remember that in the village where you spent your infancy—"

"Do you know the name of that village?" asked the prisoner.

"Noisy-le-Sec, monseigneur," Aramis firmly replied.

"Go on," said the young man, his face neither avowing nor denying.

"Listen, monseigneur," said Aramis. "If you'd absolutely rather keep playing this game, let's call it a day. I've come to tell you a lot of things, that's true. But you have to show me for your part that you want to hear them. Before speaking, before exposing the important things that I'm concealing, I need a little help if not frankness, a little sympathy if not trust. You see, you've locked yourself up in a pretended ignorance that paralyzes me. . . . Oh, not for what you believe. For no matter how ignorant you may be or how indifferent you may pretend to be, you are no less than what you truly are, monseigneur. And nothing, nothing—do you hear?—will make you be anything else."

"I promise," the prisoner answered, "to hear you out patiently. But I feel I've got the right to ask you the same question that I've already asked you: Who are you?"

"Think back some seventeen or eighteen years ago in Noisy-le-Sec. Do you remember a cavalier who came with a lady? She normally wore black silk and had fiery ribbons in her hair."

"Yes," said the young man. "I once asked what the cavalier's name was, and they told me that he was the Abbé d'Herblay. I was astonished that this clergyman looked like a warrior, and I was told that it was not so astonishing, given that he was a musketeer of King Louis XIII."

"Well," said Aramis, "that man, who was a musketeer and an abbé back then, and who is now the Bishop of Vannes and your confessor today—that man is I!"

"I know. I recognized you."

"Well, then, monseigneur! If you know that, I must add something that you do not know. If the king knew of the presence here of this musketeer, this abbé, this bishop, this confessor tonight, then tomorrow the man who's risked everything to find you will see the gleam of the headman's ax in the depth of a dungeon that is far darker and more lost than your cell."

Listening to these sharply accentuated words, the young man sat up in bed and peered more and more avidly into Aramis's eyes. As a result of this scrutiny, the prisoner seemed to be gaining some trust.

"Yes," he murmured, "yes. I remember perfectly. The woman you're speaking of came with you once, and came twice with the woman . . ."

He broke off.

"With the woman who came to see you every month—isn't that right, monseigneur?"

"Yes."

"Do you know who that woman was?"

Lightning seemed to flash from the prisoner's eyes. "I knew it was a lady of the court."

"Do you remember that lady clearly?"

"Oh, my memories of her can't be too hazy," said the young prisoner. "I saw her once with a man in his mid-forties. I saw her once with you and with the woman in the black gown and the fiery ribbons. I saw her twice more with that same person. Those four people, plus my tutor and old Perronnette, my jailer and the warden, are the only people I've ever spoken to, and actually the only people I've even laid eyes on."

"But were you in prison back then?"

"If I'm in prison here, then I was relatively free back then, even though my freedom was highly restricted: a house with grounds that I never strayed from, a large garden surrounded by walls that I couldn't scale—that was my home. You know the place, you've been there. Besides, I was so used to living inside those walls, and that house, that I never wanted to leave. So, you will understand, sir, that having seen nothing of the world, I cannot desire anything, and if you tell me something, you will have to explain it thoroughly."

"And that's what I'll do, monseigneur," said Aramis, bowing, "for that's my duty."

"Very well! Then start by telling me who my tutor was."

"A fine aristocrat, monseigneur, an honest aristocrat above all, a teacher for both your body and your soul. Did you ever have occasion to complain about him?"

"Oh, no, sir. Quite the contrary. But this gentleman often told me that my parents were dead. Was he lying to me or telling the truth?"

"He was forced to carry out his orders."

"So he was lying?"

"On one point. Your father was dead."

"And my mother?"

"She's dead for you."

"But she's alive for other people, isn't she?"

"Yes."

"And I"—the young man stared at Aramis—"I'm doomed to live in the darkness of a prison?"

"Alas! I think so!"

"And that," the young man continued, "is because my presence out in the world would expose a great secret?"

"A great secret, yes."

"To lock up a child in the Bastille, my enemy must be very powerful."

"He is."

"So much more powerful than my mother?"

"Why do you say that?"

"Because my mother would have defended me."

Aramis hesitated.

"Yes, monseigneur. More powerful than your mother."

"If my nurse and my tutor were taken from me, I or they must have posed a very great danger for my enemy, right?"

"Yes," Aramis calmly replied. "A danger that your enemy escaped by making your nurse and your tutor disappear."

"Disappear?" asked the prisoner. "In what way did they disappear?"

"In the surest way," Aramis answered. "They are dead."

The young man paled slightly and drew a trembling hand across his face. "Poison?" he asked.

"Poison."

The prisoner reflected for a moment.

"If those two innocent people, my sole mainstays, were killed on the same day, then my enemy must be very cruel or constrained by necessity. For that worthy aristocrat and that poor woman had never harmed a fly."

"Necessity is harsh in your house, monseigneur. And thus it's necessity that, to my great regret, forces me to tell you that they were both assassinated."

"Oh! You've told me nothing new," said the prisoner, knitting his brow.

"What do you mean?"

"I suspected it."

"How?"

"Let me tell you."

At that instant, the young man, propped on his elbows, approached Aramis's face with such a profound expression of dignity, abnegation, and even defiance, that the bishop felt the devouring sparks of the electric enthusiasm rising from his faded heart to his steel-hard skull.

"Speak, monseigneur. I've already told you that I'm risking my life by conversing with you. Insignificant as my life may be, I beg you to receive it as a ransom of yours."

"Very well," said the young man. "This is why I suspected that my nurse and my tutor had been killed—"

"You called him your father . . ."

"Yes, I called him my father, but I knew perfectly well that I was not his son."

"What made you assume that? . . ."

"Just as you are too respectful for a friend, he was too respectful for a father."

"I have no intention of disguising myself," said Aramis.

The young man nodded and went on: "No doubt, I wasn't destined to remain eternally locked up, and the reason I think so, especially now, is the care they took to raise me as a cavalier who is as accomplished as possible. The nobleman who looked after me taught me everything he knew: mathematics, a little geometry, astronomy, fencing, and riding. Every morning I practiced fencing in a low room and rode horseback in the garden. Well, one very hot morning—it was summer—I had dozed off in that room. Aside from my tutor's respect toward me, nothing so far had enlightened me or aroused my suspicions. I lived on air and sunshine like a child, like a bird, like a plant. I had just turned fifteen."

"So that was eight years ago?"

"Yes, more or less. I've lost track of time."

"Forgive me, but what did your tutor tell you to encourage you to work?"

"He said that a man must seek his fortune out in the world if God has refused to provide him with one at birth. He added that as a poor, obscure orphan, I could rely only on myself, and that no one was or ever would be interested in me per se. Now I was in that low room, where, worn out by my fencing lesson, I had fallen asleep. My tutor was in his room on the second level, right overhead. Suddenly, I heard a muffled cry; it was my tutor. Then he called: 'Perronnette! Perronnette!' She was my nurse."

"Yes, I know," said Aramis. "Go on, monseigneur, go on."

"She must have been in the garden, for my tutor dashed down the stairs. I stood up, worried that he was worried. He opened the vestibule door that led to the garden and he kept shouting: 'Perronnette! Perronnette!' The windows of the low room faced the courtyard; the shutters were closed. But through a chink in a shutter I saw my tutor heading toward a large well located almost below the windows of his study. He leaned over the rim of the well, peered into the depth, and cried out again while gesticulating in terror. From where I was I could not only see, I could also hear. So see I did, and hear I did."

"Please, go on, monseigneur," said Aramis.

"Lady Perronnette came hurrying up in response to those cries. He stepped toward her, took her arm, and dragged her to the rim. Next, with the two of them leaning into the well, he said: 'Look! Look! How awful!'

" 'C'mon, c'mon, calm down!' said Lady Perronnette. 'What's wrong?'

" 'That letter!' cried my tutor. 'Do you see that letter?' And he pointed toward the bottom of the well.

" 'What letter?' asked my nurse.

" 'The letter you see down there. It's the queen's latest letter.'

"That word made me shudder. My tutor, who pretended to be my father, who kept recommending modesty and humility to me—that man was in correspondence with the queen!

" 'The queen's latest letter!' exclaimed Perronnette, who seemed astonished only that the letter was at the bottom of the well. 'Goodness, how come it's down there?'

" 'By chance, Lady Perronnette, by a singular chance! I was going to my study, and, when I opened the door, the window happened to be open too. The draft carried off a sheet of paper. I recognized the queen's letter. I rushed over to the window with a shout. The letter floated aloft for an instant, then dropped into the well.'

" 'So,' said Lady Perronnette, 'if the letter's dropped into the well, it's like being burned, and since the queen personally burns all her letters whenever she comes here—'

"Whenever she comes!" the prisoner interrupted himself. "So that woman who visited us once a month was the queen."

Aramis nodded.

" 'No doubt, no doubt,' the old gentleman continued. 'But this letter contains instructions. How can I follow them?'

" 'Write quickly to the queen. Tell her what happened, and she'll write you a second letter in place of the first.'

" 'The queen won't believe it was an accident,' my tutor said, wagging his head. 'She'll think that instead of handing it back to her like the others, I meant to keep this letter in order to use it as a weapon. She's so distrustful, and Monsieur de Mazarin is so . . . That Italian demon is capable of having us poisoned at the slightest suspicion!' "

Aramis smiled, imperceptibly moving his head.

" 'You know, Lady Perronnette, both of them are so skittish with regard to Philip!' "

The prisoner interrupted himself: "Philip is the name they gave me.

" 'Then there's no time to lose,' said Lady Perronnette. 'Someone has to descend into the well.'

" 'He'll just read the letter as he comes back up.'

" 'Find someone in the village who can't read. That'll put your mind at ease.'

" 'Fine! But won't that person guess the importance of a document for which we're risking a human life? However, you've just given me an idea, Lady Perronnette. Yes, someone will descend into the well, and that someone will be I.'

"Upon hearing those words, Lady Perronnette wailed so tearfully and pleaded so loudly that the old gentleman promised he'd find a ladder that was long enough, while she went to the farm to find a stouthearted boy. They would tell him that a jewel wrapped in paper had fallen down the well, and that since paper, as my tutor pointed out, unfolds in water, it would not be surprising that the letter was fully open.

" 'The ink must have dissolved by now,' said Lady Perronnette.

" 'It doesn't matter, so long as we've got the letter. When I return it to the queen, she'll see that I haven't betrayed her. And so, by not arousing Monsieur de Mazarin's distrust, we'll have nothing to fear from him.'

"Having made that decision, they separated. I pushed back the shutter and, seeing that my tutor was about to come in, I threw myself on my pillows, my head buzzing with everything I'd just heard.

"Several seconds later, my tutor half-opened the door, and, thinking I was asleep, softly closed it again.

"That same instant, I got to my feet and listened hard to the fading footsteps. Then, returning to my shutter, I watched my tutor and Lady Perronnette leaving the house.

"I was alone.

"No sooner were they out the front door than, without bothering to cross the vestibule, I jumped out the window and dashed over to the well.

"I leaned into it just as my tutor had done.

"Something whitish and luminous was quivering in the trembling circles of the greenish water. The brilliant disk fascinated and attracted me. My eyes gaped; I was panting. The well drew me with its wide mouth and its icy breath. It was as if, at the very bottom, I could read fiery characters on the paper touched by the queen.

"Next, not knowing what I was doing, and animated by one of those instinctive movements that push you out on thin ice, I unrolled one end of the rope from the foot of the windlass. Then I lowered the bucket to within three feet of the water, while struggling to avoid disturbing the precious document, whose whitish color was turning greenish. This was proof that it was sinking. Clutching a piece of soaked canvas, I slipped down into the abyss.

"When I saw I was suspended above that dark water, when I saw the sky shrinking overhead, the cold grabbed hold of me, my head whirled, my hair stood on end. But my willpower overcame everything: terror and discomfort. I reached the water and plunged in at one swoop, holding on by one hand while I stretched out the other. I seized the precious document, which came apart in my fingers.

"I hid the two halves in my jerkin and crawled and clambered up the sides of the well. Vigorous, agile, and, above all, hurrying, I reached the rim, which I flooded with water that poured down from the lower part of my body.

"Once I was out of the well with my booty, I started running in the sunshine. I reached the back of the garden, which contained a grove of small trees. That was where I sought refuge.

"As I entered my hiding place, the bell rang at the front gates, indicated that they were opening. It was my tutor coming back. I had time!

"I calculated that it would take him ten minutes to get here if, guessing where I was, he came straight to me, and twenty minutes if he had to look for me.

"That was enough time for me to read this precious letter, and I swiftly brought the two fragments together. The writing was starting to fade. Nevertheless, I managed to decipher the text."

"And what did you read, monseigneur?" asked Aramis, acutely interested.

"Enough to learn, sir, that my tutor was a nobleman, and that Perronnette, though not a grande dame, was still more than a servant. I found out that I myself was highborn, since Queen Anne of Austria and Prime Minister Mazarin so solicitously commended me to their care."

The young man broke off, deeply moved.

"What happened next?" asked Aramis.

"What happened was that the laborer summoned by my tutor found nothing after searching every nook and cranny of the well. My tutor then noticed that the rim was wet. Moreover, since I hadn't dried off completely, Lady Perronnette noticed that my clothes were still damp. Eventually, I grew feverish because of the cold water and the agitation of my discovery. My fever was followed by a delirium, in which I revealed everything. Guided by my own words, my tutor found the two fragments of the queen's letter under my pillow."

"Ah!" said Aramis. "Now I understand!"

"Beyond that, it's all conjecture. My poor tutor and that poor woman probably didn't dare keep what had happened a secret. They must have written everything to the queen and sent her the torn letter."

"After which," said Aramis, "you were arrested and dragged off to the Bastille."

"Exactly."

"Then your tutor and your nurse disappeared."

"Alas!"

"Don't worry about the dead," Aramis went on. "Let's see what we can do with the living. You told me you're resigned."

"Indeed I am."

"And unconcerned about freedom?"

"That's what I said."

"No ambition, no regret, no thought?"

The young man didn't respond.

"Fine!" said Aramis. "So you're holding your tongue?"

"I think I've said enough," the prisoner replied. "Now it's your turn. I'm worn out."

"I'll do as you say," said Aramis. He collected his thoughts, and a deep solemnity spread all over his face. One could sense that he had reached the crux of the role that he had come to play in this prison.

"One question," said Aramis.

"What is it? Speak."

"In the house you lived in, there were no mirrors or looking glasses, right?"

"What do those two words mean?" asked the young man. "I don't know them."

"A mirror or looking glass is an object that reflects things. For instance, it lets you see the features of your face in specially treated glass, just as you can see my features with your naked eye."

"No," the young man answered. "There was no mirror or looking glass in the house."

Aramis scanned the room. "And there's none here. The same precautions have been taken."

"With what aim?"

"You will know soon. Meanwhile, forgive me. You said that you were taught mathematics, astronomy, fencing, riding. But you haven't mentioned history."

"Sometimes my tutor would tell me about the glorious deeds of King Saint Louis, King Francis I, and King Henry IV."

"Is that all?"

"Just about."

"Well, I get it. That too was deliberate. Just as they removed all the mirrors, which reflected the present, they kept you ignorant of history, which reflects the past. In your imprisonment, you're not allowed to have any books, so that many things are unknown to you. Otherwise you could reconstruct the collapsed edifice of your memories and interests."

"That's true," said the young man.

"Listen," said Aramis, "I'm going to sum up for you what's

happened in France during the last twenty-three or -four years—that is, since the probable date of your birth—from the moment that concerns you."

"Tell me." And the young man resumed his serious and pensive stance.

"Do you know who the son of Henry IV was?"

"I at least know who his successor was."

"How do you know that?"

"From a coin dated 1610 and showing Henry IV, and from a coin dated 1612 and showing Louis XIII. Since only two years had passed between those two coins, I assumed that Louis XIII was the successor of Henry IV."

"So," said Aramis, "you know that the last reigning king was Louis XIII?"

"Yes." The young man blushed faintly.

"Well, as a ruler he was full of good ideas, great projects—projects that were put off by those bad times and by his minister Richelieu's struggles against the French *seigneurie*. Personally, the king had a weak character. He died young and in a dismal way."

"I know all that."

"For a long time he was preoccupied with his posterity. That is a painful concern for rulers who need to leave something more in this world than a memory. They want their thoughts to keep going, their work to continue."

"Did Louis XIII die childless?" the prisoner asked with a smile.

"No, but for a long time he was deprived of the joy of having children and he thought that his lineage would die with him. This anxiety reduced him to profound despair, when all at once his wife, Anne of Austria—"

The prisoner shuddered.

"Did you know that Louis XIII's wife was named Anne of Austria?"

"Go on," said the young man without responding.

"When all at once Queen Anne announced that she was pregnant. The news triggered great joy, and everyone prayed for a happy delivery. Finally, on September 5, 1638, she gave birth to a son."

Here, Aramis looked at the prisoner and he believed that the young man had turned pale.

"You are going to hear something," said Aramis, "that few people can now tell you, for this story is a secret that is thought to be dead with the dead or buried in the abyss of confession."

"And you're going to tell me this secret?" said the young man.

"Oh," said Aramis in an unerring tone of voice, "I don't believe I am risking anything by entrusting it to a prisoner who has no desire to leave the Bastille."

"I'm listening, sir."

"The queen gave birth to a son. But when the entire court greeted the news with cries of joy, when the king had shown the newborn to his people and the nobility, when he gaily sat down at the table to celebrate this happy event, the queen, alone in her chamber, was stricken with more contractions, and she then gave birth to a second boy."

"Oh!" said the prisoner, revealing more knowledge than he admitted. "I thought the king's brother was actually born in—"

Aramis raised his finger. "Just wait."

The prisoner sighed impatiently and waited.

"Yes," said Aramis, "the queen had a second son, a boy whom the midwife, Lady Perronnette, received in her arms."

"Lady Perronnette," the young man murmured.

"They ran to the banquet hall, where the king was dining, and whispered to him what had occurred. The king ran back to his wife's chamber. But this time his face was not merry; it expressed something like terror. Twin sons changed into bitterness the joy caused by the birth of a single son, given—I'm sure you don't know this—given that in France it is the oldest son who succeeds the father."

"I know that."

"And physicians and jurists claim that there is reason to doubt whether the first twin leaving his mother's womb is the elder by the laws of God and nature."

The prisoner uttered a muffled cry, turning whiter than the sheet he was hiding under.

"Now, you understand," Aramis went on, "the king, who had been so joyful that his lineage would continue, was in the throes of despair. He now had two sons, and the second one, whose existence was unknown, might contest the seniority claimed by the other twin, who was born two hours earlier and whose right had been recognized. The second son, banking on partisan interests or caprices, could eventually sow discord and warfare in the kingdom, destroying the dynasty that he was supposed to consolidate."

"Oh!" the young man murmured. "I understand, I understand!"

"Well," Aramis went on, "this is what's reported, this is what's asserted. This is why one of Queen Anne's sons was shamefully separated from his brother, shamefully sequestered, consigned to the deepest obscurity. This is why that second son has vanished, and vanished so thoroughly that, aside from his mother, nobody in France now knows he exists."

"Yes, his mother, who abandoned him!" the prisoner exclaimed in despair.

"Aside," Aramis went on, "from the lady in the black gown and the fiery ribbons, and, finally, aside—"

"Aside from you, right? You who've come to tell me all this, you who've come to arouse curiosity, hatred, ambition in my soul, and perhaps even a thirst for vengeance. If you, sir, are the man I've been waiting for, the man promised me in the letter, the man, finally, whom God must send me, then you must have on you . . ."

"What?" asked Aramis.

"A portrait of King Louis XIV, who now sits on the French throne."

"Here is the portrait," replied the bishop, handing the prisoner an utterly exquisite enamel that showed Louis XIV proud, handsome, and lifelike, as it were.

The prisoner avidly grabbed the portrait, gaping at it as if he wanted to devour it.

"And now, monseigneur," said Aramis, "here is a mirror."

Aramis left the prisoner time to gather his thoughts.

"So high! So high!" murmured the young man, his eyes devouring the portrait of Louis XIV and his own reflection in the mirror.

"What do you think?" said Aramis.

"I think I'm doomed," the prisoner responded. "The king will never forgive me."

"For my part, I wonder," added the bishop, gazing significantly at the prisoner, "I wonder which of the two is the king: the man in the portrait or the man in the mirror."

"The king, sir, is the one on the throne," the young man sadly replied, "the one who's not in prison and who, quite the contrary, puts others in prison. Royalty is power, and you can see that I'm powerless."

"Monseigneur," answered Aramis with a reverence that he had previously not displayed, "listen carefully. If you like, the king can be the man who will leave prison and who will sit on the throne, where his friends place him."

"Sir, don't tempt me," the prisoner said bitterly.

"Monseigneur, do not weaken," Aramis urged him vigorously. "I've brought all the evidence of your birth. Consult it, prove to yourself that you are a son of a king, and then we'll act."

"No, no! It's impossible."

"Unless," the bishop sneered, "it lies in the destiny of your breed that any brother who is excluded from the throne is worthless and dishonorable—like your uncle, Monsieur Gaston of Orléans, who hatched ten plots against King XIII, his own brother."

"My uncle plotted against his own brother?!" the prince cried in horror. "He plotted to dethrone him?"

"Of course, monseigneur. For no other reason."

"What are you telling me, monsieur?"

"The truth."

"And he had friends? Loyal followers?"

"Just as I am your friend and loyal follower."

"Well? What happened? He failed?"

"He failed, and it was always his own fault. And to buy his freedom—not his life, for the life of the king's brother is sacred—to buy his freedom, your uncle sacrificed the lives of all his friends, one after the other. And so today he is a disgrace in history and the execration of a hundred noble families in this kingdom."

"I understand, sir," the prince replied. "And why did my uncle kill his friends? Out of weakness, or treason?"

"Weakness—which is always treason among rulers."

"Can't a man also fail out of ignorance, incompetence? Do you really believe that a poor captive like myself, who was raised not only far from the court, but far from society—do you believe that he can possibly help those of his friends who would attempt to serve him?"

Before Aramis could respond, the young man suddenly exclaimed with a violence that showed his true blood: "We're talking about friends. But by what chance would I have friends, I who am totally unknown, with nothing to offer any friends—no freedom, no money, no power?"

"I believe I have the honor of offering myself to Your Royal Highness."

"Oh, don't address me like that, monsieur. It's derision or barbarity. Don't let me dream of anything but the prison walls that surround me. Let me continue to love, or at least submit to, my enslavement and obscurity."

"Monseigneur! Monseigneur! If you keep repeating those words of discouragement; if, after having proof of your birth, you remain poor in spirit, breath, and willpower—then I will respect your wishes. I will disappear; I will renounce serving a master to whom I so ardently devote my life and my help."

"Monsieur!" cried the prince. "Before telling me everything you've told me, wouldn't it have been better to realize that you've shattered my heart forever?"

"That's what I wanted to do, monseigneur!"

"Sir, in order to speak to me about grandeur, power, even kingship, did you have to choose a prison? You want to make me believe in splendor, and yet we hide in the night. You vaunt glory, and yet we muffle our words behind the curtains of this pallet! You give me a glimpse of omnipotence, and yet I hear the jailer's footsteps in the corridor—the footsteps that frighten you more than me. To make me a bit less incredulous, get me out of the Bastille. Give air to my lungs, spurs to my feet, a sword in my hand, and we'll begin to understand each other."

"Those are all my intentions, monseigneur. But do you want this?"

"Listen to me, sir," the prince broke in. "I know there are guards in every corridor, locks on every door, cannon and soldiers at every barrier. With what can you overcome the guards, spike the cannon? With what can you smash the locks and the barriers?"

"Monseigneur, the letter you've read, the letter announcing my coming—how did it reach you?"

"One can bribe a jailer for a letter."

"If one can bribe one jailer, one can bribe ten."

"Fine. I admit that it's possible to sneak a poor captive out of the Bastille. It's possible to hide him so well that the king's men will never catch him. It's even possible to comfortably care for this unhappy man in an unknown retreat."

"Monseigneur!" Aramis smiled.

"I admit that the man who did that for me would be more than a mortal. But since you say that I'm a prince, a brother of the king, how will you help me regain the rank and the power that were taken from me by my mother and my brother? Since I'm to live a life of combat and hatred, how will you make me victorious in combat and invulnerable to my enemies? Ah, sir! Think about it! Throw me into some black cavern tomorrow, deep inside a mountain. Give me the joy of hearing the sounds of a river and a plain in freedom, of seeing the sunny sky or the stormy sky in freedom—and that would be enough. Don't promise me anything more, for you can't really give me more, and it would be a crime to deceive me since you call yourself my friend."

Aramis continued listening in silence. "Monseigneur," he then said after reflecting for a moment, "I admire the sound, resolute common sense that dictates your words. I'm happy that I've discovered my king's mind."

"Again! Again! Ah! For pity's sake!" the prince cried out, his icy hands squeezing his brow, which was burning with sweat. "Don't abuse me! I don't need to be king, sir, in order to be the happiest of men."

"And I, monseigneur, I need you to be king for the happiness of mankind."

"Ah!" said the prince, his defiance further kindled by that word. "Ah! What does mankind reproach my brother for?"

"I neglected to tell you, monseigneur, that if you deign to follow my guidance, and if you consent to become the most powerful ruler on earth, you will have served the interests of all the friends whom I dedicate to the success of our cause, and those friends are numerous."

"Numerous?"

"More powerful than numerous, monseigneur."

"Please explain!"

"Impossible. I swear to God, who hears me, that I will explain everything on the very day that you will sit on the French throne."

"What about my brother?"

"You will decide his fate. Do you pity him?"

"The man who leaves me to rot in a dungeon? No, I don't pity him!"

"Fine!"

"He could have come to this prison himself, he could have taken my hand and said, 'My brother, God created us to love each other, not to fight. A barbaric prejudice condemned you to die obscurely, far from all men, deprived of all joys. I want to seat you next to me, I want to attach our father's sword at your side. Will you take advantage of this attachment to stifle or constrain me? Will you use this sword to spill my blood?'

" 'Oh, no!' I would have answered him. 'I regard you as my savior and I will respect you as my master. You will give me a lot more than God gave me. You have given me freedom and the right to love and to be loved in this world.' "

"And would you have kept your word, monseigneur?"

"Yes! On my life!"

"Whereas now . . ."

"Whereas now I've got culprits to punish."

"Punish how, monseigneur?"

"What do you say to my God-given resemblance to my brother?"

"I say that this resemblance teaches a providential lesson that the king should not have neglected. I say that your mother committed a crime by the way she treated so differently the sons that nature had created so similarly in her womb. And I personally conclude that the punishment should be confined to redressing the balance."

"Which means . . ."

"That I will restore your place on your brother's throne, and your brother will take your place in your prison."

"Alas! A man can duly suffer in prison, especially if he has drunk deeply of the goblet of life!"

"Your Royal Highness will always be free to do as he wishes. He can, if he so chooses, grant a pardon after punishing."

"Very well. And now, do you know what, sir?"

"Tell me, my prince."

"I will no longer listen to you until we are outside the Bastille . . ."

"I was about to tell Your Royal Highness that I will no longer have the honor of seeing him but once."

"When?"

"The day my prince will leave these black walls."

"Your words in God's ear! How will you notify me?"

"By coming for you."

"Yourself?"

"My prince, do not leave this room except with me. If someone forces you to do so without me, then you will know that I have no part in it."

"So I must not breathe a word to anyone but you?"

"Not anyone but me." Aramis bowed deeply.

The prince held out his hand. "Sir," he stated in a heartfelt tone, "I've got one last thing to say to you. If you have turned to me in order to doom me, if you're simply an instrument in the hands of my enemies, if our dialogue—in which you've thoroughly sounded me out—results in something worse than imprisonment (namely, death), well, then, bless you! For you will have terminated my sufferings and substituted peace of mind for the feverish tortures that have been devouring me for eight years."

"Monseigneur," said Aramis, "wait until you can judge me."

"I've said that I bless you and forgive you. If, on the contrary, you've come to restore the place that God destined me for in the sunlight of fortune and glory; if, thanks to you, I can live in human memory and do honor to my race through several illustrious deeds or several services for my subjects; if, from the bottommost rank where I am languishing, I can ascend to the acme of honors, supported by your generous hand—well, then, I bless you and thank you, and you will have half my power and glory! You will nevertheless be terribly underpaid, your share will still be incomplete. For I will never succeed in sharing with you all the happiness that you will have given me."

"Monseigneur," said Aramis, deeply moved by the young man's pallor and élan, "the nobility of your heart fills me with joy and admiration. It is not for you to thank me; that will be chiefly for the people whom you will make happy, for your descendants whom you will make illustrious. Yes indeed, I will have given you more than life, I will give you mortality."

The young man held out his hand to Aramis, who knelt and kissed it.

"Oh!" cried the prince with charming modesty.

"That was the first homage rendered to our future king," said Aramis. "When I see you again, I will greet you with: 'Good day, sire.' "

"Until then," the young man exclaimed, placing his white, emaciated fingers on his heart. "Until then, no more dreams, no more shocks in my life—otherwise my life would burst! Oh, sir! How small my prison is and how low that window! How narrow are those doors! How could so much pride, so much splendor, so much felicity have passed through them and remain here?"

"Your Royal Highness makes me proud," said Aramis, "because you claim that it was I who brought all those things."

He hurried over to the door.

The jailer came, accompanied by Baisemeaux, who, devoured with worry and fear, was reluctantly starting to eavesdrop at the door of the room.

Luckily, neither Aramis nor the prisoner had forgotten to muffle their voices, even in their most daring outbursts of passion.

"What a lengthy confession!" said the warden, trying to laugh. "Could anyone believe that a recluse with one foot in the grave could have committed so many sins and taken so long in listing them?!"

Aramis held his tongue. He was eager to get out of the Bastille, where his overwhelming secret doubled the weight of the walls.

When they arrived at Baisemeaux's quarters, Aramis said, "My dear warden, let's get down to brass tacks."

"Alas!" replied Baisemeaux.

"You've asked me for my receipt for one hundred fifty thousand pounds," said the bishop.

"And to pay me the first third of the sum," the poor warden added with a sigh. He took three paces toward his iron strongbox.

"Here is your receipt," said Aramis.

"And here is the money," Baisemeaux responded with a triple sigh.

"My orders were to give you a receipt for only fifty thousand," said Aramis. "I was not told to receive any money. Good-bye, Warden."

And Aramis walked out, leaving Baisemeaux more than suffocated by joyful surprise in regard to the royal present given so grandly by the extraordinary confessor of the Bastille.

2
How Mouston Had Gained Weight Without Warning Porthos, and How This Spelled Trouble for This Worthy Nobleman

Since Athos's departure for Blois, Porthos and d'Artagnan had seldom gotten together. One man had performed a wearying service for the king; the other had been shopping for a lot of furniture that he planned to send to his estates. He was hoping to provide his diverse residences with a bit of the court's luxury, which he had glimpsed in dazzling clarity when he had been in the company of His Majesty.

One morning, when his work had left him some spare time, d'Artagnan, ever loyal, thought about Porthos; and, worried after not hearing anything about him for over two weeks, d'Artagnan headed for Porthos's town house, where he found him just getting up.

The worthy baron seemed pensive; more than pensive: melancholy. He sat on his bed, half-naked, his legs dangling. He was contemplating a throng of suits, which, with their fringes, braids, embroideries, and clashing colors, were strewn across the parquet floor.

Porthos, sad and wistful like the rabbit in La Fontaine's fable, didn't see d'Artagnan enter; the visitor was hidden by Monsieur Mouston, whose corpulence, sufficient to conceal any man from another, was doubled at that moment by a scarlet suit that the steward was displaying to his employer, holding it up by its sleeves so that it was fully visible on all sides.

D'Artagnan halted at the threshold and scrutinized his wistful friend. Then, since the sight of those countless garments scattered on the floor was drawing profound sighs from the worthy host, d'Artagnan felt it was time to rouse him from his painful contemplation. So he coughed to announce himself.

"Ah!" said Porthos, his face brightening with joy. "Ah! Ah! It's d'Artagnan! He'll finally give me an idea!"

At those words, Mouston, inferring what a visitor was behind him, stepped out of the way while smiling tenderly at his employer's friend. The steward thus removed the material obstacle that prevented Porthos from seeing d'Artagnan. Porthos's robust knees cracked as he stood up, and, crossing the room in two bounds, he stood face-to-face with d'Artagnan, whom he hugged with an affection that seemed to gather new strength with each passing day.

"Ah!" he repeated. "You're certainly always welcome, my friend. But today you're more welcome than ever."

"What's wrong?" asked d'Artagnan. "Are you down in the dumps today?"

Porthos responded with a look that expressed his low spirits.

"Well, tell me everything, Porthos, my friend, unless it's a secret."

"First of all, my friend," said Porthos, "you know that I have no secrets from you. Let me tell you why I'm so sad."

"Wait, Porthos. First let me disentangle myself from this whole litter of satin and velvet."

"Go ahead! Go ahead!" Porthos said woefully. "It's all nothing but garbage!"

"Damn it! Garbage, Porthos?! At twenty pounds a yard! Magnificent satin! Royal velvet!"

"So you find these clothes—"

"Splendid, Porthos, splendid! I bet you're the only man in France who's got this many suits. And even if you don't order any more and you live to be a hundred, which wouldn't surprise me, you'll still be wearing new clothes the day you die—without having to see the nose of a single tailor between now and then."

Porthos shook his head.

"C'mon, old friend," said d'Artagnan. "This melancholy isn't typical of you; it scares me. My dear Porthos, shake it off! The sooner the better!"

"Yes, my friend. Let's shake it off," said Porthos. "If that's possible."

"Have you received bad news from Bracieux, my friend?"

"No. They chopped down the forest, and it yielded a third more than the estimate."

"Is there any leakage in the Pierrefonds ponds?"

"No, my friend. They've been dragged for fish, and there's enough left over from the sale to stock all the ponds in the area."

"Has Le Vallon collapsed in an earthquake?"

"No, my friend, quite the contrary. The lightning struck a hundred paces from the castle and it uncovered a wellspring in a place that was totally devoid of water."

"Well, then, what's wrong?"

"What's wrong is that I received an invitation to the celebration at Vaux," said Porthos with a lugubrious air.

"Well, poor you! The king has alienated over a hundred courtiers by not inviting them. Ah, my friend! You're really and truly heading for Vaux? Good for you!"

"Yes, by God!"

"The celebration will be magnificent, my friend!"

"Alas! I don't doubt it!"

"The grandest names in France will be there!"

"Ah!" said Porthos. In his anguish, he yanked out a lock of hair.

"Well, for God's sake!" said d'Artagnan. "Are you sick, my friend?"

"I'm as fit as a fiddle! Damn it! That's not it!"

"Then what is it?"

"I've got nothing to wear!"

D'Artagnan was dumbfounded. "Nothing to wear, Porthos? Nothing to wear?! Why, you've got over fifty suits right there on the floor!"

"Fifty, yes, and not a single one that fits me!"

"What do you mean not a single one that fits you? Doesn't your tailor take your measurements when he makes you a suit?"

"Certainly!" Mouston pitched in. "But, unfortunately, I've gained weight."

"What do you mean you've gained weight?"

"It's that I've gotten fatter, a lot fatter, than the baron. Can you believe it, sir?"

"Damn it! I think it's obvious!"

"You see, imbecile?" Porthos berated Mouston. "It's obvious!"

"But, my dear Porthos," said d'Artagnan, slightly impatient, "I don't see why your clothes don't fit you just because Mouston's gained weight."

"Let me explain, old friend," said Porthos. "Remember you once told me the story of the Roman general, Antony, who always had seven boars skewered and roasted to different degrees of doneness so he could have his dinner whenever he felt like it? Well, since I could be summoned to court at any moment and remain there for a week, I resolved to always have seven suits ready just in case."

"Sound reasoning, Porthos! But a man has to have your fortune to gratify such whims. Aside from the time lost in getting your measurements taken. Fashions change so often!"

"That's precisely my point," said Porthos. "I can pat myself on the back for hitting on such an ingenious idea!"

"Well, out with it. God knows I don't doubt your genius."

"Do you recall that Mouston used to be thin?"

"Yes. Before he shortened his name from Mousqueton [blunderbuss]."

"And do you also recall when he started gaining weight?"

"No, not exactly. Forgive me, my dear Mouston."

"Oh, it's not your fault, sir," said Mouston amiably. "Monsieur was in Paris, and we were in Pierrefonds."

"Anyway, my dear Porthos, there was a moment when Mouston started gaining weight. That's what you're driving at, isn't it?"

"Yes, my friend, and I was so delighted."

"By God! I can believe it!" said d'Artagnan.

"You understand," Porthos continued, "that it spared me a lot of trouble!"

"No, my dear friend, I still don't understand. But by explaining—"

"Hear me out, my friend. First of all, as you said, getting measured is a waste of time, even if it's just every other week. And besides, a man may be traveling, and if you're always dragging seven suits around . . . Well, old friend, I hate getting measured. A man is a nobleman or he isn't, damn it! Getting scrutinized and verified by some rascal who analyzes you by the foot, the inch, the line is humiliating. Those people find that you stick in too much here, stick out too much there; they know your strong points and your weak points. Look, when you emerge from a measurer's hands, you resemble a stronghold after a spy has ferreted out its angles and thicknesses."

"Honestly, my dear Porthos, you've got ideas that belong to you alone!"

"Oh, you understand . . . If a man's an engineer . . ."

"And he's fortified Belle-Île, that's natural, my friend."

"I had an idea, and it would have been good, no doubt, without Monsieur Mouston's negligence."

D'Artagnan glanced at Mouston, who responded with a slight motion of his body, which meant: You'll see if any of this is my fault.

"So I applaud myself," Porthos went on, "for watching Mouston gain weight, and I even helped him as much as I could by feeding him substantial fare. I kept hoping he'd reach my girth, so he could be measured in my place."

"Aha!" cried d'Artagnan. "I get it. . . . It spared you time and humiliation."

"Damn it! Imagine my joy when after a year and a half of judiciously combined fare, for I went to great pains to feed that rascal myself—"

"Oh! I did my bit, sir," Mouston modestly tossed in.

"That's true. Well, imagine my surprise when one morning I realized that Mouston was forced to step aside, just as I was forced to step aside in order to pass through the small secret door that those diabolical architects had made in the late Madame du Vallon's bedchamber at the castle of Pierrefonds. Apropos of that door, my friend, let me ask you, since you know everything, why did those good-for-nothing architects, who ought to have an accurate eye, build doors which only skinny people can squeeze through?"

"Those doors," replied d'Artagnan, "are meant for lovers. Now, a lover is generally svelte and slender."

"Madame du Vallon had no lover," Porthos interrupted majestically.

"Perfectly true, my friend," said d'Artagnan. "But the architects figured that you might remarry."

"Ah! That's impossible," said Porthos. "And now that I've been given the explanation for the overly narrow doors, let's get back to Mouston's fattening. Take note, however, that those two issues overlap. I've always noticed that ideas run in parallel lines. It's an admirable phenomenon, d'Artagnan. I was talking about Mouston and his fatness, and we've come to Madame du Vallon . . ."

"Who was slender."

"Hmm! Marvelous, isn't it?!"

"Old friend, a scholar that I know, Monsieur Costar, made the same observation about ideas running parallel, and he used a Greek term that I no longer remember."

"Ah! So my observation isn't new?" cried Porthos, stupefied. "I thought I'd invented it."

"My friend, it was a known fact before Aristotle—that is, some two thousand years ago."

"Well, it's no less accurate," said Porthos, delighted to be hobnobbing with the sages of antiquity.

"Fabulous. But let's get back to Mouston. I believe we left him as he was visibly growing fat."

"Yes, sir!" said Mouston.

"Here we go," said Porthos. "Mouston got so fat that he reached my girth, outweighing my fondest hopes. It hit home one day when I saw this rascal wearing a waistcoat of mine that he had made into a suit—a waistcoat that was worth a hundred pistoles for the embroidery alone!"

"I was just trying it on, sir," said Mouston.

"As of that moment," Porthos went on, "I decided that Mouston would be in contact with my tailors and be measured in my place."

"An imaginative solution, Porthos. But Mouston is a foot and a half shorter than you."

"Exactly! The tailor would measure him down to the floor, and the bottom of the suit would come down almost to my knees."

"You're a lucky man, Porthos! Those things happen only to you!"

"Yes, congratulate me, and for good reason! It was precisely around that period—some two and a half years ago—that I left for Belle-Île after telling Mouston to always keep swatches of all fashionable fabrics just in case and to order a new suit every month."

"And did Mouston disobey that recommendation? Ah, that would be bad, Mouston!"

"On the contrary, sir, on the contrary!"

"No, he didn't forget to order suits, but he forgot to inform me that he was getting fatter."

"Damn! It wasn't my fault, sir. Your tailor never told me."

"And so," Porthos went on, "his waist size increased by eighteen inches during those two years. As a result, my last dozen suits are progressively between twelve and eighteen inches too large for me."

"But what about your other suits? The ones that were made when his waist was the same size as yours?"

"They're hopelessly out of style, old friend. If I wore them,

I'd look as if I were coming straight from Siam after not being at the French court for the past two years."

"I understand your quandary. How many new suits do you have? Thirty-six? And you don't have even one. Well, you'll have to order a thirty-seventh suit, and the other thirty-six will be for Mouston."

"Ah! Sir!" said Mouston in a satisfied tone of voice. "The fact is that Monsieur has always been so good to me."

"Damn it! Don't you think that idea has occurred to me or that I was held back by the expenditure? The celebration at Vaux is in two days. I got my invitation yesterday. So I had Mouston bring me my entire wardrobe. It was only this morning that I noticed the disaster, and there's not even a slightly fashionable tailor who can make me a suit by the day after tomorrow."

"You mean a suit covered with gold, don't you?"

"I want gold everywhere!"

"We'll take care of that. You're not leaving until three days from now. The invitation's for Wednesday, and it's now Sunday morning."

"True enough. But Aramis told me to arrive in Vaux twenty-four hours ahead of time."

"Aramis?"

"He's the one who brought me the invitation."

"Ah, fine! Now I get it. You're invited through Monsieur Fouquet."

"Not at all. I'm invited directly by the king, old friend. The invitation is written out in full: 'The Baron du Vallon is hereby informed that the king has deigned to place him on the list of guests . . .' "

"Very good, but you'll be leaving with Monsieur Fouquet."

"And when I think," cried Porthos, stamping loudly, "when I think that I have no suits, I could explode! I'd love to strangle someone or smash something!"

"Don't strangle anyone, don't smash anything, Porthos! Leave it all to me. Put on one of your thirty-six suits, and let's go to a tailor."

"Forget it! My courier has tried all the tailors since this morning."

"Even Monsieur Percerin?"

"Who the hell is Monsieur Percerin?"

"Why, he's the king's tailor, damn it!"

"Ah! Yes, yes," said Porthos, pretending to know that even though this was the first time he'd heard that name. "Yes, Monsieur Percerin, the king's tailor, by God! I figured he'd be too busy."

"He probably is, but keep calm, Porthos. He'll do for me what he won't do for anybody else. Only you'll have to put up with getting measured, old friend."

"Ah!" Porthos sighed. "That's annoying. But what can you do?"

"Damn it! You'll do what everyone else does, my dear friend. You'll do what the king does."

"What? The king gets measured too? And he endures it?"

"The king likes to look stylish, old friend, and so do you, no matter what you may claim."

Porthos smiled triumphantly. "Well, then, let's go to the king's tailor! And since he measures the king, by God, then I guess I can let him measure me."

3
Who and What Master Jean Percerin Was

The king's tailor, Master Jean Percerin, inhabited a rather grand mansion on rue Saint-Honoré, near rue de l'Arbre-Sec (dry tree). He was a man who loved beautiful fabrics, beautiful embroideries, beautiful velvets. His forebears had been tailors to kings all the way back to Charles IX, who, as we know, often launched bravura fantasies that are rather difficult to act out.

The Percerin of that era had been a Huguenot like Ambroise Paré and his life had been spared by the Queen of Navarre, la belle Margot, in consideration of his services. For he was the only tailor who had ever managed to create those wondrous riding habits that she loved to wear because they obscured certain anatomical defects that she so meticulously concealed.

Percerin was so grateful to her for saving his life that he

made some very inexpensive black bodices for Queen Catherine, who, after disliking him for such a long time, was ultimately glad that the Huguenot had survived. However, Percerin was a prudent man. He had heard that nothing was so life-threatening for a Huguenot as Queen Catherine's smiles. And noticing that she smiled at him more often than usual, he quickly converted to Catholicism along with his entire family. Having thereby become irreproachable, he achieved the supreme position of master tailor to the French crown.

Under Henry III, a clotheshorse if ever there was one, that position reached the height of one of the most sublime peaks of the Cordilleras. Percerin had been a resourceful man all his life, and, in order to preserve his reputation beyond the grave, he made sure not to die a bad death. He passed away very skillfully, at the precise moment when his imagination was about to go into its decline.

He left a son and a daughter. Both were worthy of the name that they had been called upon to bear. The boy, a cutter, was as precise and intrepid as a square rule; the girl did embroidery and designed ornaments.

The wedding of Henry IV and Marie de Médicis, the beautiful garments for mourning the above-mentioned queen, plus a few words dropped by Monsieur de Bassompierre, the king of dandies during that period—all those things established the fortune of that second generation of Percerins.

Monsieur Concino Concini and his wife, Galigai, who subsequently shone at the France court, wanted to Italianize the wardrobes, and so they sent for a few Florentine tailors. Percerin, however, cut to the quick in his patriotism and his self-esteem, sent those foreigners packing with his designs for brocades and inimitable satin stitchings. As a result, Concino was the first to abandon his compatriots. Indeed, he held the French tailor in such high regard that he refused to let anyone else clothe him. Cancino was actually wearing a Percerin doublet the day that Vitry blew the Italian's brains out on the small bridge of the Louvre.

It was this doublet from Master Percerin's studio that the Parisians had the pleasure of tearing to shreds, along with the human flesh that it contained.

Despite the favor that Percerin had enjoyed with Concino Concini, King Louis XIII was generous enough to bear his tailor no grudge and to keep him in his service. When Louis the Just was setting this great example of fairness, Percerin had raised two boys. One of them performed his trial shot at the wedding of Anne of Austria, inventing that lovely Spanish outfit in which Cardinal Richelieu danced a saraband; Percerin's son also made the costumes for Saint-Sorlin's tragedy *Mirame*, and stitched the pearls on Buckingham's mantle—those famous pearls that were fated to scatter across the parquets of the Louvre.

A tailor becomes readily illustrious if he has clothed the likes of Monsieur de Buckingham, Monsieur de Cinq-Mars, Mademoiselle Ninon, Monsieur de Beaufort, and Marion Delorme. Thus Percerin III had reached the apogee of his glory by the time his father died.

That same Percerin III, old, renowned, and wealthy, was still dressing Louis XIV; and, being childless, which caused him great distress, he realized that his dynasty would expire with him. He therefore trained several highly promising disciples. Percerin III had a coach, a country estate, lackeys (the tallest in Paris), and, by the king's special authorization, a pack of hounds. He clothed Monsieur de Lyonne and Monsieur le Tellier under something like a patronage. But, political as he was and nourished on state secrets, he had never managed to design an outfit for Monsieur Colbert. This is to be sensed rather than explained. Great minds of any ilk live on invisible, intangible perceptions; they act without quite knowing why themselves. The Great Percerin—for, contrary to the usual dynastic habit, it was above all the last Percerin who merited the epithet "Great"—the Great Percerin was utterly inspired when he cut a skirt for the queen or a trunk hose for the king; he created a mantle for the king's younger brother or a stocking clock for the latter's wife. But for all his supreme genius, Percerin could never take Monsieur Colbert's measure. "That man," the tailor often said, "is beyond my talent; my needles will never design for him."

Needless to say, Percerin was the tailor of Monsieur Fouquet, the superintendent of finances, who praised him to the skies.

Monsieur Percerin was close to eighty, and yet he was still hale and hearty, and indeed so lean as to be brittle, according to the courtiers. His renown and his fortune were large enough for Monsieur le Prince, that king of the coxcombs, to take his arm when chatting with him about clothes; and even the worst deadbeats at court never dared to get too far behind in their accounts with him, for Master Percerin made clothes on credit once only, but never twice if he was not paid the first time.

One can imagine that such an important tailor, instead of running after clients, was fussy about accepting new ones. He turned down members of the middle class and people who had been raised to the nobility too recently. It was even rumored that one fine day Monsieur de Mazarin, in exchange for the full ceremonial vestments of a cardinal, had slipped a patent of nobility into the tailor's pocket.

Percerin had wit and malice. He was reputed to have a ribald spirit. At eighty he still measured a woman's bodice with a firm hand.

It was to the house of this artist–cum–grand seigneur that d'Artagnan took his desolate friend.

Rolling along, Porthos said, "Please don't, my dear d'Artagnan, please don't compromise the dignity of a man like me by exposing me to the arrogance of this Percerin, who must be totally uncivil. For I warn you, dear friend, if he shows me any disrespect, I will punish him."

"If I present you," d'Artagnan replied, "you have nothing to fear, dear friend, even if you . . . were what you're not."

"Ah! So . . ."

"What's wrong? C'mon, Porthos, do you have something against Percerin?"

"I think that a long time ago . . ."

"What was a long time ago?"

"I think I sent Mouston to a scoundrel with that name."

"Well, and then?"

"And then that scoundrel refused to clothe me."

"Oh! A misunderstanding, no doubt, which we have to urgently clear up. Mouston must have made a mistake."

"Maybe."

"He confused some names."

"It's possible. That rascal Mouston is bad with names."

"I'll take care of it."

"Fine."

"Tell the coachman to stop, Porthos, we're here."

"This is the place?"

"Yes."

"How can that be!? We're at Les Halles, and you said the house was at the corner of rue de l'Arbre-Sec."

"That's right, but take a look."

"Well, I'm looking, and I see . . ."

"What?"

"That we're at Les Halles, damn it!"

"You certainly don't want our horses to climb on top of the coach in front of us, do you?"

"No."

"Or the coach in front of us to climb on top of the one in front of it?"

"Even less so."

"Or the second coach to ride down the thirty or forty others that arrived before us?"

"Damn it, you're right!"

"Ah!"

"So many people, old friend, so many people."

"Huh!"

"And what are all those people doing?"

"It's quite simple. They're waiting their turn."

"Have the actors of the Hôtel de Bourgogne moved?"

"No, it's their turn to enter Monsieur Percerin's home."

"So we're going to wait too?"

"We're going to be more ingenious than they and less proud."

"What are we going to do?"

"We're going to get out, pass through the pages and lackeys, and enter the tailor's home, which I'll answer for, especially if you take the lead."

"Let's go," said Porthos.

And they both got out and walked toward the house.

The traffic had jammed because Monsieur Percerin's door was closed. A lackey standing there was explaining to the illustrious clients of the illustrious tailor that Monsieur Percerin was not receiving anyone for now. The people in the street repeated what the tall lackey had, in strictest confidence, told a grand seigneur whom he favored: namely, that Monsieur Percerin was making five suits for the king, and that, given the urgency of the situation, he was in his studio pondering the cuts, colors, and ornaments of those five suits.

Several people, satisfied with this explanation, turned around, happy to relay it; but several more tenacious souls demanded that the door be opened. Among them were three Blue Ribbons (Knights of the Order of the Holy Ghost) meant for a ballet that was certain to flop if those three Blue Ribbon Knights didn't have suits from the fingers of the great Percerin.

D'Artagnan, pushing Porthos, who shoved his way through the crowd, reached the counters, behind which the apprentices were struggling to reply as best they could.

We neglected to mention that the footmen at the doorway had tried to keep Porthos out like the others; but d'Artagnan had merely uttered these words: "The king's order!" And the two friends were promptly admitted.

Those poor apprentices had their work cut out for them as they did their best to represent their absent employer and respond to the demands of the clients. They would stop in mid-stitch to utter a sentence, and when wounded pride or useless waiting brought them overly rough treatment, the boy who was attacked dived under the counter.

The procession of dissatisfied lords offered a tableau teeming with curious details.

Our musketeer captain, whose eyes were swift and sure, took in the entire scene with a single glance. But after sweeping through the groups, his eyes rested on a man in front of him. This man, perching on a stool, barely loomed over the sheltering counter. About forty years old, he had a pale, mournful face and soft, bright eyes. With his chin propped on one hand, this calm and curious observer gazed at d'Artagnan and the others. No doubt recognizing our captain, he pulled his hat down over his eyes.

That gesture may have been what drew d'Artagnan's attention. If such was the case, then the man had achieved the exact opposite of his intention.

The man's garb was quite simple, and his hair was cut evenly enough so that unheeding clients might take him for a mere assistant tailor squatting behind the oak board and punctiliously stitching cloth or velvet.

Nevertheless, this man raised his head too often to be working fruitfully with his fingers.

D'Artagnan was no dupe, and he fully saw that if this man was working, it was assuredly not with fabrics.

"Hey!" said d'Artagnan, addressing the man. "Have you become a tailor's apprentice, Monsieur Molière?"

"Shush, Monsieur d'Artagnan," the man murmured. "Shush! For God's sake. You're going to expose me!"

"So what's the harm?"

"There's no harm, but—"

"But you mean that it's not so harmless either, right?"

"Alas, it's not! You see, I was busy looking at some intriguing faces."

"Go ahead, go ahead, Monsieur Molière. I can understand your interest, and . . . I won't interfere any further with your studies."

"Thank you!"

"But there's one condition. You have to tell me where Monsieur Percerin really is."

"Oh, gladly. He's in his studio. Only . . ."

"Only no one can enter?"

"Inaccessible!"

"To everyone?"

"To everyone. He had me come in here so I could be comfortable while making my observations, and then he went away."

"Well, my dear Monsieur Molière, you will go and announce me, won't you?"

"I?" cried Molière, sounding like a good dog losing the bone that it has legitimately won. "I? Move? Ah! Monsieur d'Artagnan, you're treating me so badly!"

"If you don't go and announce me immediately," d'Artagnan

murmured, "I can warn you about one thing: I won't let you see the friend I've brought."

Molière imperceptibly motioned toward Porthos. "This one, right?"

"Yes."

Molière perused Porthos with the kind of focus that probes minds and hearts. The object of his scrutiny must have seemed very promising, for Molière promptly stood up and went to the next room.

4
The Swatches

During those moments, the crowd slowly dissipated, leaving a murmur or a threat at each angle of the counter, just as ebbing waves leave a bit of foam or crushed seaweed on the ocean's sandbanks.

Molière reappeared ten minutes later, signaling to d'Artagnan under the tapestry. D'Artagnan hurried, pulling along Porthos through rather intricate corridors until they reached Percerin's studio. With his sleeves rolled up, the old man was twisting a piece of brocade with large gold flowers, trying to produce beautiful reflections. Catching sight of d'Artagnan, he left his fabric and went over to him, not radiant, not courteous, but, in sum, quite civil.

"Monsieur Captain of the Guards," he said, "please excuse me, but I'm up to my ears."

"Yes, suits for the king. I know all about it, my dear Monsieur Percerin. I was told you're making three."

"Five, my dear monsieur, five."

"Three or five, it doesn't matter to me, Master Percerin, and I know you'll make the most beautiful suits in the world."

"Yes, we know. Once they're finished, they will be the most beautiful suits in the world. I won't deny it. But before being the most beautiful suits in the world, they have to exist. And for that, Monsieur Captain, I need time."

"Bah! Two days! That's a lot more time than you need, Monsieur Percerin," said d'Artagnan, very self-possessed.

Percerin raised his head like a man who's not used to being challenged, even in his whims. . . . But d'Artagnan ignored the mood that was overcoming the illustrious tailor of brocade.

"My dear Monsieur Percerin," d'Artagnan went on, "I've brought you a client."

"Ah! Ah!" Percerin retorted sullenly.

"Baron du Vallon de Bracieux de Pierrefonds," d'Artagnan continued.

Percerin tried to bow, which did not appeal to the terrible Porthos, who had been scowling at the tailor ever since arriving in his studio.

"A good friend of mine," d'Artagnan wound up.

"I will serve Monsieur," said Percerin, "but later on."

"Later on? When?"

"Well . . . when I have the time."

"You already said that to my valet," Porthos broke in, annoyed.

"Could be," said Percerin. "I'm almost always pressed for time."

"My friend," said Porthos sententiously, "a man's always got the time he wants."

Percerin flushed crimson, which is always disturbing in old men hoary with age.

"Goodness," he said. "Monsieur is quite free to try elsewhere."

"C'mon, c'mon, Percerin," d'Artagnan tossed in. "You're not very amiable today. Well, I'm going to say one last word, it's going to make you fall to your knees before us: Monsieur is not only a friend of mine, he's also friends with Monsieur Fouquet."

"Aha!" said the tailor. "Now, that's a horse of a different color." Turning to Porthos, he asked, "Is Monsieur Baron attached to Monsieur Fouquet?"

"I'm attached to myself!" Porthos blew up at the very moment that the tapestry was lifted to allow a newcomer to pass through.

Molière was observing. D'Artagnan was laughing. Porthos was fuming.

"My dear Percerin," said d'Artagnan, "you will make a suit for the baron. I'm the one asking you."

"I won't say no to you, Captain."

"But that's not all. You will make his suit immediately."

"Impossible in less than a week."

"You might as well refuse to make it, because the suit is destined to be worn at the celebration in Vaux."

"I repeat: it's impossible," the obstinate oldster retorted.

"Don't say that, dear Monsieur Percerin, especially since I'm the one asking you." At the sound of that gentle, silvery voice, d'Artagnan pricked up his ears. It was Aramis.

"Monsieur d'Herblay!" cried the tailor.

"Aramis!" murmured d'Artagnan.

"Ah! Our bishop!" said Porthos.

"Hello, d'Artagnan; hello, Porthos; hello, dear friends. C'mon, c'mon, dear Monsieur Percerin, make the suit for Monsieur, and, I guarantee that by doing this, you'll be pleasing Monsieur Fouquet." And he accompanied those words with a sign that meant: "Consent and dismiss."

Apparently, Aramis had greater influence on Master Percerin than even d'Artagnan, for the tailor nodded his head by way of agreement. Turning to Porthos, he snapped, "Get your measures taken on the other side."

Porthos blushed formidably.

D'Artagnan, in the face of the brewing storm, murmured to Molière, "My dear monsieur, the man you see before you feels dishonored when somebody scrutinizes his God-given flesh and bones. Study this type, Master Aristophanes, and take advantage of the opportunity."

Molière didn't need encouragement. His eyes were glued to Baron Porthos.

"Monsieur," said Molière, "if you'll come with me, I'll have you measured for a suit without your being touched."

"Oh!" said Porthos. "How would you do that, my friend?"

"Neither a yard nor a foot will be applied to your seams. This is a new procedure, which we thought up to measure people of quality who are touchy about being touched by yokels. We have hypersensitive people who cannot bear being measured—a ceremony that, in my opinion, offends man's natural majesty. And if, sir, you happen to be one of those people . . ."

"Damn it! I do believe I am!"

"Well, that's excellent, Baron, you can be the first to use our invention."

"But how in God's name do we go about it?" asked Porthos, beaming.

"Sir," said Molière with a bow. "If you care to follow me, you will see."

Aramis gaped at these goings-on. Perhaps, he figured, d'Artagnan's lively conduct indicated that he would leave with Porthos so as not to miss the conclusion of a scene that had begun so nicely. But perspicacious as Aramis may have been, he was wrong. Porthos and Molière left together. D'Artagnan remained with Percerin. Why? Out of sheer curiosity, that was all. He must have been planning to enjoy a few more minutes of his good friend Aramis's presence. Once Molière and Porthos had vanished, d'Artagnan went over to the Bishop of Vannes, which seemed to annoy the latter very greatly.

"A suit for you too, right, dear friend?"

Aramis smiled. "No."

"But you're still going to Vaux?"

"I'm going, but not in a new suit. You're forgetting, dear d'Artagnan, that a poor Bishop of Vannes doesn't have the wherewithal to order new clothes for every celebration."

The musketeer laughed. "And what about poems? Have we stopped writing them?"

"Oh, d'Artagnan!" Aramis rejoined. "I haven't thought about those foolish things in quite a while."

"Fine," said d'Artagnan, unconvinced.

As for Percerin, he had plunged back into his contemplation of brocades.

Aramis smiled. "Don't you notice, dear d'Artagnan, that we're troubling this good man terribly?"

"Ah, ah!" the musketeer muttered. "You mean I'm troubling him, dear friend." Then aloud: "Fine! Let's go. I've got no other business here, and if you're as free as I am, dear Aramis—"

"No! I myself wanted—"

"Ah! You've got something private to tell Percerin? Why didn't you say so immediately?"

"Private," repeated Aramis. "Yes, certainly. But not private from you, d'Artagnan. Please believe me when I say that I would never have anything private enough to keep from a friend like you."

"Oh, no, no! I'm leaving," d'Artagnan insisted, though his voice had a sharply inquisitive touch. For Aramis's embarrassment, however well disguised, had not eluded him. D'Artagnan knew that in Aramis's impenetrable soul, everything, even the most ostensible trivia, usually headed toward a goal. And though the goal was unknown, the musketeer knew it was important, given his familiarity with his friend's character.

Aramis, for his part, inferring that d'Artagnan suspected something, urged him: "Please stay. This is what it's about." Next he addressed the tailor: "My dear Percerin . . ." Then: "I'm actually quite glad that you're here, d'Artagnan."

"Ah! Really!" said d'Artagnan a third time, less hoodwinked than before.

Percerin didn't budge. Aramis violently woke him up from his meditation by snatching the fabric that was its object. "My dear Percerin, I've got Monsieur Le Brun nearby, he's one of Monsieur Fouquet's painters."

"Ah! Very good!" d'Artagnan mused. "But why Le Brun?"

Aramis looked at d'Artagnan, who seemed to be peering at some engravings by Marcantonio Raimondi.

"And you want me to make a suit like that of the Epicureans," the worthy tailor responded, listening with only half an ear as he tried to recapture his brocade.

"An Epicurean suit?" asked d'Artagnan inquisitively.

"Well," said Aramis with his most charming smile, "our dear d'Artagnan is fated to know all our secrets this evening. Yes, my friend, you've heard of Monsieur Fouquet's Epicureans, haven't you?"

"I think so. Isn't it a kind of secret society of poets, including La Fontaine, Loret, Pellisson, Molière, and goodness knows whom else? And isn't its academy in Saint-Mandé?"

"Exactly. Well, we're giving our poets a uniform and forming them into a regiment in the king's service."

"I get it: Monsieur Fouquet wants to surprise the king. Don't worry! If that's Monsieur Le Brun's secret, I won't breathe a word."

"Always agreeable, my friend. No, Monsieur Le Brun has nothing to do with this. His secret is far more important!"

"Well, if it's all that important, I'd rather not know it," said d'Artagnan, acting as if he were about to leave.

"Come in, Monsieur Le Brun, come in," said Aramis, his right hand opening a side door and his left hand holding d'Artagnan back.

"Goodness, I don't understand at all," said Percerin.

Aramis did a double take, as we say in the theater: "My dear Monsieur Percerin. You're making five suits for the king, right? One in brocade? One for hunting? One in velvet? One in satin? And one in Florentine cloth?"

"Yes. But how do you know all that, monseigneur?" Percerin was dumbfounded.

"It's quite simple, my dear monsieur. There's going to be a hunt, a feast, a concert, a promenade, and a reception. Those five fabrics are prescribed by etiquette."

"You know everything, monseigneur!"

"And a lot more too," murmured d'Artagnan.

"But," the tailor cried triumphantly, "what you don't know, monseigneur, even though you're a prince of the church, and what nobody will know, except for the king, Mademoiselle de la Vallière, and myself, is the colors of the fabrics and the kinds of ornaments. Those are what constitute the cut, the harmony, the overall appearance!"

"Well," said Aramis, "that's precisely what I'm asking you to reveal to me, dear Monsieur Percerin."

"Bah!" exclaimed the terrified tailor even though Aramis had spoken those words in the sweetest and most honeyed voice. On reflection, his request sounded so exaggerated, so ludicrous, so outrageous, that Monsieur Percerin first giggled very softly, then chuckled more loudly, then finally burst into laughter. D'Artagnan copied him, not because he also found the request profoundly hilarious but to keep Aramis from cooling off.

Aramis let them laugh. Then, once they'd calmed down, he said: "At first blush, I seem to be making an absurd request, don't I? But d'Artagnan, who is wisdom incarnate, is about to tell you that I have no choice but to make this request."

"Let's see!" said the attentive musketeer. With his marvelous flair, he sensed that so far they had only been skirmishing and that the moment of battle was now at hand.

"Let's see!" said Percerin, incredulous.

"Why," Aramis continued, "is Monsieur Fouquet throwing a party for the king? To please him, right?"

"Assuredly," replied Percerin.

D'Artagnan nodded in approval.

"Out of what attentiveness? What fine imagination? In a chain of surprises like the ones we were just talking about in regard to a regiment for our Epicureans?"

"How splendid?"

"Well, this is the surprise, my good friend. Monsieur Le Brun, who is here, is a man who draws very precisely."

"Yes," said Percerin, "I've seen his paintings and I noticed that the clothes were rendered meticulously. That's why I instantly agreed to make him a suit, either in harmony with those of the Epicureans or for him personally."

"Dear monsieur, we accept your promise. And we will come back to it later on. But for the moment, Monsieur Le Brun doesn't need the suits you'll make for him, he needs the suits you're making for the king."

Percerin jumped back, which d'Artagnan, a calm and appreciative man par excellence, did not consider exaggerated. After all, Aramis's perilous statement had such bizarre and hair-raising aspects.

"The king's suits! Hand over the king's suits to just anybody! Oh, goodness, Your Lordship! You're crazy!" cried the poor tailor, his back against the wall.

"Help me, d'Artagnan," said Aramis, more and more tranquil and beaming. "Help me to persuade Monsieur, for you understand, don't you?"

"Mmm, mmm! Not really, I must admit."

"C'mon, my friend. You don't understand that Monsieur Fouquet wants to surprise the king, who'll find his portrait when he reaches Vaux. The resemblance will be striking, and the king's likeness will be wearing the same clothes as the king."

"Ah, yes, yes!" exclaimed the musketeer, almost persuaded, since the explanation sounded so plausible. "Yes, my dear Aramis, you're right. Yes, it's a wonderful idea. I bet you thought it up, didn't you?"

"I'm not sure," the bishop replied nonchalantly. "It was either me or Monsieur Fouquet. . . ." Then, scouring Percerin's face after noticing d'Artagnan's hesitance, Aramis asked: "Well, Monsieur Percerin, what do you say?"

"I say that—"

"That you are free to refuse, no doubt. I'm well aware of it and I have no intention of forcing you, my dear sir. I'll go further: I even understand all your tact in refusing to go along with Monsieur Fouquet's plan—you're afraid you'd seem to be fawning on the king. A noble heart, Monsieur Percerin! A noble heart!"

The tailor stammered.

"It would indeed be a fine way of flattering the young prince," Aramis went on. "But Monsieur Fouquet said to me: 'If Percerin refuses, tell him that I'll never hold it against him and I'll respect him as much as ever. Only . . .' "

"Only . . . ?" Percerin echoed nervously.

" 'Only,' Monsieur Fouquet went on, 'I will be forced to tell the king: "Sire, I had planned to offer Your Majesty his effigy, but with a perhaps exaggerated yet nevertheless respectable sense of tact, Monsieur Percerin was against it." ' "

"Against it?" cried the tailor, horrified at the thought of bearing full responsibility. "I against Monsieur Fouquet's wish, his desire to give pleasure to the king?! Oh, what an ugly word you've used, Your Lordship! I 'against'? Oh, it wasn't I who used that word, thank goodness! Captain d'Artagnan of the Musketeers can bear witness to that. Isn't that so, Monsieur d'Artagnan? I'm not against anything, am I?"

D'Artagnan held up his hands, indicating that he'd rather stay neutral. He sensed an intrigue—a comedy or a tragedy. He couldn't for the life of him guess what it was, but he preferred to wait on the sidelines.

Meanwhile, Percerin, haunted by the fear that someone could tell the king that the tailor was opposed to the king's surprise, had pulled a chair over to Le Brun. Next the tailor removed four resplendent outfits from an armoire (the fifth suit being still in the hands of his assistants). He slipped the four suits over four Bergamo dummies, which, arriving in France during Concini's period, had been given to Percerin II by Marshal d'Ancre after the Italian tailors had been routed by their competition.

Le Brun began to draw, then paint the garments.

But Aramis, who was carefully watching all the phases of the painter's work, stopped him abruptly: "I don't think you're quite capturing the colors, my dear Monsieur Le Brun. They won't come up to your expectations, and the perfect resemblance that's absolutely necessary will be lost on the canvas. We'd need more time to observe the nuances closely."

"That's true," said Percerin. "But time is what we're lacking, and that, Your Lordship will agree, is beyond my power."

"Then we'll fail," said Aramis calmly, "and only for lack of accuracy in the colors."

However, Le Brun copied fabrics and ornaments with the most solemn fidelity, while Aramis looked on with unconcealed impatience.

C'mon, c'mon! d'Artagnan kept wondering. For God's sake, what kind of imbroglio are you hatching here?

"It's definitely not going to work, Monsieur Le Brun," said Aramis. "Close your boxes and roll up your canvases."

"The light is terrible here," cried the chagrined painter.

"I've got an idea, Monsieur Le Brun, an idea. If we had, say, a swatch of the fabrics, and with time and better light—"

"Great!" exclaimed Le Brun. "I can give you my guarantee."

"Fine!" said d'Artagnan. "That should do it! We need a swatch of each fabric. Damn it! Can we get that from Percerin?"

The tailor, left without a leg to stand on, taken in by Aramis's pseudo-simplicity, cut out five swatches, which he then handed to the Bishop of Vannes.

"That's much better, isn't it?" Aramis said to d'Artagnan. "Don't you agree?"

"I agree, my dear Aramis," said d'Artagnan, "that you're still the same."

"And, consequently, I'm still your friend," said the bishop in a somewhat engaging tone.

"Yes, yes," said d'Artagnan out loud. Then more softly: "If I'm your dupe—double Jesuit that you are—I at least don't want to be your accomplice, and so as not to be your accomplice I really ought to leave.

"Good-bye, Aramis," he added out loud. "Good-bye, I'm joining Porthos."

"Wait for me," said Aramis, pocketing the swatches. "I'm done. And I won't regret saying a final word to our friend."

Le Brun packed up. Percerin put his creations back in the armoire. Aramis pressed his pocket to make sure the swatches were nicely tucked away. And the visitors all left the studio.

5

Where Molière Might Have Drawn His Inspiration for The Burgher As Aristocrat

D'Artagnan found Porthos in the next room. But this was no irritated Porthos, no disappointed Porthos. It was a beaming, charming, radiant Porthos, chatting with Molière, who gazed at him with virtually idolatrous eyes, like a man who not only had never seen anything better, but who'd never seen anything as good.

Aramis headed straight for Porthos and held out his fine, white hand, which was about to be engulfed in his old friend's gigantic paw—an action that d'Artagnan never risked without a quiver of malaise. But, having submitted to the amicable pressure without suffering too greatly, the Bishop of Vannes turned toward Molière.

"Well, sir, will you accompany me to Saint-Mandé?"

"I'll go wherever you like, Your Lordship," Molière replied.

"To Saint-Mandé!?" cried Porthos, surprised to see the

proud Bishop of Vannes on such familiar terms with a tailor's assistant. "What, Aramis!? You're taking Monsieur to Saint-Mandé?"

"Yes," Aramis smiled. "Time is of the essence."

"And besides, my dear Porthos," d'Artagnan continued, Monsieur Molière is not quite what he appears to be."

"How's that?" asked Porthos.

"Monsieur is one of Master Percerin's top assistants and he's expected in Saint-Mandé. He's to have the Epicureans try on the party suits that were ordered by Monsieur Fouquet."

"That's right!" said Molière. "Yes, monsieur."

"Well, then, come, my dear Monsieur Molière," said Aramis, "so long as you're done with Monsieur du Vallon."

"We're done," replied Porthos.

"And you're satisfied?" asked d'Artagnan.

"Completely satisfied," answered Porthos.

Molière took leave of Porthos, bowing and scraping, and he shook the hand that was furtively held out to him by the Captain of the Musketeers.

"Monsieur," Porthos concluded with a simper, "above all, be on time."

"You will have your suit tomorrow, Baron," replied Molière. And he left with Aramis.

D'Artagnan took Porthos's arm: "You're so content with this tailor, my dear Porthos! Just what did he do for you?"

"What did he do for me, old pal?!" Porthos enthusiastically cried. "What did he do for me?"

"Yes, that's what I'm asking. What did he do for you?"

"My friend, he did what no other tailor has ever done: he took my measurements without touching me."

"You don't say! Tell me all about it, old pal."

"First of all, old pal, he rustled up a whole bunch of dummies in all sizes, hoping he'd find one with my measurements. But the biggest dummy, that of a Swiss Guard drum major, was two inches too short and half a foot too skinny."

"Really?"

"It's as I have the honor of telling you, my dear d'Artagnan. However, this Monsieur Molière is a great man, or, at the very least, a great tailor. He wasn't the slightest bit put off."

"So what did he do?"

"Oh, it was very simple. Goodness, I just can't believe that all other tailors are too dense to have hit on this idea in the first place. How much pain and humiliation I'd've been spared!"

"Not to mention suits, Porthos, old pal."

"Yes, thirty suits."

"Well, my dear Porthos, why don't you describe Monsieur Molière's approach."

"Molière? That's his name, isn't it? I'll make sure to remember it."

"Yes, or Poquelin, if you prefer."

"No, I prefer Molière. If I want to recall his name, I'll think of the word 'volière' [aviary], and I've got an aviary in Pierrefonds. . . ."

"Fabulous, old pal. And what is this Monsieur Molière's approach?"

"This is it. Instead of chopping me up like all those good-for-nothings, making me bend my back, strain my joints—nothing but contemptible and dishonoring practices."

D'Artagnan nodded in approval.

" 'Monsieur,' he told me, 'a man of honor has to measure himself. Please be so kind as to step over to this mirror.' So I stepped over to the mirror. I must confess that I didn't quite see what that good Monsieur Volière wanted of me."

"Molière."

"Ah, yes. Molière, Molière. And since I was still scared of getting measured, I told him: 'Watch what you're doing. I warn you, I'm very ticklish.' But in his gentle voice (he's a courteous fellow, old pal, you must agree). In his gentle voice he said: 'Sir, if the suit is to fit properly, it has to be made in your image. And your image is reflected exactly by the mirror. We're going to measure your reflection.' "

"In fact," said d'Artagnan, "you saw yourself in the mirror. But where did they dig up a mirror that shows you from head to foot?"

"Old pal, it's the same mirror that the king sees himself in."

"Yes, but the king is a foot and a half shorter than you."

"Well, I don't know how it happened—it was probably a way of flattering the king—but the mirror was too big for me.

It's true that its height was made up of three superimposed plates of Venetian glass and its width was made up of three juxtaposed plates of Venetian glass."

"Yes, old friend! Your words are so admirable! Where the devil did you acquire them?"

"In Belle-Île. Aramis explained them to the architect."

"Ah! Very good! Let's get back to the mirror, dear friend."

"Well, our good Monsieur Volière—"

"Molière."

"That's right: Molière. You'll see: now I'll be remembering his name all too well. This good Monsieur Molière used a little whiting to trace lines on the mirror, outlines of my arms and shoulders, and he recited this maxim, which I find admirable: 'A suit should never constrain its wearer.' "

"Honestly," said d'Artagnan, "that's a fine maxim, which, unfortunately, is not always practiced."

"That's why I found it all the more astonishing, especially when he expounded on it."

"Ah, he expounded on it?"

"Damn right!"

"Let's hear how he expounded."

" 'Allowing,' Molière went on, 'that, in a difficult circumstance, or in an awkward situation, one may have one's coat on one's shoulder and refuse to take it off.' "

"That's true," said d'Artagnan.

" 'Thus,' Monsieur Volière went on—"

"Molière."

"Molière, right. 'Thus,' Monsieur Molière went on, 'you need to draw your sword, monsieur, but you have your coat on your back. What do you do?'

" 'I take it off,' I replied.

" 'Absolutely not!' he retorted.

" 'Why not?'

" 'Your coat, I tell you, must be so well crafted that it never constrains you, even when you draw a sword.'

" 'Aha!'

" 'Take the en garde position,' he went on. And I did with such marvelous aplomb that two windowpanes burst. 'It's nothing, it's nothing,' he said. 'Stay like that.' I raised my left arm, my forearm was gracefully bent, my sleeve drooping, my wrist sharply curved, while my semi-extended right arm shielded my waist with my elbow and my chest with my wrist."

"Yes," said d'Artagnan, "it's the true en garde, the classical en garde."

"You've hit the nail on the head, old friend. Meanwhile, Volière—"

"Molière."

"Now, frankly, dear friend, I prefer calling him—how did you pronounce his other name?"

"Poquelin."

"I prefer calling him Poquelin."

"And why should you remember this name better than the other?"

"Listen. . . . His name is Poquelin, right?"

"Right."

"I'll remember Madame Coquenard."

"Fine."

"I'll change 'Coc' to 'Poc,' 'nard' to 'lin,' and so instead of Coquenard I'll have Poquelin."

"That's wonderful!" cried d'Artagnan, dumbfounded. "Go on, my friend. I'm all ears with admiration."

"So Coquelin sketched my arm on the mirror."

"You mean Poquelin."

"What did I say?"

"You said Coquelin."

"Ah! You're right. So Poquelin sketched my arm on the mirror. And he took his sweet time, he kept looking at me. The fact is that I cut a fine figure.

" 'Are you getting tired?' he asked me.

" 'A little,' I answered, my knees bending. 'But I can hold out for another hour.'

" 'No, no, I won't allow it!' he said. 'We've got willing boys here who'll make it their business to support your arms, just as people used to support the arms of prophets who were invoking the Lord.'

" 'Very well.'

" 'It won't humiliate you?'

" 'My friend,' I told him, 'there is, I believe, a vast difference between being supported and being measured.' "

"That distinction makes perfect sense," d'Artagnan broke in.

"Well," Porthos went on, "he signaled. Two boys came over. One supported my left arm, while the other boy supported my right arm with infinite skill.

" 'A third boy!' he said. And a third boy came over. 'Support Monsieur's waist.' The boy supported my waist."

"So that you were posing?" asked d'Artagnan.

"Absolutely, and Pocquenard sketched me on the mirror."

"Poquelin, my friend."

"Poquelin, you're right. Well, I certainly prefer calling him Volière."

"Yes, and then it was over, wasn't it?"

"During that time, Volière drew me on the mirror."

"That was gallant of him."

"I love that method. It's respectful and it puts everyone in his place."

"How did it end?"

"It ended, my friend, without anyone having touched me."

"Except for the three boys who supported you."

"True enough, but I believe I've already described the difference between supporting and measuring."

"Very true," said d'Artagnan, who then muttered to himself, "Goodness, if I'm not mistaken, I've brought a windfall to that rascal Molière, and I'm sure we'll find the scene true to life in some comedy."

Porthos smiled.

"What's so funny?" d'Artagnan asked.

"Must I tell you? Well, I'm laughing because I'm so happy."

"That's very true. I don't know any happier man than you. But what new happiness has come to you?"

"Well, my friend, congratulate me."

"I couldn't ask for more!"

"Apparently, I'm the first person who's been measured in that way."

"Are you sure?"

"Pretty sure. I figured it out on the basis of certain signals that Volière exchanged with his boys."

"Well, my friend, from what I know of Molière that's not surprising."

"Volière, my friend."

"Get off it, for God's sake! I'm willing to let you say Volière, but I'll continue saying Molière. Well, as I was saying: That doesn't surprise me about Molière. He's an ingenious fellow, and you were his inspiration for that fine idea."

"He'll make use of it eventually, I'm sure."

"What do you mean: 'Make use of it'!? Of course he'll make use of it—lots of use! Look, old friend: Of all our well-known tailors Molière is the one who does the best job of dressing our barons, our counts, and our marquis . . . to their measure."

Upon that utterance, of which we shall not discuss the depth or the relevance, d'Artagnan and Porthos left Percerin's studio and got into their carriage. If the reader doesn't mind, we'll leave them there and return to Molière and Aramis in Saint-Mandé.

6

The Hive, the Bees, and the Honey

The Bishop of Vannes, annoyed at having run into d'Artagnan in Master Percerin's studio, was in a foul mood when he went back to Saint-Mandé.

Molière, on the contrary, was delighted at stumbling upon an excellent character and knowing where to get hold of the original when he wanted to re-create the scene. And so his mood on returning to Saint-Mandé was utterly elated.

The left side of the entire second floor was occupied by the most illustrious Epicureans in Paris and the most frequent visitors of the house. Like bees in their cells, each person was in his own compartment, absorbed in producing a honey for the royal cake that Monsieur Fouquet planned to serve His Majesty Louis XIV during the celebration at Vaux.

Pellisson, propping his head on his hand, was digging the

foundation for the prologue of *Les Fâcheux* (*The Nuisances*), a comedy in three acts, to be mounted by Poquelin de Molière, as d'Artagnan put it, or Coquelin de Volière, as Porthos put it.

Loret, in all his naïveté as a newsmonger (newsmongers of all ages have always been naïve), was composing his account of the Vaux celebration before that celebration even took place.

La Fontaine was wandering about from one person to the next: a distraught and distracted shadow, tedious, unbearable, buzzing and humming poetic blather a thousandfold on every shoulder. He annoyed Pellisson so often that the latter, testily lifting his head, said: "C'mon, La Fontaine, at least cull a rhyme! After all, you say you're walking in the gardens of Parnassus."

"What rhyme would you like?" asked the fabulist (as Madame de Sévigné had dubbed him).

"I want a rhyme for 'lumière' [light]."

" 'Ornière' [rut]," replied La Fontaine.

"Well, old friend," said Loret, "it's impossible to talk about ruts when you're vaunting the delights of Vaux."

"Besides, they don't rhyme," cried Pellisson.

"What do you mean they don't rhyme?" La Fontaine exclaimed in surprise.

"You have a detestable habit, old friend—a habit that will forever prevent you from becoming a poet of the first water. Your rhymes are sloppy!"

"Oh! You really think so, Pellisson?"

"Yes indeed, old friend, I really think so. Remember: A rhyme is never good enough if you can find a better one."

"Fine. Then from now on I'll stick to writing prose," said La Fontaine, who was taking the reproach seriously. "Ah, I've often suspected that I was a rascal of a poet! Yes, that's the plain, honest truth."

"Don't say that, old friend. You're too opinionated, and there's a lot of good stuff in your fables."

"I'll start right in," La Fontaine continued, engrossed in his idea, "by burning a hundred lines that I've just composed."

"Where are they?'

"In my head."

"Well, if they're in your head, you can't burn them."

"True enough," said La Fontaine. "But if I don't burn them . . ."

"Well? What'll happen if you don't burn them?"

"They'll haunt me forever, and I'll never forget them."

"Damn it!" Loret cried. "That's a dangerous fix to be in. You could go crazy!"

"Damn it, damn it, damn it!" La Fontaine reiterated. "What should I do?"

"I've got a solution," said Molière, who had just come in during those last few words.

"Namely?"

"Jot them down. Then burn them."

"How simple! I'd never have hit on that! What a mind he's got—that devil Molière!" said La Fontaine. Striking his forehead, he added: "You'll never be anything but an ass, Jean de La Fontaine!"

"What did you say, my friend?" Molière broke in as he approached the poet after hearing his aside.

"I said that I will never be anything but an ass, dear colleague." La Fontaine heaved a deep sigh, and his eyes puffed up with sadness. "Yes, my friend," he went on, growing more and more woeful, "I guess I'm a sloppy rhymer."

"You're wrong."

"You can see! I'm a lowlife!"

"Who told you that?"

"Damn it! Pellisson told me. Didn't you, Pellisson?"

The latter, again absorbed in his work, refused to answer.

"Why, if Pellisson called you a lowlife," cried Molière, "then he's grievously offended you!"

"You think so? . . ."

"Ah! Dear friend. Since you're a nobleman, I advise you not to let such an insult go unpunished."

"Pooh!" said La Fontaine.

"Have you ever dueled?"

"Once, my friend, with a lieutenant in the light cavalry."

"What had he done to you?"

"Apparently, he'd seduced my wife."

"Aha!" said Molière, blanching slightly.

But since the others had returned upon those last few words, Molière's lips kept his sarcastic smirk, which had nearly faded. The playwright kept drawing out La Fontaine: "What was the upshot of your duel?"

"The upshot was that my adversary knocked my sword out of my hand, then apologized and promised never to set foot in my home again."

"And you were satisfied?" asked Molière.

"Absolutely not! Quite the opposite! I picked up my sword and said: 'Pardon me, monsieur, I'm not dueling with you because you were my wife's lover, but because I was told that I had to fight you. Now, since I've never been happy except when you were seeing her, do me the favor of visiting my home as before, or, damn it, we'll continue the duel.' And so," La Fontaine went on, "he was forced to remain my wife's lover, and I continue being the happiest husband on earth."

They all burst out laughing. Molière was the only one to pass his hand over his eyes. Why? Perhaps to wipe a tear, perhaps to stifle a sigh. Alas, as we know, Molière was a moralist, but he was not a philosopher.

"It doesn't matter," he said, going back to the topic under discussion. "Pellisson has offended you."

"Ah, how true, I totally forgot."

"And I'm going to call him out on your behalf."

"You can if you feel it's indispensable."

"I feel it's indispensable, and I'm going there now."

"Wait!" said La Fontaine. "I need your advice."

"About what? This offense?"

"No. Tell me if 'ornière' really doesn't rhyme with 'lumière.' "

"I'd rhyme them."

"Damn! I knew it!"

"And I've composed a hundred thousand similar verses in my life."

"A hundred thousand!" cried La Fontaine. "That's four times the length of Monsieur Chapelain's *Maid of Orleans.* Did your hundred thousand verses deal with the same subject, old friend?"

"Listen to me, you eternal scatterbrain," said Molière.

"It's certain," La Fontaine went on, "that 'légume' [vegetable], for instance, rhymes with 'posthume' [posthumous]."

"Especially in the plural."

"Yes, especially in the plural, given that in the plural it's not just the last three letters that rhyme, it's the last four as in 'ornière' and 'lumière.' Put them in the plural, my dear Pellisson," said La Fontaine, patting his colleague on the back, "and it'll rhyme." He had forgotten all about the insult.

"Huh?" said Pellisson.

"Damn it! Molière says so, and Molière knows a thing or two. He himself states that he's composed a hundred thousand verses."

"C'mon!" Molière laughed. "He's taken off!"

"It's like 'rivage' [shore], which rhymes admirably with 'herbage.' I'd stake my life on it."

"But . . ." said Molière.

"I'm telling you all this," La Fontaine went on, "because you're preparing a divertissement for Sceaux, aren't you?"

"Yes, *The Nuisances*."

"Ah, *The Nuisances*, that's it. Yes, I remember. Well, I figured that a prologue would go very well with your divertissement."

"Certainly! That would be marvelous!"

"So you agree with me?"

"I agree so much that I asked you to write this prologue."

"You asked me? Me?"

"Yes, you. And when you turned me down, I asked you to ask Pellisson, who's working on it now."

"Ah! So that's what he's doing? Goodness, my dear Molière, you could be right at times."

"When?"

"When you call me scatterbrained. It's an awful fault! I'll get rid of it and I'll write your prologue."

"But Pellisson is already doing it!"

"That's right! Ah, I'm a twofold brute! Loret was right when he called me a lowlife!"

"That wasn't Loret, my friend."

"Well, whoever said it—so what! So your divertissement is

titled *The Nuisances*? Fine. Wouldn't you rhyme 'heureux' [happy] with 'fâcheux' [nuisance]?"

"In a pinch."

"And even with 'capricieux' [whimsical]?"

"Oh no! Absolutely never!"

"That would be foolhardy, wouldn't it? But just why would it be foolhardy?"

"Because the endings are too different."

"I imagined," said La Fontaine, leaving Molière and going over to Loret. "I imagined—"

"What did you imagine?" Loret cut him off in midsentence. "C'mon! Out with it!"

"You're writing the prologue for *The Nuisances*, aren't you?"

"No, damn it! Pellisson's doing it!"

"Ah, Pellisson!" cried La Fontaine, now looking for Pellisson. "I imagined that the nymph of Vaux—"

"Ah! Lovely!" exclaimed Loret. "The nymph of Vaux! Thank you, La Fontaine. You've just handed me the final two lines of my gazette:

> The nymph of Vaux gave them the prize
> For their hard work in her soft eyes.

"Excellent! Now, that's a rhyme," said Pellisson. "If you rhymed like that, La Fontaine, you'd be doing a fine job."

"But apparently I do rhyme like that. For Loret says I gave him the last two lines, which he just read out loud."

"Well, if you rhyme like that, then tell me: How would you begin my prologue?"

"I would say, for instance: 'Oh, nymph . . . that . . .' I'd put a verb after 'that,' the second person singular of the present indicative, and I'd go on like this: 'This profound grotto.' "

"But the verb—what about the verb?" asked Pellisson.

" 'To come admire the greatest king that's found,' " La Fontaine continued.

"But what about the verb?" Pellisson obstinately nagged him. "This second person singular of the present indicative?"

"Fine: 'Leave.'

Oh, nymph, that leaves that grotto so profound,
To come admire the greatest king that's found.

"You'd write 'who leaves'?"

"Why not?"

" 'That'—'that'!"

"Ah, my friend," said La Fontaine. "You're a terrible pedant."

"Not to mention the fact," said Molière, "that the second verse, 'come admire,' is weak, my dear La Fontaine."

"So you can see that I'm a cad, a lowlife, as you said."

"I never said that!"

"Well, then it was Loret."

"It wasn't Loret either, it was Pellisson."

"Fine. Pellisson was right on target. But what angers me most, my dear Molière, is that we won't have our Epicurean suits."

"You were counting on yours for the celebration?"

"Yes, for the celebration, and then for after the celebration. My housekeeper warned me that mine has seen better days."

"Damn it, your housekeeper's right! It's seen much better days!"

"Look," said La Fontaine. "I left it on the floor in my study, and my cat . . ."

"Your cat?"

"My cat gave birth to kittens on it, which made it fade a little."

Molière cracked up. Pellisson and Loret followed his example.

At that moment, the Bishop of Vannes walked in, carrying a roll of plans and parchments under his arm.

As if the angel of death had frozen all wild and cheerful fancies, as if that pallid face had frightened away the Graces, to whom Xenocrates made his offerings, the studio instantly hushed up, and each person regained his composure and his quill.

Aramis distributed the invitations to the assistants, thanking them on behalf of Monsieur Fouquet, the superintendent of finances. The superintendent, he said, had too much work to leave his office and so he couldn't come to see them. But he was asking them to send him a bit of their daily work to help him forget the fatigue of his nightly work.

At these words all heads were lowered over the work. La Fontaine himself sat down at a table and sent his quill racing across the vellum. Pellisson wrote a fair copy of the prologue. Molière sketched fifty new verses, which were inspired by his visit with Percerin. Loret penned his article on the marvelous celebration that he prophesied. And Aramis, laden with booty like the king of bees, that big, black drone with gold-and-purple ornaments, set out for his home, silent and occupied. But before going, he said:

"Don't forget, gentlemen, we're all leaving tomorrow evening."

"In that case," said Molière, "I have to inform my household."

"Ah, yes! Poor Molière!" said Loret with a smile. "*He loves* at home."

"*He loves,* yes," replied Molière with his sad and gentle smile. "*He loves,* which doesn't mean that *he is loved.*"

"Well," said La Fontaine, "I'm loved at Château-Thierry, I'm quite certain."

At that instant Aramis came back after a moment's disappearance. "Is anyone joining me?" he asked. "I'm driving through Paris after seeing Monsieur Fouquet for fifteen minutes. My carriage is at your disposal."

"Great! Count me in!" said Molière. "I accept, I'm in a hurry."

"I'm dining here," said Loret. "Monsieur de Gourville has promised me snails."

He has promised me snails.

"Find a rhyme for that, La Fontaine."

Aramis left, laughing for all he was worth. Molière followed him. They were at the bottom of the stairs when La Fontaine half-opened the door and cried:

With his words he regales,
He has promised us snails.

The Epicureans laughed harder than ever, and their mirth reached the ears of the superintendent when Aramis opened the door to Monsieur Fouquet's office.

As for Molière, he took charge of ordering the horses while Aramis spoke briefly with the superintendent.

"My oh my, they're really laughing their heads off!" said Fouquet with a sigh.

"You're not laughing, monseigneur?"

"I'm no longer laughing, Monsieur d'Herblay."

"The celebration is coming."

"Money is leaving."

"Haven't I told you that that's my business?!"

"Yes, you promised me millions."

"You'll have the money the day after the king enters Vaux."

Fouquet stared hard at Aramis and passed his icy hand across his moist forehead. Aramis sensed that the superintendent either doubted him or felt he was powerless to get the money. How could Fouquet assume that a poor bishop, an ex-priest, an ex-musketeer, could dig up that much cash?

"Why doubt me?" asked Aramis.

Fouquet smiled and shook his head.

"Man of little faith!" the bishop added.

"My dear Monsieur d'Herblay," replied Fouquet, "if I fall—"

"Well, if you fall? . . ."

"I'll at least fall from such a great height that I'll break every bone in my body." Then, shaking his head as if to escape himself, he asked, "Where are you coming from, dear friend?"

"From Paris."

"From Paris? Ah!"

"Yes, from Percerin."

"And what were you doing there, for I don't assume that you attach such great importance to the wardrobes of our poets?"

"No, I was ordering a surprise."

"A surprise?"

"Yes—your surprise for the king."

"Will it be costly?"

"Oh! A hundred pistoles, which you will give to Le Brun."

"A painting? Ah! All the better! And what should this painting depict?"

"I'll tell you. Then, at the same time, no matter what you say about it, I checked out the clothes of our poets."

"Bah! And they must be rich, elegant?"

"Superb! There aren't too many noblemen who can hold a candle to them! We'll see the difference between the courtiers of wealth and the courtiers of friendship."

"Always witty and generous, dear prelate!"

"A follower of your school."

Fouquet shook Aramis's hand. "And where are you going?" he asked.

"I'm going to Paris once you've given me a letter."

"A letter to whom?"

"A letter to Monsieur de Lyonne."

"And what do you want from him?"

"A *lettre de cachet*—an order under the king's private seal."

"A *lettre de cachet*! Do you want to put someone in the Bastille?"

"No, quite the opposite. I want to get someone out."

"Ah! And who would that be?"

"A poor wretch, a young man, a child, who's been incarcerated for almost ten years because of two Latin verses he wrote against the Jesuits."

"For two Latin verses? The poor wretch!"

"Yes."

"And he committed no other crime?"

"Apart from those two verses he is as innocent as you or I."

"Your word?"

"On my honor!"

"And his name? . . ."

"Seldon."

"That's too much, damn it! And you knew about it and didn't tell me?!"

"His mother only told me about it yesterday, monseigneur."

"And this woman is poor?"

"She's mired in poverty."

"My God," said Fouquet, "you sometimes tolerate so much injustice that I can understand why there are poor wretches who are suspicious of you. Here you are, Monsieur d'Herblay."

And Fouquet, picking up a quill, swiftly wrote several lines to his colleague Lyonne.

Aramis took the letter and was about to leave.

"Wait," said Fouquet. He opened his drawer and produced ten vouchers. Each was worth a thousand francs. "Here, get the son out and give this to the mother. But don't tell her . . ."

"What, monseigneur?"

"That she is ten thousand francs richer than I. She'll say that I'm a poor superintendent! Go on, and I hope that God will bless those who think of His poor."

"I hope so too," Aramis replied, kissing Fouquet's hand.

And, with the letter for Lyonne and the vouchers for Seldon's mother, he hurried away, dragging along Molière, who was starting to lose patience.

7
Another Supper at the Bastille

The huge clock of the Bastille was striking seven in the evening—that famous clock, which, like all the torturous accessories of the state prison, reminded the inmates of the intended purpose of every single hour of their torment. The clock of the Bastille, decorated with figures like most timepieces of that era, depicted Saint Peter in bonds.

It was suppertime for the poor inmates. The gates, groaning on their enormous hinge pins, made way for the trays and baskets of food, whose delicacy, as Monsieur de Baisemeaux has already told us, was geared to each captive's rank.

We know the theories of Monsieur de Baisemeaux, sovereign dispenser of gastronomic delights, head chef of the royal fortress, whose full baskets mounted the steep stairways, bringing the prisoners some consolation in the depths of honestly filled bottles.

Seven P.M. was also suppertime for the warden. Tonight he had a guest, and the spit was turning more heavily than usual.

Roast partridges, flanked by quails and flanking a larded young hare; chickens in bouillon, fried ham basted in white wine, prawns from Guipúzcoa and crawfish bisque: that, along with soups and hors d'oeuvres, made up the warden's bill of fare.

Baisemeaux, seated at his table, rubbed his hands as he gazed at the Bishop of Vannes, who, booted like a cavalier, wearing gray and with his sword at his side, kept talking on and on about how hungry he was and kept revealing the keenest impatience.

Monsieur de Baisemeaux de Montlezun was not accustomed to hobnobbing with His Grace the Bishop of Vannes; and that evening, Aramis, livelier than ever, shared one confidence after another with his host. The prelate had regained a touch of the musketeer. His conversation was bordering on the risqué. As for Monsieur de Baisemeaux: with the ease of vulgar people, he abandoned himself entirely to the bishop's lack of restraint.

"Monsieur," said the warden, "for tonight I really don't dare address you as 'Monseigneur.' "

"You certainly mustn't," said Aramis. "Address me as 'Monsieur'—I'm wearing boots."

"Fine! Monsieur, do you know whom you remind me of tonight?"

"Goodness, no!" said Aramis, pouring himself some wine. "But I do hope I remind me of a good guest."

"You remind me of two, monsieur. François, my friend, close that window. The draft could be unpleasant for His Grace."

"Send him away!" Aramis added. "The supper is fully served, we can eat it easily enough without a servant. I prefer a small, informal gathering, I like being with a friend. . . ."

Baisemeaux respectfully bowed.

"I love," Aramis continued, "serving myself."

"François, leave!" Baisemeaux exclaimed. "I was saying that Your Grace reminded me of two people. One of them is quite illustrious: it's the late cardinal, the great Cardinal of La Rochelle, who wore boots like you. Isn't that so?"

"Yes indeed," said Aramis. "And the other person?"

"The other is a certain musketeer, very handsome, very brave, very courageous, very happy. He was a priest who became a musketeer, and a musketeer who became a priest."

Aramis deigned to smile.

"The priest," Baisemeaux went on, emboldened by His Grace's smile, "the priest became a bishop, and the bishop—"

"Stop right there—please!" Aramis broke in.

"I tell you, monseigneur, you look like a cardinal."

"Stop, my dear Monsieur de Baisemeaux. You've pointed out that I'm wearing a cavalier's boots, but, nevertheless, I don't wish to be at loggerheads with the Church even just tonight."

"Still, you have wicked intentions, monseigneur."

"Oh, I admit I do. As wicked as anything in society."

"You haunt the town and the streets in disguise?"

"As you say: 'in disguise.' "

"And you still indulge in sword fighting?"

"I think so, but only when I'm forced. Please be so kind as to summon François."

"Don't you have enough wine?"

"It's not about the wine, it's because the room is hot and the window is shut."

"I keep the windows shut during supper in order to muffle the noise of the patrols and the arrivals of couriers."

"Ah, I see! You can hear them when the window's open?"

"All too clearly, and it's very annoying. You do understand."

"But still, I'm suffocating. François!"

François entered.

"Master François," said Aramis, "please open the window—if that's all right with you, dear Monsieur de Baisemeaux?"

"Monseigneur is at home here," the warden answered.

The window was opened.

"Do you know," said Monsieur de Baisemeaux, "that you're going to be quite solitary now that Monsieur de La Fère has returned to his home in Blois? The two of you go way back, don't you?"

"You know that as well as I do, Baisemeaux. After all, you were in the musketeers with us."

"Bah! With friends I count neither bottles nor years."

"And you're right. But, dear Monsieur de Baisemeaux, I more than care for Monsieur de La Fère, I venerate him."

"Well, it's strange," said the warden, "but I prefer Monsieur d'Artagnan. Now that's a man who drinks well and long! People like him certainly reveal their innermost thoughts."

"Baisemeaux, get me drunk tonight, let's live it up the way we used to. And if I have any pain at the bottom of my heart, I promise that you will see it as clearly as a diamond at the bottom of your glass."

"Bravo!" said Baisemeaux. He filled his large wineglass and drained it, trembling with joy at participating in a bishop's deadly sin.

While drinking, the warden failed to see how attentively Aramis was listening to the sounds in the grand courtyard.

Around eight a courier arrived, during the fifth bottle of wine brought in by François, and, though the courier was very noisy, Baisemeaux heard nothing.

"To hell with him!" cried Aramis.

"What's wrong? To hell with who?" asked Baisemeaux. "I hope it's not the wine you're drinking or the person who's offered you the wine?"

"No, it's a horse that's making as big a racket in the courtyard as an entire squadron could make."

"Bah! It's some courier," the warden answered, refilling his glass to the brim. "Yes, he can go to hell! And so fast that we don't hear another peep out of him! Hurray! Hurray!"

"You're forgetting me, Baisemeaux! My glass is empty," said Aramis, pointing to a dazzling crystal goblet.

"You're delightful, I swear. François, wine!"

François entered.

"Wine, you rascal; the best wine!"

"Yes, monsieur, but . . . there's a courier."

" 'To hell with him,' I said."

"But, monsieur—"

"He can leave his message at the registry, we'll take care of it tomorrow. Tomorrow there'll be time, tomorrow there'll be daylight," said Baisemeaux, chanting the last two phrases.

"Ah! Monsieur!" The soldier François grumbled in spite of himself. "Monsieur!"

"Be careful," said Aramis, "be careful."

"About what, dear Monsieur d'Herblay?" asked Baisemeaux, half-drunk.

"A letter brought by a courier to the commanding officer of a citadel can sometimes be an order."

"Nearly always."

"Don't the orders come from ministers?"

"Yes, of course, but—"

"And aren't those ministers simply countersigning the king's signature?"

"You may be right. But it's quite annoying when a man is sitting at a rich table, having a private supper with a friend! Ah, forgive me, monsieur, I forgot that I'm the host and that I'm talking to a future cardinal."

"Don't worry, dear Baisemeaux. Let's get back to your soldier, François."

"Well, what's he done?"

"He grumbled."

"He was wrong."

"But he grumbled all the same, you understand. Something extraordinary must be afoot. Perhaps it's not wrong of François to grumble; perhaps it's wrong of you not to listen."

"In the wrong? Me in the wrong with François? That sounds harsh!"

"An irregularity, if you'll forgive my saying so. But I felt I had to make an observation that I find important."

"Oh! You may be right," Baisemeaux stammered. "An order from the king is sacred! But when an order arrives during supper, then I repeat: To hell with it!"

"If you'd have said that to the grand cardinal, my dear Baisemeaux, and if this order were at all important—"

"I'm ignoring it so as not to annoy a bishop. Isn't that excusable, damn it?"

"Don't forget, Baisemeaux, that I was a soldier and that I habitually see orders everywhere."

"So you want—?"

"I want you to do your duty, my friend. Please do so at least in front of this soldier."

"No sooner said than done!" Baisemeaux exclaimed.

François was still waiting.

"Bring me this order from the king," said the warden, drawing himself up. And he very softly added: "Do you know what it says? Let me tell you. Something fascinating such as: 'Be careful with fire in the vicinity of gunpowder'; or: 'Watch out for so-and-so—he's an escape artist!' Ah, monseigneur, if you only knew how often I've been startled out of my gentlest and deepest sleep by orderlies galloping up to tell me or rather bring me a message that says: 'Monsieur de Baisemeaux, any news?' It's obvious that the people who waste their time writing such orders have never slept at the Bastille. If they had, they'd have a better knowledge of the thickness of the walls, the vigilance of my officers, the frequency of our rounds. Well, what do you expect, monseigneur? Their job is to write so as to torment me when I'm relaxed and to disturb me when I'm happy," Baisemeaux added, bowing to Aramis. "So let them do their job!"

"And you do yours," the bishop added with a smile. His sharp gaze commanded the situation despite his friendly attitude.

François came back. He handed Baisemeaux the ministry's order. The warden slowly unsealed the envelope and read the letter. Aramis pretended to be drinking in order to observe his host through the crystal.

After reading the text, Baisemeaux said, "What did I tell you?"

"Yes, what?"

"A release order! Honestly! What fine news to disturb us!"

"It's fine news for the prisoner—don't you agree, my dear warden?"

"And at eight P.M.!"

"That's charity."

"Charity, granted. But it's charity for that wretch who's bored and not for me when I'm having fun!" said Baisemeaux, exasperated.

"Are you losing anything? Is he on the general list?"

"That he is! A rogue, a rat—for five francs!"

"Let me see," said Monsieur d'Herblay, "if I'm not being indiscreet."

"Not at all! Read it."

"The letter says, 'Rush!' You can see that, can't you?"

"That's admirable: 'Rush!' A man who's been here for ten years! They're in a rush to get him out today, tonight, at eight P.M.!" And Baisemeaux, with a superbly disdainful shrug, tossed the order on the table and resumed eating.

"They have their whims," he said, his mouth full. "They grab a man one fine day, feed him for ten years, and write you, 'Watch out for this wretch!' Or, 'Hold him rigorously!' And then, when you've grown used to treating him as dangerous—all of a sudden, without a why or wherefore, without prior notice, they write you, 'Set him free!' And they add, 'Rush!' You will agree, monseigneur, that it's enough to shrug at."

"What do you expect? You rail against the order and you carry it out!" said Aramis.

"Fine! Fine! We carry it out! . . . Oh, patience! You mustn't think I'm a slave."

"Goodness, my dear Monsieur de Baisemeaux, who says so? We know how independent you are!"

"Thank the Lord!"

"But we also know what a good heart you have."

"Ah! Please!"

"And how obedient you are to your superiors! Once a soldier, always a soldier, Baisemeaux!"

"Fine, I'll obey strictly. And tomorrow, at the crack of dawn, the prisoner will be released!"

"Tomorrow?"

"At the crack of dawn."

"Why not tonight? After all, both the envelope and the letter say 'Rush!' "

"Because tonight we are having supper and we're also in a rush."

"Dear Baisemeaux, despite my boots, I feel like a priest, and charity drives me more than hunger and thirst. This miserable man has suffered long enough—you've just told me that he's been your boarder for ten years. Shorten his torment. His moment has come, give it to him quickly. God will reward you with years of bliss in paradise."

"You want me to?"

"I beg you."

"Just like that? In the middle of supper?"

"Please do so. Your action will be worth ten blessings!"

"Then I'll do it! Except that our meal will grow cold!"

"Don't worry!"

Baisemeaux leaned back to summon François, and, with a very natural movement, he turned toward the door.

The order remained on the table. While Baisemeaux's eyes were averted, Aramis took advantage of those moments to produce a letter from his pocket and switch the two.

"François," said the warden, "get me the major with the turnkeys of La Bertaudière."

François bowed and left, and the two diners found themselves alone.

8
The General of the Order

There was a moment of silence, during which Aramis's eyes were glued to the warden. The latter seemed only half-inclined to trouble himself in the middle of his supper, and it was obvious that he was trying to come up with a reason, good or bad, to put off his duty until after dessert. All at once, he appeared to have hit on a pretext.

"It's impossible!" he cried.

"Why is it impossible?" asked Aramis. "Give me a glimpse of why it's impossible."

"It's impossible to release the prisoner at this time of night. Where will he go? He doesn't know Paris."

"He'll go wherever he can."

"You can see for yourself! It's like releasing a blind man!"

"I've got a carriage, I'll take him to wherever he wants to go."

"You've got an answer for everything. François! Tell the major to release Monsieur Seldon, number three, La Bertaudière."

" 'Seldon'?" Aramis asked very simply. "You said 'Seldon,' I believe?"

"I did say 'Seldon.' That's the name of the man who's being released."

"Don't you mean 'Marchiali'?" asked Aramis.

" 'Marchiali'? Aha! No, no, I mean 'Seldon.' "

"I believe you're mistaken, Monsieur Baisemeaux."

"I've read the order."

"So have I."

"And I saw 'Seldon' in letters this big." He held up a finger.

"Well, I read 'Marchiali' in letters this big." And Aramis held up two fingers.

"Why don't we clear it up?" said Baisemeaux, sure of himself. "The letter's here; all we have to do is read it."

"I read 'Marchiali,' " said Aramis, unfolding the document. "Look!"

Baisemeaux looked, and his arms flexed. "Yes, yes," he said, dumbstruck. "Yes, 'Marchiali.' He did write 'Marchiali'! It's true!"

"Ah!"

"What? The man we've talked about so much? The man I'm to take special care of?"

"It says 'Marchiali,' " the inflexible Aramis repeated.

"Indeed it does, monseigneur. But I'm totally at sea."

"You can believe your eyes, however."

"Goodness! To think that it's Marchiali!"

"And in good handwriting to boot."

"It's phenomenal. I can still see the order and the name of Seldon, an Irishman. I can see it. Ah! And I remember a blot of ink under the name."

"There's no ink, there's no blot."

"Oh! I tell you there was. The proof is that I rubbed the powder on the blot."

"Well, however that may be, dear Monsieur Baisemeaux, and whatever you may have seen, the order is signed and it requires you to release Marchiali with or without a blot."

"The order is signed that requires me to release Marchiali," Baisemeaux muttered mechanically, trying to pull himself together.

"And you will release this prisoner. If your heart tells you to release Seldon too, I declare that I will not oppose you in the least."

Aramis punctuated his statement with an ironic grin that sobered Baisemeaux up and lent him courage.

"Monseigneur," he said, "this Marchiali is the same prisoner who was so imperiously and so secretly visited the other day by a priest, a confessor of *our order.*"

"I plead ignorance, monsieur," the bishop replied.

"Yet it wasn't so long ago, dear Monsieur d'Herblay."

"True enough, but among us, monsieur, it is better if today's man doesn't know what yesterday's man did."

"In any case," said Baisemeaux, "the Jesuit confessor must have brought this man luck."

Aramis didn't respond. Instead, he resumed eating and drinking.

Baisemeaux, touching nothing that was on the table, picked up the order again and examined it with a fine-tooth comb.

In ordinary circumstances, this inquisition would have made our impatient Aramis turn crimson; but the Bishop of Vannes refused to hit the roof for such a flimsy reason, especially since he had murmured to himself that it would be dangerous to lose his temper.

"Are you gonna release Marchiali?" he said. "Oh! my dear warden! Just get a whiff of this mellow and fragrant Jerez sherry."

"Monseigneur," replied Baisemeaux, "I'll release the prisoner Marchiali once I call back the courier who brought the order. I'll question him and make sure—"

"Orders are sealed, and a courier doesn't know their contents. So how, I ask you, can you make sure?"

"True, monseigneur. But I'll write to the ministry, and Monsieur de Lyonne will either withdraw the order or approve it."

"What's the point of all that?" said Aramis coolly.

"What's the point?"

"Yes, I ask you, what's the point?"

"The point is that I must make no mistakes, monseigneur. A subaltern must never lack the respect that every underling owes his superiors, and he must never fail in the duties of the service that he has agreed to perform."

"Fine. You speak so eloquently that I have to admire you. It's true, a subaltern owes respect to his superiors. If he makes a mistake, he is the culprit, and he will be punished if he fails in his duties or flouts the rules of his service."

Baisemeaux gaped at the bishop in astonishment.

"The bottom line," Aramis went on, "is that you're going to consult Monsieur de Lyonne in order to ease your conscience, right?"

"Yes, monseigneur."

"And if a superior gives you an order, you will obey?'

"Do not doubt it, monseigneur."

"You do know the king's signature, Monsieur de Baisemeaux?"

"Yes, monseigneur."

"Doesn't it appear on the release order?"

"That's true, but it can—"

"Be forged, right?"

"It's been known to happen, monseigneur."

"True enough. But what about Monsieur de Lyonne's signature?"

"I do see it on the order, but, just as one can forge the king's handwriting, one can all the more easily forge Monsieur de Lyonne's handwriting."

"Your reasoning is overwhelming, Monsieur de Baisemeaux," said Aramis, "and your argumentation is invincible. But if you think these are forgeries, what do you base your assumption on?"

"On this: the absence of the signatories. We cannot verify His Majesty's signature, and Monsieur de Lyonne isn't here to tell me that he signed this."

"Very well, Monsieur de Baisemeaux," said Aramis, with his penetrating glare. "I so unreservedly accept your doubts and your way of illuminating them that I'm going to take a quill if you give me one."

Baisemeaux handed him a quill.

"A blank sheet of paper," Aramis added.

Baisemeaux handed him a sheet of paper.

Aramis continued: "And I will write an order—I too, I present, I incontestable, right? An order that I'm sure you'll believe, incredulous as you are."

Baisemeaux blanched before this glacial self-assurance. Aramis's voice, so cheerful, so merry an instant ago, now sounded eerie and funereal. The torches seemed to have changed into the tapers in a sepulchral chapel, and the glasses of wine looked like chalices of blood.

Aramis took the quill and wrote. A terrified Baisemeaux read over Aramis's shoulder. "A.M.D.G.," wrote the bishop, adding a cross above those four letters, which stand for *Ad majorem Dei gloriam* (For the greater glory of God). And he went on:

> I hereby guarantee that the order brought to Monsieur de Baisemeaux de Montlezun, the king's warden for the stronghold of the Bastille, is both good and valid and is to be executed immediately.
>
> *Signed:* D'HERBLAY, General of the Order, by the grace of God

Baisemeaux was struck so profoundly that his features remained tense, his mouth agape, and his eyes gawking. He didn't stir; he didn't let out a peep.

All that could be heard in the vast room was the buzzing of a tiny fly that was flitting around the torches.

Aramis, without so much as deigning to glance at the man whom he'd reduced to such a miserable state, pulled out a small case containing black wax. He secured the letter and sealed it with a seal that hung on his chest behind his doublet. And when the operation was completed, Aramis, still silent, presented the missive to Monsieur de Baisemeaux.

The latter, whose hands were trembling piteously, gazed with wild, lackluster eyes at the seal. A final gleam of emotion appeared on his features, and, as if struck by lightning, he collapsed on a chair.

"C'mon, c'mon," said Aramis after a long silence, during which the warden of the Bastille gradually regained his self-control. "Don't make me believe that the presence of the general of the order is as terrible as the presence of God. The sight of the general won't kill anyone. Courage! Get up, give me your hand, and obey."

Reassured, if not satisfied, Baisemeaux obeyed. He kissed Aramis's hand and straightened up. "Immediately?" he murmured.

"Oh, don't overdo it, monsieur. Sit down at the table again and let's do justice to this fine dessert."

"Monseigneur, I'll never recover from this shock. I laughed with you, joked with you! I dared to treat you on a footing of equality."

"Hold your tongue, old comrade," replied the bishop, who sensed how tight the cord was and how dangerous it would be to make it snap. "Hold your tongue. Let's each of us live his life. I will be your friend and protector, and you will obey. With these two tributes paid precisely, let's enjoy ourselves."

The warden reflected. All at once he realized the consequences of releasing a prisoner on the basis of a forged order. Comparing the possibility with the general's guarantee, he didn't set great store by the latter.

Aramis read his mind.

"My dear Baisemeaux, you're a moron. You must shake off this habit of reflection when I go to the trouble of thinking for you."

And in response to Aramis's gesture, the warden bowed again. "How should I go about it?" he asked.

"How do you normally release an inmate?"

"I've got the regulations."

"Well, then, follow the regulations, my friend."

"I go to the inmate's room with my major, and, if the inmate is a person of importance, I accompany him out."

"Well, this Marchiali is not a person of importance."

"I wouldn't know," replied the warden, as if saying, It's your job to inform me.

"Well, if you don't know, then I must be right. So act toward him as you act toward unimportant people."

"Fine. The regulations spell it out."

"Ah!"

"The regulations stipulate that the turnkey or one of the

low-ranking officers should take the prisoner to the warden in the office."

"Fine! That makes a lot of sense. And then?"

"Then the prisoner is given the valuables he had when he was incarcerated—the clothes, the papers—unless the minister's order indicates otherwise."

"What does the minister's order say about Marchiali?"

"Nothing. The poor man arrived here with no jewels, with no papers, with almost no clothes."

"Look how simple it all is! Honestly, Baisemeaux, you're making mountains out of molehills. Stay here, and have the prisoner taken to the office."

Baisemeaux obeyed. He called his lieutenant and gave him instructions, which he calmly transmitted to an authorized person.

Half an hour later, they heard a door closing in the courtyard: it was the door to the dungeon, which had just restored its prey to the free air.

Aramis snuffed all the candles in the room. He kept only one burning behind the door. The flickering prevented the eyes from focusing on any one object. The faltering, wavering flame created many aspects and nuances.

Footsteps were approaching.

"Go meet your men," Aramis told Baisemeaux.

The warden obeyed.

The sergeant and the jailers disappeared.

Baisemeaux returned, followed by a prisoner.

Aramis stood in the shadows; he could see without being seen.

Baisemeaux, in an agitated tone of voice, informed the young man about the order to release him.

The prisoner listened without speaking or even gesturing.

"These are the regulations," the warden added. "You swear that you will never reveal anything that you have seen or heard in the Bastille."

The prisoner spotted a crucifix. He reached out and swore by kissing it with his lips.

"Now, monsieur, you are free," said the warden. "Where are you planning to go?"

The prisoner turned his head as if searching behind him for a protection he could rely on.

It was at this point that Aramis emerged from the shadows. "Here I am," he said, "to provide Monsieur with whatever service he pleases to request of me."

The prisoner blushed faintly and he unhesitatingly locked arms with Aramis.

"God keep you in His holy protection!" Both his words and the firmness of his voice made the warden shudder.

Aramis, shaking Baisemeaux's hand, said: "Does my order pose a problem for you? Are you afraid someone might find it if he searched the place?"

"I want to keep it, monseigneur," said Baisemeaux. "If it were found here, that would be a sure sign that I'd be doomed; and, in that case, you'd be a powerful and final helper."

"You mean your accomplice?" Aramis shrugged. "Adieu, Baisemeaux."

The horses were waiting, shaking the carriage in their impatience.

Baisemeaux accompanied the bishop to the foot of the staircase.

Aramis let his companion precede him into the carriage, climbed in after him, and, giving the coachman no further order, he said, "Get going!"

The vehicle rumbled noisily over the paving stones of the courtyard. An officer clutching a torch walked ahead of the horses, ordering each guard to let them pass.

During the time it took to open each door, Aramis held his breath. You could have heard the bishop's heart pounding against his ribs.

Nor did the prisoner, buried in a corner of the carriage, give any sign of existence.

Finally, a jolt stronger than the rest announced that the final barrier had been crossed. The final gate, leading to rue Saint-Antoine, closed behind them. No more walls to the right and the left; the sky everywhere, freedom everywhere, life everywhere.

The horses, reined in by a vigorous man, headed slowly toward the middle of the suburb. There they broke into a gallop.

Little by little, whether warming up or being spurred on, the horses charged faster and faster. Their ardor was so intense that once the carriage reached Bercy, it virtually flew. The coursers dashed all the way to Villeneuve-Saint-Georges, where the relay had been prepared. Now four horses instead of two dashed off toward Melun, halting for a moment in the forest of Sénart. The order had, no doubt, been given to the postilion in advance, for Aramis didn't even have to signal him.

"What's wrong?" asked the prisoner as if awakening from a long dream.

"Monseigneur," said Aramis, "before proceeding, we need to talk—Your Royal Highness and I."

"I look forward to it, monsieur," the young prince replied.

"The best place and time, monseigneur, would be right here, in the middle of the forest. No one can hear us."

"What about the postilion?"

"The postilion of this relay is deaf and dumb, monseigneur."

"I am at your disposal, Monsieur d'Herblay."

"Do you wish to remain in this carriage?"

"Yes, we're sitting comfortably, and I like this carriage: it's restored my freedom."

"Wait, monseigneur, there's one more precaution."

"Namely?"

"We're on the highway here. Horsemen and carriages might be passing by, traveling like us. When they see that we've stopped, they may think we're in trouble. We have to avoid friendly offers of help—they'd be inconvenient."

"Tell the postilion to hide our carriage on a side road."

"That's exactly what I had in mind, monseigneur."

Aramis signaled the deaf mute, touching his arm. The mute climbed down, took the two front horses by their bridles, and led them to the velvety heather, the mossy grass of a winding lane, beyond which, on this moonless night, the clouds formed a curtain that was blacker than ink.

Next, the mute lay down on an embankment by his horses, which tore out the young acorn shoots left and right.

"I'm listening," the young prince said to Aramis, "but what are you doing?"

"I'm disarming myself of my guns, we've got no further need of them, monseigneur."

9
The Tempter

"My prince," said Aramis, turning toward his companion in the carriage, "I may be a feeble creature, with a mediocre mind, a creature so low in the hierarchy of thinking beings. But I've never spoken to any man without reading his thoughts through the living mask that's thrown over our intelligence in order to keep it from expressing itself. However, tonight, given these shadows and your reserve, I'm unable to read your features, and something tells me that I'll have a hard time extracting a single sincere word from you. I therefore beg you—not out of love for me, for a subject should weigh nothing in a ruler's scales. For love of yourself, retain my every last syllable, my every last inflection, each of which, in these grave circumstances, will have a meaning and validity that are as important as anything ever uttered in the world."

"I'm listening," the young prince repeated decisively, "without aspiring to anything, without fearing anything of what you're about to tell me."

And he buried himself deeper in the thick carriage cushions, trying to deprive his companion of not only the sight of him, but also the sheer notion of his presence.

The blackness, broad and opaque, stretched from the tops of the intertwining trees. The carriage, closed off by a vast roof, wouldn't have received the smallest particle of light even if a luminous atom had slipped through the columns of mist that were spreading over this forest lane.

"Monseigneur," Aramis resumed, "you're acquainted with the history of the government that now rules France. The king emerged from a captive childhood like yours, as obscure as yours, as confined as yours. Only instead of being enslaved in a prison, in the darkness of solitude, the narrowness of a hidden life, the king had to suffer all his miseries, all his embarrassments, all his humiliations in broad daylight, in the pitiless sun of royalty—a place flooded with light, in which every blemish feels like a vile stain and every glory feels like a blemish. The king has suffered, he harbors a grudge, he intends to get even. He'll be a bad king. I'm not saying he'll spill blood like Louis XI or Charles IX—he has no mortal insults to avenge. What I mean is that he'll devour the money and subsistence of his subjects, because he's endured offenses in his own interest and money. So, first off, I'm protecting my conscience when I face this ruler's merits and defects, and, if I condemn him, my conscience absolves me."

Aramis paused. Not to hear whether the forest silence was still the same. Rather, he wanted to gather his thoughts from the depths of his mind and give those uttered thoughts enough time to ingrain themselves in the mind of his companion.

"God does right whatever He does," the Bishop of Vannes went on. "And I'm so convinced of this that I've long patted myself on the back because He's entrusted me with the secret that I helped you uncover. The God of justice and foresight needed a sharp, earnest, persevering instrument in order to accomplish a great work. And I am that instrument. I'm acute, I'm earnest, I'm persevering. I rule a mysterious brotherhood, which has taken God's motto for its own: '*Patiens quia aeternus,*' 'He is patient because He is eternal'!"

The prince stirred.

"I sense, monseigneur, why you've raised your head and why you're astonished by this brotherhood that I rule. You didn't realize you were dealing with a king—the king of a very humble nation, the king of a completely disinherited nation. My subjects are humble because they have no strength except when they're creeping, and they are disinherited because they virtually never harvest the crops they sow and virtually never eat the fruits they grow. They toil for an abstraction. They mass together all the molecules of power and form them into a man, and, with the sweat of his brow, they compose a cloud around this man, and, with his genius, this man must, in turn, shape this cloud into an aureole gilded with all the crowns of Christendom. That's the man you've got at your side, monseigneur. He has to tell you that he has drawn you from the abyss for a great purpose, and that, for this magnificent purpose, he wants to elevate you beyond the powers of the earth, beyond himself."

The prince lightly grazed Aramis's arm:

"You're speaking about the religious order that you head. I infer from your words that if ever you want to hurl down the man you've elevated, you'll do so, and you'll also keep your creature of yesterday under your hand."

"Don't you believe that, monseigneur!" Aramis replied. "I wouldn't go to the trouble of playing this dreadful game with Your Royal Highness if I didn't have two advantages in winning. Once you are elevated, you will be elevated forever. You will overturn the footstool on which you mount the throne, you will send it rolling so far that the sight of it will never remind you of its right to your gratitude."

"Oh! Monsieur!"

"Your reason, monseigneur, comes from an excellent constitution. Thank you! Believe me, I strive for more than gratitude. I'm certain that once you've reached the pinnacle, you'll judge me more worthy of being your friend. And then the two of us, monseigneur, will achieve things that people will talk about for centuries!"

"Do tell me, monsieur, and do not mince your words. Tell me who I am today and who you claim I will be tomorrow."

"You are the son of King Louis XIII, you are the brother of King Louis XIV, you are the natural and rightful heir to the French throne. By keeping you near him, just as he kept Monsieur, your youngest brother, the king reserved for himself the right to be the legitimate sovereign. Only the doctors and God could challenge his legitimacy. And doctors always prefer the king who rules to the king who does not. God would put Himself in the wrong by harming a decent ruler. But God wanted you to be persecuted, and this persecution anoints you today as king of France. You therefore had the right to reign because your right was contested, you therefore had the right to be declared king because you were confined illegally. You are therefore of divine blood because they did not dare spill your blood as they spilled the blood of your servants.

"Now see what's being done for you by God, this God whom you have so often accused of having done everything against you. He gave you your brother's features, his size, his age, his voice, and all causes of your persecution will become the causes of your triumphant resurrection. Tomorrow, the day after, at the first moment, you, the royal phantom, the living shade of Louis XIV—you will sit on his throne, from which the will of God, carried out by a human arm, will hurl him with no hope of return."

"I understand," said the prince. "My brother's blood will not be spilled."

"You will be the sole arbiter of his fate."

"The secret by which they abused me . . ."

"You will use against him. What did he do to conceal it? He concealed you. As his living image, you'd betray the plot hatched by Mazarin and Anne of Austria. You, my prince, will have the same interest in concealing the man whom you resemble as a prisoner just as he resembles you as king."

"Let me go back to what I was saying. Who will guard him?"

"Who guarded you?"

"You know the secret, you used it for my benefit. Who else knows it?"

"The queen mother and Madame de Chevreuse."

"What will they do?"

"Nothing, if you wish."

"What do you mean?"

"How will they recognize you if you act in such a way that you won't be recognized?"

"That's true. But there are more serious problems."

"What are they, my prince?"

"My brother is married, I cannot take my brother's wife."

"I'll see to it that Spain agrees to a repudiation. It's in the interest of your new policies, it's human morality. Everything that is truly noble in this world and truly useful will be satisfied."

"The imprisoned king will speak."

"Whom will he speak to? The walls?"

"You call the men you trust walls?"

"If necessary. And besides, Your Royal Highness . . ."

"Besides . . ."

"I was about to say that it would be a pity if God's design were to stop after such a good start. Every plan of such a scope is completed by its results, like a geometric calculation. The imprisoned king won't be the obstacle that you were for the reigning king. God gave him a haughty and impatient soul. He also weakened him, disarmed him by getting him accustomed to honors and sovereign power. God wants the geometric calculation that I have the honor to tell you about to conclude with your accession to the throne and the destruction of whatever might harm you. God has therefore decided that the vanquished man will soon end his sufferings with your own. And so He has prepared his soul and his body for the brief agony. When you were imprisoned as a private individual, incarcerated with your doubts, stripped of everything, habituated to a hard life, you resisted. But when your brother is confined and forgotten, he will not endure the misery, and God will take his soul in due time—that is, soon."

At this point in Aramis's grave assessment, a nocturnal bird in the depths of the forest uttered the prolonged and plaintive ululation that makes every creature tremble.

"I'll exile the dethroned king," said Philip, shuddering. "It will be more humane."

"The king will decide at his discretion," Aramis responded. "Meanwhile—have I presented the problem nicely? Is my solution consistent with the desires or expectations of Your Royal Highness?"

"Yes, monsieur, yes. You've forgotten nothing except for two items."

"What is the first one?"

"Let's talk about it now with the same frankness of our conversation so far. Let's talk about the things that could shatter the hopes we've pinned on this project. Let's talk about the dangers we'll be facing."

"The dangers would be immense, infinite, terrifying, insurmountable if, as I've told you, everything didn't work toward nullifying them completely. There is no danger for you or for me so long as Your Royal Highness's boldness and staunchness equal nature's gift of your perfect resemblance to the king. I repeat: There are no dangers, there are only obstacles. I've found that word in all languages, but I've never understood it, and, if I were king, I'd have it deleted as absurd and useless."

"Fine, monsieur, but you're forgetting a mountable danger."

"Ah!" said Aramis.

"There is conscience, which cries out; there is remorse, which tears us apart."

"Yes, that's true," said the bishop. "There is weakness of the heart—you've reminded me. Oh! You're right! It's an immense obstacle, that's true. The horse that's scared of a ditch jumps into it instead of over it and is killed! The man who trembles when he crosses swords leaves loopholes for the enemy blade, openings for the passage of death! That's true, that's true!"

"Do you have a brother?" the young man asked Aramis.

"I'm alone in the world," the bishop replied, his voice as dry and sharp as the click of a trigger.

"But there's someone you love on earth?"

"No one! Oh yes, I love you."

The young man lapsed into a silence so profound that the sound of his own breathing became a tumult for Aramis.

"Monseigneur," Aramis went on, "I haven't told Your Royal Highness everything I have to say. I haven't offered my prince all the helpful advice and useful resources that I possess. It's not a question of dazzling the eyes of a man who loves the darkness. It's not a question of making a cannon roar in the ears of a gentle man who loves relaxation and the countryside. Monseigneur, your happiness occupies my mind, my words. My words are going to drop from my lips. Gather them up very carefully for yourself—you who love the sky, the green meadows, the pure air. I know a land of delights, an unknown paradise, a corner of the world, where you can be free, alone, and anonymous in the woods, amid the flowers, amid the spring waters, where you'll forget all the recent misery inflicted on you by human folly—God's tempter. Oh, listen to me, my prince, I'm not joking! I have a soul, you see, I can sense the abyss of your soul. I will not take you as an unfinished man and throw you into the crucible of my will, my caprice, or my ambition. All or nothing. You're hurt, sick, almost wiped out by all the extra breathing that you've been doing in your first hour of freedom. For me, it's a sure sign that you don't wish to keep taking long, deep breaths. So let's stick to a humbler life, a life more consistent with our strength. As God is my witness, and I attest to His omnipotence, I wish to create your happiness after this ordeal that I've put you through."

"Speak! Speak!" exclaimed the prince, with an alertness that caught Aramis's attention.

"I know," the prelate went on, "of a certain canton in Bas-Poitou, and no one in France has the slightest inkling of its existence. It runs to some twenty leagues of countryside—that's immense, isn't it? Twenty leagues, monseigneur, chock-full of water, pasture, and rushes, and all interspersed with islands crowded with forests. Those vast marshes, which are densely cloaked with reeds, sleep there, silent and profound, under a smiling sun.

"Several fishermen's families drift lazily in their large houseboats, which are made of poplar and alder. The floors are beds of reeds, and the roofs are braids of thick rushes. These houseboats are steered by random breezes. At times, they happen to strike a bank purely by chance, and they bump so softly that they never wake the sleeping fisherman. If he wants to land, it's because he's spotted a large flock of crakes or lapwings, ducks or plover, teal or snipes, which he either traps or shoots with his musket.

"Masses of silvery shad, enormous eels, skittish pike, gray-and-pink perch tumble into his nets. All a man has to do is choose the fattest fish and release the rest. No urbanites, no soldiers—no one has ever penetrated that area. The sun there is sweet. Vines grow in clumps, which nourish black and white grapes with a fragrant juice. Once a week, a boat sails to the community oven and picks up the warm yellow bread, whose aroma draws and caresses you from far away.

"You'll live there like a man in ages past. As the powerful master of your barbet spaniels, your fishing lines, your guns, and your lovely house of reeds, you'll live on your rich prey and game, in complete safety and security. You'll spend years there until, transformed and unrecognizable, you'll have forced God to rework your fate.

"There are a thousand pistoles in this bag, monseigneur. It's more than you'll need to buy up that entire marshland. It's more than you'll need to live there for as many years as you have days to live. It's more than you'll need to become the richest, freest, happiest man in that district. Accept this as I offer it: sincerely and joyfully. On the spot. I'll unhitch two of the horses from this carriage, and you'll be conducted by my mute servant. You'll travel by night and sleep by day, until you reach your destination. And I'll at least have the satisfaction of telling myself that I've rendered the service that my prince desired. I'll have made a man happy. God will be more grateful than if I'd made a man powerful. The latter's much more difficult.

"Well, what do you say, monseigneur? Here's the money! Oh, don't hesitate! You risk nothing in Poitou except catching a fever. And if you do, then the witch doctors in that region can cure you for a few of your pistoles.

"If you make the other choice, the one you know about, you risk getting assassinated on a throne or strangled in a prison. I swear to you, now that I've weighed both possibilities—I swear to you, I'd waver."

"Monsieur," the young prince replied, "before I make up my mind, let me step out of this carriage, walk on the ground, and consult the voice with which God speaks in the great outdoors. Ten minutes, and you'll have my decision."

"As you please, monseigneur," said Aramis, bowing respectfully—so solemn and majestic was his companion's voice.

10

Crown and Tiara

Aramis had descended before the young man, for whom he held the door open. He watched him set foot on the moss, his entire body trembling as he took a few unsteady, almost reeling steps. One might have thought that the poor prisoner was not accustomed to walking on God's earth.

It was August 15, around eleven at night. Huge clouds, heralding a storm, had invaded the sky, and their folds concealed all light and all vistas. The distant ends of the forest lanes barely stood out against the copses in a gray, opaque penumbra, which, after some scrutiny, grew visible in the midst of that total darkness. However, the perfumes were rising from the grass, fresher and more penetrating than those exhaled by the essence of the oaks. And for the first time in years, the prince was fully enveloped by the warm and balmy air and filled with the ineffable delight of freedom in the depths of the countryside. All these things spoke a language so seductive for the prince that, despite his restraint, we might almost say his dissimulation, which we have tried to sketch, he was so overwhelmed by his feelings that he heaved a sigh of joy.

Then, little by little, he raised his heavy head and inhaled the different puffs of fragrant air that wafted into his beaming face. Crossing his arms on his chest as if to prevent it from exploding at the invasion of this new rapture, he deliciously breathed the unknown air that imbues the night under the dome of a high forest. That sky he was contemplating, that water he heard ripple, those creatures he saw stirring—weren't they reality? Wasn't Aramis a madman for believing that there was anything else to dream of in this world?

Those intoxicating images of country life, exempt from worry, distress, and hardship, that ocean of happy days that sparkles incessantly before any young imagination—those things were the real bait for tempting a miserable captive worn down by the stones of the dungeon, enfeebled by the meager air in the Bastille. That, we recall, was how Aramis lured the prince when he offered him the thousand pistoles along with the enchanted Eden that the wilderness of Bas-Poitou concealed from the eyes of the world.

Such were Aramis's reflections as, with an indescribable anxiety, he followed the silent development of the joys of Philip, who lapsed deeper and deeper into his meditation. Indeed, the absorbed prince was touching the earth only with his feet, while his soul, which had flown up to God's feet, was imploring Him to send a ray of light to this hesitation, this matter of life and death.

This moment was dreadful for the Bishop of Vannes. Never before had he been faced with such great misery. His iron soul, accustomed to hurdling flimsy obstacles, was never inferior or defeated—and was his vast plan about to miscarry because he hadn't foreseen the effect of some leaves and a few puffs of air on a human body?

Aramis, transfixed by the torment of uncertainty, therefore watched Philip's agony, the struggle between the two mysterious angels. This torture lasted for the ten minutes that the young man had asked for. During this eternity, Philip's sad, moist eyes kept gazing at the heavens, beseeching them. And Aramis kept gazing at Philip with eager, blazing, devouring eyes.

All at once, the young man bowed his head. His thoughts came back to earth. His eyes hardened, his forehead creased, his mouth armed itself with fierce courage. Then he began staring again, but this time his eyes reflected the flame of earthly splendors, this time they resembled the eyes of Satan on the mountain when he tried to seduce Jesus with the kingdoms and powers of the earth.

Aramis's eyes became as gentle as they had been somber.

Then Philip grabbed his companion's hand with a swift, nervous movement. "Let's go!" he cried. "Let's go to where we'll find the crown of France!"

"Is that your decision, my prince?" Aramis asked.

"That's my decision!"

"Irrevocable?"

Philip did not even deign to respond. He stared resolutely at the bishop as if asking him whether it was ever possible for a man to go back on his word.

"Those gazes are flashes of fire that depict a character," said Aramis, bowing over Philip's hand. "You will be great, monseigneur, I can assure you!"

"Let's resume our conversation, please. I believe I told you that I *wanted* to agree with you on two matters. One is the dangers or obstacles, and that point is settled. The other point is the conditions you'll stipulate. You have the floor, Monsieur d'Herblay."

"The conditions, my prince?"

"Exactly. You won't stop me midway for such a bagatelle and you won't insult me by having me assume that you have nothing to gain from this business. So be frank and don't be afraid. Open up to me completely."

"I'll do that, monseigneur. Once you're king—"

"When will that be?"

"That will be tomorrow evening—or, rather, tomorrow night."

"Explain how!"

"Let me first ask Your Royal Highness a question."

"Go ahead."

"I'd sent Your Highness a man assigned to bring you a notebook containing finely penned, unerring notes. These notes would thoroughly familiarize Your Highness with all the people making up your court at present and in the future."

"I've read all those notes."

"Carefully?"

"I know them by heart."

"And do you understood them? Forgive me, but I'm allowed to ask the poor man abandoned in the Bastille. It goes without saying that, one week from now, I'll have no more questions for a mind like yours, a mind enjoying its freedom in its omnipotence."

"Well, then, ask away! I want to be the pupil who is told to repeat his lesson by the erudite tutor."

"First, about your family, monseigneur."

"My mother, Anne of Austria? All her troubles, her dismal illness. Oh, I know her, I know her!"

"Your second brother?" Aramis bowed.

"Your notes were accompanied by such marvelously sketched, drawn, or painted portraits that I promptly recognized the individuals whose characters, mores, and backgrounds were described in the notes. My second brother is a handsome brunet with a pale face. He doesn't love his wife, Henriette, whom I—I, Louis XIV—once had a crush on and still flirt with, even though she drove me to tears when she wanted to get rid of Mademoiselle de la Vallière."

"Be very cautious with her," said Aramis. "She sincerely loves the present king. It's hard to trick a woman in love."

"She's blond, she's got blue eyes whose tenderness will reveal her identity to me. She has a slight limp. She writes a letter every day, to which I have Monsieur de Saint-Aignan reply."

"Do you know him?"

"Like the back of my hand, and I know the latest poems he wrote for me, as well as the ones I composed in response to his."

"Very good. And do you know your ministers?"

"Colbert, a gloomy, ugly, but intelligent face, with hair covering his forehead, and a big, full, heavy head. Monsieur Fouquet's mortal enemy."

"As for Fouquet, don't worry about him."

"I won't, since you're inevitably going to ask me to exile him, am I right?"

Aramis, filled with admiration, contented himself with saying: "You're going to be very great, monseigneur."

"You can see," the prince added, "that I've learned my lesson thoroughly and, with God's help, then yours, I'll avoid any mistakes."

"You've still got a pair of troublesome eyes to deal with, monseigneur."

"Yes, your friend d'Artagnan, the captain of the guards."

"My friend, I must say so."

"The man who escorted Mademoiselle de la Vallière to Chaillot, who delivered Monck in a chest to King Charles II, the man who's served my mother so loyally, the man to whom the French crown owes so much, owes everything. Are you going to ask me to exile him too?"

"Never, sire. D'Artagnan is a man to whom I plan to tell everything in due time. But be careful. If he finds out before I reveal it to him, you or I will be captured or killed. He's a man of action."

"I'll think about it. Tell me about Monsieur Fouquet. What do you want to do with him?"

"One more moment, please, monseigneur. Forgive me if I sound disrespectful by questioning you further."

"It's your duty, and it's also your right."

"Before discussing Monsieur Fouquet, I wouldn't care to forget another friend of mine."

"Monsieur du Vallon, the Hercules of France. Don't worry, his fortune is secure."

"No, that's not whom I mean."

"Well, then, is it Count de La Fère?"

"Yes, and his son, the son of all four of us."

"The boy who is dying of love for Mademoiselle de la Vallière, whom my brother so disloyally deprived him of? Don't worry, I'll help him get her back. Tell me one thing, Monsieur d'Herblay: Does a man forget insults when he's in love? Does he forgive the woman who betrayed him? Is that a custom of the French mind? Is it a law of the human heart?"

"A man who loves profoundly, as Raoul de Bragelonne does, ultimately forgives his beloved's crime. But I don't know whether Raoul will forget."

"I'll make sure he does. Is that all you want to tell me about your friend?"

"That's all."

"Now for Monsieur Fouquet. What would you like me to do with him?"

"Please keep him on a superintendent of finances."

"Fine! But today he's prime minister."

"Not quite."

"We'll need a prime minister for a king as ignorant and hampered as I will be."

"Your Majesty will need a friend."

"I've got only one friend: you."

"You'll have others later on. But none so devoted, none so zealous for your glory."

"You'll be my prime minister."

"Not right away, monseigneur. It would be too offensive and astonishing."

"Monsieur de Richelieu, prime minister for my grandmother Marie de Médicis, was merely the Bishop of Luçon, just as you are the Bishop of Vannes."

"I see that Your Royal Highness has profited nicely from my notes. I'm overwhelmed by your miraculous perspicacity."

"I'm fully aware that Monsieur de Richelieu soon became cardinal thanks to the queen's protection."

"It will be better," said Aramis with a bow, "if I don't become prime minister until after you name me cardinal."

"You'll be cardinal within two months, Monsieur d'Herblay. But that's little enough. You won't offend me by asking for more, and you'll distress me by staying on that level."

"In that case, there's something else I hope for, monseigneur."

"Tell me, tell me!"

"Monsieur Fouquet won't be doing his job forever; he's getting long in the tooth. He loves pleasure, which is presently still compatible with his work, thanks to the vestige of youth that he enjoys. But this youthfulness is vulnerable to the first chagrin or first illness that comes his way. We'll spare him any chagrin because he's a gallant man with a noble heart. But we cannot shield him against illness. So that's established. Once you've settled all of Monsieur Fouquet's debts and put finances back on a solid basis, he can remain king with his court of poets and painters—we'll have made him rich. Then, when I become prime minister for Your Royal Highness, I'll be able to think about my interests and yours."

The young man looked at his interlocutor.

"Monsieur de Richelieu," said Aramis, "made a very big mistake when he focused purely on governing France. He let two kings, Louis XIII and himself, sit on the same throne, whereas he could have seated them more comfortably on two different thrones."

"On two thrones?" the young man asked pensively.

"Exactly," Aramis continued tranquilly. "A cardinal as prime minister of France, helped by the favor and support of the Very Christian King, a cardinal to whom the king, his master, lends government funds, lends his armies, his counsel—such a man would be committing a double injustice by applying his resources to France alone.

"Besides," Aramis added, gazing into the very depths of Philip's eyes, "you won't be a king like your father: with a sluggish mind, a delicate body, and weary of everything. You will reign with your mind and your sword. You will rule purely to the extent that you can do so unaided, I'd only be in your way. Indeed, our friendship should never be—I won't say altered—our friendship should never be ruffled by a secret thought. I will have given you the French throne, you will give me Saint Peter's throne. Your firm, armed, loyal hand will be joined by the pope's hand, *my* hand, and then neither Charles V, who owned two-thirds of the earth, nor Charlemagne, who owned the entire earth, will be able to hold a candle to you.

"I have no alliances, I have no biases, I won't pressure you to persecute heretics, and I would not push you into any family wars. I will say: 'The universe is ours! I'll take care of the souls, you'll take care of the bodies.' And since I'll die first, you will inherit my entire estate. What do you say to my plan, monseigneur?"

"I can say that merely understanding you makes me proud and happy. Monsieur d'Herblay, you will be cardinal. And as cardinal, you'll be my prime minister. And then you'll tell me what I can do to have you elected pope, and I'll do it. You may ask me for guarantees."

"Don't bother. I'll never do anything that won't be to your advantage, and I'll never climb without hoisting you to the next rung. I'll always remain far enough away from you to avoid arousing your jealousy and close enough to maintain your benefit and watch over your friendship with me. All the contracts in the world are broken because they tend to favor one side over the other. This will never be the case with us. I don't need guarantees."

"So . . . my brother . . . will disappear? . . ."

"Simply. We'll kidnap him from his bed by means of a plank that yields to the touch of a finger. He'll have fallen asleep under the crown and he'll awaken in captivity. From that moment on, you alone will be in command, and nothing will be more precious to you than keeping me close by."

"I'm sure of it. Here is my hand, Monsieur d'Herblay."

"Allow me, sire, to kneel before you very respectfully. We will embrace on the day that you put on the crown and I the tiara."

"Embrace me today, and be more than great, more than skillful, more than a sublime genius. Be good to me, be my father."

Aramis was deeply moved. He felt a stirring in his heart that he had never felt before. But it faded quickly.

"His father!" he mused. "Yes, Holy Father."

And they reentered the carriage, which then flew along the road leading to Vaux-le-Vicomte.

11

The Castle of Vaux-le-Vicomte

The Castle of Vaux-le-Vicomte, located several miles from Melun, had been built by Fouquet in 1653. At that point, there was little money in France. Mazarin had taken most of it, and Fouquet was spending the rest. However, as certain men have fertile defects and useful vices, Fouquet, in recklessly dumping millions into this castle, had contrived a way of gathering three illustrious men: Le Vau, the architect; Lenôtre, the landscape architect; and Le Brun, the interior decorator.

If the castle had any fault, it was its graceful and grandiose magnificence. People still traditionally count up its acres of roofing, the maintenance of which is the ruin of fortunes, which are now restricted like everything else in our era.

Once you go past the sumptuous iron gates, which are supported by caryatids, the main building spreads out in the vast main courtyard, which is ringed by deep ditches and edged by a stone balustrade. Nothing could be nobler than the middle forecourt, which rises on its perron like a king on his throne; it is surrounded by four pavilions, which form angles, and whose immense and majestic Ionic columns rise as high as the edifice itself. The friezes adorned with arabesques and the frontons crowning the pilasters add wealth and grace everywhere. The domes surmounting the entire castle provide splendor and amplitude.

This castle, built by a subject, resembles a royal structure more than those royal buildings that Cardinal Wolsey felt compelled to give Henry VIII for fear of arousing his jealousy.

But if the fine taste and exaltation burst out in a special place in this castle, if any one thing can be preferred to the glorious disposition of the interiors, to the luxury of the gilts, to the profusion of paintings and statues, it is the park—the gardens of the castle. The jets of water, already marvelous in 1653, are still marvelous today; the cascades were admired by all kings and princes. And as for the famous grotto, the theme of so many renowned poems, the residence of that illustrious nymph who was spoken about by Pellisson and La Fontaine, we need not discuss all of the grotto's beauties, for we would not care to elicit the criticism contemplated by Boileau in *The Art of Poetry*:

> Those things are mere festoons, mere astragals.
> . . . .
> And so I barely flee across the garden.

We will do as Despréaux did: we will step into the just eight-year-old park, whose already superb treetops spread out and blush in the first sunbeams. Lenôtre, the landscape designer, had hurried to give pleasure to his patron: all the nurseries had produced trees that had grown quickly thanks to their thorough culture and rich fertilization. Every promising tree in the area had been transplanted, roots and all, to the park. Fouquet could easily obtain trees to decorate his gardens since he had bought three villages and their contents to expand his park.

Monsieur de Scudéry claimed that in order to irrigate those gardens Monsieur Fouquet had divided a stream into a thousand fountains and had merged a thousand fountains into torrents. Volume X of *Clélie*, his sister's novel, to which he contributed a little, says a lot of other things about the Palace of Valterre, whose charms he minutely describes. It would be wiser to send curious readers to Vaux than to *Clélie*. Nonetheless, there are as many leagues between Paris and Vaux as there are volumes in that saga.

This splendid abode was ready to receive "the greatest king in the world." Some of Monsieur Fouquet's friends had brought their actors and their stage sets, other friends had brought their teams of sculptors and painters, and still others their finely sharpened quills. Lots of impromptus were in the offing.

The cascades, untamed though passing through nymphs, disgorged water that, more brilliant than crystal, swept over the bronze tritons and nereides, and the foam was iridescent in the blazing sun.

An army of waiters dashed through the courtyards and the vast corridors, while Fouquet, who had only arrived that morning, strolled about, calmly and shrewdly issuing his final orders after his stewards inspected the troops.

It was, as we have said, the fifteenth of August. The sun, directly overhead, burnished the bronze and marble shoulders of gods; the sunlight warmed the water in the conches, shining on the vineyards and ripening the peaches that the king was to miss fifty years later: "You're too young to have eaten Monsieur Fouquet's peaches."

Quite certain that Aramis had distributed the masses of guests throughout the castle, that he had made a point of stationing guards at doors and preparing the lodgings, Fouquet dealt purely with the overall cohesion. Gourville showed him the arrangements of the fireworks while Molière led him to the theater. Finally, after visiting the chapel, the salons, and the galleries, an exhausted Fouquet was going back down when he spotted Aramis on the stairs. The prelate signaled to him.

The superintendent joined his friend, who stopped him in front of a large, barely completed painting. Struggling over this picture, the artist Le Brun, bathed in sweat, splattered with pigments, pale with fatigue and inspiration, threw on the final touches with his rapid brush. It was the portrait of the king in the ceremonial garb that Percerin had deigned to show the Bishop of Vannes ahead of time.

Fouquet stood in front of this painting, which was alive, so to speak, with its moist warmth and rosy complexion. He gazed at the figure, admired it, calculated the work that had gone into it, and, unable to hit on a compensation worthy of this labor of Hercules, he flung his arm around the painter's neck and embraced him. The superintendent had just ruined a suit worth a thousand pistoles, but he had satisfied Le Brun.

It was a wonderful moment for the artist, it was a horrible moment for Monsieur Percerin, who had likewise come up behind Fouquet and was idolizing Le Brun's depiction of the suit that the couturier had made for His Majesty—an "objet d'art," he said, the likes of which could only be found in the superintendent's wardrobe.

The pain and the cries were interrupted by the signal given from the top of the edifice. Beyond Melun, in the already empty plain, the sentinels of Vaux had sighted the cortege of the king and the two queens: His Majesty was entering Melun with his long file of horsemen and carriages.

"In one hour," Aramis said to Fouquet.

"In one hour," Fouquet repeated with a sigh.

"And to think some people wonder what use such royal festivities are!" the Bishop of Vannes went on, laughing with his false laugh.

"Alas!" said Fouquet. "I'm not people and I wonder the same thing."

"I'll reply within twenty-four hours, monseigneur. Put on a happy face, this is a day of joy."

"Well, believe it or not, d'Herblay," said Fouquet effusively as he pointed toward Louis's retinue on the horizon, "he scarcely likes me, and I don't much care for him. But I don't understand why it is that the closer he gets to my home . . ."

"What do you mean?"

"What I mean is that the closer he gets, the more sacred he becomes for me. He is my king, he is almost dear to me."

" 'Dear'? Yes," said Aramis, toying with that word, just as the Abbé Terray did later on with Louis XV when he called the wedding of the king's son "inestimable."

"Don't laugh, d'Herblay. I sense that if he wanted me to, I would love this young man."

"It's not I you should be telling that to," said Aramis, "it's Monsieur Colbert."

"Monsieur Colbert?" exclaimed Fouquet. "Why?"

"Because once he's superintendent, he'll award you a pension from the king's privy purse."

After that final shot, Aramis took his leave.

"Where are you off to?" asked Fouquet, now somber again.

"I'm going to change clothes, monseigneur."

"Where are you staying, d'Herblay?"

"In the Blue Chamber on the third floor."

"The room right over the king's apartment?"

"Precisely."

"What slavery you've taken on! Condemning yourself not to move about!"

"I sleep or read in bed all night long, monseigneur."

"What about your men?"

"I've only brought one person."

"That's little!"

"My reader is enough for me. Good-bye, monseigneur, do not wear yourself out. Stay fresh for the king's arrival."

"Will we see you? And will we see our friend du Vallon?"

"I've lodged him near me. He's getting dressed."

And Fouquet, bowing with a smile, strode on like a commander in chief who visits the outposts after the enemy catches his attention.

12
The Wine of Melun

The king had actually entered Melun with the intention of just passing through. The young monarch craved pleasure. During the trip he had spotted Mademoiselle de la Vallière only twice, and, figuring that he would manage to speak to her in the gardens at night and only after the ceremony, he was in a hurry to get to Vaux and settle in. However, he reckoned without his captain of the musketeers and without Monsieur Colbert.

Like Calypso, who was unable to console herself after Odysseus's departure, our Gascon musketeer was unable to console himself for failing to determine why Aramis had asked Percerin to exhibit the king's new clothes.

"Still and all," said the man with inflexible logic, "my friend the Bishop of Vannes is up to something."

And he racked his brains to no avail.

D'Artagnan, so accustomed to all the court intrigues; d'Artagnan, who knew Fouquet's situation better than Fouquet himself, had developed the most bizarre suspicions at the announcement of that festivity, which would have ruined a rich man, and which was becoming an insane, an impossible labor for a ruined man. Meanwhile, Aramis had returned from Belle-Île and had been named master of ceremonies by Monsieur Fouquet, and Aramis persevered in sticking his nose in all of Fouquet's affairs. All these shady things, including Monsieur de Vannes's visits with Baisemeaux, had been haunting d'Artagnan for weeks now.

"With men of Aramis's stamp," he said, "you're the stronger only if you're holding a sword. So long as he was a soldier, there was some hope of overcoming him. But now that he's added a stole to his breastplate, we're doomed. Just what is Aramis after?"

And d'Artagnan fell to musing: What does it matter in the end if he only wants to overthrow Monsieur Colbert? . . . What else can he want?

D'Artagnan scratched his forehead, that fertile soil where his plowing nails had so often unearthed such wonderful ideas.

He thought of drawing Monsieur Colbert out, but d'Artagnan's friendship with Aramis, his oath—"All for one and one for all!"—attached him too strongly to the bishop. He hesitated. Besides, he hated the financier.

D'Artagnan wanted to open up to the king. But he realized the king wouldn't understand his suspicions, which were flimsier than a shadow.

The musketeer decided to confront Aramis directly the very next time he saw him. I'll grab him when he least expects it. I'll put my hand on his heart and he'll tell me . . . What will he tell me? Yes, he'll tell me something, because, damn it, there's more here than meets the eye!

A calmer d'Artagnan prepared for his trip and made sure that the king's military household, anything but large, was properly staffed and operated despite its middling size. The captain proceeded by trial and error, so that the king was traveling at the head of the musketeers, his Swiss mercenaries, and a picket of his French Guard when he reached Melun. You could have mistaken this force for a private army. Monsieur Colbert gazed with delight at these soldiers. He wished there were a third more.

"Why?" asked the king.

"To bring greater honor to Monsieur Fouquet," Colbert replied.

"To ruin him more quickly," d'Artagnan mused.

The army drew up at the entrance to Melun, whereupon the leading citizens presented the king with the keys to the city and invited him to imbibe the wine of honor at the town hall.

The king, who expected to ride through and reach Vaux immediately, turned red with chagrin.

"Who's the moron who's causing this delay?" he grumbled under his breath while the alderman gave his speech.

"It wasn't me," d'Artagnan answered. "I think it was Monsieur Colbert."

Colbert heard his name. "What is it, if you please, Monsieur d'Artagnan?"

"It would please me to know if it was you who compelled the king to sip Brie wine?"

"Yes, monsieur."

"Well, then, it was you whom the king gave a name to."

"Namely, monsieur?"

"I'm not quite sure . . . Wait! 'Imbecile'—no, no . . . 'Idiot, idiot . . . moron'! That's what His Majesty called the man who led him to the wine of Melun."

After that broadside, d'Artagnan calmly stroked his horse. Monsieur Colbert's big head was more bloated than ever.

D'Artagnan, seeing him turn ugly with anger, did not halt. The orator was still speechifying, and the king was visibly reddening.

"Damn it!" the musketeer said imperturbably. "The king is about to have a fit. How did you ever dream this up, Monsieur Colbert? You're out of luck."

"Monsieur," said the financier, sitting up straight, "I was inspired by my eagerness to serve the king."

"Bah!"

"Monsieur, Melun is a town, a good town, which pays a lot of taxes. So it shouldn't be slighted."

"Imagine that! I'm no financier, but I caught an ulterior motive on your part."

"Namely, monsieur?"

"To give Monsieur Fouquet something to fret about. He's doing his utmost to wait for us."

The blow was hard and true. Colbert was knocked for a loop. He rode off with his tail between his legs. Luckily, the alderman's discourse was finished. The king drank. Then the cortege prepared to continue its passage across the town.

The king chewed his lips because night was setting in and any hope of his strolling with Mademoiselle de la Vallière was fading.

Given all the arrangements, it would take at least four hours to get the king into the palace at Vaux. Thus the king, who was seething with impatience, pressed the two queens to hurry so that he'd arrive before nightfall. But the moment the cortege began moving, all sorts of difficulties emerged.

"Isn't the king going to spend the night in Melun?" Monsieur Colbert whispered to d'Artagnan.

Monsieur Colbert was quite poorly inspired that day by addressing the head of the musketeers. D'Artagnan, who had guessed that the king was anxious to leave, wanted to make sure that he was properly escorted when entering Vaux. He therefore wanted His Majesty to have the full train. On the other hand, d'Artagnan sensed that these delays would irritate the impatient ruler. How could the captain reconcile these two problems? He went to the king and repeated Colbert's question:

"Sire, Monsieur Colbert has asked whether Your Majesty is spending the night in Melun."

"Spend the night in Melun?! For what?" cried Louis XIV. "Spend the night in Melun?! Who in God's name could have thought of that if Monsieur Fouquet is expecting us this evening?!"

"I was worried," Colbert exclaimed, "about delaying Your Majesty. According to protocol, Your Majesty cannot enter any building, aside from a royal residence, until the lodgings have been marked out by his quartermaster and the garrison has been properly distributed."

D'Artagnan listened, all ears and biting his mustache.

The two queens likewise listened. They were exhausted and

wanted to sleep. And more than anything else, they wanted to prevent the king from taking an evening stroll with Monsieur de Saint-Aignan and the ladies of the court. For while etiquette kept the princesses at home, the noblewomen were at liberty to go strolling after performing their duties.

We can see that all these clashing interests, clustering into vapors, were bound to produce clouds, and that the clouds would swirl into a tempest. The king had no mustache to chew: he greedily gnawed the handle of his whip. How should they resolve this dilemma? D'Artagnan made sheep's eyes, and Colbert pouted. Whom should the king bite?

"We'll consult Queen Marie-Thérèse," said Louis XIV, bowing to the ladies.

His graciousness filled the heart of Marie-Thérèse, a kind and generous woman. Allowed to make a free choice, she respectfully answered: "It will always be my pleasure to go along with the king's wishes."

"How long will it take us to reach Vaux?" asked Anne of Austria, dwelling on each syllable and holding her hand on her suffering heart.

"An hour for Their Majesties' carriages," said d'Artagnan. "The roads are quite decent."

The king glared at him.

"A quarter hour for the king," d'Artagnan quickly added.

"Will we arrive in daylight?" asked Louis XIV.

Colbert objected softly: "No matter how fast we reach Vaux, we'll lose so much time quartering the military household."

What an imbecile! d'Artagnan thought to himself. If I wanted to destroy your standing, I would do it in ten minutes. Out loud, he added: "If I were the king, I would trust Monsieur Fouquet and leave my retinue. After all, Monsieur Fouquet is a man of honor. I would go there as a friend, I would enter his home alone with my captain of the guards. It would make me greater and nobler."

The king's eyes shone joyfully. "That's excellent advice, my ladies. Let's visit a friend, as friends. My carriages may advance slowly, but we, gentlemen, will charge forward!"

And off he dashed, followed by all the horsemen.

Colbert hid his large head and his scowl behind his horse's neck.

"I'll be free," said d'Artagnan as he galloped, "to chat with Aramis tonight. And then, Monsieur Fouquet is a man of honor. Damn it! I said so, and we have to believe it."

And so, toward seven P.M., without trumpets or his advance guard, without scouts or musketeers, the king presented himself at the gates of Vaux, where a bareheaded Fouquet, notified ahead of time, had been waiting for half an hour in the middle of his home and his friends.

13
Nectar and Ambrosia

Monsieur Fouquet clutched the stirrup of the king, who, after setting foot on the ground, nodded graciously, and, even more graciously, held out his hand, which Fouquet, despite the king's casual resistance, brought respectfully to his lips.

The king wanted to wait inside the first enceinte until the carriages arrived. He did not wait for long. The superintendent had made sure the roads were thoroughly prepared. You wouldn't have found a pebble the size of an egg between Melun and Vaux. And so the carriages, rolling on a virtual carpet, without jolting or tiring the passengers, delivered all the ladies at eight P.M. They were welcomed by Madame Fouquet, and, the instant they appeared, a light as radiant as daylight spurted from all the trees, all the vases, all the marbles. This bewitchment lasted until Their Majesties were inside the castle.

All these marvels, which the chronicler packed into, or, rather, preserved, in his narration, almost vying with a novelist; all these splendors, which outdid nature and turned night into day; all these pleasures and luxuries combined to satisfy the mind and the senses—Fouquet actually offered them to his king in that enchanted retreat, the likes of which no European monarch could boast of possessing.

We won't speak of the grand banquet that Their Majesties

participated in, or the concerts, or the magical metamorphoses. We'll content ourselves with painting a portrait of the king, who, at first cheerful, open, happy, soon grew somber, starchy, irritated. He was musing about his own residence and its meager luxury, which was merely the trappings of royalty and not his personal property. The huge vases of the Louvre, the old furniture and crockery of Henry II, Francis I, Louis XI, were simply historic monuments. They were simply art objects, the cast-offs of the royal position. In Fouquet's palace, the value of an item lay in the craftsmanship as in the material. Fouquet ate from gold dishware that his artists had smelted and sculpted for him. He drank wines that the king of France had never even heard of; and each goblet that Fouquet drank from was more precious than the entire royal wine cellar.

And what can we say about the apartments, the tapestries, the paintings, the servants, the officers of every description? What can we say about the service, in which order replaced etiquette; about the comfort, which replaced rigidity; about the pleasure and satisfaction that were the supreme law of all those who were at the beck and call of the host?

This noiseless swarm of busy people, this multitude of guests outnumbered by servants, these myriad food, of gold and silver vases, these floods of light, these masses of unknown flowers of which the hothouses were stripped as if overloaded, for they were lavishly beautiful; this harmonious whole, which was solely the prelude to the promised celebration, delighted all the visitors, who repeatedly expressed their admiration, not with voices or gestures, but with silence and attention—those two languages of the courtier who is no longer curbed by any master.

As for the king, his eyes swelled with tears; he no longer dared to look at the queen. Anne of Austria, still haughtier than any other creature, crushed her host by scorning everything she was served.

The young queen, kindhearted and curious about life, praised Fouquet, ate with gusto, and asked for the names of several fruits that appeared on the table. Fouquet replied that he didn't know their names. They came from his own stores; he had often grown them himself, since he had a green thumb when it came to exotic plants. The king, sensing the delicacy of Fouquet's response, was all the more humiliated. He found the young queen's behavior ever so slightly common, and Anne of Austria a wee bit Junonian. He focused entirely on staying aloof, at the edges of extreme disdain or simple admiration.

But Fouquet had foreseen all this: he was one of those men who foresee everything.

The king had explicitly stated that during his visit with Monsieur Fouquet he wanted to avoid mealtime protocol and, consequently, dine with everyone else. But the superintendent made sure that the king was served separately, if we may put it this way, in the middle of the general table. This marvelous dinner comprised all the king's favorites, all that he normally chose. Louis, enjoying the premier appetite in his kingdom, had no excuse for saying he wasn't hungry.

Monsieur Fouquet did even better. After following the king's order by sitting down at the table, he got up the moment the soups were brought out and he waited on the king himself, while Madame Fouquet stood behind the queen mother. Juno's disdain and Jupiter's grouchiness could not prevail against this extravagant cordiality. The queen mother nibbled on a biscuit dipped in Sanluca wine, and the king partook of everything, saying to Monsieur Fouquet: "Monsieur Superintendent, it would be impossible to provide a better dinner."

At which time the entire court pounced on the food with the enthusiasm of hosts of Egyptian locusts swooping down on fields of green rye.

But even satisfying his hunger didn't prevent the king from feeling sad: sad in proportion to the good mood he felt he ought to display; and sad, above all, because of the deference his courtiers were showing Fouquet.

D'Artagnan, who was stuffing his gut and drinking hard without letting on, never missed a mouthful; instead, he made lots of useful observations.

After supper, the king didn't want to lose out on his stroll. The park was lit up. With its diamonds and phosphorus, the moon, as if at the orders of the lord of Vaux, tinted the trees and the lake a silvery hue. The cool air was balmy, and the lanes were shadowy and graveled so softly as to delight the feet. The king had every reason to feel merry, for, coming upon Madame de la Vallière at a bend in a grove, he managed to squeeze her hand and say, "I love you." No one heard those words except for Monsieur d'Artagnan, who was behind the king, and Monsieur Fouquet, who was in front of him.

That enchanted night went on. The king asked to be shown to his private chambers. Everyone was promptly on the move. The queens went to their chambers, accompanied by flutes and theorbos. Upon climbing the grand perron, the king found his musketeers, whom Monsieur Fouquet had sent for and invited to supper.

D'Artagnan's suspicions disappeared. He was tired, he had eaten well, and, for once in his life, he wanted to fully indulge in a truly royal celebration.

"Monsieur Fouquet," he said, "is the man for me!"

The king was ceremoniously led to the Morpheus Chamber, of which we owe our readers a brief description. This was the biggest and most beautiful chamber in the palace. On the cupola Le Brun had painted the joyful dreams and woeful dreams that Morpheus arouses in kings and in commoners. The painter had enriched his frescoes with all the graceful things that sleep gives birth to, all the honey and fragrance, the flowers and the nectar, the delicious rapture or the repose of the senses. The images were as pleasurable in one part as they were sinister and horrifying in another part. The goblets that poured the poisons, the blade that shone over the sleeper's head, the sorcerers and the phantoms with their hideous masks, the half-shadows more frightening than the dazzling flame or the black depth of night—all those things were Le Brun's pendants to his blissful fancies.

Upon stepping into that magnificent chamber, the king shuddered. Fouquet asked him for the cause.

"I'm sleepy," the monarch answered, rather pale.

"Does Your Majesty wish to have his attendants right now?"

"No," said the king, "I have to chat with a few people. Notify Monsieur Colbert."

Fouquet bowed and left.

14
For a Gascon and a Gascon and a Half

D'Artagnan had lost no time; he wasn't accustomed to doing so. After learning Aramis's whereabouts, d'Artagnan dashed over to see him. Now, once the king had ridden into Vaux, Aramis had retired to his room, no doubt planning some intrigue for the king's enjoyment.

D'Artagnan had himself announced to Aramis and found him two flights up, in a beautiful room known as the Blue Chamber because of its hangings. The Bishop of Vannes was in the company of Porthos and several modern Epicureans.

Aramis came over to embrace his old friend and offered him the best chair; and since the others sensed that the musketeer desired some privacy for a secret conversation with Aramis, the Epicureans said their good nights and left.

Porthos didn't budge. Actually, having eaten a lot, he dozed in his chair. He didn't interfere with the conversation. His snoring was harmonious, and they could speak over that bass as if it were an ancient chant.

D'Artagnan felt that it was his job to start the dialogue. Since he was seeking a stringent commitment, he cut to the chase.

"Well, so here we are in Vaux!" he said.

"Yes indeed, d'Artagnan! Do you like it here?"

"A lot, and I also like Monsieur Fouquet."

"Isn't he charming?"

"As charming as they come."

"They say that initially the king had it in for him, but now he's mellowed."

"You say, 'They say.' So you didn't witness it personally?"

"No, I was totally involved with those men who've just left. We were dealing with tomorrow's theatrical production and tournaments."

"Aha! So you're in charge of the festival arrangements?"

"As you know, I enjoy the pleasures of the imagination. I've always had a touch of the poet."

"I remember your poems. They were delightful."

"I've forgotten them, but I love reading other poets—if those poets are named Molière, Pellisson, La Fontaine, and so on."

"Do you know what I thought of during supper, Aramis?"

"No, tell me, I couldn't guess it—you have so many ideas."

"Well, it occurred to me that the real French king is not Louis XIV."

"What?" cried Aramis, his eyes involuntarily locking with the musketeer's eyes.

"The real king is Monsieur Fouquet."

Aramis heaved a sigh of relief and smiled.

"You're just like all the rest: jealous. I bet it was Monsieur Colbert who put that bee in your bonnet."

To draw Aramis off the trail, d'Artagnan described Colbert's misadventures with the wine of Melun.

"What a rat that Colbert is!" said Aramis.

"Damn right!"

"And to think," added the bishop, "that that rat is going to be your minister four months from now."

"Ugh!"

"And that you'll serve him the way you served Richelieu and Mazarin."

"As you serve Fouquet," said d'Artagnan.

"With the difference, old friend, that Monsieur Fouquet is not Monsieur Colbert."

"True enough."

And d'Artagnan pretended to be sad.

"However," he went on a moment later, "why did you tell me that Monsieur Colbert is going to be a minister in four months?"

"Because Monsieur Fouquet will be out of a job," replied Aramis.

"He's going to be broke, isn't he?" said d'Artagnan.

"Flat broke."

"Then why these celebrations?" asked the musketeer, and his tone sounded so genuinely benevolent that it fooled the bishop for an instant. "Why didn't you try to talk him out of it?"

Those last few words went too far. Aramis was suspicious once more.

"It's a matter," he said, "of humoring the king."

"By going broke."

"By going broke for the king—yes."

"A bizarre reckoning!"

"A necessity."

"I don't see why, dear Aramis."

"Really? Well, you do notice Monsieur Colbert's burgeoning antagonism, don't you?"

"Oh, yes!"

"And you do see that Monsieur Colbert keeps urging the king to get rid of the superintendent?"

"It's as plain as day."

"And that a clique has formed against Monsieur Fouquet?"

"It's well known."

"How likely would it be for the king to support the faction that opposes a man who spent everything for the king's pleasure?"

"Not very likely," d'Artagnan slowly said. He was unconvinced and eager to broach another theme.

"There are follies and there are follies," he went on. "I don't like some of yours."

"Which ones?"

"You have my blessing for the supper, the ball, the concert, the play, the tournaments, the cascades, the bonfires, the fireworks, the illuminations, the presents—all well and good. But aren't those appropriate expenditures enough? Did you have to—"

"What?"

"Did you have to buy whole new wardrobes for the entire household?"

"You're right! I said as much to Monsieur Fouquet, but he replied that he was rich enough. He would offer the king a new castle, refurbished from the cellars to the weathercock. It would be new with everything in it. And once the king had gone, Monsieur Fouquet would burn everything so that no one else could use it."

"That's pure gibberish!"

"I told him so. And he said, 'The man who advises me to save my money is my enemy!' "

"It's crazy, I tell you. Like that portrait."

"What portrait?" asked Aramis.

"The portrait of the king. It's a surprise."

"A surprise?"

"Yes. That's why you got those swatches from Percerin."

D'Artagnan paused. He had shot the arrow. Now all he had to do was measure its impact.

"It's merely an act of courtesy," Aramis replied.

D'Artagnan strode over to his friend, took his hands, and peered into his eyes. "Aramis, do you still care for me a little?"

"How can you ask!?"

"Fine! Then do me a favor. Tell me why you got those swatches from Percerin."

"Come and ask that poor Le Brun, who worked on that portrait two days and two nights."

"Aramis, that may convince anyone else, but I . . ."

"Honestly, d'Artagnan, I'm surprised at you."

"Be kind to me. Tell me the truth. You wouldn't want to drive a wedge between us, would you?"

"Old friend, I don't get it. What the devil do you suspect?"

"Do you trust my instincts? You used to in the past. Well, instinct tells me that you're carrying out a secret project."

"A project? Me?"

"I'm not sure."

"Damn it!"

"I'm not sure, but I'd swear to it!"

"Damn it, d'Artagnan! That really hurts! Look, if I have a project that I have to keep from you, then I'll keep it from you—won't I? And if I had a project that I had to reveal to you, I'd've done so by now."

"No, Aramis, no. There are projects that can be revealed only at the right moment."

"Well, old friend," the bishop laughed, "I guess the right moment hasn't come yet."

D'Artagnan mournfully shook his head. "Friendship, friendship," he said. "An empty word! Here I have a man who'd let himself be chopped to bits if I asked him!"

"That's true," said Aramis nobly.

"And yet this man, who'd give me every last drop of blood in his veins, refuses to show me a tiny corner of his heart!

Friendship, I tell you, you're nothing but a shadow and a decoy like everything else that shines in this world!"

"Don't speak like that about our friendship," the bishop retorted in a firm and earnest tone. "It's nothing like the false friendships you're talking about."

"Look at us, Aramis. There are three of us out of the old four. You're deceiving me, I'm suspicious of you, and Porthos is asleep. A fine trio of friends, aren't we? A fine remnant!"

"I can tell you only one thing, d'Artagnan, and I will swear on the Gospels. I love you as much as before. If ever I distrust you, it's because of others and not because of you or me. Whatever I do, whatever my success, you'll have your share. Make me the same promise—go ahead!"

"If I'm not mistaken, Aramis, your words are totally generous at the moment you speak them."

"That could be."

"So you're conspiring against Monsieur Colbert. If not, then tell me what's going on, damn it! I've got the tool and I'll rip out the tooth!"

Aramis could not wipe away a cavalier smile that flashed across his noble face.

"And if I *were* conspiring against Colbert, would that be so bad?"

"It would be too negligible for you, and Colbert's not the reason why you asked Percerin for those swatches. Oh, Aramis! We're not enemies, we're brothers. Tell me what you're after, and I swear by all that's holy that if I can't help you I'll remain neutral."

"I'm not after anything," said Aramis.

"Aramis, a voice inside me is talking to me, illuminating me; and this voice has never misled me. You're conspiring against the king."

"The king?!" cried the bishop, feigning dismay.

"Your face won't convince me otherwise. I repeat: You're conspiring against the king."

"Will you help me?" asked Aramis, still with an ironic smile.

"Aramis, I'll do more than help you, I'll do more than remain neutral, I will save you!"

"You're crazy, d'Artagnan!"

"I'm the only one who's sane here."

"You suspect me of wanting to assassinate the king!"

"Who says so?" asked the musketeer.

"Let's understand each other. I don't see what you can do to a legitimate king like ours other than assassinate him."

D'Artagnan held his tongue.

"Besides, you've got your guards and your musketeers here," said the bishop.

"That's true."

"You're not in Fouquet's castle, you're in your own."

"That's true."

"At this very moment, you've got Monsieur Colbert, who's trying to turn the king against Monsieur Fouquet, giving him all the advice you'd want if I weren't involved."

"Aramis! Aramis! For God's sake! The words of a true friend."

"The words of a true friend are always true! If I think of letting even one finger touch the son of Anne of Austria, the true king of this land of France; if I don't have the adamant intention of prostrating myself before his throne; if I don't plan to help make the next few days, here in Vaux, the most glorious days in the life of my king, then may lightning strike me dead!"

Aramis had turned his face toward the alcove, while d'Artagnan, his back toward that alcove, could not suspect that someone was hiding there. The gravity of Aramis's words, their deliberate slowness, the solemnity of the pledge gave the musketeer the most complete satisfaction. He took both of Aramis's hands and squeezed them in the most heartfelt way.

Aramis had endured the reproaches without blanching. But he did turn crimson upon listening to the praises. A deceived d'Artagnan did him honor, a trusting d'Artagnan made him feel ashamed.

"Are you leaving?" asked Aramis, embracing him to hide his redness.

"Yes, duty calls. I have to get the watchword."

"Where will you sleep?"

"In the king's antechamber, I guess. What about Porthos?"

"Take him along! He snores like a cannon!"

"Ah! He's not staying with you?"

"Not for all the tea in China. I don't know where he's lodged."

"Excellent!" said the musketeer, his final suspicion removed by the separation of the two friends. And he heartily slapped Porthos's shoulder. Porthos let out a roaring yawn.

"C'mon!" said d'Artagnan.

"Hey! D'Artagnan, old friend! What are you doing here? Oh, that's right. I'm at the Vaux celebration."

"With your gorgeous suit."

"That's very nice of Monsieur Coquelin de Volière, isn't it?"

"Shush!" said Aramis. "You're trekking heavily enough to break through the floor!"

"That's true," said the musketeer. "This room is over the dome."

"I didn't take it for a fencing hall," the bishop added. "The ceiling of the king's chamber has the sweet things of slumber. Don't forget that my floor is the cover of his ceiling. Good night, my friends. In ten minutes I'll be fast asleep."

And Aramis saw them out with a gentle chuckle. Once they were gone, he quickly bolted the door, made the windows airtight, and called out: "Monseigneur! Monseigneur!"

Philip emerged from the alcove after pushing a sliding door behind the bed. "Monsieur d'Artagnan is quite suspicious," he said.

"Ah! So you recognized him?"

"Before you even used his name."

"He's your captain of the musketeers."

"He's devoted to *me*," replied Philip, stressing the pronoun.

"Faithful as a dog. And at times he bites. If d'Artagnan doesn't recognize you before the *other one* disappears, you can count on d'Artagnan till the end of time. For if he sees nothing, he will remain faithful. If he sees when it's too late, he's a Gascon and he'll never admit that he's wrong."

"I thought so. And what do we do now?"

"You're going to observe carefully and watch the king's evening bedroom ceremony."

"Fine. Where should I be stationed?"

"Sit down on this folding chair. I'm going to slide back a part of the floor. You'll watch through that opening, which corresponds to the false windows in the king's chamber. Can you see?"

"I see the king." And Philip shuddered as if encountering an enemy.

"What's he doing?"

"He's seating a man at his side."

"Monsieur Fouquet?"

"No, not at all. Wait . . ."

"The notes, my prince, the portraits!"

"That man is Monsieur Colbert."

"Colbert sits in the king's presence?!" exclaimed Aramis. "Impossible!"

"See for yourself."

Aramis peered through the aperture in the floor. "Yes," he said, "it's Colbert in the flesh. Oh, monseigneur! What are we about to hear, and what will be the result of this intimacy?"

"Nothing good for Monsieur Fouquet, I assume."

The prince was not mistaken. We have seen that Louis XIV had sent for Colbert, and that Colbert had arrived. Their conversation began with one of the highest favors that the king had ever granted. Though it's true that the king was alone with his subject.

"Colbert, sit down."

Colbert, who was overjoyed, who had feared that he was going to be dismissed, refused this remarkable honor.

"Is he accepting it?"

"No, he's remaining on his feet."

"Let's listen, my prince."

The future king and the future pope eagerly listened to those mere mortals under their feet, ready to crush them if they felt like it.

"Colbert," said the king, "you really annoyed me today."

"Yes, sire . . . I know."

"Very good! I like your answer. Yes, you know. And it took courage."

"I risked annoying Your Majesty, but I also risked concealing your true interests."

"What? You were afraid of something concerning me?"

"Yes, sire," said Colbert, "even if it was a slight indigestion, for people give their king such banquets only to crush him under the mass of good food!"

Colbert pleasantly waited to see the effect of his broad joke. Louis XIV, the vainest and most difficult man in his kingdom, forgave Colbert for his jest too.

"You're right," said the king. "Monsieur Fouquet went a bit overboard with his feast. Tell me, Colbert, where does Fouquet get all the money for these enormous undertakings? Do you know?"

"Yes, sire, I know."

"Can you more or less give me a detailed account?"

"Easily, down to the last penny."

"I know that you're very exact."

"It's the first quality that one can demand of an intendant of finances."

"Not everyone has that quality."

"I am grateful to Your Majesty for such flattering praise."

"So Monsieur Fouquet is rich, very rich, and that's something everyone knows."

"Everyone, the living and the dead."

"What does that mean, Monsieur Colbert?"

"The living see Monsieur Fouquet's wealth, they admire the end result and they applaud it. The dead, however, are more knowledgeable than we: they know the sources and they accuse."

"Well? What are the sources of Monsieur Fouquet's wealth?"

"The position of intendant often favors those who occupy it."

"You have to speak more confidentially. Don't be afraid, we're quite alone."

"I'm never afraid of anything, sire, so long as I'm under the aegis of my conscience and under the protection of my king." And Colbert bowed.

"So if the dead were to speak . . ."

"They do speak sometimes, sire. Read this."

"Ah!" murmured Aramis to the prince, who, at his side, listened without missing a syllable. Aramis went on: "Since you're placed here, monseigneur, to learn how to be a king, listen to a totally royal infamy. You're about to witness one of those scenes that are conceived and executed by God alone—or, rather, by the devil. Listen carefully, it will be to your benefit."

The prince, doubly attentive, saw Louis XIV take a letter that Colbert held out to him.

"The late Cardinal Mazarin's handwriting!" said the king.

"Your Majesty has an excellent memory," replied Colbert with a bow. "For a king who's fated for arduous work, it's a wonderful aptitude to recognize a handwriting at first glance."

The king read the letter. "I don't quite understand," he said with keen interest.

"Your Majesty is not yet in the habit of reviewing public finances."

"I believe that the issue is money that was given to Monsieur Fouquet."

"Thirteen million. A tidy sum!"

"Oh, yes! Well, so those thirteen million are missing from the overall accounts? I tell you, I don't quite understand that. Why and how is this deficit possible?"

"I don't say it's possible, I do say it's real."

"You say that thirteen million is missing from the overall accounts?"

"It's not I who say so, it's the ledger."

"And Monsieur de Mazarin's letter indicates the use of that sum and the name of the person it was deposited with?"

"As Your Majesty can check for himself."

"Yes indeed. So the bottom line is that Monsieur Fouquet has not yet rendered the thirteen million."

"No, sire. Not according to the ledgers."

"And so . . ."

"And so, sire, if Monsieur Fouquet has not rendered the thirteen million, then he must be keeping them for himself. And with thirteen million, a man can spend over four times as much on splendor and magnificence—which Your Majesty was unable to do at Fontainebleau, which cost a mere three million in toto, if you recall."

For an awkward man the memory of that celebration was anything but awkward. It was at Fontainebleau that the king had first realized his own inferiority to Monsieur Fouquet. Colbert was paying back at Vaux what Fouquet had done to him at Fontainebleau, and, good financier that he was, he paid both principal and interest. Having thus manipulated the king, Colbert didn't have much more to do. He sensed this, for the king had grown somber. Colbert waited for the king's next few words as impatiently as Philip and Aramis from their high observation post.

"Do you grasp the consequences, Monsieur Colbert?" asked the king after some reflection.

"No, sire, I don't."

"If the appropriation of the thirteen million were proved—"

"It *has* been proved."

"I mean if it were declared and validated, Monsieur Colbert."

"I think it would be tomorrow, if Your Majesty—"

"—were not in Monsieur Fouquet's home," the king stated with some dignity.

"The king's home is everywhere, sire, especially the homes that his money has paid for."

"It seems to me," Philip murmured, "that the architect of this dome could have foreseen its use and contrived to make it collapse on scoundrels like this Monsieur Colbert!"

"I was thinking the same thing," said Aramis, "but Monsieur Colbert is too close to the king at this moment!"

"You're right. It would open the succession."

"Of which your younger brother would reap all the fruits, monseigneur. But let's keep still and continue eavesdropping."

"We won't have to eavesdrop for long," said the young prince.

"What do you mean, monseigneur?"

"I mean that if I were the king, I would not respond at all."

"What would you do?"

"I would think about it until tomorrow morning."

Louis XIV finally looked up and found Colbert hanging on his every word. The king brusquely changed the subject: "Monsieur Colbert, I see it's getting late. I'm going to bed."

"Ah!" said Colbert. "I'll—"

"Wait till tomorrow. I'll make by decision by morning."

"Very well, sire," exclaimed Colbert, beside himself, though he held back in the king's presence.

The king gestured, and the intendant backed up toward the door.

"My attendants," cried the king.

The royal attendants entered his chamber.

Philip was about to leave his observation post.

"One moment," said Aramis, as gentle as ever. "What just happened is merely a detail, and we won't even worry about it tomorrow. But the bedtime attendants, the etiquette of the evening ceremony—ah, monseigneur! That is crucial! Learn, learn your bedtime ritual, sire. Watch, watch."

15
Colbert

History will tell us or rather has told us about the next day's events, the splendid festival that Monsieur Fouquet presented to his king. There was joy and amusement, there were strolls, banquets, and performances—and Porthos, to his great surprise, recognized Monsieur Coquelin de Volière acting in *The Nuisances*. That was the title given by Monsieur de Bracieux de Pierrefonds.

Furthermore, La Fontaine sang Molière's praises, and Porthos heartily agreed: "Damn it! This Molière is my man! But only for his suits!"

Meanwhile, preoccupied with last night's scene, the king had slept off the venom poured by Colbert. Throughout that dazzling, surprising, eventful day, in which all the marvels of *The Arabian Nights* seemed to emerge under his feet, the king stayed aloof, reserved, and taciturn. Nothing could cheer him up. People sensed a profound resentment coming from far away, increasing little by little like a wellspring that turns into a stream fed by a thousand trickles. And this animosity trembled at the core of his soul. It was only toward noon that he started to regain a modicum of serenity. He most likely had made up his mind.

Aramis, following him step-by-step in both thought and deed, concluded that the event he was expecting was about to take place.

This time, Colbert seemed to be walking in unison with the Bishop of Vannes, and had he received a direction from Aramis for every pinprick that he, Colbert, had inflicted on the king, he could not have done better.

All that day, the king, who, no doubt, needed to get rid of his somber thoughts, appeared to seek out Mademoiselle de la Vallière as actively as he fled Colbert or Fouquet.

Evening set in. The king had not wished to go on a stroll until after the card games. So they played several hands between the supper and the stroll. The king won a thousand pistoles, which he pocketed. He then rose, saying, "Gentlemen, to the park."

There they found the ladies. While the king had won a thousand pistoles, Monsieur Fouquet had somehow contrived to lose ten thousand, so that one hundred ninety thousand pounds was subdivided among the courtiers and the military officers—a circumstance that made their faces the most joyous in the world.

But that wasn't true of the king. Despite his winnings, to which he was not insensitive, a wisp of cloud hovered over his features. Colbert was waiting for him at a bend in a garden path. They must have had an appointment, for Louis XIV, who had been avoiding Colbert, or pretending to avoid him, signaled him, and they vanished in the depths of the park.

However, Mademoiselle de la Vallière had also seen the king's scowling face and blazing eyes. She had seen them, and since nothing that brewed in his soul was impenetrable to her love, she realized that his suppressed anger was aimed at a specific person standing on the road of vengeance like an angel of mercy.

Utterly sad, utterly confused, half-insane after her long separation from her lover, distressed by his emotions, which she had sensed, she initially displayed embarrassment, which the king, in his poor frame of mind, interpreted unfavorably.

They were alone—or nearly so, given that Colbert, upon spotting the girl, had halted respectfully and was stationed ten paces away. And now the king approached her and took her hand: "Mademoiselle, may I be so indiscreet as to ask you what's wrong? Your bosom looks swollen, your eyes are moist."

"Oh, sire! If my bosom is swollen, if my eyes are moist, if I'm sad, it's because Your Majesty is sad."

"Sad? Oh, you're mistaken, mademoiselle, it's not sadness I feel."

"And what is it you feel?"

"Humiliation."

"Humiliation? What are you saying?"

"I am saying, mademoiselle, that wherever I may be, no one else should be the master. Well, look around, see if I'm not eclipsed—I, the king of France—by the king of this domain." Gritting his teeth and making a fist, he went on. "And when I think that this king . . ."

"Yes, sire?" said the frightened girl.

"That this king is a disloyal servant who makes himself house-proud with property he has stolen from me! I'm going to turn this impudent minister's celebration into a tableau of mourning that the nymph of Vaux, as his poets say, will remember for a long time."

"Oh! Your Majesty! . . ."

"What, mademoiselle? Are you going to side with Fouquet?" the king snapped impatiently.

"No, sire, I only wonder if you're well informed. Your Majesty has learned the value of any number of court accusations."

Louis XIV signaled Colbert to come over: "Speak, monsieur, for I do believe that Mademoiselle de la Vallière needs to hear your words in order to confirm the words of the king. Tell Mademoiselle what Monsieur Fouquet has done. And as for you, mademoiselle, it won't take long. I beg you, please be so kind as to listen."

Why was Louis XIV so insistent? It was quite simple. His heart wasn't tranquil, his mind wasn't fully convinced. He sensed some dark, obscure, tortuous intrigue behind that story of the thirteen million. And so he counted on Mademoiselle de la Vallière's pure heart. Revolted by the mere idea of a theft, she would approve his resolution with a single word—the conclusion he had come to, but nevertheless hesitated to act on.

"Speak, monsieur," she said to Colbert, who had come over. "Speak, because the king wants me to listen to you. Now, tell me, what is Monsieur Fouquet's crime?"

"Oh, nothing grave," said the dark personage. "A mere abuse of trust . . ."

"Go on, go on, Colbert, and when you're done go and inform Monsieur d'Artagnan that I have orders to give him."

"Monsieur d'Artagnan!" cried Mademoiselle de la Vallière. "Why notify him? I beg you to tell me!"

"Damn it! To arrest that arrogant titan, who, faithful to his motto, threatens to climb to my stars."

"Arrest Monsieur Fouquet, you say?"

"Ah! You're amazed?"

"In his own home?"

"Why not? If he's guilty, then he's as guilty here as anywhere else."

"Monsieur Fouquet, who is ruining himself to honor his king?"

"Why, I do believe that you are actually defending this traitor, mademoiselle!"

Colbert chuckled softly. The king turned toward that sound.

"Sire," said the girl, "I'm not defending him, I'm defending you!"

"Me?! . . . You're defending me?!"

"Sire, you're dishonoring yourself by issuing such an order."

"Dishonoring myself?" murmured the king, livid with anger. "Honestly, mademoiselle, your words reveal a strange passion!"

"I'm passionate not about my words but about my service to Your Majesty," the noble-hearted girl retorted. "I would stake my life, if need be, and with the same passion, sire!"

Colbert started muttering something. But then Mademoiselle de la Vallière, that gentle lamb, drew herself up and imposed silence upon him with her flaming eyes.

"Monsieur," she said, "if the king, by doing good, wrongs

me or my near and dear, then I hold my tongue. But if the king, by helping me or those I love, acts badly, I will tell him so."

"Why, it seems to me, mademoiselle," Colbert ventured to reply, "that I too love the king."

"Yes, monsieur, we both love him, each in his way," she declared so emphatically that her retort filled the young king's heart. "Except that I love him so powerfully that everyone knows about it, and so purely that the king himself never doubts my love. He is my king and my master. I am his humble servant. But anyone who meddles with his honor meddles with my life. Let me repeat my statement: Anyone who advises the king to arrest Monsieur Fouquet in his own home is dishonoring the king."

Colbert lowered his head, he felt abandoned by the king. Nevertheless, he murmured, "Mademoiselle, I have only one thing to say."

"Do not say it, monsieur, for I will not listen. And just what can you say to me? That Monsieur Fouquet has committed crimes? I know it because the king has said so. And the instant the king says 'I believe,' I don't need someone else to say 'I can testify to it.' But—and I say so out loud—even if Monsieur Fouquet were the most wretched of men, he is still sacred to the king, because the king is his guest. Even if Monsieur Fouquet's home were a den of thieves, even if Vaux were a lair of counterfeiters or highwaymen, his home is sacred, his castle is inviolable, because that's where his wife lives with him. And it's a place of asylum that no headsman would desecrate!"

Mademoiselle de la Vallière lapsed into silence. The king couldn't help admiring her. He submitted to the ardor of her voice, to the noble way she championed her cause. As for Colbert, he yielded to her words, crushed as he was by the inequality of the struggle. Finally, the king drew a long breath, shook his head, and held out his hand to Mademoiselle de la Vallière.

"Mademoiselle," he murmured, "why do you speak against me? Do you know what that scoundrel will do if I give him a chance to catch his breath?"

"Isn't he a prey that you can capture any time you like?"

"What if he escapes, what if he flees?" cried Colbert.

"Monsieur, letting him escape will be to the king's eternal glory. And the guiltier Monsieur Fouquet, the greater the king's glory—compared with this misery, the shame of arresting him here!"

Louis kissed her hand as he slipped to his knees.

I'm doomed! Colbert thought. But suddenly his features brightened: No, no! Not yet! he said to himself.

The king, shielded by the density of an enormous linden tree, hugged Mademoiselle de la Vallière with all the fervor of ineffable love. Meanwhile, Colbert, after calmly rummaging through his portfolio, removed a sheet of paper that was folded like a letter. The document was slightly yellow, but it must have been quite precious because it elicited a smile from the intendant. Then his hateful eyes focused on the attractive couple in the shade: the girl and the king, who were about to be illuminated by the approaching torches.

Louis saw the flames reflected by the girl's white gown.

"Leave me, Louise," he said, "they're coming."

"Mademoiselle, mademoiselle, they're coming!" Colbert chimed in, trying to hasten her departure.

Louise quickly vanished among the trees, while the kneeling king got back on his feet.

"Ah! Mademoiselle de la Vallière has dropped something!" said Colbert.

"What is it?" asked the king.

"A document, a letter, something white. Here it is, sire."

The king swiftly bent down and picked up the letter, crumpling it.

At that instant, the torches arrived, inundating the dark tableau with a flood of light.

16
Jealousy

This intense glare, this eager throng, this new ovation by Monsieur Fouquet, suspended a decision that the girl had already shaken in the king's heart.

He gazed at Fouquet with something like gratitude for enabling Mademoiselle de la Vallière to reveal her generosity, her power over the king's heart.

This was the moment of the final marvels of the celebration. Scarcely had Fouquet led the king back toward the castle when a mass of flames, as dazzling as dawn, burst from the dome with a blinding roar and lit up the tiniest details of the gardens.

The fireworks commenced. Standing some twenty paces from the king, who was surrounded and celebrated, Colbert, with his obstinate, funereal mind, was trying to retain Louis's attention, which was already too distracted by the magnificent spectacle.

Suddenly, as the king was about to hold out his hand to Fouquet, he felt the document that his mistress had supposedly dropped while hurrying away.

The stronger magnet of the thought of love aroused the memory of his mistress in the young king. Amid the more and more beautiful light of the fireworks, which drew shouts of admiration from the surrounding villages, the king read the letter, which he figured was a love letter that Louise had written to him.

As he read, his face grew paler and paler, and his muffled anger, illuminated by the thousand colors of the fireworks, created a horrifying spectacle. Indeed, it would have terrified anyone who could read the king's heart, which was ravaged by the most sinister passions. There was no pause in his rage and jealousy. The instant he discovered the dark truth, everything disappeared: pity, kindness, the sanctity of hospitality.

A keen grief twisted his heart, which was still too weak to dissimulate his suffering, and he very nearly uttered a shriek of alarm, very nearly called for his guards.

The letter, as the reader might know, was penned by Fouquet

when he had tried to capture the heart of Mademoiselle de la Vallière.

Fouquet saw the king's pallor but was unaware of its cause. Colbert saw the king's fury and delighted in the gathering storm.

Fouquet's voice tore the king from his fierce reverie: "What is wrong, sire?" the superintendent graciously asked.

Louis made an effort to pull himself together—a violent effort. "Nothing," he said.

"I'm afraid that Your Majesty seems to be suffering."

"I *am* suffering, I've told you so, monsieur, but it's nothing."

And the king, without waiting for the end of the fireworks, headed toward the castle.

Fouquet accompanied him. Everyone else followed them.

The final rockets burned sadly for their own entertainment.

Fouquet tried to ask the king again, but received no answer. He assumed that the king had quarreled with his mistress in the park, that they had had a falling-out, and that the king, not sulky by nature, but totally devoted to his amorous rage, hated the whole world so long as his mistress was sulking. This assumption was enough to console Fouquet; he even had a friendly and comforting smile when the young king wished him good night.

That wasn't the end of things for Louis XIV; he also had to endure the bedtime ritual, which was particularly ceremonious this evening. The guests were scheduled to leave the next day. They certainly had to thank Monsieur Fouquet and show some gratitude for his thirteen million.

The only amiable words that the king could come up with for his host were: "Monsieur Fouquet, you'll be hearing from me. Please send for Monsieur d'Artagnan."

And the blood of Louis XIII, who had dissimulated so much, was boiling in his veins; he was ready to cut Fouquet's throat just as the previous king had assassinated Marshal d'Ancre. In this way, Louis XIV disguised the horrible decision with one of those royal smiles that flash like lightning prior to a national crisis.

Fouquet took the king's hand and kissed it. Louis shuddered

from head to foot, but he let his hand be touched by Monsieur Fouquet's lips.

Five minutes later, d'Artagnan, after receiving the royal order, entered the bedroom of Louis XIV.

Aramis and Philip were in their room, eavesdropping as attentively as ever.

The king didn't leave the captain of his musketeers enough time to reach his armchair. He dashed over to him. "Make sure," he exclaimed, "that no one else joins us!"

"Of course, sire," replied the soldier, who had been analyzing the ravages of the king's physiognomy for some time now. D'Artagnan transmitted the order to the sentry guarding the door, then returned to the king.

"Does Your Majesty have any news?"

The king ignored the question. "How many men do you have here?"

"For what purpose, sire?"

"How many men do you have here?" he repeating, stamping his foot.

"I've got the musketeers."

"And then?"

"I've got twenty guards and thirteen Swiss mercenaries."

"How many men would it take to . . ."

"To?" asked the musketeer with large, calm eyes.

"To arrest Monsieur Fouquet?"

D'Artagnan recoiled. "Arrest Monsieur Fouquet!" he gasped.

"Are you too going to tell me that it's impossible?" yelled the king with cold, hateful fury.

D'Artagnan was cut to the quick. "I never say that anything is impossible."

"Then do it!"

D'Artagnan turned on his heel and veered toward the door. It was a short distance, six paces. Once there, he halted. "Excuse me, sire."

"What is it?" said the king.

"I would like a written order to make this arrest."

"For what purpose? And since when is the king's word not enough for you?"

"When a king's word is spoken in anger, it may change when the anger changes."

"Don't mince matters, monsieur! You've got an ulterior thought."

"Oh, I've always got some kind of thought—including thoughts that don't, unfortunately, cross other people's minds," d'Artagnan retorted impertinently.

The king, although in the heat of passion, yielded to this man the way a horse kneels under the robust hands of its trainer.

"Tell me your thoughts!" he cried.

"This is it, sire," said d'Artagnan. "You're arresting a man in his own home; you're acting in anger. Once you've gotten over your anger, you'll repent. At that point, I'd like to show you your signature. While it may not rectify anything, it will at least prove that the king is wrong to lose his temper."

"Wrong to lose his temper!?" yelled the king in his frenzy. "Christ Almighty! Didn't the king my father, didn't the king my grandfather, ever lose their temper?!"

"The king your father and the king your grandfather lost their temper only in private."

"The king is the master everywhere."

"That's flattering claptrap, and it probably comes from Monsieur Colbert. But it's not true. The king is at home in every house from which he's driven out the owner."

Louis bit his lip.

"What's wrong?" asked d'Artagnan. "This man has ruined himself to please you, and you want to arrest him! Damn it, sire. If I were Fouquet, and I were treated like that, I'd swallow a dozen Roman candles, ignite them, and blow up myself and everyone else! But no matter! You desire it, and I'll do it!"

"Go ahead!" said the king. "But have you got enough men?"

"Do you think I need backup? Arresting Monsieur Fouquet is like taking candy from a baby! Arresting Monsieur Fouquet is like drinking a jigger of absinthe: you make a face and that's that!"

"What if he puts up a fight?"

"Monsieur Fouquet? Come on! Put up a fight when these harsh measures make him a king and a martyr?! If he's got a million left—which I doubt—he'd spend it all on this! Fine, sire, I'm going."

"Wait," said the king.

"Ah! What is it?"

"Do not arrest him in public."

"That would be more difficult."

"Why?"

"Because nothing would be easier than to go into the midst of the thousand enthusiastic people around him and say to Monsieur Fouquet: 'Sir, I arrest you in the name of the king!' But to go up to him, turn him again, stick him in some inescapable corner of the chessboard, steal him away from all his guests and keep him as your prisoner without hearing him so much as heave a sigh—now, that's a real, true, supreme difficulty, too much for even the most skillful men."

"Tell me again that it's impossible and you'll be done with it! Oh, God! Oh, God! Why am I surrounded by people who prevent me from doing what I want!"

"I'm not preventing you from doing anything. Have you made up your mind?"

"Guard Monsieur Fouquet until tomorrow, when I'll reach my definitive decision."

"I will do so, sire."

"And attend my morning ceremony, so I can give you my new orders."

"Yes, sire."

"And now leave me alone."

"You don't even need Monsieur Colbert?" said the musketeer, shooting his final arrow as he left.

The king shuddered. Fully absorbed in his revenge, he had forgotten the why and wherefore of the crime, the corpus delicti.

"No, nobody!" he said. "Nobody! Leave me!"

D'Artagnan left. The king shut the door himself and started racing furiously through the room like a wounded bull dragging its streamers and iron darts. Finally, he consoled himself by shouting his misery: "That scoundrel! Not only does he steal my finances, but he uses the money to corrupt my secretaries, my friends, my generals, my artists, and he even takes my mistress! . . . Ah! That's why that conniving cheat defended him so bravely! . . . Out of gratitude! . . . Who knows? Perhaps even out of love!"

For an instant he was lost in his painful reflections.

"A satyr!" he mused, with that deep hatred that young men feel toward mature men who still think about love. "A man who's never met any resistance, a man surrounded by silly females, a man who gives them gold and diamonds and who has artists paint his mistresses in the costumes of goddesses!"

The king shook with despair. "He soils everything for me! He ruins everything for me! He's going to be the death of me! He's too much for me! He's my mortal enemy! That man is going to fall! I hate him! . . . I hate him! . . . I hate him! . . ."

While uttering these words, he banged his fists on the arms of his chair and then struggled to his feet like an epileptic. "Tomorrow! Tomorrow!" he murmured. "Oh, the wonderful day when the sun will rise as my only rival! That man will fall so low that when people see the wreckage caused by my anger, they'll have to admit at last that I am greater than he!"

The king, unable to control himself any further, knocked over a table near his bed, and, fully clothed, drowning in grief, suffocating, almost weeping, he collapsed on his sheets, to chew them and find some rest for his body. The bed groaned under that weight, and, apart from a little sighing and panting, nothing more could be heard from the Morpheus Chamber.

17
Lèse-Majesté

The hotheaded king's fury, ignited by Fouquet's letter to Mademoiselle de la Vallière, subsided gradually into painful fatigue.

Youth, brimming with health and life, needs to repair any damage the very instant it occurs; nor does youth experience those endless sleepless nights that recall the fable of Prometheus with the vulture feeding eternally on his liver. A middle-aged man constantly feeds his sorrow in his vigor, as does an old man in his feebleness. On the other hand, a young man, surprised by the sudden revelation of misfortune, weakens himself in cries and direct struggles, and is more quickly overwhelmed by his inexorable enemy. Once overwhelmed, he stops suffering.

Louis was crushed within a quarter hour. He then stopped clenching his fists and glaring at the invisible objects of his hatred; he stopped hurling violent accusations at Monsieur Fouquet and Mademoiselle de la Vallière. He plunged from fury to despair, and from despair to prostration.

After Louis stiffened and twisted on the bed for several moments, his inert arms dropped to his sides. His head languished on the lace pillow, his exhausted limbs shivered, his muscles contracted lightly, his chest heaved only occasional sighs.

The god Morpheus, who reigned supreme in the chamber bearing his name; the god, to whom Louis turned his angry, tearful, bloodshot eyes—Morpheus poured his handfuls of poppies upon the king, who gently closed his eyes and fell asleep.

As often happens in the sweet and light beginning of slumber, which raises the body above the bed, the soul above the earth, images flickered in Louis's mind. The god Morpheus, painted on the ceiling, seemed to be gazing at him with human eyes; something appeared to be shining and stirring in the dome; and the swarms of eerie dreams, shifting for an instant, exposed a man's face, his hand leaning against his mouth, his features absorbed in deep meditation. And, oddly enough, this man so thoroughly resembled the king that Louis took him for his own reflection in a mirror. Except that the man was saddened by a look of profound pity.

Next, the dome gradually seemed to be fleeing, fading, and Le Brun's painted figures and attributes melted farther and farther away into darkness. The immobility of the bed was replaced by a gentle, regular, cadenced movement like that of a vessel pitching on the waves.

The king must have been dreaming, and in his dream the gold crown that fastened the curtains together slipped away just like the dome from which the crown was suspended, so that the winged genius holding it with both hands appeared to be uselessly calling to the king, who was vanishing in the distance.

The bed was still sinking. Louis, opening his eyes, was inveigled by that cruel hallucination. Finally, as the light of the royal chamber kept waning, something cold, somber, inexplicable was invading the atmosphere. Gone were the paintings, the gold, the velvet curtains: the walls were now a dull gray that thickened more and more into a shadow. And after a minute that dragged by like a century, the bed reached a stratum of black, icy air. And there the bed stopped.

The king saw the light of his chamber as if he were peering at the daylight from the bottom of a well.

This is a horrible dream! he thought. It's time I awoke! C'mon! Wake up!

There is no one who hasn't experienced what we're describing. There is no one who, in the throes of a suffocating dream, but with the aid of the lamp that glows at the core of the brain when all human light has been extinguished, hasn't told himself, It's only a dream!

That was what Louis XIV told himself. But, upon hearing the words "Wake up!," he realized not only that he was awake but that his eyes were open as well. And he scanned the room.

To his right and his left stood two armed men, each enveloped in a vast coat and with a mask on his face. One man was clutching a small lantern, its red glow illuminating the saddest tableau that a king could envisage.

He couldn't help thinking that he was still dreaming and that all he needed to do was to move his arms or hear his voice. He jumped out of bed and found himself on a moist floor. He then asked the lantern holder: "What's going on, monsieur? What kind of a joke is this?"

"It's no joke!" the lantern holder retorted in a hollow voice.

"Are you working for Monsieur Fouquet?" asked the bewildered king.

"It doesn't matter who we're working for," said the phantom. "We are your masters, and that's that!"

The king, more impatient than intimidated, turned toward

the second mask: "If this is some sort of performance, tell Monsieur Fouquet that I find it quite improper, and I order you to stop!"

The second masked man was a tall hulk. He stood as straight and motionless as a block of marble.

"C'mon!" added king, stamping his foot. "Answer me!"

"We will *not* answer you, my little man!" the giant boomed. "There is no reason to answer you—except to say that you are the first 'nuisance,' and that Monsieur Coquelin de Volière has neglected to include you in his roster of nuisances!"

"Just what is it you want?" cried Louis, angrily crossing his arms.

"You'll know soon enough!" replied the lantern holder.

"Where am I?"

"Have a look!"

Louis did have a look. But all he could make out in the glow of the lantern was damp walls with silvery trails of slugs glittering here and there.

"Is this a dungeon?" asked the king.

"It's an underground passage."

"Leading where?"

"Please follow us!"

"I won't budge an inch!" cried the king.

"If you resist, my young friend," the more robust of the two men retorted, "I'll pick you up and roll you up in a coat. And, if you suffocate, then tough!"

And the speaker held out a hand that Milo of Crotona would have wanted to possess on the day that he had the unfortunate idea of splitting his last oak tree.

The king was terrified of violence, for he realized that these two men had not gone this far merely to retreat. They would stick to their mission until the very end. Louis shook his head. "I guess I've fallen into the hands of two assassins. Let's go!"

Neither man responded. The lantern holder took the lead, the king followed him. The second mask brought up the rear. They marched through a long, winding gallery with as many stairways as are to be found in Ann Radcliffe's gloomy and mysterious palaces. All these twists and turns, during which the king heard water overhead several times, finally brought them to a lengthy corridor with an iron door. The lantern holder unlocked the door with keys that had been jingling from his belt all the while.

When the door opened, letting in air, Louis recognized the fragrances exhaled by trees after a hot summer day. He hesitated for an instant, but the robust guard pushed him on.

"I repeat," said the king, turning toward the man who had committed that audacious act of touching his sovereign, "what are you planning for the king of France?"

"Try to forget that phrase," replied the lantern holder, his voice brooking no retort any more than the famous decrees of Minos.

"You ought to be broken on the wheel for those words!" the giant added, extinguishing the light that his companion handed him. "But the king's heart is all too human."

Hearing that threat, Louis moved brusquely as if trying to flee, but the giant's hand lay on the king's shoulder, fixing him in place.

"At least tell me where we're going," said the king.

"Come along," the first of the two men answered somewhat respectfully as he led his prisoner to what looked like a waiting carriage. This carriage was entirely hidden in the foliage. Two horses, their feet shackled together, were attached by a halter to the lowest branches of an enormous oak tree.

"Get in," said the guard, opening the padded door of the carriage and lowering the step. The king obeyed, and, when he sat down inside the carriage, the door was instantly locked behind him and his guard. As for the giant, he undid the horses' shackles and fetters, hitched the horses to the carriage, and climbed up to the empty box. They trotted off briskly, swerved into the highway to Paris, and, in the forest of Sénart, they found relay horses likewise tied to trees and without a postilion. The driver changed the pair and flew on toward Paris, which he reached at three A.M. The carriage rolled across the Faubourg Saint-Antoine and, after shouting "By order of the king" to the sentinel, the coachman guided the horses into the Bastille's circular enclosure, which led to the warden's courtyard. The steaming horses drew up at the perron. A sergeant of the guards came running.

"Wake up the warden," the driver thundered.

Aside from his voice, which could be heard all the way to the Faubourg Saint-Antoine, everything remained calm in both the carriage and the stronghold. Ten minutes later, Monsieur de Baisemeaux, clad in a dressing gown, appeared on the threshold.

"What's this all about?" he asked. "And who are you bringing me?"

The lantern holder opened the carriage door and mumbled something to the coachman. The latter promptly got down from his box, grabbed a musketoon wedged between his feet, and shoved it into the prisoner's chest. The man descending from the carriage muttered: "If he opens his mouth, shoot him!"

"Fine!" replied the other man with no further comment.

Next, the man escorting the king climbed the steps, where Baisemeaux was waiting at the top.

"Monsieur d'Herblay!" he exclaimed.

"Shush!" said Aramis. "Let's go to your apartment."

"For God's sake! What brings you here in the middle of the night?"

"A mistake, my dear Monsieur de Baisemeaux," Aramis responded tranquilly. "Apparently, you were right the other evening."

"About what?" asked the warden.

"Why, about that release order, my friend."

"Please explain, monsieur—no, monseigneur!" said the warden, choking with both surprise and terror.

"It's quite simple. Do you remember the release order you were sent, dear Monsieur de Baisemeaux?"

"Yes, for Marchiali."

"Right! We all thought it was for Marchiali, didn't we?"

"Exactly. But don't you remember? I had my doubts, I didn't want to. It was you who forced me."

"Oh, what a harsh word, my dear Monsieur de Baisemeaux! . . . I merely recommended, that was all!"

"Recommended, yes, to have me hand him over to you, and you drove off with him in your carriage."

"Well, my dear Monsieur de Baisemeaux, I was wrong. The ministry noticed the mistake, and so I've brought you a royal order to release . . . Seldon, that poor Scotsman, you know."

"Seldon? Are you sure this time?"

"Damn it all! Read it for yourself!" added Aramis, handing him the order.

"But," said Baisemeaux, "this is the same order that passed through my hands."

"Really?"

"It's the one I assured you I'd seen the other evening! Damn it! I recognize the blob of ink."

"I don't know if it's the same order, but the fact remains that I'm bringing it to you."

"And what about the other man?"

"Which other man?"

"Marchiali?"

"Here he is."

"But that's not enough. I need a new order to take him in."

"Don't talk nonsense, my dear Baisemeaux! You sound like a child. Where's the order you received concerning Marchiali?"

Baisemeaux hurried over to his strongbox and produced the document. Aramis grabbed it, coolly ripped it into four pieces, set fire to them, and burned them up.

"What are you doing?!" cried Baisemeaux in sheer terror.

"Consider the situation, my dear warden," said the unflappable Aramis, "and you'll see how simple it is. You no longer have an order justifying Marchiali's release."

"That's right! My God! I'm doomed!"

"Not at all! You see, I've brought Marchiali back! It's as if he'd never left!"

"Ah!" The warden was flabbergasted.

"Don't worry! Just lock him up on the spot!"

"Definitely!"

"And you'll give me Seldon, who's been liberated by this new order. This way, everything's accounted for. Do you understand?"

"I . . . I . . ."

"You do understand," said Aramis. "Very good!"

Baisemeaux wrung his hands. "Just why have you brought me Marchiali after taking him away?" exclaimed the miserable warden in a paroxysm of agony and stupefaction.

"From a friend like you," said Aramis, "from a devoted aide like you, I have no secrets." And then he whispered into Baisemeaux's ear, "You can see the resemblance between this poor man and . . ."

"And the king. Yes."

"Well, the first thing Marchiali did with his freedom was to maintain—can you guess what?"

"How do you expect me to guess?"

"To maintain that he's the king of France."

"Oh, the poor man!"

"He put on clothes similar to the king's clothes and he pretended that he was the king."

"God Almighty!"

"That's why I've brought him back to you, dear friend! He's insane, and he displays his insanity in front of everyone."

"So what can we do?"

"It's quite simple: don't let him communicate with anybody. You see, when this insanity reached the king's ears, the king, who'd felt sorry for the poor man, and had then been rewarded for his goodness with grim ingratitude—the king was furious! As a result—bear this in mind, dear Monsieur de Baisemeaux, for it concerns you directly—as a result, anyone who lets this man communicate with anybody but myself, not even the king, will be sentenced to death. Do you understand, Baisemeaux? Sentenced to death!"

"Do I *ever* understand, by God!"

"And now come down and take this poor devil back to his dungeon cell, unless you'd rather he went up there?"

"What good would that do?"

"Yes, it would be better to imprison him immediately, don't you think?"

"Right, damn it!"

"Fine, then let's go."

Baisemeaux had someone beat the drum and ring the bell, warning his men to get to their quarters so as not to run into a mysterious prisoner. Then, once the corridors were empty, he went over to the carriage, where Porthos, faithful to his instructions, still kept the musketoon on the prisoner's throat.

Upon seeing the king, Baisemeaux said: "Ah! There you are, you poor man! It's fine! It's fine!"

Helping the prisoner step out of the carriage, Baisemeaux was accompanied by Porthos, who still wore his mask, and Aramis, who had put his mask back on. When they reached the second Bartaudière, Baisemeaux opened the door to the room where Philip had sighed for the last six years.

The king entered the cell without saying a word. He was pale and haggard.

Baisemeaux shut the door, turned the key twice in the lock, and came back to Aramis. "He really does resemble the king," the warden murmured, "but less than you say."

"So you won't be fooled into any kind of substitution?"

"Of course not!"

"You are a valuable man, my dear Baisemeaux!" said Aramis. "Now release Seldon."

"Right! I forgot! . . . I'll go and give the order."

"Oh, you can wait till tomorrow, you've got time."

"Tomorrow!? No, I'll do it immediately! God won't let me wait a second longer!"

"Well, go about your business, and I'll see to mine. But it's understood, isn't it?"

"What's understood?"

"That no one will enter the prisoner's cell without the king's order, which I will bring to you personally."

"I'll make sure of it, monseigneur. Good-bye."

Aramis returned to his companion. "C'mon, c'mon, Porthos old friend. Let's get to Vaux! And fast!"

"A man is light when he's faithfully served his king, and, by saving him, saved his country." said Porthos. "The horses will have a field day! Let's go!"

And the carriage, which had delivered a prisoner who could have seemed quite heavy to Aramis, crossed the Bastille's drawbridge, which was then drawn up and closed.

18
A Night in the Bastille

Suffering in life is in proportion to human strength. We are not saying that God always measures an individual's God-given anguish to his strength. That would be inaccurate, for God permits death, which is sometimes the only refuge of a soul crushed in a body. Suffering is in proportion to strength—that is, all things being equal, the weak suffer more than the strong. Now, just what are the elements of human strength? Aren't they, above all, practice, habit, experience? We need not even bother to demonstrate that: it is both a moral and a physical axiom.

When the young king, stunned and shattered, was taken to a room in the Bastille, he first imagined that death is like sleep, that it has its own dreams, that the king's bed dropped through the floor of the Vaux castle, that this had been followed by death, and that, pursuing his royal dream, the late Louis XIV was dreaming about horrors that are impossible in real life: the horrors known as the dethronement, incarceration, and degradation of a once omnipotent monarch.

To witness, as a tangible wraith, his excruciating passion; to swim in an incomprehensible mystery between illusion and reality; to see everything, hear everything, without missing a single detail of that agony—wasn't all this, the king told himself, a torture more dreadful since it could wear on forever?

"Is this what they call eternity, call hell?" Louis XIV murmured as the door closed behind him, pushed by Baisemeaux himself.

The king didn't even look around. Leaning against a wall of this room, he yielded to the horrible assumption that he had died, and he closed his eyes to avoid seeing something even worse.

"How can I be dead?" he wondered, half-incensed. "Couldn't they have lowered this bed through some mechanical contrivance? No. I don't recall any shock, any bruise. Didn't they actually poison me with food or wax fumes, just as they poisoned my great-grandmother, Jeanne d'Albret?"

All at once, the chill of this room dropped like a cloak upon Louis's shoulders.

"I saw," he said, "my dead father lying on his bed in his royal garb. That pallid face, so calm and so crumpled; those once adroit and now insensitive hands; those stiffened legs—nothing heralded a slumber filled with dreams. And yet how many dreams might God have sent that corpse!—that dead man whom so many others had preceded, precipitated by him into eternal death!!! No! This king was still the king; he was still enthroned on that funereal couch as if on the velvet armchair. He had abdicated nothing of his majesty. God, who did not punish him, cannot punish me, for I have done nothing wrong."

A strange noise drew his attention. On the mantelpiece, under a coarse fresco depicting an enormous crucifix, he spotted a monstrous rat nibbling on a remnant of stale bread while fixing curious and intelligent eyes on the new lodger.

The king was frightened, disgusted. He backed toward the door, emitting a loud cry. And, as if he needed that involuntary cry to recognize himself, Louis grasped that he was alive, astute, and filled with his natural awareness. "A prisoner!" he exclaimed. "Me, me—a prisoner!" He cast about for a bell.

"There are no bells in the Bastille," he said, "and the Bastille is where I'm locked up. How can I be imprisoned? Monsieur Fouquet must be plotting against me. I was drawn into a trap in Vaux. Monsieur Fouquet can't be acting alone. His agent . . . That voice . . . It was Monsieur d'Herblay! I recognized him. Colbert was right. But what does Monsieur Fouquet want of me? Is he going to rule in my place? Impossible! Who knows!? . . ." The king was somber now. "My brother, the Duke of Orléans, may be working against me the way my uncle spent his life working against my father. But what about the queen? What about my mother? What about Mademoiselle de la Vallière? She'll be handed over. The dear child! Yes, that's it! She's been locked up—just like me! We'll be separated for all eternity!"

And at the mere thought of that separation, the lover burst into sighs, sobs, and shouts.

"There's a warden here," the king shrieked. "I'll talk to him. Let me call him."

He called. No voice responded.

He grabbed his chair and banged it against the massive oak door. Wood struck against wood, arousing lugubrious echoes in the depths of the staircase. But not a living soul responded.

For the king, this was further evidence of how little he was respected in the Bastille. Then, after his initial fury, he noticed a barred window emitting a gilded sliver that had to be dawn. Louis started calling softly, then loudly. There was no response. Twenty more attempts were equally unsuccessful.

The prince's blood boiled and rose to his face. Accustomed to being in command, he trembled when faced with disobedience. The prisoner grew angrier and angrier. He broke the chair, which was too heavy for his hands, and he used it as a battering ram against the door. He battered the door so hard and so often that the sweat began pouring down his brow. The thudding was immense and continuous. A few muffled cries responded here and there.

They had a bizarre effect on the king. He paused to listen. Those were the voices of inmates who had once been his victims and were now his companions. The voices rose like vapors through dense ceilings and opaque walls. They condemned the man responsible for that noise, just as their sighs and tears softly condemned the man responsible for their captivity. After robbing so many people of their freedom, the king had now joined them and was robbing them of their sleep.

The realization nearly drove him insane. It doubled his strength, or, rather, his will; he was determined to obtain information or some conclusion. The chair rung resumed its work. An hour later, Louis heard something in the corridor, and a violent blow on the door made him stop his banging.

"Hey! Are you crazy?" snapped a rude, gross voice. "What's gotten into you this morning?"

"Morning?" The king was astonished. Then, more politely, he asked: "Monsieur, are you the warden of the Bastille?"

"My good man, your mind is unhinged! But that's no reason to raise such a rumpus. Shut up, damn it!"

"Are you the warden?" the king repeated.

A door closed. The jailer had left without even deigning to reply.

When the king realized this, his anger knew no bounds. As agile as a tiger, he jumped from the table to the window and began rattling the bars. He smashed a pane, and the fragments dropped into the courtyard, clinking harmoniously. His voice going hoarse, he shouted: "Warden, warden!" This fit dragged on for a feverish hour.

His hair disheveled, with strands sticking to his forehead, his clothes ripped and soiled, his linen tattered, the king stopped only with his last ounce of strength. Now he finally appreciated the merciless thickness of these walls, the impenetrability of the cement—invincible to anything but time and with despair as its sole tool.

He leaned his forehead against the door and let his heart calm down little by little; one more beat and it would have exploded.

"He'll come," he said, "when they make the food rounds. I'll see somebody then, I'll speak to him, he'll answer me."

And the king tried to remember at what time the first meal was brought to the prisoners in the Bastille. He had no idea. His remorse was a cruel, underhanded stab: he had lived for twenty-five years, a happy king, without thinking about the sufferings of a wretched man who'd been unjustly deprived of his freedom. The king turned crimson with shame. He sensed that God was imposing this terrible humiliation merely to pay him back for the tortures he had inflicted on so many people.

Nothing could have been more effective for returning to religion a soul struck down by torment. But Louis didn't even fall to his knees and beg God to end this ordeal.

"God is doing the proper thing," he said. "God is right. It would be cowardly for me to ask God for what I often denied my fellow men."

He was lost in his reflections—that is, his agony—when he again heard a sound outside the door. This time the sound was followed by the grinding of keys and the rattling of latches.

The king leaped forward to meet the man about to enter. But then suddenly figuring that this movement was unworthy of a king, he stopped, assumed a calm and noble pose, which was easy for him. His back toward the window, he waited, trying to disguise his agitation about the newcomer. It was only a turnkey lugging a basket of food.

The king gazed at this man anxiously, waiting for him to talk. "Ah!" said the turnkey, "you've broken your chair. I thought so. You must have been really furious!"

"Monsieur," said the king, "be careful what you say. The consequences could be very serious for you."

The turnkey placed his basket on the table and peered at his interlocutor: "Huh?" he said in surprise.

"Send for the warden," the king added nobly.

"C'mon, my boy," said the turnkey. "You've always been well behaved, but insanity brings out nastiness, and we have to warn you: You've smashed your chair and raised a rumpus. For that we can put you in a worse dungeon. Promise me you won't start again, and I won't tell the warden."

"I wish to see the warden," replied the king without batting an eye.

"Watch it, he'll put you in a worse dungeon!"

"I wish to see him, do you hear?"

"Ah! Your eyes are getting haggard again. Fine! I'll have to take your knife!"

And the turnkey did so, then closed the door and trudged off, leaving the king more astonished, more miserable, more alone than ever.

It was no use wielding the chair rung, no use hurling the dishes out the window: no one responded.

Two hours later, he was no longer a king, no longer a gentleman, no longer a human being, no longer a creature with a mind. He was a madman, scratching the door, trying to pull out the flooring, and shrieking so dreadfully that the old Bastille seemed to tremble to its very foundations for daring to revolt against its master.

As for the warden, he never even stirred. The turnkey and the sentinels had made their reports, but why bother? Weren't madmen typical in the fortress, and weren't the walls stronger than the madmen?

Monsieur de Baisemeaux, heeding everything that Aramis had told him and faithfully executing the king's order, hoped for only one thing: that the madman Marchiali would be crazy enough to hang himself from his bed canopy or from a window bar.

The prisoner brought the warden little profit and was becoming more troublesome than was proper. Those complications about Seldon and Marchiali, those complications of release and reimprisonment, those complications of resemblance could have a felicitous outcome. Baisemeaux felt that such an ending would not displease Monsieur d'Herblay.

"And honestly," said Baisemeaux to his adjutant, "an ordinary prisoner is already unhappy enough to be a prisoner. His sufferings are awful enough for us to be charitable and hope for his death. And it's even more charitable when the prisoner has gone crazy and he can bite and raise a rumpus in the Bastille. At this point, we're not even charitable when we hope for his death. It would be a good deed to very gently put him out of his misery."

And the good warden tucked into his lunch.

19

Monsieur Fouquet's Shadow

D'Artagnan, still feeling confused after his meeting with the king, wondered if he was in full possession of his common sense. He wondered if the scene had taken place in Vaux; if he, d'Artagnan, was really captain of the musketeers; and if Monsieur Fouquet was the owner of the castle in which Louis XIV had been welcomed so hospitably. These were not the reflections of a drunkard. Yet they had banqueted gorgeously in Vaux, and Monsieur Fouquet's wine had been highly honored. But the Gascon was as cool as a cucumber. Touching his steel sword, he knew how to raise the spirit of that cold blade on major occasions.

"Well," he said while leaving the royal apartment, "now I've been thrown historically into the fortunes of the king and the minister. Historians will write that Monsieur d'Artagnan, the youngest son of a Gascon family, collared Monsieur Nicolas Fouquet, superintendent of the finances of France. My descendants, if I have any, will pride themselves on this arrest, just as the de Luynes family did with the estate of that poor Marshal d'Ancre. I'm saddled with executing the king's orders in a proper way. Anybody can tell Monsieur Fouquet: 'Your sword, monsieur!' But nobody can keep watch over him without somebody crying havoc. How am I supposed to escort the superintendent from extreme favor to the most thorough disgrace, from his castle to a dungeon, from the incense of Assuerus to the gallows of Haman—that is, Enguerrand de Marigyn?"

D'Artagnan's face clouded over pitifully. He had his scruples. Delivering Fouquet to his death (for the king certainly hated him), delivering the gentleman who had just proved to be a man of honor—it truly plagued d'Artagnan's conscience.

"I find that if I'm not a despicable person, I ought to tell Monsieur Fouquet what the king has in store for him. But if I reveal my master's secret, that would make me a deceitful traitor, and treason is a crime that's severely dealt with in military law. In fact, during wartime, I've seen some twenty traitors strung up for offenses that were insignificant compared with the outrage that my qualms are advising me to commit. No, I think that a quick-witted man ought to escape this dilemma more skillfully. And should we admit that I've got a quick mind? It's a moot point. For the past forty years I've used up so much of my mind that I'd be lucky if I had any left!"

D'Artagnan buried his face in his hands, tore out a few random hairs from his mustache, and added:

"Why is Monsieur Fouquet out of favor? There are three reasons. The first one is that Monsieur Colbert doesn't like him, the second one is that he tried to woo Mademoiselle de la Vallière, and the third reason is that the king loves Monsieur Colbert and Mademoiselle de la Vallière. Fouquet is doomed! But should I trample him underfoot, I of all men, when he's falling prey to the intrigues of women and clerks? It's shameful.

"If he's dangerous, I'll crush him. But if he's being harassed, I'll wait and see! At this point, neither a king nor a commoner will change my mind. If Athos were here, he'd act as I'm acting. So instead of brutalizing Monsieur Fouquet, instead of apprehending him and throwing him in prison, I'll try to behave like a man of breeding. People will talk, granted, but they will speak well of me."

And d'Artagnan, fitting his crossbelt over his shoulder with a special gesture, headed straight toward Monsieur Fouquet, who, after saying good night to the ladies, was preparing to sleep calmly, resting on the day's laurels.

The air was still perfumed or polluted (whichever you prefer) by the smell of the fireworks. The candles were guttering, the blossoms were dropping from the garlands, the flocks of dancers and courtiers were scattering in the salons.

At the center of his friends, who were complimenting him and receiving his compliments, Monsieur Fouquet half-closed his weary eyes. Yearning to rest, he collapsed on the bed of laurels amassed over so many days. His head looked as if it were bowing under the weight of the new debts that he had incurred to pay for this celebration.

Fouquet had just retired for the night, smiling and half-dead with exhaustion. He heard nothing, he saw nothing. His bed drew him, fascinated him. The god Morpheus, dominating Le Brun's dome, had extended his power to the neighboring chambers and had tossed his most soporific poppies at the master of the castle.

Fouquet was practically alone, with only his valet attending to him, when Monsieur d'Artagnan appeared at the threshold.

D'Artagnan had never succeeded in making himself mundane at court, and though he was seen constantly and everywhere, he nevertheless made a fresh impact each time. That is the privilege of certain people who, in that respect, are like thunder and lightning. Everyone is familiar with them, yet their appearance is astonishing; and whenever they materialize, their latest effect is their strongest.

"Well, Monsieur d'Artagnan?" said Fouquet, his right arm already out of his sleeve.

"I'm at your service," replied the musketeer.

"Please come in, my dear Monsieur d'Artagnan."

"Thank you!"

"Are you here to critique the celebration? You're an ingenious man."

"Oh, no!"

"Are you suffering any inconvenience?"

"Not at all."

"Is there a problem with your lodging perhaps?"

"Quite the contrary."

"Well, thank you for being so gracious. In fact, I should be the one expressing gratitude for all your flattering remarks." The implication was blatant; Fouquet meant: My dear Monsieur d'Artagnan, why don't you go to bed, since you've got a bed, and let me do the same.

D'Artagnan apparently failed to catch the hint: "Are you going to bed already?"

"Yes. Do you have something you'd like to communicate to me?"

"Nothing, monsieur, nothing. So you're going to bed here?"

"As you can see."

"Monsieur, you have given the king a wonderful festival."

"Really?"

"Oh, superb!"

"Is the king satisfied?"

"He is enchanted."

"Has he asked you to tell me that?"

"He would not choose such an unworthy messenger, monseigneur."

"You're doing yourself an injustice, Monsieur d'Artagnan."

"Is that your bed?"

"Yes. Why do you ask? Are you dissatisfied with yours?"

"May I be frank?"

"Of course."

"Well, yes, I'm dissatisfied."

Fouquet trembled. "Monsieur d'Artagnan, take my room."

"Deprive you, monseigneur? Never!"

"Well, then, what would you like to do?"

"Allow me to share this room with you."

Fouquet gaped at the musketeer. "Aha! You're coming from the king?"

"Of course, monseigneur."

"And the king would like you to sleep in my chamber?"

"Monseigneur . . ."

"Very well, Monsieur d'Artagnan, very well. You are in charge here. Come on, monsieur."

"I assure you, monseigneur, that I do not wish to abuse—"

Fouquet addressed his valet: "Leave us." The valet left.

"You have something to say to me?" Fouquet asked d'Artagnan.

"I?"

"At this time of night, a man with your mind does not simply come to chat with a man with my mind. There's more here than meets the eye."

"Do not question me."

"On the contrary. What do you want from me?"

"Nothing but your company."

Suddenly, Fouquet said, "Let's go to the park."

"No," the musketeer exclaimed. "No."

"Why not?"

"The cool air . . ."

"Come, come. Admit that you're arresting me," said the superintendent.

"Never!" said the captain.

"Then you mean to watch me?"

"Yes, monseigneur, on my honor."

"Your honor? . . . That's a horse of a different color. So I'm being arrested in my own home?"

"Don't say that!"

"I'll shout it out!"

"If you shout it out, I'll be forced to demand your silence."

"Ha! Violence in my home? Very well!"

"We do not understand one another at all. Listen, you've got a chess set here. Why don't we play a round, monseigneur?!"

"So, Monsieur d'Artagnan, am I in disgrace?"

"Not at all. But—"

"But I'm not allowed out of your sight?"

"I have no idea what you're talking about, monseigneur. And if you'd like me to withdraw, just say so."

"Dear Monsieur d'Artagnan, you're driving me crazy. I was practically in the arms of Morpheus, but you've awakened me."

"I'll never forgive myself, and if you'd like me to absolve myself . . ."

"Well?"

"Well, then sleep there, in front of me. I'd be delighted."

"Under surveillance?"

"Then I'll leave."

"I don't understand you."

"Good night, monseigneur." And d'Artagnan seemed to be withdrawing.

Fouquet ran after him. "I won't go to bed. Seriously, and because you refuse to treat me like a man and you're playing games with me, I'm going to run you down the way a hunter runs down a wild boar."

"Ha!" cried d'Artagnan, forcing a smile.

"I'll send for my horses and I'll head out for Paris," said Fouquet, unsettling the captain of the musketeers.

"Ah, that's different, monseigneur."

"You'll arrest me?"

"No, I'll go with you."

"That's enough, Monsieur d'Artagnan," Fouquet snapped coldly. "There are reasons why you're reputed to be intelligent and resourceful. But with me, that's all superfluous. Let's cut to the chase. Do me a favor. Tell me why I'm being arrested. What have I done?"

"Oh, I have no idea what you've done, but I'm not arresting you . . . tonight. . . ."

"Tonight?" cried Fouquet, blanching. "And what about tomorrow?"

"This isn't tomorrow, monseigneur. You never can tell what tomorrow will bring."

"Quick! Quick! Captain! Let me talk to Monsieur d'Herblay."

"Sorry, but that's impossible, monseigneur. I've been ordered not to let you talk to anyone."

"Monsieur d'Herblay, Captain, your friend!"

"Monseigneur, is it a coincidence that my friend, Monsieur d'Herblay, is not the only person whom I'm to keep you from communicating with?"

Fouquet turned crimson, and, with an air of resignation, he

said: "Monsieur, you're correct. You've taught me a lesson that I shouldn't have provoked. A fallen man has no rights whatsoever, not even to the people whose fortunes he's made—and even less to the people whom he's never been lucky enough to help."

"Monseigneur!"

"It's quite true, Monsieur d'Artagnan. You've always behaved properly toward me, and that's the right situation for the man fated to arrest me. You've never asked anything of me!"

"Monseigneur," replied the Gascon, touched by that noble and eloquent grief, "would you please give me your word of honor as a gentleman that you won't leave this room?"

"What good would it do? After all, you're guarding me here. Are you afraid I'll fight against the most valiant sword in the kingdom?"

"That's not the issue, monseigneur. You see, I'm going to look for Monsieur d'Herblay, which means I'll have to leave you alone."

Fouquet emitted a cry of joy and surprise. "Look for Monsieur d'Herblay! Leave me alone!" he exclaimed, clasping his hands.

"Where is Monsieur d'Herblay sleeping? In the Blue Chamber?"

"Yes, my friend, yes."

"Your friend? Thank you for calling me that, monseigneur. You confer that word on me today if you haven't done so earlier."

"Ah! You're saving me!"

"It would take me a good ten minutes to go to the Blue Chamber and come back, right?"

"More or less."

"And it would take me five minutes to wake up Aramis, who's a very sound sleeper. That means I'd be gone for a total of a quarter hour. Now, monseigneur, give me your word that you won't try to flee in any way and that I'll find you here when I get back."

"I give you my word, monsieur," replied Fouquet, shaking the musketeer's hand with affectionate gratitude.

D'Artagnan disappeared.

Fouquet watched him hurrying off, waited with feverish impatience for the door to close, then pounced on his keys and opened a few secret drawers concealed in the furniture. He looked in vain for several documents that were probably in Saint-Mandé, and he seemed to regret not having them here. Next, hastily grabbing letters, contracts, records, he piled them up and quickly burned them on the marble hearth of the fireplace. He didn't even take the time to pull out the flowerpots encumbering it.

Then, like a man who has just escaped an immense danger, and whose strength is drained the instant the danger is no longer to be feared, he collapsed, exhausted, in an armchair.

When d'Artagnan returned, he found Fouquet in that same position. The worthy musketeer had never doubted for an instant that Fouquet would even dream of breaking his word. However, d'Artagnan did assume that Fouquet would take advantage of the musketeer's absence to get rid of all the papers, all the notes, all the contracts that could further imperil his already precarious situation. Thus, raising his head like a dog catching a scent, d'Artagnan caught the odor of smoke that he had expected to find, and, having found it, he nodded as a sign of satisfaction.

Fouquet, meanwhile, lifted his head. Not a single one of d'Artagnan's movements escaped the superintendent.

Their eyes locked. Both men saw that they had understood one another without exchanging a word.

"Well?" asked Fouquet. "Did you find Monsieur d'Herblay?"

"My goodness, monseigneur," replied d'Artagnan, "Monsieur d'Herblay seems to enjoy nocturnal strolls. He must be composing verses with some of your poets in the moonlight. At any rate, he wasn't in his room."

"What? Not in his room?" cried Fouquet, his last hope gone. For while not knowing how the Bishop of Vannes could save him, Fouquet nevertheless regarded him as his only hope.

"Or, if he *is* in his room, he had his reasons for not responding."

"But didn't you call him loudly enough, monsieur?"

"Monseigneur, you know that I have flouted my order not to

leave your side for even an instant. So you cannot assume that I would be foolish enough to wake up the entire household and let myself be seen near Monsieur d'Herblay's door. Had I been spotted, Monsieur Colbert could state that I had given you enough time to burn your papers."

"My papers?"

"Exactly. That's the least I'd have done in your place. If a door opens for me, I use it."

"Well, yes, thank you! I did use it."

"That was very wise of you, damn it! Every man has his little secrets that are no one else's business. But let's get back to Aramis, monseigneur."

"Well, I tell you, you didn't call him loudly enough. He probably didn't hear you."

"Monseigneur, no matter how softly one calls Aramis, he always hears when it's in his best interest to hear. So let me repeat myself: Aramis was not in his room or else he had his reasons for not recognizing my voice—reasons unknown to me, and perhaps to you, no matter how devoted to you the Lord Bishop may be."

Fouquet heaved a sigh, stood up, paced to and fro several times, and, finally, with a look of profound dejection, he sat down on his magnificent velvet bed with its splendid lace.

D'Artagnan gazed at Fouquet with utter pity. "I've seen a lot of men arrested in my time," said the musketeer in a melancholy tone. "I saw Monsieur Cinq-Mars arrested, I saw Monsieur de Chalais arrested. I was very young. I saw Monsieur de Condé arrested with the princes, I saw Monsieur de Retz arrested, I saw Monsieur Broussel arrested. Listen, monseigneur, it may be disagreeable to say so, but the one you resemble most among all those men is poor Broussel. Like him, you very nearly put your napkin in your portfolio and wiped your lips with your documents. Damn it, Monsieur Fouquet! A man like you should be above all this! If your friends saw you . . ."

"Monsieur d'Artagnan," Fouquet smiled woefully, "you don't understand me at all. It's precisely because my friends can't see me that I'm behaving this way. I don't live alone, I am nothing alone. I must point out to you that I've used every moment of my life to make friends who, I hoped, would lend me their support. In prosperous times, all those happy voices—happy, thanks to me—offered me a concert of praise and gratitude. During the slightest disfavor, those humbler voices harmoniously accompanied the murmurs of my soul. I have never known isolation. Poverty was a ragged specter that I glimpsed at the end of my road! It is the ghost with which several of my friends have been playing for so many years, which they cherish and write poetry about, which they have me love! Poverty! I do accept it, I recognize it, I welcome it like a disinherited sister. For poverty is not solitude, it's not exile, it's not prison! Will I ever be poor if I've got friends such as Pellisson, La Fontaine, Molière? Such a mistress as . . . Oh, but solitude—for a man who loves activity, who loves pleasure, who exists only because other people exist! . . . Oh, if you only knew how alone I feel at this moment! And you, who are separating me from everything I love, you seem to be the very image of solitude, nothingness, and death!"

"But, Monsieur Fouquet," replied d'Artagnan, touched to the very core of his soul, "I've already told you, you're exaggerating. The king loves you."

"No!" said Fouquet, shaking his head. "No!"

"Monsieur de Colbert hates you."

"Monsieur de Colbert? So what?!"

"He's going to ruin you."

"Let him try! I'm already ruined!"

Upon hearing that strange admission, d'Artagnan scanned the room. Though he held his tongue, Monsieur Fouquet caught his drift and added:

"What can we do with all this magnificence if we're no longer magnificent? Do you know what good most of our possessions are for rich people like us? Their very splendor serves to disgust us with everything that is inferior to that splendor. 'Vaux!' you'll say to me. 'The marvels of Vaux! Right?' Well, what? What should I do with this marvel? If I'm ruined, how will I pour water into the urns of my naiads, fire into the entrails of my salamanders, air into the lungs of my tritons? In order to be rich enough, Monsieur d'Artagnan, a man has to be too rich."

D'Artagnan shook his head.

"Oh, I know what you're thinking," Fouquet retorted. "If you owned Vaux, you'd sell it and you'd buy an estate in the country. Your property would have forests, orchards, meadows, and it would nourish its owner. With forty million you'd do nicely—"

"Ten million!" d'Artagnan broke in.

"Not one million, my dear captain. No one in France has the wherewithal to pay two million for Vaux. And no one could maintain it as is, no one could, no one knows how!"

"Damn it!" cried d'Artagnan. "In any case, one million . . ."

"Well?"

"It's not destitution."

"It's close to it, my dear monsieur!"

"What do you mean?"

"Oh, you don't understand! No, I don't wish to sell my castle. I'm giving it to you, if you want it." And Fouquet moved his shoulders with a blank look.

"Give it to the king!" said d'Artagnan. "You'd make a much better deal!"

"The king doesn't need it. He'll simply take it if he likes. That's why I'd rather see it destroyed. Look, Monsieur d'Artagnan, if the king weren't under my roof, I'd take this candle and set fire to the two cases of flares and rockets stored under the dome and I'd reduce my castle to ashes."

"Huh!" the musketeer said nonchalantly. "In any case, you wouldn't burn the gardens. That's the best part of your property."

"Good God!" Fouquet's voice was muffled. "What am I saying? Burn Vaux! Destroy my castle! But Vaux doesn't belong to me! Granted, these riches, these marvels, belong to the man who enjoys them, who paid for them. But in the long run, they belong to the men who created them. Vaux belongs to Le Brun, Vaux belongs to Lenôtre, Vaux belongs to Pellisson, to Le Vaux, to La Fontaine. Vaux belongs to Molière, who staged *The Nuisances* here. Ultimately, Vaux belongs to prosperity. You can see, Monsieur d'Artagnan, that I don't even own my own home."

"Fine!" said d'Artagnan. "That's an idea that I like, and I

recognize Monsieur Fouquet in it. That idea makes me forget all about that poor Broussel, and you no longer remind me of his whining and sniveling. If you're ruined, monseigneur, take it in stride. You too belong to posterity, by God, and you've no right to belittle yourself. Just look at me. I seem to be exercising power over you since I'm arresting you. Destiny, which assigns their roles to the actors in this world, has cast me in an unpleasant part, less agreeable than your part. Well, I'm the sort of person who thinks that the roles of kings and other powerful men are worth more than the roles of beggars or lackeys. Onstage—I mean, any stage that's not the stage of the world—onstage, it's much better to sport a fine coat and speak a fine language than to tread the boards in worn-out shoes or get your backbone caressed with tow-padded sticks.

"In short, you've misused gold, you've commanded, you've had fun. But as for me, I've dragged my halter, I've obeyed orders, I've drudged. Well, trivial as I may be compared with you, monseigneur, I tell you my memories of my actions spur me on, and they keep me from prematurely bowing my old head. I'll remain a good warhorse to the very end, and I'll perish in one piece, breathe my last, after choosing the site.

"Do as I do, Monsieur Fouquet, you won't be the worse for it. For a man like you, this occurs only once. The trick is to do it well when the opportunity arises. There's a Latin proverb—I've forgotten the exact wording but recall the meaning, because I've often mulled it over—it goes: 'The end crowns everything.' "

Fouquet stood up and threw one arm around d'Artagnan, crushing him on his chest, while his other hand clutched the musketeer's hand.

"That was a fine sermon," said Fouquet after a pause.

"A musketeer's sermon, monseigneur."

"You must like me if you tell me all that."

"Maybe."

Fouquet turned pensive again. Then, an instant later, he asked: "But what about Monsieur d'Herblay? Where could he be?"

"Aha!"

"I don't dare ask you to locate him."

"You could ask, but I wouldn't do it, Monsieur Fouquet. It would be imprudent. People would find out, and Aramis, who's not involved in any of this, might be compromised and embroiled in your disgrace."

"I'll wait till daylight," said Fouquet.

"Yes, that would be best."

"What will we do at daylight?"

"I don't know, monseigneur."

"Do me a favor, Monsieur d'Artagnan."

"Very gladly."

"You're guarding me, I'll stay here. I assume that you're acting in full compliance with your orders?"

"Of course."

"Well, then, fine, be my shadow. I prefer you as my shadow to anyone else."

D'Artagnan bowed.

"But forget that you're Monsieur d'Artagnan, captain of the musketeers. Forget that I'm Monsieur Fouquet, superintendent of finances. And let's talk about my affairs."

"Damn it! That's a ticklish business!"

"Really?"

"Yes. But for you, Monsieur Fouquet, I would do the impossible."

"Thank you. What did the king tell you?"

"Nothing."

"Ah! Is that your idea of talking?"

"You bet!"

"What do you think of my situation?"

"Nothing."

"However, unless you nurture some ill will toward me . . ."

"Your situation is difficult."

"In what sense?"

"You're in your own home."

"Difficult as my situation may be, I understand it."

"Damn it! Do you imagine I'd be this frank with anyone else?"

"Huh? This frank? You've been frank with me? You? You who refuse to tell me the slightest thing?"

"So much fuss, then."

"Fine!"

"Listen, monseigneur, let me tell you how I'd act with anyone else. Once your men were gone, I'd reach your door. Or if they weren't gone, I'd wait for them to leave. Then I'd grab them one by one like rabbits and I'd lock them up without making a sound. I'd sneak along the carpet in your corridor and, with one hand upon you, without your suspecting a thing, I'd guard you until my master's breakfast. That way, there'd be no scandal, no resistance, no commotion—and also no warning for Monsieur Fouquet, no consideration, and none of those delicate concessions that are shown by courteous men at a decisive moment. Would that approach be satisfactory to you?"

"It makes me shudder!"

"Doesn't it, though? It would be a dismal affair if I'd turn up tomorrow, with no preparation, and ask you for your sword."

"Oh, monsieur! I'd die of shame and anger!"

"Your gratitude is all too eloquent. I assure you, I haven't done enough for you."

"I'm certain, monsieur, that you will never get me to believe that."

"Well, and now, monseigneur, if you're satisfied with my conduct, if you've recovered from the shock—which I've tried to soften as much as I could—let's give it a little time. You're worn out, you've got a lot of thinking to do. I beg you, sleep, or pretend to sleep, on your bed or in it. As for me, I'll sleep in this armchair, and my sleep is always so sound that I can't even be aroused by a booming cannon."

Fouquet smiled.

"Unless, however," the musketeer went on, "somebody opens a secret or visible door to either come or go. For things like that, my ears are extremely sharp. The slightest creaking makes me shiver. It's a matter of natural antipathy. You can walk around the room; you can write, cross out, rip up, burn up—none of that will keep me from sleeping or even snoring. But don't touch the door key, don't touch the door handle, because that would rattle my nerves and make me jump up wide-awake."

"Monsieur d'Artagnan," said Fouquet, "you are truly the

wittiest and most courteous man that I know, and my only regret in knowing you is that I've met you so late in life."

D'Artagnan heaved a sigh that signified, Oh my! Perhaps you've met me too early! Then he sank into the chair, while Fouquet, propped on one elbow and half-lying on his bed, mused about his adventure.

And both men, letting the candles burn, waited for the first glimmer of daybreak; and when Fouquet sighed too loudly, d'Artagnan snored more noisily.

No visitor, not even Aramis, disturbed their peace; and no stirring could be heard anywhere in the huge castle.

On the outside, however, the guards of honor and the patrols of the musketeers made their rounds with the sand grinding under their boots. That meant even more tranquillity for the sleepers. And then the rustling wind and the swishing fountains performed their eternal tasks without worrying about the minor sounds and minor things that make up human life and death.

20
Morning

In contrast with the lugubrious fate of the king imprisoned in the Bastille and chewing the locks and the bars in his despair, the old chroniclers would not fail to present, as an antithesis, Philip sleeping under the royal canopy. It's not that rhetoric is always bad, or that it always misplants the flowers with which it tries to spangle history. But we will apologize for meticulously polishing the antithesis and for drawing the other tableau as pendant to the first.

The young prince had descended from Aramis's room just as the king had descended from the Morpheus Chamber. The dome sank slowly under Monsieur d'Herblay's pressure, and Philip found himself in front of the royal bed, which had then ascended after delivering its prisoner to the depths of the underground galleries.

Alone with this luxury, alone with all his power, alone with the role that he would be forced to play, Philip, for the first time, felt his soul opening to those thousand emotions that are the vital throbbings of a royal heart.

But he blanched upon gazing at that empty bed, which was still rumpled where his brother's body had lain.

This mute accomplice had returned after helping to perform the task. It was coming back with a trace of the crime; it was speaking to the culprit in the frank and brutal lingo that a culprit is never afraid to use with his cohort. It was speaking the truth.

Bending over the bed in order to see more clearly, Philip spotted a handkerchief that was still moist with the cold sweat that had streamed down Louis XIV's forehead. This sweat terrified Philip just as Abel's blood had terrified Cain.

"I'm face-to-face with my destiny," said Philip, his eyes blazing, his features ghastly pale. "Will my destiny be more appalling than my captivity was sorrowful? If I'm forced to constantly wield my usurped power, will I always remember to listen to the scruples of my heart? . . . Yes indeed! The king has rested on this bed. Yes indeed, it was his head that creased the pillow. Yes indeed, it was the bitterness of his tears that softened this handkerchief. I'm hesitant to lie on this bed, to clutch the handkerchief with its embroidered royal coat of arms! . . .

"Stop it. Let us imitate Monsieur d'Herblay, who wants action to be always one degree higher than thought. Let me imitate Monsieur d'Herblay, who always thinks about himself, and who calls himself an honorable man if he crosses or betrays only his enemies.

"I would be occupying this bed if Louis XIV hadn't cheated me out of it thanks to my mother's complicity. And this handkerchief, embroidered with France's coat of arms, would belong to me alone if, as Monsieur d'Herblay observed, I'd have been left in my place in the royal cradle. Philip, son of France, get back into your bed! Philip, sole king of France, take back your blazon! Philip, sole heir apparent of your father, Louis XIII, be ruthless with the usurper, who doesn't even feel remorse for all your sufferings!!!"

Having said that, Philip, despite the instinctive repugnance of his body, despite the terror and horror battering his willpower, lay down in the still-warm royal bed and forced his muscles to press down in it while he patted his fiery brow with the sweaty handkerchief.

When his head fell back, hollowing out the downy pillow, Philip saw, above his forehead, the French crown borne aloft, as we have said, by an angel with large, golden wings.

Now imagine that royal intruder, with his somber eyes and quivering body. He resembles a tiger lost in a stormy night, loping through reeds, through an unfamiliar ravine, and stretching out in the den of an absent lion. The tiger is drawn by the feline odor, that warm vapor of ordinary habitation. He has found a pallet of dry grass and broken bones that are as pasty as marrow. He arrives, and his blazing eyes explore the darkness. He shakes his soaked limbs, his muddy skin; he crouches heavily, and rests his large muzzle on his enormous paws. He is ready for sleep but also ready for combat.

From time to time, the lightning that gleams and glistens in the crevices of the cave, the banging branches, the stones that tumble down amid cries, the vague apprehension of danger, arouse him from his lethargic exhaustion.

You may be eager to lie down in the lion's bed, but you cannot expect to sleep like a baby.

Philip's ears perked up at every last sound. His heart fluttered with every terror. But confident about his own strength, aided by the intensity of his supreme resolution, he staunchly waited for a decisive circumstance that would enable him to judge himself. He looked forward to a great danger that would shine the way the phosphoric lights in a tempest show navigators the heights of the waves they are fighting.

But nothing happened. All night long, silence, that mortal enemy of uneasy hearts, that mortal enemy of ambitious men, enveloped Philip in its thick mist, enveloped the future king of France, who was sheltered under his stolen crown.

Toward morning, someone—more shadow than body—slipped into the royal chamber. Philip, who was expecting him, was not surprised.

"Well, Monsieur d'Herblay?"

"Well, sire, everything is done."

"What do you mean?"

"Everything we've been waiting for."

"Any resistance?"

"Dreadful resistance. Tears, shouts."

"Then?"

"Then stupor."

"And finally?"

"Finally, complete victory and absolute silence."

"Does the warden of the Bastille suspect anything?"

"Nothing."

"What about our resemblance?"

"It's the reason for our success."

"But the prisoner can't fail to talk. Think about it. I was able to talk, even though I had to battle a power that was much more solid than mine is now."

"I've provided for everything. Several days from now, sooner if necessary, we'll remove the prisoner and exile him so far away—"

"People can return from exile, Monsieur d'Herblay."

"So far away, I tell you, that human strength and a human lifetime would not be enough to help him return."

Once again their eyes locked in cold intelligence.

"What about Monsieur du Vallon?" asked Philip, changing the subject.

"He will be presented to you today and he will confidentially congratulate you in regard to the danger that the usurper inflicted on you."

"How will we reward him?"

"Monsieur du Vallon?"

"With a dukedom, right?"

"Yes, a dukedom," said Aramis with a strange smile.

"Why are you laughing, Monsieur d'Herblay?"

"I'm laughing at Your Majesty's farsightedness."

"Farsightedness? What do you mean?"

"Your Majesty is probably afraid that poor Porthos may become a troublesome witness, and you'd like to be rid of him."

"By making him a duke?"

"Exactly. You'll kill him. He'll die for joy, and the secret will die with him."

"Oh my God!"

"And I," said Aramis phlegmatically, "I'll lose a very good friend."

At that moment, in the midst of that frivolous dialogue, with which the two conspirators disguised their joy and their pride at their success, Aramis caught something that made him prick up his ears.

"What's wrong?" asked Philip.

"The daylight, sire."

"Well?"

"Well, before getting into this bed yesterday, you probably decided to do something at daylight."

"I told my captain of my musketeers that I'd be expecting him!" the young man declared vividly.

"If you told him that, he will assuredly come. He's a punctual man."

"I hear footsteps in the vestibule."

"It's him."

"Come on! Let's launch the attack!" the young king cried resolutely.

"Watch it!" snapped Aramis. "It would be crazy to launch the attack, especially with d'Artagnan. D'Artagnan knows nothing, he's seen nothing. He's very far from suspecting anything at all. But if he's the first to come here this morning, he'll sense that something's happened and that he ought to deal with it. Look, sire, before letting him in, we have to ventilate the room thoroughly or else bring in so many people that the finest bloodhound in the kingdom would be baffled by some twenty different scents."

"But how can we dismiss d'Artagnan? After all, I've made an appointment with him," said the young prince, eager to measure himself against such a redoubtable adversary.

"I'll take care of it," replied the bishop. "I'll start by striking a blow that will send him reeling."

"He's already striking a blow himself," the young prince exclaimed.

And indeed, they heard a knock on the door.

Aramis was not mistaken: it was d'Artagnan announcing himself.

We've seen him spend the night philosophizing with Monsieur Fouquet. But the musketeer was worn out, too exhausted even to feign sleep. And the instant the bluish aureole of dawn had started illuminating the sumptuous cornices of the superintendent's chamber, d'Artagnan had risen from his armchair, adjusted his sword, smoothed out his suit with his sleeve, and brushed his hat like a soldier about to be inspected.

"Are you leaving?" asked Fouquet.

"Yes, monseigneur. And you?"

"I'll remain here."

"Your word of honor?"

"My word of honor."

"Fine. The only reason I'm leaving is to get you that reply—you understand?"

"You mean that sentence?"

"Listen, I've got a streak of the ancient Roman in me. When I got up this morning, I noticed that my sword wasn't caught in an aiguillette and that my shoulder belt had slipped off. That's an infallible sign."

"Of prosperity?"

"Yes, believe it or not. Every time that damn belt stuck to my back, it meant that Monsieur de Tréville was punishing me or Monsieur de Mazarin was refusing to pay me something. Every time my sword got stuck in my shoulder belt, it hinted at an unpleasant duty, and I've been deluged by such chores all my life. Every time my sword bobbed up and down in its sheath, it meant a duel with a fortunate outcome. Every time my sword dangled around my calves, it meant a light wound. Every time my sword left its sheath entirely, I was trapped on the battlefield, plus I'd have to endure three months of surgeons and compresses."

"I never realized you were kept so well informed by your sword," said Fouquet with a vague smile that revealed his struggle against his own weaknesses. "What kind of sword do you have? Is your sword charmed or enchanted?"

"My sword, you see, is an added limb. I've heard that certain men receive warnings from a leg or a throbbing temple. But I receive warnings from my sword. Well, this morning it's told me nothing! Ah, yes! . . . It just fell of its own accord into the last notch in my shoulder belt. Do you know what that foretells?"

"No."

"It foretells an arrest today."

"Look here!" said Fouquet, more astonished than annoyed by that frankness. "If your sword has made no sad prediction, then you don't feel sad about arresting me, do you?"

"Arrest you? You?"

"Certainly. . . . The presage . . ."

"It doesn't concern you, since you've been under arrest since yesterday. So it's not you I'll be arresting. That's why I'm joyful, that's why I'm saying that my day will be happy."

And having uttered those words graciously and affectionately, the captain took leave of Fouquet in order to go to the king. He was just crossing Fouquet's threshold when the superintendent said: "A final mark of your goodwill."

"Certainly, monseigneur."

"Monsieur d'Herblay. Let me see Monsieur d'Herblay."

"I'll try to bring him to you."

D'Artagnan did not consider himself a soothsayer. The day was fated to make the morning's predictions come true for him.

As we have said, d'Artagnan knocked on the king's door. The door opened. The captain could have thought it was the king himself who'd opened it. This assumption might have been correct, given the king's agitation the previous evening. But instead of the royal personage whom he was about to salute respectfully, he found the long and impassive face of Aramis. His surprise was so violent that he very nearly cried out.

"Aramis!" he said.

"Good morning, dear d'Artagnan," the prelate coldly responded.

"You here?!" the musketeer stammered.

"His Majesty," the bishop went on, "asks you to announce that he is resting after a very fatiguing night."

"Ah!" said d'Artagnan, unable to grasp how the Bishop of Vannes, so little in favor last night, had become, in just six hours, the highest mushroom of fortune that had ever grown by a royal bed.

Indeed, to transmit the king's wishes at his threshold, to serve as his intermediary, to stand just two feet away from him and issue commands in his name—to have all that authority, a man had to be more powerful than Richelieu had been under Louis XIII.

D'Artagnan's expressive eyes, his parted lips, his bristly mustache revealed his amazement in the most ringing language, said all those things to the haughty favorite, who remained unfazed.

"Furthermore, Monsieur Captain of the Musketeers," the bishop went on, "please be so good as to admit only those people with special permission this morning. His Majesty wants to sleep some more."

"But," d'Artagnan rebelliously protested, his explosive suspicions aroused by the king's silence. "But, Your Grace, His Majesty asked me to come here this morning."

"Later, later," said the king from the back of the alcove. His voice terrified the musketeer.

Upon hearing those words, d'Artagnan bowed, astounded, dumbfounded, and stupefied by Aramis's crushing smile.

"Furthermore," the bishop went on, "in response to your request, here is an order that you are to execute immediately. This order concerns Monsieur Fouquet."

D'Artagnan took the document that was handed to him. "Release?" he murmured. "Ah!" Then he uttered a second "Ah!" that was more intelligent than the first. For this document explained Aramis's presence with the king. Aramis, having obtained Fouquet's pardon, must be standing very high in the king's favor—which explained Monsieur d'Herblay's incredible aplomb when issuing orders in His Majesty's name.

It was enough for d'Artagnan to grasp something in order to grasp everything. He bowed and started backing out.

"I'll accompany you," said the bishop.

"Where to?"

"To Monsieur Fouquet. I want to enjoy his delight."

"Ah! Aramis! You're very intriguing!" said d'Artagnan.

"But now you understand?"

"Damn it! Do I ever!" he cried. Then he muttered to himself, whistling softly: "Well, no, I don't! No, I don't understand. It doesn't matter. I've got my order." Next he said to Aramis: "After you, monseigneur."

D'Artagnan conducted Aramis to Fouquet.

21
The King's Friend

Fouquet was waiting fearfully. He had already dismissed a few servants and friends, who, anticipating the time of his customary receptions, had arrived at his door. Concealing the danger that hung over his head, he merely asked each of them where he could find Aramis.

When he saw d'Artagnan coming back, with the Bishop of Vannes behind him, Fouquet was overwhelmed with joy, which was as powerful as his earlier anxiety. The sight of Aramis more than made up for the misery of arrest.

The prelate was grave and silent. D'Artagnan was bowled over by this accumulation of unbelievable events.

"Well, Captain," said Fouquet, "you've brought me Monsieur d'Herblay?"

"And something even better, monseigneur!"

"What?"

"Freedom."

"I'm free?!"

"You're free. By order of the king."

Fouquet regained his full serenity, his eyes questioning d'Artagnan.

"Oh yes!" d'Artagnan continued. "You can thank the Bishop of Vannes. He's the one who got the king to change his mind."

"Oh!" said Fouquet, more humiliated by the service than grateful for its success.

D'Artagnan then spoke to Aramis: "You—you protect Monsieur Fouquet. Could you possibly do something for me?"

"Anything you like, my friend," the bishop calmly replied.

"Just one thing and I'll be satisfied. You and the king haven't exchanged more than a word or two in your life. So how have you managed to become his favorite?"

"One doesn't hide anything from a friend like you!" Aramis shrewdly responded.

"Fine! Then tell me!"

"Well, you believe that the king and I hadn't exchanged more than a word or two. But I tell you, I've seen him a hundred times. Except that it was always in secret. That's all."

And without trying to extinguish the redness that colored d'Artagnan's forehead at that revelation, Aramis turned to Monsieur Fouquet, who was as surprised as the musketeer. "Monseigneur," said the bishop, "the king has instructed me to tell you that he is your friend now more than ever and that he has been moved to the depth of his heart by the beautiful celebration that you have so generously offered him."

Aramis then bowed to Fouquet so reverentially that the superintendent, unable to fully grasp this powerful diplomacy, remained mindless, speechless, motionless.

As for d'Artagnan: realizing that these two men had something to say to one another, he was all set to obey the instinct of courtesy that compels a man to head for the door if his presence is obtrusive to others. However, d'Artagnan's ardent curiosity, spurred on by so much mystery, advised him to stay on.

Aramis now turned toward him gently. "My friend, you do recall the king's order in regard to his levee, don't you?"

The hint was clear enough. The musketeer caught the drift. He therefore bowed to Fouquet, then Aramis, with a tinge of irony, and disappeared.

Fouquet, bursting with impatience, charged toward the door, closed it, and returned to the bishop: "My dear d'Herblay, I think it's time you explained what's going on. I'm totally at a loss."

"We'll explain everything," said Aramis, sitting down, and having Fouquet sit down too. "Where should we begin?"

"Begin here. Everything else aside, why has the king ordered my release?"

"You really should ask why he had you arrested."

"I've had time to mull it over ever since my arrest, and I believe that a bit of jealousy is involved. My celebration irked Monsieur Colbert, and Monsieur Colbert devised some kind of scheme against me—Belle-Île, for instance."

"No, it wasn't Belle-Île."

"Then what was it?"

"Do you recall those receipts for thirteen million that Monsieur de Mazarin stole from you?"

"Yes indeed! What about it?"

"Well, you've been declared a thief!"

"My God!"

"That's not all. Do you remember the letter you wrote to Mademoiselle de la Vallière?"

"Unfortunately!"

"You've been declared a traitor and a suborner!"

"Then why did the king pardon me?"

"We're not up to that yet! I want you to focus on the facts. Now, listen carefully. The king feels you're guilty of embezzlement. Damn it! *I'm* quite aware that you haven't embezzled anything! But still, the king hasn't seen the receipts, and he has no choice but to consider you a criminal."

"Excuse me, I don't see—"

"You'll see! Furthermore, after reading your love letter to Mademoiselle de la Vallière, and your offers to her, the king can nurture no doubts about your intentions regarding that beauty—right?"

"Assuredly! But finish up!"

"I'm getting there. So the king is your sworn, your implacable, your eternal enemy."

"Fine. But am I so powerful that despite his hatred he wouldn't dare to destroy me with all the means that my weakness or bad luck put at his disposal?"

"It's quite clear," Aramis coolly went on, "that the king had broken with you irreconcilably."

"But he's absolved me—"

"Do you really believe that?" the bishop asked with a scrutinizing gaze.

"Without believing in the sincerity of his heart, I believe in the truth of the facts."

Aramis shrugged slightly.

"Then why," asked Fouquet, "did Louis XIV instruct you to tell me what you've reported to me?"

"The king has given me no instructions concerning you."

"No instructions?!" The superintendent was stupefied. "Well, what about that order? . . ."

"Oh, yes! There is an order. That's true." And those words were uttered with such a bizarre accent that Fouquet shuddered in spite of himself.

"Listen," he said, "you're hiding something from me, I can tell."

Aramis softly rubbed his chin with his white fingers.

"Is the king exiling me?" asked Fouquet.

"Don't play twenty questions with me!"

"Then out with it!"

"Guess."

"You're scaring me."

"Nonsense! You just haven't guessed, that's all."

"What did the king tell you? For the sake of our friendship, don't conceal it from me."

"The king said nothing."

"You're going to make me die of impatience, d'Herblay. Am I still superintendent of finances?"

"As long as you like."

"What kind of power have you suddenly gained over His Majesty's mind?"

"Ah! There you are!"

"You make him act according to your wishes."

"I believe so."

"That's incredible!"

"That's what they'll say!"

"D'Herblay, by our alliance, by our friendship, by everything you cherish in the world—speak to me, I beg you. How have you managed to get so close to the king? He didn't use to like you, I know that."

"The king will like me *now*," said Aramis, stressing that last word.

"Then there's something special going on between you?"

"Yes."

"A secret, perhaps?"

"Yes, a secret."

"A secret capable of changing His Majesty's interests?"

"You've got a superior mind, monseigneur. You've guessed

correctly. I've truly unearthed a secret capable of changing the interests of the king of France."

"Ah!" said Fouquet with the reserve of a man of honor who doesn't wish to interrogate.

"And you will judge it for yourself," Aramis continued. "You're going to tell me whether I'm wrong about the importance of this secret."

"I'm listening, since you're kind enough to open up to me. Except, my friend, that I haven't asked any indiscreet questions."

Aramis collected his thoughts for a moment.

"Don't say anything!" exclaimed Fouquet. "We've got time."

"Do you recall the birth of Louis XIV?" said Aramis, lowering his eyes.

"As if it were yesterday."

"Did you hear something special about that birth?"

"Nothing, except that the king was not really the son of Louis XIII."

"That concerns neither our interest nor that of the kingdom. According to French law, a man is his father's son if his father is recognized as such by the law."

"That's true. But it's a serious matter when the quality of breeding is at issue."

"That's a secondary question. So you didn't know anything special?"

"Nothing."

"That's the start of my secret."

"Ah!"

"The queen gave birth to two sons, not one."

Fouquet raised his head: "And the second one died?"

"You'll see. The twins were the pride of their mother and the hope of France. But the king's weakness, his superstition, made him afraid there would be conflicts between the two children, who had equal rights. So he got rid of one baby."

" 'Got rid,' you say?"

"Wait. The two children grew. One on the throne—you're his minister. The other in darkness and isolation."

"And the latter?"

"He's my friend."

"My God! What are you saying, Monsieur d'Herblay? And what is this poor prince doing?"

"First, ask me what he's done."

"Yes, yes."

"He was raised in the country, then sequestered in a fortress known as the Bastille."

"Is that possible!?" cried Fouquet, clasping his hands.

"One twin was the most fortunate of men, the other the most miserable of wretches."

"Is his mother unaware of all this?"

"Anne of Austria knows everything."

"What about the king?"

"The king knows nothing."

"All the better!" said Fouquet.

This exclamation seemed to have a strong impact on Aramis. He eyed his interlocutor anxiously.

"Forgive me, I've interrupted you," said Fouquet.

"I was saying," Aramis went on, "that this poor prince was the most wretched of men, when God, Who is concerned about His creatures, came to his rescue."

"Oh! How?!"

"You'll see. The king regnant . . . I say 'the king regnant'—can you guess why?"

"No. Why?"

"Because both children were legitimate heirs by birth and should therefore have been kings. Is that your opinion?"

"That's my opinion."

"Without reservation?"

"Without reservation. The twins are one person in two bodies."

"I like the fact that a jurist with your background and authority should have reached this conclusion. So we agree, don't we, that both twins had the same rights?"

"We're agreed. But, my goodness! What an unbelievable story!"

"You haven't heard everything yet. Patience. . . ."

"I'm patient."

"God wanted to create an avenger for that oppressed child, create a support, if you prefer. It happened that the king regnant, the usurper . . . You do agree with me, don't you? The tranquil, egotistical enjoyment of a whole heritage of which one is entitled to only half is genuine usurpation, isn't it?"

" 'Usurpation' is the right word."

"I'll go on, then. God wanted the usurper to have a talented and generous prime minister, a man with a great mind to boot."

"Fine, fine," cried Fouquet. "I catch your drift. You're counting on me—aren't you?—to help you redress the wrong done to Louis XIV's poor twin? Well, you're right: I will help you. Thank you, d'Herblay, thank you!"

"That isn't it at all. You're not letting me finish," said Aramis impassively.

"I'll hold my tongue."

"As I was saying: Monsieur Fouquet is a minister of the king regnant, who, however, has developed an aversion to his minister. Indeed, Fouquet's fortune, his freedom, and even his life are threatened by the hatred and intrigue to which the king pays too much attention. However, God—for the salvation of the sacrificed prince—allows Monsieur Fouquet to have a devoted friend. And this friend knows this state secret and feels strong enough to expose this secret after having the strength to keep this secret in his heart for twenty years."

"Go no further," said Fouquet, seething with bountiful ideas. "I catch your drift and I can guess everything. You went to the king when you heard about my arrest. You pleaded with him; he turned a deaf ear. Then you threatened to reveal his secret, and Louis XIV was so terrified of your possible indiscretion that he granted you what he had refused to your noble intercession. I understand, I understand! You've got the king in your power! I understand!"

"You understand nothing!" Aramis retorted. "And you've interrupted me yet again, my friend. Allow me to tell you: you're neglecting logic, and you're not using your memory enough."

"What do you mean?"

"Do you recall what I emphasized at the start of our conversation?"

"Yes. His Majesty's hatred for me, an invincible hatred. But what hatred could resist the threat of such a revelation?!"

"Such a revelation! That shows your lack of logic! What? Do you imagine that if I'd threatened the king with that revelation, I'd still be alive?"

"You only saw the king ten minutes ago!"

"Fine! He wouldn't have had time to kill me, but he would have had time to have me gagged and thrown into a dungeon. So use your head, damn it!"

That musketeer curse had slipped out from a man who never let things slip, and its mere utterance must have made Fouquet grasp the profound agitation afflicting the normally calm and impenetrable bishop. Fouquet shuddered.

"And then," Aramis went on after pulling himself together, "would I be the man I am, would I be a true friend, if I exposed you—you whom the king already hates—if I exposed you to an even more horrible feeling in the young king? Robbing him is nothing. Courting his mistress is little enough. But to hold his crown and his honor in your hands—why, he'd rather rip out your heart with his bare hands!"

"So you didn't even hint at the secret?"

"I'd rather have swallowed all the poisons that Mithridates sipped during twenty years of trying to avoid death!"

"So what did you do?"

"Ah, now we're coming to the point, monseigneur. I believe I'm going to arouse a little interest in you. You're still listening, aren't you?"

"I'm all ears! Go on."

Aramis walked around the room, making sure of their solitude and the surrounding hush. Then he paused at the armchair where Fouquet waited for the revelations with profound anxiety.

Aramis faced Fouquet, who was listening with extreme attention. "I forgot to mention a remarkable characteristic of those twins: God Himself made their resemblance to each other so thorough that if He summoned them to His tribunal, He alone could tell them apart. Their mother could not!"

"Is that possible?!" cried Fouquet.

"The same noble features, the same carriage, the same stature, the same voice!"

"But how about their minds? How about their intelligence? Their knowledge of life?"

"Oh, that's where the resemblance ends, monseigneur. Yes indeed, for the prisoner of the Bastille is incontestably superior to his brother. And if that poor victim were to leave prison and mount the throne, France would not—perhaps since her very birth—have known a master with a more powerful virtue and nobility of character."

For a moment, Fouquet buried his face in his hands, crushed by that immense secret. Aramis drew closer and, pursuing his efforts at temptation, he said: "That too is where the resemblance ends. However, this nonresemblance between the sons of Louis XIII concerns you, monseigneur. You see, the latter twin does not know Monsieur Colbert."

Fouquet's head snapped up, his face pale and twisted. The blow had struck not his heart but his mind. "I understand! You're asking me to join your conspiracy."

"More or less!"

"One of those attempts at changing the fate of an empire, as you said at the start of our conversation."

"And the fate of the superintendent—yes, monseigneur."

"In a word: you want me to help substitute the imprisoned son of Louis XIII for the son now sleeping in the Morpheus Chamber?"

Aramis smiled with the sinister radiance of his sinister thought. "Exactly!" he said.

"But," replied Fouquet after a painful silence, "it doesn't seem to have dawned on you that this political action could turn the whole kingdom topsy-turvy. It doesn't seem to have struck you that for tearing out this tree with its infinite roots—the tree that's known as the king—for, replacing it with another, the earth will never be firm enough to help the king brave the wind that will be left over from the ancient storm, and the earth will never be firm enough to prevent the oscillations of its own mass."

Aramis kept smiling.

Fouquet was hot and bothered—with the forceful talent that examines a plan and thrashes it out in seconds and with a broad view that foresees all the consequences and embraces all the results. "You must realize," he said, "that we have to assemble the nobility, the clergy, the Third Estate. We have to depose the prince regnant, inflict a horrible scandal on the tomb of Louis XIII, doom the life and honor of one woman, Anne of Austria, and doom the life and peace of another woman, Marie-Thérèse of Austria. And once we finish, if ever we do finish—"

"I don't understand you," Aramis snapped coldly. "You haven't uttered one sensible word in anything you've said."

"What?!" exclaimed the amazed superintendent. "You refuse to discuss the practical side—a man like you?! You limit yourself to the juvenile delights of a political illusion and you neglect the chances of success—namely, reality. Is that possible?"

"My *friend*," said Aramis, stressing that noun with a sort of disdainful familiarity, "how does God go about replacing one king with another?"

"God!" exclaimed Fouquet. "God gives an order to His agent, who snatches the condemned man, whisks him away, and seats the victor on the now empty throne. However, you're forgetting that this agent is called 'Death.' Oh my goodness, Monsieur d'Herblay! Are you thinking of—"

"Not at all, monseigneur! You're reaching past our goal. Who's even mentioned putting Louis XIV to death? Who says we mean to follow God's example in the strict practice of His works? No. I was merely saying that God acts without turning everything topsy-turvy, without scandals, without great efforts. The men inspired by God succeed, as He does, in whatever they undertake, whatever they attempt, whatever they do."

"What are you saying?"

"I'm saying, my friend," Aramis continued with the same intonation as when he had first pronounced that noun, "I'm saying that if there's been any chaos, scandal, or even great effort in substituting the prisoner for the king, I challenge you to prove it!"

"What?!" cried Fouquet, whiter than the handkerchief with which he was mopping his temples. "What was that?! . . ."

"Go to the king's bedroom," Aramis went on tranquilly.

"And since you know the secret, I challenge you to determine that the Bastille prisoner is lying in his brother's bed."

"But the king?" stammered Fouquet, who was terror-stricken by the news.

"Which king?" asked Aramis in the sweetest of tones. "The king who hates you or the king who loves you?"

"Yesterday's . . . king?"

" 'Yesterday's king'? Don't worry. He's in the Bastille, where he's taken the place that his victim occupied for too long a time."

"Good heavens! And who conducted him there?"

"I did."

"You?!"

"Yes, and in the simplest way. I kidnapped him last night, and, while he descended into darkness, the other king ascended to the light. I don't believe there was a single sound. Lightning without thunder never awakens anybody."

Fouquet emitted a dull cry as if struck by an invisible blow, and burying his face in his rigid fingers, he murmured, "You did that?"

"Quite adroitly. What do you think?"

"You've dethroned the king? You've imprisoned him?"

"It's done."

"And it happened here, in Vaux?"

"Here, in Vaux, in the Morpheus Chamber. Doesn't that chamber appear as if had been built for such an action?"

"And it really happened?"

"Last night."

"Last night?"

"Between midnight and one A.M."

Fouquet moved as if he wanted to pounce on Aramis. But he held back.

"In Vaux! In my home!" he said, choking.

"Why, I do believe so. And it's even more your home now that Monsieur Colbert can't steal it from you."

"That crime was committed in my own home!"

"That crime?!" said Aramis, stupefied.

"That abominable crime!" Fouquet continued, growing more

and more agitated. "A crime more execrable than an assassination! A crime that will dishonor my name forever and condemn me to posterity's loathing!"

"You're delirious, monsieur!" said Aramis in a shaky voice. "You're talking much too loudly! Be careful!"

"I'll yell so loudly that the entire universe will hear me!"

"Monsieur Fouquet, be careful!"

Fouquet turned back to the prelate and confronted him. "Yes, you've dishonored me by perpetrating this treason, this heinous crime, against my guest, against the man who was resting peacefully under my roof! Oh! I'm doomed!"

"Doomed is the man who planned the ruin of your fortune, of your life, under your very roof! Are you forgetting that?"

"He was my guest, he was my king!"

Aramis stood up, his eyes bloodshot, his mouth convulsive.

"Am I dealing with a lunatic?" he snapped.

"You're dealing with a man of honor."

"You're crazy!"

"A man who will prevent you from carrying out your crime."

"Crazy!"

"A man who'd rather die, who'd rather kill you, than let you implement his dishonor."

And Fouquet, grabbing his sword (which d'Artagnan had placed at the head of the bed), resolutely brandished the shiny steel blade.

Aramis frowned and reached inside his chest as if seeking a weapon. This move did not escape Fouquet's notice. Proud and noble in his magnanimity, the superintendent tossed his sword far away. As it rolled into the space between the bed and the wall, Fouquet drew close enough to touch Aramis with his disarmed hand.

"Monsieur," said Fouquet, "I would rather perish here than survive my disgrace; and if you still feel any friendship for me, I beg you: put me to death."

Aramis remained silent and motionless.

"You won't answer me?"

Aramis gently raised his head, and a shimmer of hope returned to his eyes. "Monsieur, think about everything lying ahead for us. Justice has been done, the king is still alive, and his incarceration has saved your life."

"Yes," replied Fouquet, "you may have been acting in my interest, but I refuse to accept your services. Nevertheless, I do not wish to doom you. You will leave this castle immediately."

Aramis stifled the words that flashed from his shattered heart.

"I am hospitable toward each one of my guests," Fouquet went on with ineffable majesty. "You will not be sacrificed here any more than the man you've chosen to ruin."

"You will be sacrificed," said Aramis in a hollow and prophetic voice. "You will, you will!"

"I accept your augury, Monsieur d'Herblay. But nothing will stop me. You will leave Vaux, you will leave France. I'll give you four hours to get beyond the king's reach."

"Four hours?" said Aramis, sneering incredulously.

"You have my word: no one will follow you until the four hours are up. That will give you a four-hour head start on anyone the king sends after you."

"Four hours!" Aramis howled.

"That's more than you need to set sail and reach Belle-Île, which I grant you as an asylum."

"Ah!" murmured Aramis.

"Belle-Île belongs to me on your behalf just as Vaux belongs to me on the king's behalf. Leave, d'Herblay, leave. So long as I live, not a hair on your head will be harmed."

"Thank you!" said Aramis with somber irony.

"Then leave! And let's shake hands so that we can hurry away—you to save your life, I to save my honor."

Aramis withdrew his hand from his chest. His hand was red with his blood. His nails had scourged his chest as if to punish his flesh for giving birth to so many plans that were vainer, crazier, more ephemeral than a human life. Fouquet felt horror, felt pity. He opened his arms to Aramis.

"I'm not armed," murmured the bishop, as fierce and dreadful as Dido's shade.

Then, without touching Fouquet's hand, Aramis looked

around and took two steps back. His last word was a curse. His last gesture was anathema, his red hand dripping his blood on Fouquet's face.

And both man dashed from the room and hurried down the secret staircase, which led to the inner courts.

Fouquet sent for his best horses while Aramis stopped at the bottom of the stairs that led to Porthos's room.

Aramis reflected for a long time as Fouquet's carriage flew out of the main courtyard.

Leave all alone? . . . Aramis wondered. Or warn the prince? . . . Damn it! . . . Warn the prince and then do what? . . . Leave with him? . . . Drag that incriminating evidence everywhere? . . . War? . . . Implacable civil war? . . . No resources, alas! . . . Impossible! . . . What will he do without me? . . . Without me, he'll crumble as I will. . . . Who knows?! . . . Let his fate come true! . . . He was condemned—let him stay condemned! . . . God! . . . Demon! Somber and mocking power that's called human nature! You're nothing but a puff of air that's more uncertain, more useless than the wind in the mountains. You call yourself "chance." You're nothing. Your breath embraces everything; you crumble rocks, even mountains. And then suddenly you shatter before the cross of dead wood, beyond which another invisible power resides . . . which you denied perhaps, and which gets even with you and which crushes you without even honoring you by uttering its name! . . . Doomed! . . . I'm doomed! . . . What should I do? . . . Go to Belle-Île? . . . Yes. And Porthos can stay here and talk, and tell everything to everyone! Porthos may suffer, perhaps! . . . I don't want him to suffer! He's like part of me, his pain is mine. Porthos will leave with me, he'll follow my destiny. He has to!

And, terrified that somebody might find his haste suspicious, Aramis managed to climb the stairs without encountering anyone.

Porthos, scarcely back from Paris, was already sleeping the sleep of the righteous. His enormous body was forgetting its fatigue, just as his mind was forgetting its thoughts.

Aramis entered, light as a shadow, and placed his nervous hand on the giant's shoulder.

"Wake up!" he cried. "Wake up, Porthos, wake up!"

Porthos obeyed, stood up, and opened his eyes before growing conscious.

"We're leaving," said Aramis.

"Ah!" said Porthos.

"We're leaving on horseback, and we'll gallop faster than we've ever galloped before."

"Ah!" repeated Porthos.

"Get dressed, my friend!"

And he helped the giant get dressed and put his gold and his diamonds into his pockets. As he did so, a vague noise drew his attention. D'Artagnan was watching them from the doorway.

Aramis shuddered.

"What the hell are you so agitated about?" asked d'Artagnan.

"Shush!" whispered Porthos.

"We're leaving on a special mission!" added Aramis.

"Lucky you!" said d'Artagnan.

"Oh my!" said Porthos. "I'm worn out. I'd have liked to sleep more. But we have to serve the king! . . ."

"Have you seen Monsieur Fouquet?" Aramis asked d'Artagnan.

"Yes, just now, in his carriage."

"And what did he say to you?"

"He said good-bye."

"That's all?"

"What else would you have wanted him to say to me? Am I worth anything at all now that you're both in such high esteem?"

"Listen," said Aramis, hugging d'Artagnan, "your time has come again. You won't have to be jealous of anyone!"

"Bah!"

"I predict that today a certain event will double your importance!"

"Really?"

"You know that I know all the news."

"Oh yes!"

"C'mon, Porthos, are you ready? Let's go!"

"Let's go!"

"And let's hug d'Artagnan."

"Damn it!"

"What about the horses?"

"We have no lack of them here. Do you want my horse?"

"No, Porthos has his stable. Good-bye, good-bye!"

The two fugitives mounted their horses in front of d'Artagnan, who held Porthos's stirrup for him, then gazed after his friends until they disappeared.

On any other occasion, d'Artagnan thought to himself, I'd say that those two are escaping something. But today, politics are so different that an escape is called a "mission." Let it be. I'll go about my business.

And he philosophically returned to his lodgings.

22

How Orders Were Respected in the Bastille

Fouquet's carriage ate up the road. He shook with horror at what he had just heard. What, he wondered, could their youth have been like—these prodigious men who are old and feeble and yet manage to think up such plans and carry them out without batting an eye?!

At times he asked himself whether everything Aramis had confided in him was merely a dream, whether the whole story was simply a trap, and whether, upon arriving at the Bastille, he, Fouquet, would find an arrest warrant and join the dethroned monarch. Pondering the matter while fresh horses were being harnessed to his carriage, Fouquet issued a few sealed orders. These orders were addressed to Monsieur d'Artagnan and to all the corps leaders whose loyalty was above suspicion.

This way, Fouquet mused, whether I'm a prisoner or not, I'll have performed the service I owe to the cause of honor. These orders won't arrive till after my return if I come back a free man, and, consequently, they won't be unsealed. I'll take them back. But if I'm delayed, that will mean that I've encountered some misfortune. In that case, I'll have help both for myself and for the king.

Thus prepared, the superintendent reached the Bastille. He had traveled at five and a half leagues per hour.

All the things that had never happened to Aramis at the Bastille happened to Monsieur Fouquet. He could repeat his name, repeat his title, until he was blue in the face, but they wouldn't let him in.

By pleading, threatening, commanding, he eventually managed to persuade a sentry to notify a junior officer, who notified the major. As for the warden, they didn't dare disturb him for such a trifle.

At the gates of the fortress, Fouquet was fretting and fuming in his carriage as he awaited the return of the subaltern, who finally came back in a rather sulky mood.

"Well?" Fouquet snapped impatiently. "What did the major say?"

"Well, monsieur!" replied the subaltern. "The major laughed in my face. He said that Monsieur Fouquet is at Vaux, and that even if he were in Paris, he wouldn't be awake at such an ungodly hour!"

"Damn it! You're a bunch of idiots!" exclaimed the minister, hurling himself out of the carriage.

And before the subaltern had time to shut the gate, Fouquet lunged through the aperture and raced on despite the shouts of the soldier, who yelled for help.

Fouquet gained ground, heedless of the shouts of that man, who, having finally caught up with him, yelled at the sentinel by the inner gate, "Look out, look out, sentinel!"

The sentinel leveled his pike at the minister, who, however, being robust, agile, and enraged, grabbed the pike and violently clobbered the sentry's shoulder. The junior officer, who came too close for comfort, also got his share of whacks. Both victims yelled furiously, attracting the entire corps of guards.

One of those men recognized the superintendent. "Monseigneur! Ah! Monseigneur!" he cried. "Stop that, men!" And he actually stopped the guards, who were about to avenge their comrades.

Fouquet hollered at them to open the gate, but they refused to do so without proper orders. He demanded that they summon the warden, who had already been informed about all the commotion. At the head of a picket of twenty men, he came dashing over, followed by his major. The warden was convinced that the Bastille was under attack.

Baisemeaux instantly recognized Fouquet and dropped the sword he'd been brandishing. "Ah, monseigneur!" the warden stammered. "Please forgive us!"

"Monsieur!" snapped the superintendent, his face crimson with heat and sweat. "My compliments! Your defense system is wonderful!"

Baisemeaux blanched, thinking those words were ironic, a presage of wild anger. But Fouquet had caught his breath and he motioned to the sentinel and the junior officer, who were rubbing their shoulders.

"Here's twenty pistoles for the sentry and fifty for the officer. My compliments, gentlemen, I'm going to tell the king about you! But now, Baisemeaux, a word in private."

Baisemeaux was trembling with embarrassment and anxiety. Aramis's morning visit seemed to be bearing some terrifying fruits.

It was quite another thing, however, when Fouquet, in a curt tone of voice, and with an imperious glare, said: "Monsieur, you saw Monsieur d'Herblay this morning?"

"Yes, monseigneur!"

"Fine, monsieur! And aren't you horrified by the crime that you've aided and abetted?"

Nonsense! the warden thought to himself. Then he added out loud: "What crime, monseigneur?"

"It's enough to have you drawn and quartered, monsieur! Think about it! But this isn't the moment to get annoyed! Take me to the prisoner on the spot!"

"Which prisoner?" asked Baisemeaux, trembling.

"You're feigning ignorance? That's what you can do best! Of course, if you admitted your complicity, you'd be done for! So I'll pretend to believe in your ignorance."

"I beg you, monseigneur—!"

"Fine! Take me to the prisoner."

"Marchiali?"

"Who's Marchiali?"

"He's the prisoner that Monsieur d'Herblay brought here this morning."

"He's called Marchiali?" The superintendent's conviction was troubled by the warden's naïve assurance.

"Yes, monseigneur. That's the name he was registered under."

Fouquet probed the depths of Baisemeaux's heart. With the sharp-sightedness of powerful men, Fouquet realized that the warden was absolutely sincere. Besides, if you scrutinized that face for even a moment, how could you believe that Aramis had chosen such a confidant?

"So," said Fouquet, "that's the prisoner whom Monsieur d'Herblay took away the day before yesterday?"

"Yes, monseigneur."

"And whom he brought back here this morning?" snapped Fouquet, who promptly grasped the mechanics of Aramis's plan.

"Exactly, monseigneur."

"And his name is Marchiali?"

"Marchiali. If Monseigneur wishes to take the prisoner away, that's fine with me, for I was just going to write about him."

"What is he doing?"

"He's been extremely annoying since this morning. He has fits of rage, and they're so forceful that you'd think they'd bring down the Bastille."

"I'll definitely take him off your hands," said Fouquet.

"Ah! So much the better!"

"Take me to his cell."

"Can Monseigneur give me the warrant?"

"What warrant?"

"A warrant signed by the king."

"I can sign a warrant."

"That wouldn't be enough, monseigneur. I need a warrant from the king."

Fouquet was irritated. "You're so scrupulous about getting rid of prisoners. Well, then, show me the warrant he originally came here with."

Baisemeaux showed Fouquet the release warrant for Seldon.

"All well and good," said Fouquet. "Still, Seldon is not Marchiali."

"But Marchiali hasn't been released, monseigneur, he's here."

"You said that Monsieur d'Herblay took him away and brought him back here."

"I never said that."

"You said it so clearly that I can still hear it."

"A slip of the tongue."

"Monsieur de Baisemeaux, be careful!"

"I've got nothing to fear, monseigneur, I go by the book."

"You dare to say so?"

"I would say so in front of a saint. Monsieur d'Herblay brought me a release order for Seldon, and Seldon was released."

"I tell you, Marchiali has left the Bastille."

"You'll have to prove that, monseigneur."

"Let me see him."

"Monseigneur, you who help govern this kingdom—you know very well that nobody enters a prisoner's cell without an express order from the king."

"Monsieur d'Herblay got in without such an order."

"You'll have to prove that, monseigneur."

"Once again, Monsieur de Baisemeaux, watch what you say."

"The files are here."

"Monsieur d'Herblay has been ousted."

"Monsieur d'Herblay ousted? Impossible!"

"You can see how deeply he influenced you."

"What influences me, monseigneur, is serving the king. I'm doing my duty. Give me an order signed by the king, and you can enter the prisoner's cell."

"Listen, Monsieur Warden, I give you my word: if you let me see the prisoner, I'll give you an order straightaway."

"Give it to me now, monseigneur."

"And if you refuse, I'll have you arrested on the spot, together with all your officers."

"Before perpetrating such violence, monseigneur," said Baisemeaux, blanching, "you must remember that we will obey only a royal order, that it's up to you to bring one, and that it will be just as easy to obtain an order to see Monsieur Marchiali as it would be to harm me, an innocent man."

"That's true!" shouted Fouquet furiously. "That's true! Well, Monsieur Baisemeaux," he added sonorously, pulling over the miserable warden, "do you know why I so ardently want to speak to this prisoner?"

"No, monseigneur. And please note that you're frightening me. I'm shuddering, I feel faint."

"You'll soon feel even more faint, Monsieur Baisemeaux, when I come back here with ten thousand men and thirty cannon."

"My God, monseigneur! You're losing your mind!"

"I'll sic the entire population of Paris on you and your accursed turrets, I'll batter down your gates, and I'll string you up from the battlements of the corner tower!"

"Monseigneur, monseigneur! For pity's sake!"

"I'll give you ten minutes to make up your mind," Fouquet added calmly. "I'll sit down here, in this chair, and I'll wait for you. If you refuse to budge within ten minutes, I'll leave, and, no matter how crazy you think I am, you'll see what happens!"

Baisemeaux stamped his foot in desperation but didn't reply. Seeing this, Fouquet grabbed a quill and ink and he wrote:

> Order to the provost of the merchants to assemble the burgher guard and to march against the Bastille in the service of the king.

Baisemeaux shrugged. Fouquet then wrote:

> Order to the Duke de Bouillon and to Prince de Condé to take command of the Swiss mercenaries and the guards and to march against the Bastille in the service of His Majesty.

Baisemeaux reflected. And then Fouquet wrote:

> Order to every soldier, burgher or aristocrat, to seize and hold Monsieur d'Herblay, Bishop of Vannes, and his accomplices:
>
> 1. Monsieur de Baisemeaux, under suspicion of crimes of treason, rebellion, and lèse-majesté—

"Stop, monseigneur!" cried Baisemeaux. "I haven't the foggiest clue what this is all about! But so many misfortunes—even if they were caused by madness—can occur in the space of two hours. And if the king judges me, we'll see whether I was wrong to disobey his orders in the face of so many imminent catastrophes. Let's go to the cell, monseigneur. You will see Marchiali."

Fouquet dashed out of the room, and Baisemeaux followed him, wiping the cold sweat that was pouring down his forehead. "What an awful morning! What a disgrace!"

"Hurry up!" Fouquet retorted.

Baisemeaux signaled the jailer to go ahead of them. He was scared of his companion. Fouquet noticed his fear. "Don't be so childish!" he snapped crudely. "Don't bring him along. Take the keys yourself and show me the way. Nobody must hear what happens here—do you understand?"

"Oh!" said Baisemeaux indecisively.

"Now listen!" exclaimed Fouquet. "Say no right now and I'll leave the Bastille and deliver all my orders personally!"

Baisemeaux lowered his head, took the keys, and he and Fouquet climbed the tower stairs. As they advanced up that dizzying spiral, stifled murmurs became indistinct cries and horrible curses.

"What's that?" asked Fouquet.

"It's your Marchiali. That's how lunatics howl!" His response was accompanied by a wink filled with hurtful allusions rather than courtesy toward Fouquet.

The superintendent shivered. Hearing a cry that was more terrible than the others, he recognized the king's voice.

Fouquet paused on the landing and took the keys from Baisemeaux. The warden thought that the new lunatic wanted to smash his head with one of the keys.

"Ah!" cried Baisemeaux. "Monsieur d'Herblay never spoke to me about that!"

"Those keys!" snapped Fouquet. "Which is the key to the prisoner's cell?"

"This one!"

A fearful shout, followed by a horrible bang on the door, echoed through the staircase.

"Leave me!" Fouquet told Baisemeaux in a menacing voice.

"There's nothing I'd rather do more!" muttered the warden. "Two lunatics face-to-face! Each will devour the other! I'm sure of it!"

"Leave!" Fouquet repeated. "If you set foot on those stairs before I call you, you'll take the place of the most wretched prisoner in the Bastille!"

"I'll die, I'm sure of it!" grumbled Baisemeaux, reeling away.

The prisoner's cries grew more and more horrendous. After making sure that the warden had reached the bottom step, Fouquet thrust the key into the first lock. Now he heard the strangled and raging voice of the king: "Help me! I'm the king! Help me!"

There was a different key for the second door. Fouquet had to look through the bunch.

Meanwhile, the king—wild, crazy, frantic—was shouting at the top of his lungs: "It was Monsieur Fouquet who brought me here! I'm the king! Help the king fight Fouquet!"

Those yells ripped the minister's heart. They were followed by the fearful banging of a broken chair that the king was using as a battering ram. Fouquet managed to find the right key. The king was at the end of his rope. He no longer articulated, he bellowed.

"Kill Fouquet!" he howled. "Kill that villain Fouquet!"

The door opened.

23
The King's Gratitude

The two men, about to dash toward one another, suddenly halted upon recognizing each other and they emitted cries of dismay.

"Have you come to finish me off, monsieur?" said the king.

"The king in such a state!" muttered Fouquet.

Indeed, there could be nothing more horrific than the sight of the young monarch when Fouquet surprised him. The king's garments were tattered; his shirt, torn and open, soaked up both the sweat and the blood that were oozing from his chest and his arms. Haggard, pallid, foaming at the mouth, his hair bristling, Louis XIV was the epitome of despair, hunger, and terror in a single figure. The minister was so touched, so disturbed, that he darted over to the king, his arms open, his eyes filled with tears.

Louis raised the wooden fragment that he had been using so furiously.

"Come on!" said Fouquet in a trembling voice. "Don't you recognize your most loyal friend?"

"Friend? You?!" repeated Louis, gnashing his teeth, which reverberated with vindictive hatred.

"Your respectful servant," added Fouquet, falling to his knees.

The king dropped his weapon. Fouquet approached him, kissed his knees, and tenderly took him in his arms: "My king, my child! How you must be suffering!"

Louis, brought to his senses by the new situation, looked at himself. Ashamed of his disorderliness, ashamed of his lunacy, ashamed of the protection offered by Fouquet, the king recoiled.

Fouquet couldn't understand why. He failed to sense that the king's pride would never forgive the superintendent for seeing him in this condition of profound weakness.

"Come, sire, you are free," said Fouquet.

"Free?" the king repeated. "You'd set me free after daring to raise your hand against me!"

"You don't believe it!" cried Fouquet, indignant. "You can't possibly think that I'm the culprit?!"

And swiftly, even ardently, Fouquet explained the entire intrigue, the details of which we know.

Throughout the explanation, Louis endured the most horrible anguish. And when Fouquet was done, the king understood the huge danger he was in, which struck him more forcefully than the secret pertaining to his twin brother.

"Monsieur," the king suddenly addressed Fouquet, "that story about twins is a lie! You can't possibly have been fooled by it!"

"Sire!"

"I tell you, one can't possibly sully my mother's honor, her virtue! And hasn't my prime minister brought the criminals to justice?!"

"Think it over, sire," replied Fouquet, "before you're carried away by your anger! Your brother's birth—"

"I've got only one brother, my younger brother. You know him as well as you know me. There's a conspiracy, I tell you, starting with the warden of the Bastille!"

"Be careful, sire. That man was fooled like everyone else by the resemblance between you and Marchiali."

"Resemblance? Come on!"

"That Marchiali must fairly resemble Your Majesty if he can dupe so many people!" Fouquet asserted.

"It's crazy!"

"Don't say that, sire. The men who are all set to face your ministers, your mother, your officers, your family—they must be certain of the resemblance."

"Indeed they must," murmured the king. "Where are those men?"

"Why, in Vaux!"

"In Vaux! And you allow them to stay there?"

"The most urgent task, I felt, was to free Your Majesty! I've performed that duty. Now let's carry out the king's orders. I am waiting."

Louis reflected for a moment.

"Assemble all the troops in Paris," he then said.

"The orders have already been given!" replied Fouquet.

"You've given orders?!" cried the king.

"For that purpose, yes, sire. Within the hour, Your Majesty will be at the head of ten thousand men."

By way of response, the king grabbed Fouquet's hand so effusively that it was easy to see how distrustful of his minister he had been, despite Fouquet's intervention.

"And with those troops," the king went on, "we will lay siege to the rebels, who must be established and entrenched in your home."

"I'd be astonished if they were there," Fouquet answered.

"Why?"

"Because I've unmasked their leader, the head of that operation. So their entire plan must be aborted."

"You've unmasked the false prince?"

"No, I haven't seen him."

"Then whom have you unmasked?"

"The ringleader. He's not that miserable fraud. The impostor is merely an instrument, doomed, I reckon, to a horrible life!"

"Absolutely!"

"The real leader is the Abbé d'Herblay, Bishop of Vannes!"

"Your friend!"

"He *was* my friend, sire," Fouquet replied nobly.

"That's unfortunate for you!" snapped the king in a less generous tone.

"There was nothing dishonorable about such friendships, sire, so long as I didn't know about the crime."

"You should have been more prescient."

"If I am guilty of anything, I place myself in Your Majesty's hands."

"Ah, Monsieur Fouquet! That's not what I mean!" the king retorted, annoyed that he had revealed the harshness of his thoughts. "Well, let me explain! Despite that miserable traitor's mask, I did have a vague suspicion that it could be him! But this ringleader must be in cahoots with a thug! The man who threatened me with his Herculean brawn—who is he?"

"That must be the bishop's friend, the Baron du Vallon, a former musketeer."

"D'Artagnan's friend? Count de La Fère's friend? Ah! We mustn't overlook the relationship between the conspirators and Monsieur de Bragelonne."

"Sire! Don't go too far. Monsieur de La Fère is the most honorable man in France. You can be satisfied with the men I'm handing over to you."

"The men you're handing over to me? Fine! They're the culprits, right?"

"What does Your Majesty mean by that?"

"I mean," the king replied, "that we will reach Vaux with our forces and wipe out that nest of vipers. Not a single one will escape—right?"

"Your Majesty is going to kill the conspirators?!" cried Fouquet.

"Every last one!"

"Oh, sire!"

"Let's understand one another, Monsieur Fouquet," said the king haughtily. "I no longer live in a time when assassination was a ruler's only and ultimate resource. Not at all, thank God! I've got parliaments that judge in my name, and I've got scaffolds that carry out my supreme wishes."

Fouquet blanched. "Let me be so bold as to point out to Your Majesty that any proceedings for these matters would be a mortal scandal for the dignity of the throne. The august name of Anne of Austria must not cross the smiling lips of the people."

"Justice must be done, monsieur!"

"Of course, sire. But royal blood must not flow on the scaffold."

"Royal blood! You really believe that!" the king raged, stamping his foot. "The double birth is an invention. That's what I see as Monsieur d'Herblay's worst crime. And that's the crime I want to punish, far more than their violence and insults."

"Punish by death?"

"Yes, monsieur. By death."

"Your Majesty," the superintendent declared, proudly raising his head, "if you wish, you can cut off the head of your brother, Philip of France. This concerns you, and you may consult your mother, Anne of Austria. Whatever you order will be rightly ordered. I don't wish to get involved in that, even for the honor of your crown. But I have a favor to ask of you—one favor."

"Speak," said the king, deeply troubled by the minister's words. "What do you need?"

"A pardon for Monsieur d'Herblay and for Monsieur du Vallon."

"My assassins!"

"Two rebels, sire. That's all."

"Oh! I understand that you are asking me to pardon your friends."

"My friends?" said Fouquet, deeply offended.

"Yes! Your friends! But the security of the state demands an exemplary punishment for the culprits."

"I needn't remind Your Majesty that I've just liberated himself and saved his life!"

"Monsieur!"

"I needn't remind Your Majesty that if d'Herblay were an assassin, he could have simply murdered Your Majesty this morning in the forest of Sénart, and that would have been the end of it."

The king shuddered.

"A bullet in your head," Fouquet continued, "and Louis XIV's face would be unrecognizable. And Monsieur d'Herblay would be absolved forever."

The king blanched, terrified by the thought of the peril he had escaped.

"If Monsieur d'Herblay," Fouquet went on, "were an assassin, he wouldn't have needed to reveal his plan to me. Without the true king, nobody would guess that this was the false king. If Anne of Austria had recognized the usurper, he would nevertheless still be her son. And Monsieur d'Herblay's conscience would be eased because the false king, still and all, had the blood of Louis XIII. Furthermore, the conspirator would have security on his side as well as secrecy and impunity. A pistol shot would have given him all that. Pardon him, sire, in the name of your salvation."

The king, instead of being moved by this faithful depiction of Aramis's generosity, felt cruelly humiliated. His indomitable pride could not get used to the idea that a man could have had the thread of a royal life at his fingertips. Each word that Fouquet believed could help him obtain pardons for his friends poured yet another drop of venom into the king's already embittered heart. Nothing could sway him.

The king impetuously addressed Fouquet: "Monsieur, I really don't know why you're asking me to pardon those men. Why bother requesting something you can have without soliciting it?"

"I don't catch your drift, sire."

"It's simple. Where am I now?"

"In the Bastille, sire."

"Yes, in a dungeon. They think I'm a lunatic, don't they?"

"That's true, sire."

"And the only person they know is Marchiali."

"Right!"

"Well, don't change anything in the situation. Let the lunatic rot in a dungeon of the Bastille, and Messieurs D'Herblay and du Vallon won't need my forgiveness. Their new king will absolve them."

"Your Majesty is insulting me, sire, and is wrong to do so," Fouquet dryly replied. "I am not childish enough, and Monsieur d'Herblay is not inept enough, to have avoided such reflections. If I had wanted a new king, as you say, I wouldn't have needed to fight my way into the Bastille in order to free you. It's obvious! Your Majesty is blinded by anger. Otherwise, you wouldn't gratuitously offend that servant of his who performed the most crucial service for the king."

Louis realized he had gone too far. The gates of the Bastille were still closed for him, while the floodgates holding up the anger of this generous Fouquet were gradually opening.

"I didn't say that to humiliate you," the king exclaimed. "God forbid, monsieur! But you're addressing me with a request, and I am responding in accordance with my conscience. Now, following the dictates of my conscience, I tell you that these culprits are worthy of neither a pardon nor forgiveness."

Fouquet held his tongue.

"What I am doing," the king added, "is generous, just as you are being generous, for I am in your power. I will even say that you are more generous, given that you are confronting me with a circumstance on which my life and my freedom may depend. My refusal of your request could cost me both."

"I'm truly wrong," Fouquet answered. "Yes, I seemed to be extorting a favor. I repent and I beg Your Majesty to forgive me."

"And you are forgiven, my dear Monsieur Fouquet." The king smiled, and his smile brought back the serenity to his face that so many events had altered since the previous night.

"I have your forgiveness," the minister obstinately went on. "But what about Monsieur d'Herblay and Monsieur du Vallon?"

"They will never be forgiven so long as I live." The king was inflexible. "Be so good as to never mention them again."

"Your Majesty will be obeyed."

"And you won't hold a grudge against me?"

"Oh no, sire! I anticipated your reaction."

"You anticipated that I would refuse to pardon those men?"

"Definitely, and all my measures were taken in consequence."

The king was surprised. "What do you mean?"

"Monsieur d'Herblay put himself in my hands, so to speak. He granted me the happiness of saving my king and my country. I couldn't sentence Monsieur d'Herblay to death. Nor could I expose him to Your Majesty's very legitimate anger. That would have been tantamount to killing Monsieur d'Herblay myself."

"Well, then, what did you do?"

"Sire, I gave him my best horses and a four-hour head start over any horses Your Majesty can send after him."

"Fine!" muttered the king. "But the world is big enough for my horsemen to catch up with him despite his head start."

"By giving him those four hours, sire, I knew I was giving him his life. He will have his life."

"How?"

"After outriding your musketeers, sire, he will reach my Belle-Île castle, where I have granted him asylum."

"Fine! But you're forgetting that you gave me Belle-Île."

"Not for you to arrest my friends."

"So you're taking the castle back?"

"For that purpose, sire, yes."

"My musketeers will retake it, and that will be that."

"Not your musketeers and not even your army, sire," Fouquet said coldly. "Belle-Île is invincible."

The king turned livid, his eyes flashed. Fouquet felt he was doomed, but he was not a man to recoil from the voice of honor. He endured the venomous glare of the raging king.

After a brief silence, the king asked, "Are we going to Vaux?"

"I am at Your Majesty's orders," said Fouquet with a deep bow. "But I think that Your Majesty cannot dispense with a change of clothes before appearing at court."

"We'll head out by way of the Louvre," said the king. "Let's go."

And they strode off in front of a gaping Baisemeaux, who once again watched Marchiali depart. The warden tore out what little hair he had left.

Fouquet, it is true, handed him a release document, on which the king wrote: "Seen and approved, Louis." The warden, incapable of any coherent thoughts, received this lunacy with a kill-or-cure punch in his jaw.

24
The False King

In Vaux, meanwhile, the usurped royalty was playing its role correctly.

In regard to his morning ritual, Philip ordered the introduction of the *grandes entrées*, already prepared to come before the king. He decided to issue this order despite the absence of Monsieur d'Herblay, who was not returning—and our readers know why. But like all reckless spirits, the prince, assuming that this absence would not be lengthy, wanted to test his bravery and good fortune far from any protection, any advice.

There was another reason for his effort. Anne of Austria was going to appear. The guilty mother would be in the presence of the son she had sacrificed. If Philip had a weakness, he didn't care to expose it to the man whom he henceforth needed to deploy so much force.

Philip opened wide the folding doors, and several people silently filed in. While his valets dressed him, Philip didn't budge. After watching his brother's ritual the previous day, Philip now acted the king, arousing no suspicion.

Fully clad in his hunting garb, he then received the visitors. Relying on his memory and Aramis's notes, he began with Anne of Austria, who was led in by her younger son; and they were followed by the latter's wife with Monsieur de Saint-Aignan.

Philip smiled at the sight of these faces, and he shivered upon recognizing his mother. Her noble and imposing face, ravaged by sorrow, pleaded, in his heart, the cause of that famous queen who had sacrificed a child for the good of the state. Philip saw that his mother was beautiful. He knew that Louis XIV loved her, and he promised himself that he would love her too and not inflict a cruel punishment on her old age.

He gazed at his younger brother with a tenderness that was easy to understand. His brother had usurped nothing, darkened nothing in Philip's life. A separate branch, he allowed the trunk to grow without caring about the elevation and the majesty of his own life. Philip promised himself he'd be a good brother for this prince, who needed nothing but gold for his pleasures.

Philip affectionately welcomed Saint-Aignan, who kept smiling and bowing till he was blue in the face. And then trembling as he held out a hand to Henriette, his sister-in-law, Philip was struck by her beauty. In her eyes, however, he saw a touch of coldness, which pleased him because it would clarify their future relationship.

It'll be so much easier, he thought to himself, to be this woman's brother rather than her suitor if she shows me a coldness that my brother couldn't feel toward her and that is imposed upon me as a duty.

The only visitor he feared was Louis's wife. Her heart and her mind had just been shaken by such a violent ordeal that, despite their solidity, they might endure a new shock. Luckily, the queen did not come. Next, Anne of Austria launched into a political discourse about Monsieur Fouquet's reception for the Royal Household. She mixed hostilities with compliments paid to the king, questions about his health, casual maternal flattery, and diplomatic ruses.

"Well, my son," she asked, "have you reconsidered your opinion of Monsieur Fouquet?"

"Saint-Aignan," said Philip, "please be so good as to go and inquire after the queen."

At these words, the first that Philip uttered, the slight difference between his voice and that of Louis XIV was evident to maternal ears, and Anne of Austria stared hard at her son.

Saint-Aignan left.

Philip went on: "Madame, I don't like to hear negative things about Monsieur Fouquet. You know that, and you yourself have also said positive things about him."

"True enough. That's why I'm merely questioning you about your feelings for him."

"Sire," said Henriette, "I've always liked Monsieur Fouquet. He has good taste, and he's a man of honor."

"A superintendent who never pinches pennies," added her husband, "and he always pays gold for my notes."

"You're all thinking only about yourselves," said the old queen. "No one here is concerned about the state. And it's a fact that Monsieur Fouquet is ruining the state."

"Come, come, Mother," Philip replied in a softer tone. "Are you too shielding Monsieur Colbert?"

The queen was surprised. "What do you mean?"

"I often hear you saying things that your old friend Madame de Chevreuse would be saying."

Upon hearing that name, Anne of Austria blanched and she pursed her lips. Philip had irritated the lioness. "Why are you bringing up Madame de Chevreuse?! And why are you turning against me today?"

Philip continued: "Isn't Madame de Chevreuse always conniving against someone? And hasn't she visited you recently, Mother?"

"Monsieur, when I hear you speaking like that, I can hear the king, your father."

"My father never liked Madame de Chevreuse, and he was right," said the prince. "I don't like her either. And if she takes it upon herself to come here as she used to do—sowing discord and hatred under the pretext of begging for money—well, then . . ."

"Well, then?" Anne of Austria cried proudly, thereby provoking the storm.

"Well, then," the young man snapped resolutely, "I will expel Madame de Chevreuse from the kingdom, and, along with her, all purveyors of secrets and mysteries."

Philip hadn't calculated the impact of that terrible statement, or perhaps he wanted to judge its effect. He was like a man, who, suffering from a chronic pain and trying to break the monotony of his suffering, fingers his wound in order to produce acute anguish.

Anne of Austria nearly fainted. Her eyes, open but vacant, stopped seeing for a moment. She held out her arms to her other son, who embraced her instantly and unhesitatingly, and without fear of annoying the king.

"Sire," she murmured, "you are treating your mother cruelly."

"In what way, madame?" he replied. "I am speaking only about Madame de Chevreuse, and would my mother prefer her to the security of my person and the security of the state? Well, then! I tell you that Madame de Chevreuse came to France in order to borrow money. She found none and so she turned to Monsieur Fouquet, trying to sell him a certain secret."

"A certain secret?!" cried Anne of Austria.

"Concerning supposed thefts that the superintendent had allegedly committed. He was innocent, and he indignantly showed her the door. Monsieur Fouquet preferred the king's esteem to any complicity with intriguers. So Madame de Chevreuse sold the secret to Monsieur Colbert. But she is insatiable, and it wasn't enough for her to extort a hundred thousand crowns from that clerk. So she tried to go higher, looking for deeper sources. . . . Isn't that true, madame?"

"You know everything, sire," said the queen, more worried than irritated.

Philip went on: "Now, I have the right to resent that fury, who comes to my court and plots to dishonor some people and ruin others. If God endured certain crimes and hid them in the shadow of His clemency, I refuse to let Madame de Chevreuse counteract the Lord's designs."

Those last few sentences disturbed the queen mother so profoundly that Philip felt sorry for her. He tenderly took hold of her hand and kissed it. She didn't sense that this kiss, given despite the revolts and rancors of the heart, contained forgiveness for eight years of horrible suffering.

Philip let a moment of silence overwhelm his emotions. Then he spoke with something like merriment. "We won't be leaving today. I've got a plan." And turning toward the door, he hoped to see Aramis, whose absence was beginning to weigh on the prince.

The queen mother wanted to take her leave.

"Wait, Mother," said her son. "I'd like you to make peace with Monsieur Fouquet."

"But I don't have anything against him. I was simply frightened by his lavishness."

"We'll put some order to his expenditures, and we'll have nothing from him but his good qualities."

"Just what is Your Majesty looking for?" asked Henriette, seeing the king glancing at the door. She wanted to shoot an arrow into his heart, for she assumed that he was expecting Mademoiselle de la Vallière, or a letter from her.

"Sister," said the young man. He had read her mind, thanks to his marvelous acumen, which fortune would henceforth be letting him exercise. "Sister, I am waiting for an extremely distinguished man, an eminently skillful adviser. I want to introduce him to you and recommend him to your good graces. Ah! Do come in, Monsieur d'Artagnan."

D'Artagnan stepped into the room. "What does His Majesty wish?"

"Tell me, where is your friend, the Bishop of Vannes?"

"But, sire—"

"I'm expecting him, but he hasn't shown up. Please find him."

For an instant, d'Artagnan was stupefied. But then, remembering that Aramis had left Vaux on a secret mission for the king, d'Artagnan concluded that the king wanted to guard the secret.

"Sire," he responded, "does Your Majesty absolutely wish to see Monsieur d'Herblay?"

" 'Absolutely' isn't the word. I don't need him so greatly. But if he were found—"

I guessed it, d'Artagnan thought to himself.

"This Monsieur d'Herblay," asked Anne of Austria, "isn't he the Bishop of Vannes?"

"Yes, madame."

"And he's a friend of Monsieur Fouquet?"

"Yes, madame, a former musketeer."

Anne of Austria blushed.

"One of those four brave men who once worked so many miracles?"

The queen deeply regretted that she had asked. Trying to maintain her dignity, she changed the subject. "Whatever your choice, sire, I consider it excellent."

The visitors all bowed.

"You will see," Philip went on, "the depth of Cardinal Richelieu more than the avarice of Monsieur Colbert."

"A prime minister, sire?" The king's younger brother was afraid.

"I'll explain. But it's odd that Monsieur d'Herblay hasn't come."

He called out: "Notify Monsieur Fouquet that I wish to speak to him. . . . Oh, don't leave, you can all remain."

Monsieur de Saint-Aignan returned with satisfactory news from the queen, who kept to her bed only as a precaution and to have the strength to comply with all the king's wishes.

While the servants were searching for Monsieur Fouquet and Aramis everywhere, the new king peacefully continued his tests; and everyone—family, officers, valets—recognized the king by his air, his voice, his habits.

For his part, Philip, applying Aramis's faithful note and depiction to each face, behaved in such a way as to prevent the arousal of any suspicion in the people surrounding him.

Nothing could worry the usurper. With what strange facility had Providence reversed the highest fortune in the world and replaced it with the humblest!

Philip admired God's goodness toward him and seconded it with all the resources of his admirable nature. Yet at times he felt something like a shadow flitting across the rays of his new glory. Aramis did not appear.

The conversation had languished in the royal family. A preoccupied Philip neglected to dismiss his brother and Madame

Henriette. They were amazed, and they were gradually losing patience. Anne of Austria leaned toward her son and murmured something in Spanish. Philip didn't know a word of that language—he turned pale before this unexpected obstacle. But as if the spirit of the imperturbable Aramis had cloaked him with his infallibility, an unabashed Philip rose to his feet.

"Well? Answer me," said Anne of Austria.

"What's all that noise?" asked Philip, turning toward the door of the secret staircase.

They heard shouts: "Here, here! A few more steps, sire!"

"Monsieur Fouquet's voice!" cried d'Artagnan, who was standing next to the queen mother.

"Monsieur d'Herblay can't be far off," Philip added.

But then the young man saw something that he had never expected to see this closely.

All eyes were glued to the doorway through which Monsieur Fouquet was about to enter. But he wasn't the man who came in.

Horrible cries broke out from every nook and cranny—excruciating cries uttered by the king and those around him.

Few if any men, even those whose destinies contain so many bizarre elements and wonderful experiences, are given a chance to contemplate anything like the spectacle offered by the royal chamber at that moment.

The half-closed shutters admitted only an uncertain light softened by big velvet curtains with a thick silk lining.

In that mellow penumbra, all eyes were gradually dilated, and each person saw the others with trust rather than vision. Nevertheless, in such circumstances, people manage to catch every last detail, and the new object that presents itself appears luminous, as if lit by the sun.

That was what happened to Louis XIV when he emerged, pale and frowning, through the doorway of the secret staircase.

Behind him Fouquet appeared, his face stamped with severity and sadness.

The queen mother, perceiving Louis XIV while holding Philip's hand, wailed as if seeing a ghost.

The king's younger brother, knocked for a loop, kept turning his head from one king to the other.

His wife stepped forward, believing that she saw her brother-in-law reflected in a mirror.

And, indeed, the illusion was possible.

The two princes, trembling, with their faces no longer composed (We renounce depicting Philip's dreadful shock), were each clenching a convulsive fist. They sized each other up, and their eyes were like swords thrust in the soul. Wordless, gasping, bending forward, they seemed about to pounce on an enemy.

This astounding resemblance of faces, gestures, and size was completed by the same chance costume, for Louis XIV had put on a violet velvet suit; and this perfect similarity left Anne of Austria reeling. However, she still didn't guess the truth. There are calamities that no one can accept; instead, we blame them on the supernatural, on the impossible.

Louis hadn't counted on these hurdles. He had expected to be recognized the instant he entered. As the living sun, he couldn't endure the slightest suspicion of parity with anyone at all. He refused to admit that any torch would be outshone by him the moment his vanquishing rays burst forth. And so he was more terrified than anyone else at the sight of Philip; and his silence and immobility constituted the brief meditation and tranquillity that precede a violent fit of anger.

But Fouquet! Who could paint his stupor and amazement in front of the living portrait of his master?! Fouquet thought that Aramis was right, that this newcomer was as purebred a king as the other. Having refused to participate in the coup d'état so skillfully engineered by the general of the Jesuits, Fouquet would have to be an enthusiastic fool, unworthy of ever dipping his hands in politics.

And then it was the blood of Louis XIII that Fouquet was sacrificing to the blood of Louis XIII. It was to an egotistical ambition that he was sacrificing a noble ambition. It was to the right of keeping that he was sacrificing the right of having. The extent of his mistake was revealed to him by the mere sight of the pretender.

Everything haunting Fouquet was lost on the others. He had five minutes to focus his mind on this point of conscience. Five minutes were five centuries, during which the two kings and their family barely had time to recover from the terrible shock.

D'Artagnan, his back to the wall, his face toward Fouquet, his fist on his forehead, his eyes gaping, wondered about the cause of such a wondrous spectacle. He couldn't have promptly explained why he doubted, but he certainly knew that he had good reason to doubt, and that this encounter of the two Louis XIVs contained all the problems that had made the musketeer so suspicious of Aramis during these last few days.

Nevertheless, such thoughts were enveloped in a dense mist. The actors of this scene appeared to be floating in the vapors of a heavy awakening.

Suddenly, Louis XIV, more impatient, and more accustomed to commanding, dashed over to one of the shutters and opened it while tearing away the curtain. A flood of vivid light swept into the room, pushing Philip all the way back to the alcove.

Louis, ardently seizing upon that movement, addressed the queen: "Mother, don't you recognize your son? Everyone else here has repudiated their king!"

Anne of Austria shuddered as she lifted her arm toward the heavens, unable to articulate a single word.

"Mother," said Philip in a calm voice, "don't you recognize your son?"

And this time, it was Louis who recoiled.

As for Anne of Austria, with remorse striking her mind and her heart, she lost her balance. Since everyone was too petrified to help her, she collapsed in an armchair, heaving a feeble sigh.

Louis couldn't endure this spectacle and this affront. He bounded over toward d'Artagnan, who was now so dizzy that he staggered, barely grazing the door for support.

"Musketeer!" cried Louis. "Help me! Look at our faces and see who is paler—he or I?"

That shout awoke d'Artagnan and stirred the fiber of obedience in his heart. He shook his head, and, unhesitating, he strode over to Philip and placed his hand on the prince's shoulder. "Monsieur, you are my prisoner!"

Philip didn't look, he didn't stir, he was virtually nailed to the floor, and his eyes were glued on his brother, the king. Philip's sublime silence reproached him for all his past misery, all his future torment. The king felt powerless against this language of the soul. He lowered his eyes and precipitously left with his younger brother and his sister-in-law, forgetting his mother, who was stretched out motionless. She was just three paces away from her son and she was letting him be condemned to death a second time.

Philip came over to her and murmured in a soft and nobly moved voice: "If I were not your son, I would curse my mother for having made me so unhappy."

D'Artagnan felt a shiver in the marrow of his bones. He respectfully saluted the young prince, and, half-leaning toward him, he said, "Forgive me, monseigneur, I am simply a soldier, and my oath of allegiance is to the man who has just left this room."

"Thank you, Monsieur d'Artagnan. But what has become of Monsieur d'Herblay?"

"Monsieur d'Herblay is safe, monseigneur," replied a voice behind them. "And so long as I am alive and free, no one will harm a hair on his head."

"Monsieur Fouquet!" said the prince with a melancholy smile.

"Forgive me, monseigneur," said Fouquet, kneeling down. "But the man who has just left was my guest."

Philip sighed. "There are brave friends and good hearts here. They make me regret this world. Let's go, Monsieur d'Artagnan, I'll follow you."

Just as the captain of the musketeers was about to depart, Colbert appeared, handed d'Artagnan an order from the king, and withdrew.

D'Artagnan read the document and crumpled it furiously.

"What is it?" asked the prince.

"Read it, monseigneur."

Philip read the words that had been hastily jotted down by Louis XIV:

> Monsieur d'Artagnan will conduct the prisoner to the Îles Sainte-Marguerite. There he will cover the prisoner's face with an iron visor, which the prisoner cannot remove under pain of death.

"That's just," said Philip with resignation. "I'm ready."

"Aramis was right," Fouquet whispered to the musketeer. "This one is the king, as much the other."

"More so!" retorted d'Artagnan. "All he needs is you and I."

25
Porthos Believes He Is Pursuing a Dukedom

With their speed, Aramis and Porthos, taking advantage of the head start granted them by Fouquet, were a credit to the French cavalry.

Porthos did not understand for what kind of mission he was being forced to gallop so swiftly; but since he saw Aramis fiercely spurring on his mount, he, Porthos, furiously spurred on his own.

Soon they had put twelve leagues between themselves and Vaux. Now they had to change horses and organize a kind of stage service. It was during a relay that Porthos discreetly tried to question Aramis.

"Shush!" replied Aramis. "All you need to know is that our fate depends on our speed."

As if Porthos were still the penniless musketeer of 1626, he charged forward. That magic word "fate" still means something to the human ear. It means "enough" for those who have nothing; it means "too much" for those who have enough.

"They're gonna make me a duke," said Porthos aloud. He was talking to himself.

"That's possible." Aramis smiled in his fashion as Porthos rushed ahead of him. Aramis's head was ablaze. His physical action had not yet caught up with his mental action. All roaring frenzies, all throbbing toothaches, all mortal threats chewed and twisted and grumbled in the mind of the vanquished prelate. His face revealed the highly visible traces of that brutal combat. Free at least to abandon himself to momentary impressions on the highway, Aramis did not fail to swear at every stumbling of his steed, at every bump in the road. Pale, at times sweating torrents, at times dry and icy, he whipped his horse and bloodied its flank. Porthos, who was not famed for his sensitivity, moaned and groaned about it.

And so they raced for eight whole hours and arrived in Orléans at four P.M. Aramis, racking his brain, felt that no one could possibly reach them. No troops capable of seizing him and Porthos could conceivably find enough relays to cover forty leagues in eight hours. Thus, even if someone were pursuing them—which was not necessarily the case—the fugitives had an advance of a good five hours.

Aramis figured that while it wouldn't be imprudent to rest, it would be more useful to forge ahead. If they flew another twenty leagues, devoured another twenty leagues, then nobody, not even d'Artagnan, could outstrip the enemies of the king.

So Aramis upset Porthos by climbing back on his mount. They galloped until seven in the evening, reaching the final post before Blois. But as their diabolical fate would have it, this post had no horses.

The prelate wondered by what infernal machination his foes had managed to deprive him of the means to continue his journey—Aramis, who did not view chance as a god, who found a cause for everything. The bishop preferred to believe that the postmaster, at such a time, in such a countryside, had received an order from a higher authority, an order to stop the kingmaker in his tracks.

But just as he was about to exact either an explanation or a horse, he had an idea. He recalled that the Count de La Fère resided in the area. "I'm not traveling," said Aramis, "and I'm not demanding horses for a coach. Give me two horses so that I can visit my friend, a nobleman who lives nearby."

"What nobleman?" asked the postmaster.

"The Count de La Fère."

"Oh!" replied the postmaster, respectfully baring his head. "A worthy nobleman. But much as I wish to be agreeable to him, I can't give you two horses. All the horses in my post are reserved by the Duke de Beaufort."

"Ah!" Aramis was disappointed.

"However," the postmaster went on, "if you wouldn't mind riding in a small cart that I've got, I'll harness an old, blind horse who's on his last legs. He'll take you to the Count de La Fère."

"That's worth a louis," said Aramis.

"No, monsieur, it's never worth more than a crown. That's the amount I get from Monsieur Grimaud, the count's steward, whenever he rents my cart. And I wouldn't like to have the count reproach me for overcharging a friend of his."

"As you wish," said Aramis. "And especially as the count wishes, for I wouldn't care to offend him. You'll have your crown, but I have the right to give you a louis for your excellent idea."

"No doubt about it!" replied the delighted postmaster. And he personally hitched his old jade to the creaking cart.

Meanwhile, Porthos was behaving strangely. He imagined he had discovered the secret. And he felt overjoyed: first of all, he was particularly delighted at the prospect of visiting Athos; and second, he hoped to find both a good supper and a good bed.

After harnessing the horse, the postmaster had one of his assistants drive the strangers to the Count de La Fère. Porthos, sitting in the back with Aramis, whispered to him, "I understand."

"Aha!" countered Aramis. "And what do you understand, old friend?"

"The king is sending us to offer Athos an important project."

"Pooh!" said Aramis.

"Don't tell me anything!" his worthy companion added, trying to balance his weight over bumps and jolts. "Don't tell me anything—I'll guess it."

"Well, go ahead, my friend, just keep guessing."

They arrived at Athos's home at nine P.M., in magnificent moonlight. This admirable clarity aggravated Aramis to the same degree that it left Porthos speechless. Aramis expressed something of his annoyance, and Porthos answered: "Fine! I can guess! This is a secret mission."

Those were his last words in the cart; he was interrupted by the driver. "Gentlemen, we are here."

Porthos and Aramis climbed down in front of the gates of the small château. And that's where we're going to find Athos and Raoul de Bragelonne, both of whom had disappeared after the exposure of Mademoiselle de la Vallière's infidelity.

If there is one mighty truth in the world, it is as follows: Each great sorrow contains the seed of its own consolation.

Indeed, Raoul's painful wound had brought him closer to his father, and goodness only knows how sweet the consolation was that came from Athos's eloquent lips and his generous heart.

The wound had not yet healed. But by conversing with his son and sharing something of his own life, Athos got him to endure a crucial lesson: namely, that the grief of this first experience of infidelity is necessary to any human existence, and that no one has ever loved without this adversity. Raoul listened, but he often didn't hear. In a keenly smitten heart, nothing can replace the thought and the memory of the beloved.

Raoul would then respond to his father: "Sir, everything you say is true. I certainly believe that no heart has been injured as much as yours. But you're too intelligent, you've been through too many ordeals, not to permit weakness in a soldier who's suffering for the first time. I'm paying a tribute that I won't pay twice. Allow me to plunge so deeply into my sorrow that I will forget myself totally, that I will drown even my reason."

"Raoul! Raoul!"

"Listen, sir. I will never get accustomed to the thought that Louise, the most chaste and most innocent of women, could have so cowardly deceived a man as honest and loving as I am. I will never be able to see that good, sweet face change into a hypocritical and lascivious face. Louise is lost! Louise is vile! Ah! Sir! That's far crueler for me than my being abandoned and miserable!"

Athos resorted to a time-tested remedy. He defended Louise against Raoul and justified her perfidiousness with her love. "A woman who yields to the king because he is the king would deserve to be called treacherous. But Louise loves Louis. They are both young, they are both forgetful. He's forgotten his rank, and she's forgotten her oaths. Love absolves everything, Raoul. Those two young people love each other freely and truly."

Having thrust this blade into Raoul, Athos would sigh as he watched him stagger under the cruel wound and flee into the depths of the forest or into his room, from which he would emerge an hour later: pale, trembling, but subdued. Returning to his father with a smile, Raoul kissed his hand, like a beaten dog muzzling his master in order to make up for his guilt. Raoul would make up only for his weakness and confess only his pain.

That was how the days wore by after the scene in which Athos had so violently agitated the king's indomitable pride. When conversing with Raoul, Athos never alluded to that scene, he never supplied him with details of that vigorous sortie, which might have consoled the young man by showing his rival at a disadvantage. Athos didn't want the offended lover to forget his respect for the king.

And Raoul de Bragelonne—ardent, furious, somber—would denigrate royal statements, deprecate the equivocal faith that certain madmen draw from a promise made by the throne. He would pass over two centuries with the speed of a bird flying over a strait when crossing from one continent to the next, and he would go so far as to predict an age in which kings would seem less than other men.

And whenever he mouthed such words, his father would reply in a serene and persuasive voice: "You're right, Raoul. Everything you foresee will come true. Kings will lose their prestige just as stars fade after living their lives. But by the time that day arrives, Raoul, you and I will be dead. Now, always remember what I say: In this world, everybody—men, women, and kings—must live in the present. We cannot live in the future except for God."

That was what they were discussing, as usual, when striding through the park, along the lengthy row of lindens. All at once, they heard the bell that normally served to announce a meal or a visitor. Mechanically, without attaching too much importance to the ringing, Athos and his son doubled back, and, upon reaching the start of the path, they found Porthos and Aramis.

26
The Final Farewells

Raoul let out a joyful cry and tenderly threw his arms around Porthos. Aramis and Athos embraced like old men. And since this hug was virtually a question for Aramis, he said, "My friend, we won't be staying here for long."

"Ah!" said the count.

"Long enough," Porthos interrupted, "to tell you about my bonanza."

"Ah?" said Raoul.

Athos gazed silently at Aramis, whose gloominess had struck him as out of harmony with Porthos's good news.

"What kind of bonanza? Tell me." Raoul smiled.

"The king is making me a duke," our good Porthos mysteriously whispered into the young man's ear. "A duke by a royal warrant."

However, Porthos's asides had always been raucous enough to be heard by all and sundry. His murmurs were more forceful than an ordinary roar.

Athos heard him and he emitted an exclamation that made Aramis shudder.

Aramis took Athos's arm and asked Porthos to give them a few moments of privacy.

"My dear Athos," Aramis told the count, "I'm prostrate with grief."

"Grief?" cried the count. "What's wrong, old friend?"

"I'll sum it up for you in a few words. I've plotted against the king. The conspiracy failed. And they're probably hunting for me now."

"A conspiracy? . . . Hunting you? . . . My God! What are you saying?"

"A dismal truth. I'm doomed!"

"But what about Porthos? . . . That title of duke? . . . What does it all mean?"

"That's the cause of my worst distress, my deepest wound. I believed that my success was a sure thing, and so I dragged Porthos into my plot. He gave me his all—as you know he does—without knowing anything. And now he's as compromised and as doomed as I am."

"My God!" And Athos turned toward Porthos, who smiled at them agreeably.

"You have to understand everything," Aramis went on. "Hear me out!" And he told him the entire story, which we are acquainted with. A few times during the report, Athos felt his forehead get sweaty.

"It is a grand idea," he said, "but it was a grand mistake."

"For which I'm being punished, Athos."

"That's why I won't tell you all my thoughts."

"Tell me."

"It's a crime."

"A capital crime, I know. Lèse-majesté."

"Porthos! Poor Porthos!"

"What do you expect me to do? Success, I tell you, was certain!"

"Monsieur Fouquet is an honest man."

"And I'm a fool for having such bad judgment!" said Aramis. "Oh, human wisdom! Oh, the immense millstone that grinds the world—and then one day it gets stuck on a grain of sand that somehow drops into the gears!"

"Calling it a diamond would be more accurate, Aramis. Oh well, the fat's in the fire. What are you planning to do?"

"I'm taking Porthos along. The king will never believe that this worthy man could have acted in innocence. He will never believe that Porthos thought he was serving the king by behaving as he did. His head would pay for my mistake. I don't want that to happen."

"Where are you taking him?"

"First to Belle-Île. It's an invincible refuge. Next, I've got a boat to head out to sea—maybe to England, where I know a lot of people. . . ."

"You? In England?"

"Yes. Or maybe Spain, where I have even more connections—"

"If you take Porthos into exile, you'll ruin him—the king will confiscate all his worldly goods!"

"Everything's been taken care of. Once I'm in Spain, I'll

manage to make up with Louis XIV and get Porthos back in the king's good graces."

"I see that you've got influence, Aramis!" said Athos discreetly.

"A great deal of influence. And it's in the service of my friends, Athos my friend."

Those words were underscored by a sincere pressure of the hand.

"Thank you," the count responded.

"And since we've reached this point," said Aramis, "you too are a malcontent; both you and Raoul have grievances against the king. Follow my example. Come to Belle-Île. Then we'll see what's what. I guarantee on my honor that within a month war will break out between France and Spain. The issue will be this son of Louis XIII—the son who is also an infante and whom France has inhumanely incarcerated. Now, since Louis XIV won't go to war for that reason, I guarantee that a transaction will take place, and the results will be as follows: Porthos and I will be made Spanish grandees, and you will be awarded a duchy in France—you who are already a Spanish grandee. What do you say?"

"I say no. I'd much rather have something to reproach the king for. It's a natural pride of my breed to claim superiority over royal blood. If I go along with your proposal, I'll be obligated to the king. I would certainly gain in this world, but I would lose in terms of my conscience. Thank you but no thanks."

"Fine, then let me ask you for two things. The first is your absolution."

"Oh, I give it to you so long as you really wanted to defend the weak, oppressed victim against his oppressor."

"That's enough for me," replied Aramis, his blush fading in the night. "And second, please give me your two best horses so that I can reach the next post. I was told that the horses were reserved for Monsieur, the Duke de Beaufort, who is traveling in this vicinity."

"You will have my two best horses, Aramis, and I recommend Porthos to you."

"Oh, don't be afraid! One last word: Do you feel I'm doing what's right for him?"

"Since the die is cast, yes. For the king would never forgive him. And besides, whatever he may say, you've got a mainstay in Monsieur Fouquet. He'll never abandon you since he's deeply compromised too, despite his heroic actions."

"You're right. Going straight to sea would brand me as scared and guilty. That's why I'm remaining on French soil. However, Belle-Île is whatever soil I want it to be—English, Spanish, or Roman. The whole thing hinges on whatever flag will fly."

"What do you mean?"

"I was the one who fortified Belle-Île, and no one will storm it so long as I defend it. And besides, as you've just said, Monsieur Fouquet is there. No one will attack Belle-Île without Fouquet's signature."

"That's true. Nevertheless, be wary. The king is cunning, and he's powerful."

Aramis smiled.

"I recommend Porthos to you," the count repeated with a cold insistence.

"Whatever I achieve, Count," replied Aramis in the same tone, "our brother Porthos will likewise achieve."

Athos bowed as he shook Aramis's hand and then embraced Porthos effusively.

"I was born lucky, wasn't I?" a joyful Porthos murmured as he wrapped himself in his cloak.

"Let's go, old friend," said Aramis.

Raoul had gone on ahead to issue orders and have the two horses saddled.

The group had already split up. Athos saw that his two friends were about to depart. Something hazy passed before his eyes and weighed on his heart.

That's strange! he thought to himself. Why do I feel an urge to embrace Porthos again?

At that instant, Porthos turned and headed toward his old friend, his arms outstretched. That last embrace was youthfully tender, as in the days when their hearts had been hot and their lives happy.

And then Porthos mounted his horse. Aramis also turned around and threw his arms around Athos.

The latter watched them as they galloped along the highway, their shadows elongated in their white cloaks. Like two phantoms, they seemed to grow as they floated above the ground; and they didn't disappear in the mist, they vanished in a dip in the road. At the far end of the vista, they surged upward, virtually melting into the clouds.

Thereupon, Athos, with a heavy heart, turned toward the house while saying to his son, "Raoul, something tells me that this was the last time I'll ever see those two men."

"I'm not surprised, sir, that you think so. I feel the same way—I don't think I'll ever see Monsieur du Vallon and Monsieur d'Herblay again!"

"Oh c'mon!" said the count. "Something else is eating away at you. You're looking at the gloomy side of everything. But you're young, and if you never see old friends again, it'll mean that they're no longer in the world, whereas you've still got a lot of years ahead of you. I, however . . ."

Raoul gently nodded and leaned against the count. Neither man could come up with a single word even though their hearts were ready to explode. All at once, they were distracted by the sounds of horses and human voices at the far end of the road.

Mounted torchbearers joyfully brandished their torches against the roadside trees, galloping back from time to time to avoid losing the riders following them.

In the middle of the night, the flames, the din, the dust kicked up by a dozen richly caparisoned steeds contrasted strangely with the muffled and funereal disappearance of those two shadows, Porthos and Aramis.

Athos kept striding toward the house. But he hadn't even reached his lawn when the entrance gate seemed to burst into flame. All the torches halted and lit up the road.

A shout echoed: "The Duke de Beaufort!"

And Athos leaped toward his front door.

The duke had already dismounted and was scanning his surroundings.

"Here I am, monseigneur," said Athos.

"Ah! Good evening, dear count," the duke replied with the

frank cordiality that endeared him to everyone. "Is it too late for a friendly visit?"

"Not at all, monseigneur. Please come in."

And with the duke leaning on Athos's arm, they stepped inside the house, followed by Raoul, who strode modestly and respectfully among the duke's men, some of whom were Raoul's friends.

27
The Duke de Beaufort

The duke turned just as Raoul, leaving him alone with Athos, closed the door and prepared to go to another room with the officers.

"Is that the young man," the duke asked, "of whom the prince sings the praises?"

"Yes, monseigneur, that's my son."

"The boy's quite a soldier! He's not *de trop*. Let him remain, Count."

"Stay here, Raoul," said Athos. "Monseigneur permits it."

"Why, he's certainly tall and handsome!" the duke went on. "Will you let him serve me if I ask you, monsieur?"

"How do you mean that, monseigneur?" asked Athos.

"Well, I've come here to make my farewells."

"Your farewells, monseigneur?"

"Exactly. Don't you have any notion of what's to become of me?"

"Why, what you've always been, monseigneur: a valiant prince and an excellent nobleman."

"I'm about to become an African prince and a Bedouin nobleman. The king is sending me to conquer the Arabs."

"What are you saying, monseigneur?"

"That's odd, isn't it? I, the Parisian par excellence; I, who've reigned over the Parisian suburbs and who am known as the king of Les Halles—I'm passing from Place Maubert to the minarets of Gigelli. The Frondeur has become an adventurer!"

"Oh, monseigneur! If it weren't you telling me this . . ."

"It wouldn't be credible, right? But believe me, and let us say farewell. This is what comes of being restored to favor."

"Favor!?"

"Yes. You're smiling? Ah, my dear count. Do you know why I accepted this honor? Do you really know?"

"Because Your Highness loves glory above anything else."

"Oh, no! It's not glorious at all to fire muskets at those savages. That's no glory for me, and I'll more likely find something very different. . . . But, listen carefully, my dear count. After all the bizarre roles that I've played during these past fifty years, I wanted and I still want to give my life this final challenge. After all, you must admit that my life has been quite strange. I was born the son of a king, I've waged war against kings, I'm considered one of the powers of the century, I've held on to my rank, I feel the spirit of Henry IV inside me, I'm the Grand Admiral of France—and now I'm supposed to get killed in Gigelli among those Turks and Moors and Saracens."

"Monseigneur, you have a curious way of dwelling on this subject," said a troubled Athos. "Why do you think that such a brilliant destiny will be snuffed so miserably?"

"You're a fair and straightforward man, Count. Do you really believe that if I'm going to Africa for such a ludicrous reason, I won't try to come out of it without being ridiculed? Won't I be talked about? There is the prince, Monsieur de Turenne, and several others of my contemporaries—while I'm the Grand Admiral of France, the son of Henry IV, the king of Paris. So if I'm talked about nowadays, do you think I've got any choice but to let myself get killed? Damn it! People will talk about me, I tell you! And I'll be killed one way or other. If not there, then somewhere else."

"Come on, monseigneur," replied Athos. "You're going too far! And you've never gone too far in anything but bravery!"

"Damn it, dear friend! It's very brave to endure scurvy, dysentery, locusts, and poisoned arrows like my ancestor, Saint Louis. Do you know that those savages still use poison arrows? And besides, you know me—I've been thinking about it all for a long time now. And you know that when I want to do something, I do it very intensely."

"You wanted to escape from Vincennes, monseigneur."

"Oh, you did help me with that, my master. Incidentally, I've been looking every which way but I don't see my old friend Monsieur Vaugrimaud. How is he?"

Athos smiled: "Monsieur Vaugrimaud is still Your Highness's very respectful servant."

"I've got a hundred pistoles for him here as a legacy; my will's been draw up, Count."

"Ah! Monseigneur! Monseigneur!"

"And you understand that if his name appeared in my will—" The duke burst out laughing. Then, turning to Raoul, who'd been lost in a deep reverie throughout this conversation, the duke said, "Young man, I know of a certain Vouvray wine that's to be found here, and I believe . . ."

Raoul hurried out to get the wine. Meanwhile, the duke took Athos's hand. "What do you plan to do with your son?"

"Nothing for the moment, monseigneur."

"Ah, yes! I know! Since the king's passion for . . . Mademoiselle de la Vallière."

"Yes, monseigneur."

"So it's all true? . . . I think I knew her. I don't believe she's beautiful. . . ."

"No, monseigneur," said Athos.

"Do you know whom she reminds me of?"

"She reminds Your Highness of someone?"

"She reminds me of a rather disagreeable girl whose mother lived in Les Halles."

"Aha!" Athos smiled.

"The good old days!" the duke added. "Yes, Mademoiselle de la Vallière reminds me of that girl."

"She had a son, didn't she?"

"I think so," replied the duke with insouciant simplicity and complaisant forgetfulness—nor could any words describe his tone and vocal quality. "Now, here we have poor Raoul, who is your son, isn't he?"

"Yes, he's my son, monseigneur."

"And the poor boy has been dismissed by the monarch and he's sulking?"

"Worse than that, monseigneur. He's abstaining."

"You're going to let the boy go rusty—that would be wrong. Count, let me have him."

"I want to keep him here, monseigneur. He's all I've got left in the world, and so long as he wants to stay . . ."

"Fine, fine," replied the duke. "However, I'd set him to rights very soon. I can assure you that he's got the stuff of a Marshal of France, and I've seen quite a lot of marshals made of that stuff."

"That could be, monseigneur. But it's the king who appoints the Marshals of France, and Raoul will never accept anything from the king."

They broke off because Raoul was returning. He was preceded by Grimaud, whose still steady hands carried a tray with a glass and a bottle of the duke's favorite wine. Upon seeing his old protégé, the duke emitted a cry of pleasure. "Grimaud! Good evening, Grimaud! How are you?"

The servant bowed deeply; he was just as happy as the noble visitor.

"Two friends!" said the duke, vigorously shaking Grimaud's shoulder.

Grimaud returned the greeting more profoundly and more joyously.

"What's this I see, Count? A single goblet?"

"I don't drink with Your Highness unless Your Highness invites me to join him," said Athos with noble humility.

"Damn it! You're right to supply only one glass. We'll both drink out of it like two brothers in arms. You first, Count."

"Please do me the great honor," said Athos, gently nudging back the goblet.

"You're a delightful friend!" replied the duke, who had a sip, then passed the golden goblet to his companion. "But that's not all!" he went on. "I'm still thirsty, and I'd like to honor this handsome fellow who's standing here. I bring happiness, Viscount," he said to Raoul. "Wish for anything when you drink from my goblet, and damn me if I won't make your wish come true!"

He held out the goblet to Raoul, who swiftly moistened his lips. He said, equally promptly: "I did make a wish, monseigneur." The young man's eyes blazed with a somber fire, the blood had risen to his cheeks. His very smile frightened Athos.

"And what did you wish for?" asked the duke, flopping down into an armchair. He then handed Grimaud the bottle and a purse.

"Monseigneur," said Raoul, "do you promise to make my wish come true?"

"By God! I promise!"

"I wish to accompany you to Gigelli, monseigneur!"

Athos blanched, unable to hide his agitation.

The duke looked at him as if helping his friend to parry that unforeseen stroke.

"That would be difficult, my dear viscount, very difficult!" he murmured.

"Forgive me, monseigneur. That was indiscreet of me," Raoul spoke on in a firm voice. "But since you yourself invited me to make a wish . . ."

"A wish to leave me," said Athos.

"Oh, sir! How can you believe that?"

"Well, damn me," cried the duke, "he's right—the little viscount. What's he going to do around here? He'll rot with grief."

Raoul turned crimson.

The hotheaded duke went on: "War is destruction. You gain everything; you lose only one thing: life. So much the worse!"

"You mean memory," Raoul exclaimed. "So much the better!"

Upon seeing Athos stand up and open a window, the young man regretted that he had blurted out his feelings. The father's actions must have hidden some deep emotions. Raoul hurried over to the count. But Athos had already swallowed his anguish, for he reappeared in the light with a serene and impassive face.

"Fine!" said the duke. "Let's have it! Is he coming with me or not? If he does come with me, Count, he'll be my aide-de-camp, my son!"

"Monseigneur!" exclaimed Raoul, bending his knee.

"Monseigneur!" exclaimed Athos, taking the duke's hand. "Raoul will do as he wishes—!"

"Oh, no, sir!" the young man broke in. "It's totally up to you!"

"Damn it all!" the duke cried in turn. "It's up to neither the count nor the viscount. I'm taking the boy with me. The navy offers a superb future, my friend!"

Raoul smiled so sadly that this time it broke Athos's heart. Athos glared at Raoul. The boy caught his father's drift. He calmed down and kept watch on his tongue: not another word escaped him.

Noticing how late it was, the duke stood up and spoke very quickly: "I'm in a hurry. But if anyone told me that I've wasted my time chatting with a friend, I'd say that I've gained a fine recruit."

"Forgive me, monseigneur," Raoul interrupted. "Please don't say that to the king, it's not the king whom I'll be serving."

"Huh, my friend? Then whom will you be serving? The days are past when you might have said, 'I belong to the Duke de Beaufort.' No! Nowadays, great or small, we all belong to the king. If you're going to serve on my ships, my dear viscount, you can't have it both ways. It's the king whom you'll be serving."

With a sort of impatient smile, Athos was waiting for Raoul—the king's rival and intractable foe—to answer the duke's perplexing question. The father hoped that this obstacle would be too big for the son's desire. He nearly thanked the duke, whose lightheartedness and generous reflection were interfering with the departure of Athos's son, his only joy.

But Raoul, still firm and tranquil, said: "Monseigneur, I've mentally resolved your objection. I'll serve on your vessels since you're doing me the honor of taking me along. However, I'll be serving a master who's more powerful than the king—I'll be serving God!"

"What do you mean?" Athos and the duke asked simultaneously.

"My intention is to take vows and become a Knight of Malta," said the Viscount of Bragelonne, articulating his words one by one—words that were icier than the drops falling from bare trees after a blizzard.

Under that last blow, Athos reeled and the duke was deeply

shaken. Grimaud moaned obscurely, dropping the bottle, which shattered on the carpet, but no one paid it any heed. The duke eyed the young man, reading the fire of resolution in his features even though Raoul's eyes were cast down. It was a determination to which everything had to submit.

As for Athos, he was well acquainted with his son's tender and inflexible soul. He knew he couldn't make that soul deviate from the fateful path that Raoul had just chosen. Athos shook the hand held out by the duke.

"Count," said the duke, "I'm leaving for Toulon in two days. Could you come to Paris and let me know your decision?"

"Monseigneur, I'll have the honor of thanking you for all your generosity," replied the count.

"And," added the duke, "please bring along the viscount whether or not he resolves to follow me. He has my word, and I ask him only for yours."

Having poured a little balm on the wound in that paternal heart, the duke pulled old Grimaud's ear. The servant's eyes blinked more than usual as the duke rejoined his escort in the courtyard. The horses, relaxed and refreshed by that beautiful night, soon put a great distance between the château and their master. Athos and Raoul were alone, face-to-face.

The clock struck eleven P.M.

Both father and son maintained a silence that, as any intelligent observer would have sensed, was filled with cries and sobs. But both men were such that any emotions would have been lost forever once they had resolved to compress them in their hearts. And so they spent the hour before midnight wordless and almost breathless. Only the striking clock indicated the length of this painful journey that their hearts undertook in the immensity of memories of the past and anxieties about the future.

Athos was the first to stand up. "It's getting late. . . . I'll see you tomorrow, Raoul."

His son got up in turn and embraced his father. The latter, holding him to his chest, said in a husky voice, "Two days from now, you'll have left me, left me forever, Raoul!"

"Sir," replied the young man, "I had made up my mind to

drive my sword through my heart. But you would have found that cowardly. So I gave up that plan. And, besides, we had to separate."

"When you go away, you'll be leaving me, Raoul."

"Hear me out, sir, I beg you. If I don't go away, I'll die here of pain and love. I know how little time I've got to keep living like this. Send me away quickly, sir, or you'll see me die like a coward before your very eyes—in your house. I can't help it, I don't have the strength. You can see that I've aged thirty years in the past month and that I'm at the end of my life."

"Then," Athos snapped coldly, "you're planning to get yourself killed in Africa? Just tell me. . . . Don't lie."

Raoul blanched and said nothing for two seconds, which were two hours of agony for his father. All at once, the son exclaimed: "Sir, I've promised to dedicate myself to God. In exchange for this sacrifice of my youth and my freedom, I will ask the Lord for only one thing: to preserve me for you, because you are the sole bond that still attaches me to the world. God alone can give me the strength to remember that I owe you everything and that nothing must come before you."

Tenderly hugging his son, Athos said: "You've just spoken like a man of honor. In two days we'll be seeing the Duke de Beaufort in Paris. And you will then do the right thing for yourself. You are free, Raoul. Farewell."

And Athos slowly trudged to his bedroom.

Raoul went out alone to the garden, where he spent the night on the path that was flanked by rows of linden trees.

28
Preparations for Departure

Athos didn't waste his time combating that unalterable resolution. During the two days granted by the duke, Athos focused all his energy on preparing the entire equipment for Raoul. The work was done chiefly by that good Grimaud, who instantly applied himself with the generosity and intelligence that he was known for. Athos ordered this worthy servant to head for Paris once the equipment was ready. To avoid making the duke cool his heels, or, at the very least, delaying Raoul if the duke noticed his absence, Athos and his son set out for Paris the day after the duke's visit.

It is easy to understand how upset the poor young man was at the thought of returning to Paris amid all the people who had known and loved him. Every face brought back suffering to this man who had suffered so harshly, brought back a circumstance of love to this man who had loved so deeply. Upon approaching Paris, Raoul felt as if were about to die. Once in Paris, he no longer really existed. When he arrived at de Guiche's residence, he was told that Monsieur de Guiche was at the Luxembourg Palace.

Raoul then rode to the palace, which he reached without suspecting that this was a place where Mademoiselle de la Vallière had lived. Here, the young man heard so much music and smelled so much perfume, he heard so much joyous laughter and saw so many dancing shadows. And had it not been for a charitable lady, who noticed his mournful pallor in a doorway, he would have spent only a few moments here, then left forever. However, as we have said, he kept to the first few antechambers simply to avoid dealing with all these happy people that he heard in the adjacent rooms.

A servant, who recognized him, asked him whether he wished to see Monsieur (the king's younger brother) or Madame (Monsieur's wife). Barely responding, Raoul collapsed upon a bench near the velvet doorway and gazed at a clock that had stopped an hour ago. The servant went away and was replaced by a more knowledgeable one, who asked Raoul whether to inform Monsieur de Guiche of his presence. This name did not arouse poor Raoul's attention. The persistent servant was explaining that de Guiche had invented a new game of lottery, which he was teaching the ladies.

Raoul, gaping like the absentminded figure of Theophrastus, failed to respond. But he was a shade sadder. With his head hanging, his legs sluggish, his mouth half-open to allow the passage of sighs, Raoul was thus forgotten in the antechamber, when, all at once, he heard a gown rustling past the door to a lateral salon that led to it. A young, pretty, mirthful woman, rebuking an officer as she emerged, chattered vivaciously.

The officer retorted with calm but firm words. It was more like a lovers' spat than a disagreement between members of the court, and the quarrel was stopped by a kiss on the lady's hand.

Suddenly, spotting Raoul, the lady held her tongue as she pushed away the officer. "Go away, Malicorne. I didn't realize there was someone here. Damn your eyes if anyone's heard us or seen us!"

Malicorne did in fact hurry off. The young woman then approached Raoul and bent over him, pouting playfully. "Monsieur is a gallant man, and, no doubt—" She broke off with a cry. "Raoul!" she exclaimed, blushing.

"Mademoiselle de Montalais!" said Raoul, paler than death.

He staggered to his feet and tried to escape across the slippery mosaic of the floor. But she had understood his cruel and savage grief. She sensed that Raoul's flight involved an accusation against her, or, at the very least, a suspicion. Always vigilant, she didn't want to miss a chance for justification. Apparently, however, Raoul, whom she stopped in the middle of that gallery, didn't care to surrender without a struggle. His tone was so frigid and embarrassed that if either of them had been exposed here, the entire court would have had no doubts about Mademoiselle de Montalais's design.

"Ah, monsieur!" she said disdainfully. "Your action is scarcely worthy of a gentleman. My heart longs to speak to you. And you compromise me with an almost uncivil reception. You are wrong to do so, monsieur, and you confuse your enemies with your friends. Good-bye."

Raoul had sworn to himself that he would never again talk about Louise, never again look at people who might have set eyes on Louise. He was stepping into another world to avoid encountering anything that Louise had seen, anything that she had touched. But after the first shock to his pride, after glimpsing Louise's companion, Mademoiselle de Montalais, who reminded him of the small turret in Blois and the joys of youth, his self-justification vanished.

"Forgive me, mademoiselle. I would never dream, I could never dream, of being uncivil."

"Do you wish to speak to me?" she said with her earlier smile. "Well, let's go somewhere else. Someone might find us here."

"Where should we go?" he asked.

She glanced irresolutely at the clock. Then, upon reflection, she continued: "My room. We'll have an hour to ourselves." And slipping off more lightly than a fairy, she hurried up to her room, followed by Raoul. Once there, she closed the door and handed her chambermaid her cloak, which she'd been holding under her arm.

"Are you looking for Monsieur de Guiche?" she asked Raoul.

"Yes, mademoiselle."

"I'll ask him to join us in a bit, after I've spoken with you."

"Please do so, mademoiselle."

"Do you bear me a grudge?"

Raoul gazed at her for a moment, then lowered his eyes. "Yes."

"You believe that I was involved in the plot that caused her to break with you?"

"Break!" he said bitterly. "Oh, mademoiselle! There is no break if there has never been love."

"You're wrong," replied Mademoiselle de Montalais. "Louise did care for you."

Raoul shuddered.

"Not madly, I know. But she did care for you, and you should have married her before you left for London."

Raoul burst into sinister laughter, which made the young woman shiver.

"You say that so glibly, mademoiselle! Can people marry whom they wish? You're simply forgetting that the person we are discussing was already the king's mistress."

"Listen," replied the young woman, taking hold of Raoul's cold hands, "you were wrong in every way. A man of your age shouldn't leave a woman of her age to her own devices."

"So then there's no such thing as faith in the world?"

"No, Viscount," the young woman responded calmly. "However, I must tell you that instead of loving Louise coolly and philosophically, you should have awoken her to love."

"Enough, mademoiselle, I beg you," said Raoul. "I sense that all of you, male and female, are of a different century than I. You know how to laugh and to banter agreeably. As for me, I loved Mademoiselle de—" He was unable to pronounce her name. "I loved her! Well, I believed in her! But today I've stopped loving her altogether."

"Oh, Viscount!" said Mademoiselle de Montalais, gesturing toward his image in a mirror.

"I know what you're going to say, mademoiselle. I've totally changed, haven't I? And do you know why? It's because my face is the mirror of my heart. I've changed both inside and out."

"Then you're consoled?" Mademoiselle de Montalais snapped sharply.

"No, I'll never be consoled."

"People won't understand you, Monsieur de Bragelonne."

"Who cares? I understand myself all too well."

"Didn't you even try to speak to Louise?"

"I?" cried the young man, his eyes fiery. "I? Honestly! Why don't you advise me to marry her. Maybe the king would consent today!" And he stood up in a rage.

"I see," said Mademoiselle de Montalais, "that you're not cured and that Louise has one more enemy."

"One more enemy?"

"Yes. The king's mistresses are not very popular at the French court."

"Oh, so long as her lover defends her, isn't that enough? She has chosen a man of such quality that no enemy could prevail against him." Raoul paused for a moment. "And besides, she's got you for a friend, mademoiselle," he added with a tinge of irony that didn't slip through a chink in his armor.

"Who? Me? Oh, no! I'm not one of those people whom Mademoiselle de la Vallière deigns to look at. However—"

That "however," so ominous and tempestuous—that "however" made Raoul's heart pound. That word presaged sufferings for the woman he had once loved so deeply. That terrible word, so meaningful for a woman like Mademoiselle de Montalais, was interrupted by a rather loud noise originating in the alcove behind the woodwork.

Mademoiselle pricked up her ears, and Raoul was all set to leave, when a woman very calmly entered through the secret door, which she closed behind her.

"Madame!" cried Raoul, recognizing the king's sister-in-law.

"Oh, God!" murmured Mademoiselle de Montalais, throwing herself at the princess's feet. But it was too late. "I got the time wrong!"

Still, she had enough time to warn Madame, who was walking toward Raoul.

"Monsieur de Bragelonne, madame!"

At the mention of that name, the princess recoiled, uttering a cry in her turn.

"Your Royal Highness," Mademoiselle de Montalais said glibly, "will be good enough to think about that lottery. . . ."

The princess was bewildered.

Raoul made haste to leave, without guessing everything; however, he sensed that he was intruding.

The visitor was preparing some words of transition to pull herself together when an armoire opened across from the alcove and Monsieur de Guiche emerged, beaming with joy. The palest of these four people, it must be said, was Raoul. But the princess, nearly fainting, leaned against the foot of the bed. Nobody dared to support her. Several minutes wore on in a dreadful hush.

Raoul broke the silence. Going over to the count, whose knees were shaking with inexpressible agitation, Raoul took his hand: "Dear count, please tell Madame that I'm too unhappy not to merit forgiveness. Tell her also that I have loved in my life and that the horror of the treachery inflicted on me makes me inexorable toward any other treason committed around me." He smiled at Mademoiselle de Montalais. "That is why I will never divulge the secret of my friend's visits here. Obtain from Madame—Madame, who is so clement and so generous and who's caught you unaware—obtain her forgiveness. You are both free. Love each other; be happy."

The princess had a moment of unspeakable despair. Notwithstanding Raoul's delicacy, she hated being at the mercy of an indiscretion. She also hated accepting the escape hatch offered by that subtle deceit. Queasy, nervous, she struggled against the double assault of those two agonies.

Raoul understood her and went to her aid again. "Madame," he murmured very softly, "in two days I will be far from Paris. In two weeks, I will be far from France, and no one will ever see me again."

"You're leaving?" She was overjoyed.

"With Monsieur de Beaufort."

"For Africa!" cried de Guiche. "You, Raoul! Oh, my friend! Africa, where men die!"

And forgetting everything, forgetting that his very forgetfulness compromised the princess more eloquently than his presence, he said: "You ingrate! You didn't even consult me!" And he hugged Raoul.

Meanwhile, Mademoiselle de Montalais had helped Madame disappear. And she too disappeared.

Raoul passed his hand across his forehead and smiled. "I've been dreaming!"

Then he vividly said to de Guiche, who was taking him in more and more: "My friend! You're my closest friend, I won't hide anything from you. I'm going to die in Africa. And so your secret won't last for more than a year."

"Oh, Raoul! What a man you are!"

"Can you read my mind, de Guiche? These are my thoughts. I'll be living more vividly under the earth than I have lived this past month. We're Christians, my friend. And if my suffering dragged on, I wouldn't be responsible for my soul."

De Guiche tried to object.

"Not another word about me," said Raoul. "But let me give you some advice, dear friend. It's of quite a different importance."

"What do you mean?"

"You're no doubt risking far more than I because you are loved."

"Oh!"

"It's such a wonderful delight talking to you like this! Well, de Guiche, watch out for Mademoiselle de Montalais!"

"She's a good friend."

"She was the friend of . . . you know who I mean. . . . She ruined her by way of pride."

"You're mistaken."

"And now that she's ruined her, she wants to rob her of the only thing that makes that woman excusable in my eyes."

"What?"

"Her love."

"What do you mean?"

"I mean that a plot has formed against the king's mistress—a plot hatched in Madame's very home."

"Do you really believe that?"

"I'm certain of it!"

"Because of Mademoiselle de Montalais?"

"She's the very least of the enemies that I fear for . . . the mistress!"

"Explain it carefully, my friend, and if I can understand you . . ."

"In a word, the king's sister-in-law was jealous of the king!"

"I know that. . . ."

"Oh, you've got nothing to fear. You are loved, de Guiche, you are loved. Do you sense the full value of that phrase? It means that you can lift your head, that you can sleep peacefully, that you can thank God every minute of your life. You are loved. It means that you can hear everything, even the advice of a friend who wants to assure your happiness. You are loved, de Guiche, you are loved! You won't spend those atrocious nights, those endless nights suffered by doomed people, with their dry eyes and tormented hearts. You will have a long life if you behave like the miser who heaps up and fondles gold and diamonds, bit by bit, speck by speck. You are loved! Permit me to tell you what you must do in order to be loved forever."

De Guiche stared for a while at this wretched young man, who was half-crazy with despair; and something like remorse for his own happiness passed through de Guiche's mind.

Raoul recovered from his feverish exaltation and assumed an impassive tone and visage. "They'll bring sufferings to the woman whose name I'd still like to be able to pronounce. Swear to me not only that you won't help them, but that you'll defend her whenever possible, just as I would have done myself."

"I swear it," replied de Guiche.

"And," Raoul went on, "someday, when you've rendered some great service for her, someday when she thanks you, say to her, 'I've done this for you, madame, at the recommendation of Monsieur de Bragelonne, whom you wounded so terribly.' "

"I swear it!" murmured de Guiche, deeply moved.

"That's all. Farewell. I'm leaving for Toulon tomorrow or the day after. If you've got a few hours to spare, give them to me."

"Everything! Everything!" cried de Guiche.

"Thank you!"

"And what will you do now?"

"I'm going to meet the count at Planchet's, where we hope to find Monsieur d'Artagnan."

"Monsieur d'Artagnan?"

"I want to embrace him before my departure. He's a fine man, and he cared for me. Go on, dear friend, someone must be waiting for you. You'll find me again at the count's home whenever you wish. Farewell."

The two young men embraced. Anyone seeing them like that would not have failed to motion toward Raoul and say, "He's the happy one."

29
Planchet's Inventory

While Raoul was at the Luxembourg Palace, his father had gone to Planchet, d'Artagnan's former servant, to ask for news from d'Artagnan. Upon arriving, Athos found the grocer's store thoroughly congested; but it wasn't the congestion of a fortunate sale or an arrival of merchandise. Planchet wasn't throning upon sacks and barrels as usual. Not at all. A boy with a quill behind his ear and a boy with a ledger were recording throngs of numbers while a third boy was counting and weighing. They were doing an inventory.

Athos, not being a shopkeeper, felt slightly crushed by the material hurdles and by the majestic actions of the stocktakers. He watched as several customers were shown the door and he wondered whether he, who wasn't planning to buy anything, might be even more in the way. So he very politely asked the boys if he might speak to Monsieur Planchet. The careless retort was that Monsieur Planchet was packing his trunks.

Athos pricked up his ears. "What do you mean 'his trunks'? Is Monsieur Planchet going on a trip?"

"Yes, monsieur, right away."

"Well, sirs, please inform him that the Count de La Fère would like to speak to him for a moment."

At the count's name, one of the boys, accustomed no doubt to hearing that name uttered with respect, went off to notify Planchet.

It was at this moment that Raoul, free at last after that cruel scene with Mademoiselle de Montalais, arrived at the grocery store. Planchet, summoned by his employee, left his work and came hurrying over.

"Ah, Your Grace! What joy! And what lucky star has brought you here?"

"My dear Planchet," said Athos, taking the hands of his son after glimpsing his sad mood, "we've come to ask you . . . But I've caught you at a bad time. You're as white as a miller. What have you been up to?"

"Ah, damn it! Be careful, monsieur, and don't venture near me until I've thoroughly shaken myself."

"Why not? Flour or powder only make you turn white."

"Not at all! Not at all! What you see on my arms is arsenic!"

"Arsenic?!"

"Yes. I'm making my supplies for the rats."

"Oh well. In an establishment like yours, rats must play a major part."

"It's not this establishment that I'm occupied with, monsieur. The rats here have eaten more than they will ever eat of mine."

"What do you mean?"

"Why, you could have seen it, monsieur. We're doing my inventory."

"You're giving up your business?"

"Yes, by God! I'm selling it to one of my boys."

"Huh? Are you rich enough?"

"Monsieur, I've had it up to here with the city. I don't know if it's because I'm getting long in the tooth. And Monsieur d'Artagnan once told me when a man grows old, he thinks more often about the days of his youth. For some time now, I've felt drawn to the country and to gardening. I used to be a farmer, you know."

And Planchet punctuated his avowal with some chuckling, which sounded a bit pretentious in a man professing his humble origins.

Athos approved of Planchet's intention. "Are you buying some land?"

"I've already bought some, monsieur."

"All the better."

"A small cottage in Fontainebleau with some twenty acres all around."

"Very good, Planchet. Congratulations."

"Goodness, monsieur. We're in a bad way here. My damn dust is making you cough. Damn it all! I'm unconcerned about poisoning the worthiest gentleman in the kingdom."

Athos did not smile at this little joke, with which Planchet was trying his hand at social banter. "Yes," said the count. "Let's talk in private. At your home, for instance. You do have a home, don't you?"

"Certainly, monsieur."

"Upstairs, perhaps?" And Athos, noting Planchet's embarrassment, wanted to help him over it by going first.

"You see . . ." Planchet hesitated.

Athos misunderstood this hesitation, attributing it to the grocer's anxiety about offering mediocre hospitality. "It doesn't matter, it doesn't matter," said the count, going up. "In this neighborhood a merchant has the right not to live in a palace. Let's go."

Raoul preceded him nimbly and was the first to enter the room upstairs.

Two cries resounded simultaneously; and you might say three. One cry stood out. It was uttered by a woman. The other cry emerged from Raoul's lips. It was an exclamation of surprise. No sooner had he uttered that cry then he slammed the door. The third cry was one of fear. It was blurted out by Planchet. "Forgive me," he said. "You see, my wife is getting dressed."

Raoul had most likely seen that Planchet was telling the truth, for the young man was about to go back down.

"Your wife . . ." said Athos. "Ah! Forgive me, Planchet. I didn't realize you had someone upstairs. . . ."

"That's Trüchen," added Planchet, a bit crimson.

"That's whomever you please, my good Planchet. I apologize for our lack of discretion."

"No, no! Please go up, sirs."

"We'll do nothing of the sort," said Athos.

"Oh! Madame was warned. She'll have had time to—"

"No, Planchet. Good-bye."

"Please, gentlemen! You wouldn't want to disoblige me by remaining on the stairs or leaving my home without first sitting down."

"If we'd known that you had a lady up there," Athos replied with his habitual sangfroid, "we would have asked to pay our respects to her."

Planchet was so unnerved by this exquisite impertinence that he pushed his way up and opened the door to admit the count and his son.

By now Trüchen was fully dressed in the rich and stylish garb of a merchant's wife: a German eye grappling with French eyes. After curtsying twice, she went down to the shop—though first eavesdropping at the door to hear what the noble visitors said about her to Planchet. Athos, who guessed what she was up to, steered clear of that topic. As for Planchet, he was itching to provide revelations, which Athos was trying to sidestep.

But some tenacities are stronger than any others. And so Athos was forced to hear Planchet recount his idylls of delight, which were translated into a language more chaste than that of Longus in his pastorals. Planchet explained that Trüchen had charmed the middle-aged shopkeeper and brought luck to his business, as Ruth did for Boaz.

"All you need now," said Athos, "is heirs to your prosperity."

"If I had an heir," replied Planchet, "he'd be getting three hundred thousand pounds."

"You need an heir," Athos said phlegmatically, "if only to avoid losing your little fortune."

Those two words, "little fortune," made Planchet fall in, just as the sergeant had done when Planchet had been a mere outrider in the Piedmont regiment. Athos realized that the grocer would be marrying Trüchen and, willy-nilly, starting a family. This was even more obvious when Athos learned that the boy who was buying Planchet's business was Trüchen's cousin. This boy, as Athos recalled, had frizzy hair, square shoulders, and a face as red as a gillyflower.

Athos knew all one could know, all one should know, about the grocer's fate. Trüchen's beautiful gowns were not enough to make up for the boredom she would suffer, gardening and living amid nature with a graying husband.

As we have said, Athos understood everything. And, abruptly changing the subject, he asked: "Where is Monsieur d'Artagnan? We couldn't find him at the Louvre."

"Ah, sir! Monsieur d'Artagnan has disappeared."

"Disappeared?!" Athos was dumbstruck.

"Oh, monsieur. We know what that means."

"Well, I for one don't know."

"Whenever Monsieur d'Artagnan disappears, he's either on a mission or embroiled in some affair or other."

"Did he talk to you about it?"

"Not a word."

"But you did know that he'd sailed to England, didn't you?"

"Because of speculation," Planchet retorted without thinking.

"Speculation?"

Planchet was embarrassed. "I mean . . ." he broke in.

"Fine, fine. Neither your business nor our friend's business is at stake. My sole reason for questioning you was the interest he inspires in us. Since the captain of the musketeers isn't here, since we can't get anything of his whereabouts out of you, we'll be taking our leave. Good-bye, Planchet, good-bye. Let's go, Raoul."

"Monsieur," said Planchet, "I wish I could tell you—"

"Not at all! Not at all! I would never dream of reproaching a servant for his discretion."

That word, "servant," knocked the semimillionaire for a loop. But his natural respect and naïveté overcame his pride. "There's nothing indiscreet, monsieur, about telling you that d'Artagnan came by here the other day."

"Aha!"

"And that he spent several hours here, poring over a map."

"You're right, my friend. Say no more."

"And here, by way of proof, is that map," Planchet added. He went over to an adjacent wall, on which a suspended strand formed a triangle with the window bar to which the map was affixed.

Planchet brought over this map of France, on which the count's experienced eye could discern an itinerary marked by tiny pins. Any missing pin had left a tiny perforation.

Following the pins and the holes, Athos saw that d'Artagnan must have headed for the south of France, toward Toulon on the Mediterranean. The marks and punctures stopped near Cannes. For several instants, the count racked his brain, trying to figure out what the musketeer was doing there and why he had gone to observe the banks of the Var. But nothing came to Athos's mind. His customary perspicacity failed him. Nor did Raoul hit on anything either.

"It doesn't matter," he said to his father, who, with his forefinger, had silently indicated d'Artagnan's route. "We must admit that Providence is constantly occupied with linking our destiny to Monsieur d'Artagnan's. There he is, near Cannes, and you, sir, will take me at least as far as Toulon. You can be certain that we'll have an easier time finding him on our route than on this map."

Next, taking leave of Planchet, who was berating his employees, including his successor, Trüchen's cousin, the two noblemen set out to visit the Duke de Beaufort. Upon leaving the grocery shop, they spotted a coach—the future depository of Mademoiselle Trüchen and Monsieur Planchet's bags of money.

"Each person," Raoul mused sadly, "goes toward happiness on the road of his own choosing."

"The road to Fontainebleau!" Planchet cried to the coachman.

30
The Duke de Beaufort's Inventory

Having discussed d'Artagnan with Planchet, having seen Planchet abandon Paris in order to sequester himself in his retirement, Athos and Raoul viewed it as a final farewell to the noisy capital and their earlier life.

And just what were they leaving? The father had exhausted the entire past century with glory, and the son had exhausted the entire new age with misery. Obviously, neither man had anything to ask of his contemporaries. All that remained was to call on the Duke de Beaufort and settle the conditions for departure.

The duke was magnificently lodged in Paris. He enjoyed the superb lifestyle of great fortunes that certain old men recalled as having flourished thanks to the generosity of Henry III. Back then, a few grand noblemen had indeed been richer than the king. They knew it, they used their wealth, and they didn't forgo the pleasure of slightly humiliating His Royal Majesty. It was this selfish aristocracy that Cardinal Richelieu had compelled to donate its blood, its purses, and its reverence to what was known henceforth as the king's service. How many families had lifted their heads during the period from Louis XI, that dreadful reaper of nobles, to Richelieu! And how many families, during the period from Richelieu to Louis XIV, had bowed their heads—never to raise them again! However, the duke was born a prince, and his blood wasn't the kind that is shed on scaffolds except by a ruling of the people.

This prince had thus preserved his opulent way of life. How did he pay for his horses, his servants, his table? Nobody knew—least of all he. However, the sons of the king were privileged: no one declined to extend them credit—out of respect, out of devotion, out of the conviction that they would someday be repaid.

Upon arriving at the duke's mansion, they found it as congested as Planchet's store. The duke had done his inventory; that is, he was distributing his truly valuable possessions to his friends and to all his creditors. Owing roughly two million pounds, an enormous figure back then, the duke had calculated that he couldn't leave for Africa without a nice round sum. And to gain that sum, he was giving his past creditors tableware, weapons, jewels, and furniture, which would net him twice what he'd earn by selling them outright.

Indeed, how could a man who is owed ten thousand pounds refuse to carry off a present of six thousand with the additional merit that it belonged to a descendant of Henry IV? And how, after carrying off this present, could the creditor refuse to lend this generous duke another ten thousand pounds?

And that was what had happened. The duke no longer had a house—something that becomes useless for an admiral, whose home is his ship. He had no superfluous arms, once he was among his cannon; he had no jewels, which the sea could devour. But he did have a cool three or four hundred thousand crowns in his coffers. And the mansion was filled with the joyous commotion of would-be plunderers.

The duke possessed to a supreme degree the art of making the most pitiful creditors happy. Every empty purse, every man who was pressed for money, found patience and understanding in him.

He told some of them: "I'd love to have what you have. I'd give it to you." And he told others: "All I've got is this silver ewer. It must still be worth a good five hundred pounds. Take it."

And so, charm being a font of legal currency, the duke managed to endlessly renew his debts. This time, he didn't stand on ceremony: it was a scene of pillage. He was handing over everything. There is an Oriental fable about a poor Arab who, after helping to sack a palace, walks off with a big pot containing a hidden bag of gold, so that everyone lets him pass freely without envy. This story had come true for the duke. A number of tradesmen were taking advantage of his good offices. Thus, the creditors, looting the saddleries and vestiaries, failed to appreciate the trifles that are valued so highly by saddlers and tailors. Eager to bring their wives preserves given by the duke, they leaped for joy under the weight of terrines or bottles gloriously bearing the ducal coat of arms.

Eventually, the duke gave away his horses and the hay from his haylofts. He made over thirty people happy with kitchen utensils and three hundred people with the contents of his cellar. Furthermore, all these beneficiaries left with the conviction that the duke was getting rid of all this stuff because he would make a new fortune under the Arabian tents. While ravaging his mansion, the filchers kept telling one another that the king was sending him to Gigelli in order to restore his vanished wealth. The African treasures would be divided equally between the duke and the king—treasures that consisted of mines yielding diamonds and other precious stones. The gold and silver mines of the Atlas Mountains were not even paid the honor of getting mentioned. Aside from the mines, which would be worked only after the campaign, there would be the army's booty. The duke would lay hands on everything that the rich pirates had stolen from Christendom since the Battle of Lepanto, when Don Juan of Austria had defeated the Turks (1571). The millions were beyond all counting.

So why should the duke bother with these poor utensils of a past life if he was going in quest of the rarest treasures? And, conversely, how could anyone care for the property of a man who cared so little for himself? That was the situation.

Athos, with his inquiring eyes, instantly realized what was going on. He found the Grand Admiral of France a bit scattered, for he was just getting up from a feast. The table was set for fifty diners, who'd drunk countless toasts to the prosperity of the expedition. At dessert, the leftovers had been abandoned to the servants and the empty plates to the curious. The duke was intoxicated with both his ruin and his popularity. He had drunk his past wine to the health of his future wine.

Upon seeing Athos and Raoul, he exclaimed: "Here's my aide-de-camp. Come on over, Count; come on over, Viscount."

Athos looked for a passage through the chaos of linen and tableware.

"That's right! Just step over it!" said the duke. And he offered Athos a full glass.

Athos accepted it; Raoul barely moistened his lips.

"Here is your commission," the duke told the young man. "I prepared it because I was counting on you. You will go ahead of me as far as Antibes."

"Yes, sir."

"Here is your order."

And the duke handed it to Raoul. "Are you at all acquainted with the sea?"

"Yes, sir. I've gone on voyages with Monsieur le Prince."

"Fine. All those scows, all those lighters will be waiting to escort me and carry my supplies. The army has to embark within two weeks at the latest."

"As you command, sir."

"This present order gives you the right to visit and explore all the coastal islands. There, you will perform as many raids and impressments as you wish for me."

"Yes, Your Grace."

"And since you're an active man and you'll be doing a lot of work, you'll be spending large sums of money."

"I hope I won't, sir."

"I'm sure you will. My administrator has prepared one-hundred-thousand-pound vouchers for you, payable in the towns of the Midi. Now go, dear Viscount."

Athos broke in: "Keep your money, monseigneur. War against the Arabs is waged with gold and not just lead."

"I'll try sticking to lead," the duke retorted. "And besides, you know how I feel about the expedition: lots of noise, lots of fire, and I'll vanish—in the smoke, if necessary."

Having spoken, the duke wanted to laugh again, but he instantly saw that his visitors didn't share his mirth. "Ah!" he said with the courteous egotism of his rank and his age. "You're the type of people whom one mustn't see after dinner—cold, stiff, dry people—while I'm all fire, all suppleness, and all wine. No, damn it! I'll always find you sober, Viscount. As for you, Count: if you make such a face at me, you'll never see me again."

He spoke while shaking hands with Athos, who replied with a smile: "Monseigneur, don't speak so exaltedly just because you've got a lot of money. I predict that before the month is up, you'll be left dry, stiff, and cold with your war chest. And with a once sober Raoul at your side, you'll be surprised at seeing him cheerful, impetuous, and generous because he'll have new cash to offer you."

"Your words in God's ear!" cried the delighted duke. "Count, why not stay with me?"

"No, I'm accompanying Raoul. The mission you're assigning him is troublesome and arduous. If he's alone, he'll have a difficult time carrying it out. You don't seem to realize, monseigneur, that you've given him a command of the first order."

"You don't say!"

"And in the navy to boot!"

"True enough. But won't a man like him do anything he's told?"

"Monseigneur, you won't find a more zealous, intelligent, and absolutely courageous man. But if Raoul fails you in your embarkment, you'll have no one to blame but yourself."

"Why, you're scolding me!"

"Monseigneur, for provisioning a fleet, rallying a flotilla, and enrolling the military manpower, an admiral would need a whole year. Raoul is only a cavalry captain and you're giving him just two weeks."

"I can assure you he'll pull it off."

"I believe it! But I'm going to help him."

"I'm counting on you, and I'm counting on the fact that you won't let him leave Toulon all by himself."

"Oh!" said Athos, nodding.

"Patience! Patience!"

"Monseigneur, allow us to take our leave."

"Go, then. And I wish you the best of luck."

"Farewell, monseigneur, and the best of luck to you too."

"We're off to a great start!" Athos told his son. "No food! No reserves! No cargo flotilla! How will you manage?"

"Don't worry!" Raoul murmured. "If everyone does as I do, there'll be no shortage of grub."

"Sir!" Athos snapped. "Don't be cruel and unjust in your egoism or in your sorrow—whatever you call it. If you're going off to this war with the intention of dying, then you don't need anybody, and it wasn't worth the trouble recommending you to the duke. But now that you've been introduced to him, now that you've accepted the responsibility of an army post, your problems are no longer at stake. Think of all those poor soldiers who've got a heart and a body just like you, and who'll weep for their country and suffer all the hardships of their human condition. Remember, Raoul, an officer is a minister who's as useful as a priest and who must have more humanity than a priest."

"Sir, I know that, and I've practiced it. I'd continue to do so. . . . But . . ."

"You're also forgetting that our country is proud of its military glory. Go and die, if you like! But do not die without honor and without benefit for France! Go on, Raoul. Don't let what I say get you down. I love you and I want you to be perfect."

"I like your rebukes, sir," the young man murmured. "They have a healing effect. They remind me that someone still loves me."

"And now, Raoul, let's go! The weather is so beautiful, the sky is so pure! We'll always find that sky above us, and it will be even purer in Gigelli. It will speak to you there about me, just as it speaks to me here about God."

After agreeing on this point, the two noblemen talked about the duke's wild behavior. They both felt that France would be served incompletely by the spirit and practice of the expedition. Having summed it up with the word "vanity," they set out, obedient to their will rather than to their destiny.

The sacrifice was consummated.

31
The Silver Plate

The journey went smoothly. Athos and his son crossed the whole of France, riding fifteen leagues a day, sometimes more whenever Raoul's grief doubled its intensity. It took them two weeks to reach Toulon, whereby they lost any trace of d'Artagnan in Antibes. They had to assume that the captain of the musketeers wanted to remain incognito in this area; for Athos, upon making inquiries, was told that people had seen a horseman of d'Artagnan's description in Avignon, where he had exchanged his horses for a tightly shut carriage. Raoul despaired of finding d'Artagnan. The young man's tender heart yearned for the farewell and the consolation of that heart of steel.

Athos knew by experience that d'Artagnan always became impenetrable when dealing with a grave matter, whether for himself or for the king. The count even feared offending his comrade or harming him by gathering too much information. However, when Raoul began his task of organizing the flotilla, assembling scows and lighters to send to Toulon, one of the fishermen told Athos that he had put his boat in dry dock for repairs after ferrying an aristocrat who'd been in a terrible hurry to embark. Believing that this man was lying in order to stay free and earn more money by fishing after all his comrades had left, Athos pressed him for details. The fisherman explained that, six nights ago, a man had rented his boat in order to visit the island of Saint-Honorat. They had agreed on a price, but the gentleman had wanted to take along a large coach despite the variety of difficulties that this would involve. The fisherman had wanted to back out. He even threatened his would-be passenger, but all he got for his threats was a long, harsh, nasty caning. The fuming boatman had appealed to the syndic of Antibes, a guild of fishermen that protects its members and administers justice among them. However, the gentleman had whipped out a document, and, upon seeing it, the syndic had bowed to the ground and enjoined the fisherman to obey, even scolding him for his recalcitrance. The vessel had then set sail with its freight.

"But none of this," Athos retorted, "tells us how you managed to wreck your boat."

"This is what happened. I was steering toward Saint-Honorat, according to my passenger's wishes, but he changed his mind. He claimed that I couldn't pass to the south of the abbey."

"Why not?"

"Because of Monks' Reef in front of the square tower of the Benedictines, monsieur."

"A reef?" asked Athos.

"On the surface and underneath. It's a dangerous passage, but I've cleared it a thousand times. The gentleman wanted me to put him ashore on the isle of Sainte-Marguerite."

"Well?"

"Well, monsieur!" cried the fisherman in his Provençal accent, "either a man's a mariner or he ain't. Either you know your course or you're a landlubber! I insisted on charging ahead. But my passenger grabbed my collar and he calmly announced that he would strangle me. My first mate armed himself with a hatchet, and I tried to do the same. We wanted to get even for last night. However, the gentleman pulled out his sword and waved it so powerfully that neither of us could get near him. I wanted to smash his head with my hatchet, and I was well within my rights—wasn't I, monsieur? After all, a mariner is the master of his vessel, just as a man's home is his castle. So, to defend myself, I was about to slice my passenger in half, when, all at once, believe it or not, monsieur, the coach opened up—I don't know how—and a sort of phantom emerged, wearing a black cap and a black mask. It was a terrifying sight, and he threatened us with his fist."

"Who was it?" asked Athos.

"The devil, monsieur. For when the joyful gentleman saw him, he shouted: 'Ah! Thank you, monseigneur!' "

"An odd business!" muttered the count, glancing at Raoul.

"What did you do next?" Raoul asked the fisherman.

"You understand, monsieur, two poor men like us were already no match for two gentlemen. But the devil?! Oh, no! We didn't consult each other, my mate and I. We jumped into the sea—we were only seven or eight hundred feet from shore."

"And then?"

"And then, monsieur, since there was a southwesterly breeze, the boat drifted to the sands of Sainte-Marguerite."

"Oh! But what about the two passengers?"

"Huh! Don't worry! Here's proof that one was the devil and he was protecting the other. When we swam back to the boat, instead of finding those two shocked creatures, we found nothing—not even the coach."

"Odd! Odd!" the count repeated. "And what did you do after that, my friend?"

"I complained to the governor of Sainte-Marguerite, but he shook his finger at me and said that if I tried to foist such rubbish on him he'd give me a sound thrashing."

"The governor?"

"Yes, monsieur. And meanwhile, my boat had shattered, thoroughly shattered, for the prow had remained on the headland of Sainte-Marguerite. And the carpenter wants a hundred and twenty pounds to fix it up."

"Fine," replied Raoul. "You're exempted from service. You may go."

"Should we go to Sainte-Marguerite?" Athos then asked his son.

"Yes, sir. There's something there that needs clarification, and that man didn't strike me as truthful."

"I feel the same way, Raoul. With that tale about a masked aristocrat and a vanished coach, the man sounds as if he's concealing the violence he may have perpetrated out at sea. He could have gotten back at the passenger who was forced on him."

"I suspect as much too. And the coach probably contained valuables rather than a man."

"We'll see, Raoul. That aristocrat certainly resembles d'Artagnan—I'm familiar with his behavior. Alas! We're no longer the invincible young men we used to be. Who knows whether that hatchet or an iron bar succeeded in doing what the finest swords in Europe, the bullets and the cannonballs, failed to achieve during the last forty years!"

That very same day, they ordered a lugger from Toulon, boarded it, and set sail for Sainte-Marguerite.

Their first impression of this island was that of a singular well-being. The soil was replete with fruit and flowers, whereby the cultivated area served as the governor's garden. Fig trees, orange trees, pomegranate trees bent under their weight of gold and azure crops. In the uncultivated surroundings, coveys of red partridge scampered through blueberries and tufts of juniper. And along the way, a startled rabbit left the heather and the marjoram and scooted back into its hole.

Actually, this blissful island was uninhabited. With its flat terrain offering only a small bight for arriving vessels, it was under the protection of the governor. The latter shared the booty of smugglers, who used the island as a temporary warehouse, provided they didn't kill the game or ravage the garden. Through this arrangement, the governor was content with an eight-man garrison for guarding his fortress, in which a dozen cannon were growing moldy. The governor was thus a happy farmer, harvesting grapes, figs, olives, and oranges, and preserving his lemons and citrons in the sunshine of his casemates. The fortress, circled by a deep moat—its only sentry—sported three pinnacles on three turrets, which were connected by a moss-covered terrace.

For a while, Athos and Raoul strode along the garden fences without finding anyone who could take them to the governor. Eventually, they stepped into the garden. It was the hottest part of the day, when everything hides under grass and under rocks. The sky extends its fiery veils as if to muffle all suns and envelope all creatures. The partridges under the furze, the flies under the leaves, fall asleep like the waves under the heavens.

Between the second and third courtyards of the terrace, Athos spotted a soldier carrying a basket of provisions on his head. The man returned almost instantly without his basket and vanished in the shade of the lookout turret. Athos inferred that this soldier had brought someone's dinner and had then gone to his own meal.

All at once, Athos heard somebody call him. He looked up and caught something white inside the frame of a barred window: a moving hand, dazzling like a weapon struck by sunbeams. And before Athos could digest what he'd seen, a bright, hissing streak drew his attention from the dungeon to the ground.

A second dull noise was heard in the moat, and Raoul hurried over to pick up a silver plate, which had just rolled across the dry sand. The hand that had tossed the plate signaled to the two gentlemen; then it disappeared. Athos and Raoul, approaching one another, began exploring the dusty plate; on it, someone had carved a message with the point of a knife:

> I am the brother of the French king—a prisoner today, a madman tomorrow. French and Christian gentlemen, pray to God for the mind and the soul of the son of your masters!

The plate dropped from Athos's hands while his son tried to grasp the mystery of those lugubrious words. At that same instant, a shout came from the top of the dungeon. Raoul, swift as lightning, lowered his head and forced the count to do likewise. A musket barrel gleamed on the crest of the wall. A plume of white smoke purled from the mouth of the musket, and a bullet flattened on a stone within six inches from the two gentlemen. Another musket appeared and aimed downward.

"Damn it!" cried Athos. "Are they killing people here? Get down here, you cowards!"

"Yes, get down here!" Raoul echoed furiously, shaking his fist at the castle.

The assailant who was about to shoot his musket responded with an exclamation of surprise. And since his partner wanted to continue the attack with his loaded musket, the assailant shoved the barrel up so that the bullet shot into the air.

Athos and Raoul, seeing them vanish from the platform, assumed the two sentries were coming for them, and so father and son stood their ground.

Less than five minutes had dragged by when the beat of a drum summoned the eight garrison soldiers, who emerged with their muskets on the other side of the moat. These men were led by an officer whom Raoul recognized as having fired the first musket shot. The officer ordered his men to prepare arms.

"We're gonna be gunned down!" screamed Raoul. "Let's at least hold our swords and jump into the moat! We'll each kill one of the scoundrels when their muskets are empty!"

And following his advice, Raoul and Athos charged forward, when a very familiar voice resounded behind them: "Athos! Raoul!"

"D'Artagnan!" the two gentlemen responded.

"Lower your arms, damn it!" cried the captain to the soldiers. "I was sure I wasn't wrong!" The soldiers lowered their muskets.

"What's happening to us!" asked Athos. "Were they gonna shoot us without warning?"

"It was I who was gonna shoot you," replied d'Artagnan. "And if the governor would've missed you, I wouldn't have missed you, my dear friends. Luckily, I'm in the habit of aiming for a long time before firing out of instinct! I thought I recognized you! Ah, my dear friends! What good luck!"

"What?!" exclaimed the count. "The man who fired at us is the governor of the fortress?"

"In person."

"And why was he shooting at us? What had we done to him?"

"Damn it! You received something the prisoner threw down to you."

"That's true!"

"That plate. . . . The prisoner wrote something on it, didn't he?"

"Yes."

"I figured as much. Oh, God!" And d'Artagnan, with all the marks of a lethal anxiety, grabbed the plate and read the message. He turned white. "Oh, God!" he repeated.

"So it's true?" asked Athos sotto voce. "So it's true?"

"Silence! The governor's coming!"

"What's he gonna do? Was it our fault?"

"Silence, I tell you! Silence! If they think you can read, if they assume that you understood . . . I love you, dear friends, I'd die for you. . . . But . . ."

"But . . . ?" said Athos and Raoul.

"But I wouldn't save you from lifelong imprisonment if I saved you from death. So silence! Silence!"

Having crossed the moat on a plank footbridge, the governor was approaching. "Well?" he hollered. "What's stopping us?"

D'Artagnan whispered vividly to his friends: "You're Spaniards! You don't know a word of French!" He then addressed the governor: "Well, I was right. These two men are Spanish captains whom I met last year in Ypres. They don't speak a word of French."

"Ah!" said the governor attentively, trying to read the message on the plate.

D'Artagnan took the plate, wiping away its message with several blows of his sword.

"Huh?" exclaimed the governor. "What are you doing? Can't I read it?"

"It's a state secret," d'Artagnan sharply retorted. "And you know that, according to the king's order, no one can penetrate it under pain of death. So I can let you read it if you like, but then I'll have you shot!"

During that apostrophe, half serious, half ironic, Athos and Raoul coolly held their tongues.

"But," said the governor, "these two men must know at least a few words of French."

"Let them be! Even if they understood us when we speak, they couldn't read what we write. They can't even read Spanish. You must remember that a Spanish aristocrat must never know how to read."

The governor ought to have been satisfied with that explanation. But he dug in his heels. "Ask these gentlemen to come to the fort."

"I want to, and I was about to suggest it," said d'Artagnan.

Actually, he had a very different plan, and he wanted to see his friends a hundred leagues away. But he was forced to make the best of the situation. He invited the two gentlemen, in Spanish, and they accepted.

The group headed toward the entrance to the fort, which had been emptied by the incident. The eight soldiers returned to their pleasant leisure, which had been momentarily ruffled by that unexpected adventure.

32
Captive and Jailers

Once they entered the fort, the governor made some preparations to receive his guests. Meanwhile, Athos said to d'Artagnan, "C'mon. Now that we're alone, please explain what's going on."

"It's very simple. I've brought a prisoner whom the king won't permit anyone to see. When you arrived here, the prisoner tossed something out the window. I was dining with the governor and I saw the object being thrown, I saw Raoul picking it up. I'm no fool—I understood, and I thought you were communicating with my prisoner. So . . ."

"So you ordered the soldiers to shoot us down."

"By God . . . I admit it. But, luckily, while I was the first to grab a musket, I was the last to aim it."

"If you had killed me, d'Artagnan, I would have had the good fortune to die for the Royal House of France—and the tremendous honor of perishing at the hands of d'Artagnan, the king's noblest and most loyal defender."

"C'mon, Athos! Why are you talking about 'the Royal House'?!" d'Artagnan stammered. "How come? You're wise and knowledgeable, Count. How can you believe the ravings of a lunatic?"

"I believe them."

"All the more reason, my dear cavalier," Raoul continued, "for that order to shoot anyone who believes them."

"Because," replied the captain of the musketeers, "because if slander is absurd, it's almost certain to become popular."

"No, d'Artagnan," Athos murmured, "because the king doesn't want the family secret to be revealed among the people and to cover the executioners of Louis XIII's son with shame."

"C'mon! C'mon! Stop talking nonsense, Athos, or I'll question your sanity. By the way, please explain to me how Louis XIII could have a son in the Sainte-Marguerite Islands."

"A son whom you conducted here," said Athos, "a masked man, in a fishing boat. Why not?"

D'Artagnan paused. "Aha! How do you know that a fishing boat—?"

"Brought you to Sainte-Marguerite with the carriage holding the prisoner? With the prisoner whom you address as 'Monseigneur'? Oh, I know all about it!"

D'Artagnan chewed his mustache. "If it were true that I brought a masked prisoner here by boat and carriage, nothing proves that this prisoner is a prince . . . a prince of the House of France."

"Why don't you ask Aramis," Athos retorted coldly.

"Aramis?" cried the dumbfounded musketeer. "You've seen Aramis?"

"Yes. I saw him after his mortifying setback in Vaux. He was a fugitive—pursued, doomed. And he told me enough for me to believe the lament that the unfortunate man engraved on the silver plate."

A dejected d'Artagnan lowered his head. "This is how God toys with what men call their 'wisdom'! A fine secret that a dozen or so people share the scraps of! Athos, I curse the fluke that makes you confront me in this affair, because now—"

"C'mon!" said Athos, both gentle and severe. "Is your secret exposed just because I know it? Haven't I kept equally profound secrets in my time? Just rack your memory, old friend."

"You've never shared a secret this perilous," d'Artagnan retorted sadly. "I have a foreboding that everyone who's touched by this secret will die—and die horribly!"

"God's will be done, d'Artagnan. But here comes your governor."

D'Artagnan and his friends slipped back into their roles.

The harsh and suspicious governor showed d'Artagnan a courtesy that bordered on obsequiousness. As for the visitors, he was content to welcome them and keep an eye on them. Athos and Raoul noticed that the governor often tried to confuse them, to catch them off guard with sudden attacks. But neither guest was disconcerted. What d'Artagnan had said could seem probable, even if the governor wasn't fully convinced.

They left the table and went off to relax.

"What's that man's name?" said Athos to d'Artagnan in Spanish. "I don't care for the looks of him."

"Saint-Mars," the captain replied.

"So he's the young prince's jailer?"

"How should I know? I might have to stay in Sainte-Marguerite forever."

"C'mon, now! You?"

"My friend, I'm like a man who's found a treasure in the middle of the desert. He wants to carry it off, but he can't. He wants to leave it here, but he doesn't dare. The king let me depart—he's afraid that someone else would do a worse job of guarding the prisoner. The king regrets that I'm not at his side—he feels that nobody will serve him as thoroughly as I do. Oh, well! It's in God's hands!"

"The very fact that you've got nothing certain," said Raoul, "would indicate that your stay here is temporary and that you'll be returning to Paris."

Saint-Mars broke in: "Ask these gentlemen what they're doing in Sainte-Marguerite."

"They've come here in regard to the Benedictines in Saint-Honorat, and in regard to the excellent hunting in Sainte-Marguerite."

"The game is at their disposal," replied Saint-Mars, "and at yours."

D'Artagnan thanked him.

"When are they leaving?" the governor added.

"Tomorrow," d'Artagnan answered.

Leaving d'Artagnan alone with the pseudo-Spaniards, Monsieur de Saint-Mars went to make his rounds.

"Oh my!" cried the musketeer. "This life and this society aren't quite my cup of tea. I command this man, and he annoys me, damn it! Listen, would you like to shoot a few rabbits? The stroll will be beautiful and not tiring. The island is only a league and a half long and half a league wide. A real park. Let's have some fun."

"We'll go wherever you like, d'Artagnan. Not for diversion but to talk freely."

D'Artagnan signaled to a soldier, who brought them sporting guns, then went back to the fort.

"And now," said the musketeer, "please answer the question that our sulky Saint-Mars asked you. What are you doing in these islands?"

"We've come to say good-bye to you."

"Good-bye? What do you mean? Is Raoul leaving?"

"Yes."

"With the Duke de Beaufort, I bet."

"With the Duke de Beaufort. You always guess right, dear friend."

"Out of habit. . . ."

While the two friends were conversing, Raoul, with his solemn head and his burning heart, sat down on some mossy rocks and placed his musket on his lap. Gazing at the sea, gazing at the sky, listening to the voice of his soul, he let the hunters gradually move away.

D'Artagnan noticed Raoul's absence. "He's still reeling from the blow, isn't he?"

"It was lethal."

"Oh, I think you're exaggerating. Raoul's got stamina. Every noble heart's got a second envelope that acts as armor. The first envelope bleeds, the second resists."

"No!" retorted Athos. "Raoul is going to die."

"Damn it!" d'Artagnan snapped gloomily. Nor did he add a single word to his exclamation. Then, a moment later: "Why are you letting him leave?"

"Because he wants to leave."

"And why don't you go with him?"

"Because I don't want to see him die."

D'Artagnan peered into Athos's face.

"There's one thing you know about me," said the count, leaning against the captain's arm. "You know that I've been afraid of few things in my life. Well, I'm being devoured by an endless and insurmountable fear. I'm terrified of the day when I'll hold the corpse of that child in my arms."

"Oh!" d'Artagnan replied. "Oh!"

"He'll die, I know it, I'm convinced of it. And I don't want to see him die."

"C'mon, Athos! You stand in front of the most serious man

you say you've ever known—your d'Artagnan, that peerless man, as you used to call him. And you cross your arms and tell him that you're scared of seeing your son dead—you who've seen everything a man can see in this world! Well, why are you scared of that, Athos? On this earth a man must expect anything, confront anything."

"Listen, my friend," said Athos. "I've worn myself out on this earth, which you're talking about, and I've kept only two religions: the religion of my life, my friendships, my paternal duty; and the religion of eternity, my love and respect for God. Now I've got inside me the revelation that if God allowed my friend or my son to breathe his last in my presence . . . Oh, no! I don't even want to say those words, d'Artagnan."

"Say them! Say them!"

"I'm tough in regard to anything except the death of someone I love. And there's no remedy for that. The man who dies wins, the man who watches somebody die loses. No. Listen, I'd know that I will never again, never again on this earth, meet the person that I now see with joy. I'd know that d'Artagnan is nowhere, that Raoul is nowhere. . . . Oh! . . . I'm old, you know, I've got no courage left. I pray to God to spare me in my feebleness. But if He struck me full-face, and in that way, then I would curse Him. A Christian gentleman mustn't curse his God, d'Artagnan. It's quite enough to have cursed a king!"

"Hmm . . . !" said d'Artagnan, a bit shaken by this violent tempest of sorrow.

"D'Artagnan, my friend, you love Raoul. Just look at him." Athos pointed at his son. "Look at that sadness that never leaves him. Do you know anything more horrible than to witness, minute by minute, the incessant agony of that poor heart?"

"Let me talk to him, Athos. Who knows?"

"Try it. But I'm convinced you won't succeed."

"I won't console him. I'll serve him."

"You?"

"Precisely. Is this the first time that a woman's regretted an infidelity? I'll go to him, I tell you."

Athos shook his head and walked on alone. D'Artagnan, cutting across the undergrowth, returned to Raoul and held out his hand.

"Well," said d'Artagnan, "you wish to speak to me?"

"I want to ask you a favor."

"Ask."

"You're returning to France someday?"

"I hope so."

"Should I write to Mademoiselle de la Vallière?"

"No, you mustn't."

"I've got so much to tell her."

"Then go and tell her."

"Never!"

"Well, what virtue do you attribute to a letter that you can't assign to your speech?"

"You're right."

"She loves the king," d'Artagnan snapped brutally. "She's a decent girl."

Raoul shuddered.

"And as for you, whom she's abandoned, she may love you more than she loves the king, but in a different way."

"D'Artagnan, do you believe that she loves the king?"

"She worships him. Her heart is inaccessible to any other feeling. You might continue by living near her as her best friend."

"Ah!" cried Raoul with a passionate outburst of his painful hope.

"Would you like that?"

"It would be cowardly."

"That's a preposterous word. It would make me contemptuous of your mind. Listen, Raoul, it is never cowardly to do something under duress. If your heart says go there or die, then go there. Was she cowardly or courageous—the woman who loved you but who preferred the king, the woman whose heart imperiously commanded her to prefer him to you? No. She was the bravest of all women. Do as she did—obey yourself. Do you know the one thing I'm sure of, Raoul?"

"What?"

"Seeing her close up, with a jealous man's eyes. . . ."

"Well? . . ."

"Well, you'll stop loving her."

"You've decided for me, my dear d'Artagnan."

"To go back and see her?"

"No. To go away and never see her again. I want to love her forever."

"Frankly," the musketeer continued, "that's a resolution that I was far from expecting."

"Listen, my friend. You're going to see her and you'll give her this letter, which, if you find it appropriate, will explain both to her and to you what is occurring in my heart. Read the letter. I wrote it last night. Something told me that I would see you today."

Raoul handed the letter to d'Artagnan, who read it:

Mademoiselle,

In my eyes you are doing nothing wrong by not loving me. You are guilty of only one mistake: letting me believe that you loved me. This error will cost me my life. I forgive you for this error, but I do not forgive myself. They say that happy lovers are deaf to the laments of scorned lovers. This will not be the case with you since you did not love me except out of fear. I am certain that if I had tried more intensely to change your friendship into love, you would have yielded for fear of making me die or lessening the esteem I had for you. It is far sweeter for me to die, knowing that you are free and content.

How much, then, will you love me once you no longer fear my look or my reproach? You will love me, because, as charming as a new love may appear to you, God has not in any way made me the inferior of the man whom you have chosen. Indeed, in your eyes, my devotion, my sacrifice, my sorrowful end assure my genuine superiority over him. In the naïve incredulity of my heart, I allowed my treasure to escape. Many people tell me that you loved me enough to finally love me deeply. This impression abolishes all my bitterness and leads me to regard only myself as my enemy.

You will accept this final farewell, and you will bless me for

> taking refuge in the inviolable asylum where all hate is snuffed, where all love endures.
>
> Farewell, mademoiselle. If it took all my blood to purchase your happiness, then I would give you all my blood. I gladly sacrifice it to my misery.
>
> RAOUL, VISCOUNT DE BRAGELONNE

"It's a fine letter," said the captain. "I've got only one objection."

"Tell me!" cried Raoul.

"It describes everything except the thing that is exhaled like a deadly poison by your eyes, by your heart: the insane love that is still burning you."

Raoul blanched and was silent.

"Why didn't you simply write: 'Mademoiselle, instead of cursing you, I love you and I die'?"

"That's true," said Raoul with a sinister joy. And ripping up the letter that he had taken back, he wrote:

> For having the happiness to still tell you that I love you, I commit the cowardice of writing to you; and for punishing me for this cowardice, I die.

And he signed the letter. "You'll give this to her, won't you, Captain?" he said to d'Artagnan.

"When?"

"The day," said Raoul, showing him the last sentence, "the day you write the date under these words." And he dashed away, joining Athos, who came trudging back.

As they reentered the fort, the sea rose; and with the swift vehemence of the squalls that disturb the Mediterranean, the bad mood of the element became a tempest. A shapeless, tormented something emerged just off the coast.

"What's that?" asked Athos. "A wrecked boat?"

"That's not a boat," said d'Artagnan.

"Forgive me," Raoul put in, "but that's a boat, and it's dashing toward the harbor."

"There actually is a boat in the bay, and it's wisely seeking shelter here. But what Athos is pointing to on the sand . . . that stranded object . . ."

"Yes, yes. I see it."

"It's the carriage that I dumped into the sea when I was landing with the prisoner."

"Well!" said Athos. "If you want my advice, you'll burn the carriage to a crisp. Otherwise, the fishermen of Antibes, who thought they were dealing with the devil, will try to prove that your prisoner was a mere mortal."

"That's excellent advice, Athos, and I'm going to have it followed tonight—or, rather, follow it myself. Meanwhile, let's get indoors. It's about to rain, and the lightning is fearful."

As they passed across the rampart and into a gallery for which d'Artagnan had the key, they saw Monsieur Saint-Mars heading toward the prisoner's room. At d'Artagnan's signal, they hid in a corner of the staircase.

"What is it?" asked Athos.

"You'll see. Just look. The prisoner is returning from the chapel."

And by the flashes of red lightning, amid the violet mist that the wind blurred in the depths of the sky, they saw a man gravely walking six paces behind the governor. The man wore black, and his head was entirely enveloped in a visor and helmet of polished steel. The flaming sky cast lurid reflections on the burnished metal, and these shimmers, flitting capriciously, seemed to be the angry gaze of this unfortunate, who could not curse.

Reaching the middle of the gallery, the prisoner halted for a moment to contemplate the infinite horizon, inhale the sulfurous aroma of the storm, and greedily drink the hot rain. He then heaved a sigh that sounded like a roar.

"Come on, monsieur!" Saint-Mars snapped at the prisoner. The governor was unnerved at seeing the prisoner stare and stare beyond the walls. "Monsieur, come on!"

"Hey, monseigneur!" Athos shouted at Saint-Mars, and his voice was so grave and dreadful that the governor shuddered from head to foot. The count insisted on respect for the fallen majesty.

The prisoner turned around.

"Who spoke?" asked Saint-Mars.

"I did," replied d'Artagnan, emerging instantly. "You know very well that this is the order."

"Don't call me 'Monsieur' or 'Monseigneur,' " said the prisoner, his voice moving Raoul to the core of his being. "Call me 'Accursed.' " And he walked on.

The iron door ground behind him.

"Now, that's an unhappy man!" d'Artagnan muttered, showing Raoul the prince's chamber.

33
Promises

No sooner had d'Artagnan stepped into his room with his friends than one of the soldiers came to announce that the governor was looking for him. The boat that Raoul had spotted as it flew toward the harbor had brought an important dispatch to the captain of the musketeers. Upon opening it, he recognized the king's handwriting:

> I assume that you have already implemented my orders, Monsieur d'Artagnan. Return to Paris immediately and come to see me in my Louvre.

"My exile's over!" the musketeer joyfully shouted. "God be praised—I'm no longer a jailer!" And he showed the letter to Athos.

"So you're leaving us?" Athos sadly responded.

"Yes—but to meet again, given that Raoul is an adult who can depart by himself with the Duke de Beaufort. Raoul would rather see his father return with d'Artagnan than force him to travel the two hundred leagues to go back to La Fère all alone. Isn't that so, Raoul?"

"Certainly," stammered the young man with an expression of tender regret.

"No, my friend!" Athos interrupted. "I won't leave Raoul

until the day his ship disappears on the horizon. We won't be separated while he's in France."

"As you please, dear friend. But we can at least get away from Sainte-Marguerite together. Let's use the boat, which is taking me to Antibes."

"With all my heart. We won't leave this fort and that heart-wrenching spectacle too soon."

So, after bidding farewell to the governor, the three friends quit Sainte-Marguerite. And, among the final glimmers of the receding tempest, they saw the white walls of the fort for the last time.

That very same night, d'Artagnan said good-bye to his friends after watching the burning coach, which he had told Monsieur de Saint-Mars to set on fire.

After embracing Athos and mounting his horse, the captain said: "Friends, you look too much like soldiers abandoning their posts. Something tells me that Athos will need to be maintained in his rank by you. Would you like me to get permission to go to Africa with one hundred good musketeers? The king won't refuse me, and I'll take you with me."

"Monsieur d'Artagnan," replied Raoul, effusively shaking the captain's hand, "thank you for your offer, which will give us more than the count and I want. I'm young, I need mental work and physical fatigue, while my father requires the deepest rest. You're his best friend. I recommend him to your care. By watching over him, you'll hold both our souls in your hand."

"I have to get going, my horse is losing patience!" said d'Artagnan, for whom the most blatant sign of deep feelings was to change the subject. "Listen, Count, how many more days does Raoul have to stay here?"

"Three days at the most!"

"And how long will it take you to reach your home?"

"Oh, a long time," replied Athos. "I don't want Raoul and me to separate all too soon. Time will push him quickly enough for me not to help him in the distance. I'll travel only by half stages."

"Why do that, my friend? It's a sad thing to go slow, and hostelry life no longer suits a man like you."

"My friend, I rode here on post-horses, but I want to buy

two fine mounts. Now, if I'm to get them home in a fresh state, I shouldn't ride them for more than seven or eight leagues a day."

"Where's Grimaud?"

"He arrived with Raoul's equipment yesterday morning, and I let him sleep."

"There's no going back!" The words slipped out. "Well, then, good-bye, dear Athos," D'Artagnan went on. "And if you hurry, I'll embrace you all the sooner." Having spoken, he put his foot in the stirrup, which Raoul held for him.

"Farewell," said the young man, embracing him.

"Farewell," said d'Artagnan, mounting the saddle. His horse lurched forward, leaving the friends behind.

This scene took place in front of the house chosen by Athos at the gates of Antibes; and that was where d'Artagnan, after supper, had ordered his horses to be brought to him. That was also the start of the road, which stretched out, white and sinuous, in the nocturnal vapors. The horse forcefully inhaled the briny aroma exuded by the marshes.

D'Artagnan trotted off, and Athos sadly headed back together with Raoul. Suddenly, they heard the pounding of hooves and at first they mistook them for the strange, deceptive clattering that echoes from each twist of a road. But then the rider came back. It was d'Artagnan galloping toward his friends, who shouted in joyful surprise. The captain, jumping down like a man half his age, threw his arms around the cherished heads of Athos and Raoul. He hugged them for a long time without breathing a word and without emitting the sigh that was bursting his chest. Then, as swiftly as he had come, he dashed away, digging his spurs into the flanks of his furious mount.

"Alas!" the count whispered. "Alas!"

"A bad omen!" d'Artagnan thought to himself, trying to make up for lost time. "I couldn't smile at them. A bad omen!"

The next day, Grimaud was on foot again. The service ordered by the Duke de Beaufort had been performed successfully. The flotilla assembled by Raoul had left for Toulon, hauling tiny, almost invisible skiffs that carried the wives and the friends of the smugglers and the fishermen requisitioned for the navy. The few remaining moments for father and son to spend together were racing by twice as fast as usual—like the growing speed of everything that is about to plunge into the abyss of eternity.

Athos and Raoul returned to Toulon, which was filling up with the hubbub of carriages, the banging of arms, the neighing of horses. The trumpets blared their haughty marches, the drums boomed their vigor, the streets regurgitated soldiers, servants, and tradesmen. The Duke de Beaufort was everywhere, plodding along the embarkment with the zeal and devotion of a good officer. He cajoled even his humblest companions; and he hectored even his highest-ranking lieutenants. Artillery, provisions, baggage—he wanted to see everything for himself. He examined each soldier's equipment, checked each horse's state of health. You felt that this aristocrat, so shallow, boastful, and selfish in his mansion, was once more a soldier, a grand seigneur as a captain, fulfilling the responsibility that he had accepted.

Nevertheless, it must be said that however rigorous his preparations for departure, you readily spotted carefree haste and the absence of all precaution—two features that make the French soldier the finest soldier in the world, because he is left, more than any other, to his own devices, both mental and physical. Satisfied, or apparently so, the admiral paid his compliments to Raoul and issued the final orders for setting sail at the crack of dawn.

The duke invited the count and his son to dinner; but they begged off, citing a few things they had to do. And they then kept to themselves. At the hostelry, located under the trees of the large square, they wolfed down their meal. Next, Athos took Raoul to the cliffs overlooking the town. The vast, gray mountains offer infinite views embracing a liquid horizon, which is so far away that it seems barely higher than the cliffs themselves.

The night was beautiful as always in these happy climes. The moon, rising from behind the rocks, unfurled like a silvery sheet across the blue carpet of the sea. In the roadstead, the vessels maneuvered silently, taking their ranks to ease the embarkment. The sea, charged with phosphorus, opened up under the hulls of the ships transporting baggage and ammunition. Each dip of the prow swept up that gulf of white flames, and each oar dripped liquid diamonds. The sailors, delighted with the admiral's generosity, hummed their slow and artless shanties. At times, the grinding of chains mingled with the dull thuds of cannonballs rolling in the holds. These spectacles and harmonies wrenched each heart like fear and gladdened each heart like hope. All this life suggested death.

Athos and Raoul settled on the moss and heather of the promontory. Huge bats soared around their heads, swept along in the horrendous whirlwind of their blind pursuit. Raoul's legs hung over the cliff, dangling in the dizzying void, which tempts us with nothingness.

When the moon was fully risen, with its light caressing the nearby mountain peaks; when the entire surface of the water was illuminated; and when small red lights dug holes in the black masses of the ships, Athos, gathering his thoughts and his courage, told his son:

"God made everything we see, Raoul. He also made us—poor atoms lost in this great universe. We glow like those fires and those stars, we sigh like those waves, we suffer like those huge vessels that are worn out in their passages, obeying the wind that drives them toward a destination, just as God's breath drives us toward a port. And everything is beautiful in living things."

"Sir," replied the young man, "we're watching a magnificent spectacle."

"What a good man D'Artagnan is!" Athos broke in. "What a rare pleasure leaning on a friend like him all one's life! That's something you've missed, Raoul."

"A friend?!" cried the young man. "I've missed having a friend?!"

"Monsieur de Guiche is a charming companion," the father spoke coldly. "But I believe that nowadays people are more concerned with their business and their pleasure than in my time. You've sought a life of seclusion; it's made you happy, but it's also drained your strength. We four musketeers have been slightly deprived of the abstract delights that bring joy; but we've put up a lot more resistance when we've been confronted with misfortune."

"Sir, I didn't interrupt you to say that I've got a friend and that this friend is Monsieur de Guiche. He's certainly fine and generous and he cares for me. But I've lived under the aegis of another friendship, sir, a friendship as strong and precious as those you're talking about: I mean *your* friendship."

"I haven't been a friend to you, Raoul," said Athos.

"Why do you say that, sir?"

"Because I've given you reason to believe that life has only a single face. Because, sad and severe as I am, I've always cut for you—unintentionally, God knows—the joyful buds that spring nonstop from the tree of youth. In short, at this point, I regret that I've never made you very effusive, very dissolute, very boisterous."

"I know why you're saying that, sir. But you're wrong. It's not you who've made me what I am. It was love, which took hold of me when most children only feel affection. It was my natural constancy, which in others is merely a habit. I believed that I would always remain as I was. I believed that God had thrown me on a very clear, very straight path lined with fruit and flowers. I had your strength, your vigilance over me. I believed that I was strong and vigilant. Nothing prepared me for what happened. I fell once, and that one fall exhausted my courage for the rest of my life. I can truthfully say that I was shattered. Oh, no, sir! You've given me only happiness in the past and you'll give me only hope in the future. No, I've got no complaints about the life you've made for me. I bless you and I love you deeply."

"My dear Raoul, your words make me feel good. They prove that you'll be acting slightly for me in the time that lies ahead."

"I will act only for you, sir!"

"Raoul, from now on I am going to be for you what I have never been for you. I will be your friend and no longer your father. When you return, we will be lavish with ourselves instead of living as prisoners. You'll return soon, won't you?"

"Of course, sir. This kind of expedition doesn't take long."

"So then soon, Raoul, soon. Rather than sticking modestly to my income, I'll give you the capital of my estates. It will be enough to launch you in the world until my death, and I hope that before I pass on you'll give me the consolation of not letting my lineage die out."

"I'll do whatever you order me to do," said Raoul, profoundly shaken.

"Raoul, as aide-de-camp you mustn't run too many risks. You've proved your mettle, people know that you're brave under fire. Just remember that war with the Arabs is a war of snares, ambushes, and carnage."

"Yes, sir, that's what I'm told."

"There's little glory in being killed in an ambush. It's the kind of death that hints at a little rashness or lack of foresight. Many such victims aren't even mourned. And such unmourned soldiers die in vain, Raoul. Furthermore, the victor laughs, and we must not allow those stupid infidels to triumph because of our faults. Do you fully grasp what I'm saying, Raoul? God forbid that I should exhort you to give a wide berth to encounters!"

"I'm prudent by nature, sir, and I'm very lucky," said Raoul with a smile that froze his poor father's heart. The son then hastened to add: "I've seen action twenty times, and so far I've been scratched only once!"

"The climate also has to be feared," said Athos. "Dying of fever is an ugly affair. King Saint-Louis prayed to God to send him an arrow or the plague rather than a fever."

"Oh, sir. With sobriety, with reasonable exercise—"

Athos broke in: "The Duke de Beaufort has promised me that he'll send dispatches to France every other week. You, as his aide-de-camp, will be in charge of transmitting them. I can assume you won't forget me?"

"No, sir," said Raoul, choking with emotion.

"Finally, Raoul, since you're a good Christian, and so am I, we can count on special protection from God or His guardian angels. Promise me that if any harm comes to you, you'll think of me first."

"I certainly will! Oh, yes!"

"And you'll summon me?"

"Oh! At once!"

"Do you ever dream about me, Raoul?"

"Every night, sir. In my childhood, I saw you in my dreams. You were calm and gentle and you slipped your hand under my head. That's why I always slept so well . . . long ago."

"Now that we're separating, we love each other too much not to have a piece of one another's souls travel with us and live with us. Whenever you'll feel sad, Raoul, I sense that my heart will drown in sorrow, and when you'll want to smile while thinking of me, remember to send me a ray of your joy."

"I won't promise to be joyful," replied the young man. "But you can be certain that I won't let an hour pass without my thinking of you. Not an hour, I swear to you, unless I'm dead."

Athos could hold back no longer: he threw his arms around his son and with all his strength he clasped him to his heart.

The moon had faded into the twilight, and a golden band rose on the horizon, announcing the coming of day.

The father threw his cloak over Raoul's shoulders and brought him to town, which was already like a vast anthill, teeming with porters and carriers and everyone else. As Athos and Raoul left the edge of the plateau, they saw an indecisive black shadow, which seemed embarrassed to be spotted. It was Grimaud, who, worried about his master, had followed his trail and was now waiting for them.

"Oh, our good Grimaud!" cried Raoul. "What can we do for you? You've come to tell us it's time to leave, haven't you?"

"All alone?" asked Grimaud, pointing at Raoul. His reprimanding voice showed how flabbergasted he was.

"You're right!" exclaimed the count. "No, Raoul won't leave all alone! No, he won't remain on foreign soil without a friend to console him and remind him of everything he loves."

"Me?" said Grimaud.

"You? Yes, yes!" cried Raoul, touched to the quick.

"Alas!" sighed Athos. "You're quite long in the tooth, my good Grimaud!"

"All the better!" Grimaud retorted with a wealth of inexpressible emotion and intelligence.

"But the embarkment is moving forward," said Raoul, "and you're not the least bit prepared."

"Sure I am!" said Grimaud, showing the keys to his coffers—keys that were mixed with those of his young master.

Raoul objected. "You can't leave my father all alone. You've never left him before."

Grimaud focused his dimmed eyes on Athos as if measuring each man's strength. The count didn't respond.

"The count would rather I went," said Grimaud.

Athos nodded.

At that moment the drums all boomed in unison, and the clarions filled the air with joyful peals. The regiments taking part in the expedition began emerging from the city. There were five regiments, each made up of forty companies. The Royals, who were recognized by their blue-trimmed white uniforms, headed the parade. The regimental colors, quartered crosswise, violet and *feuille-morte* brown, with a scattering of golden fleurs-de-lys, let the white flag dominate with its fleur-de-lys cross. Musketeers at the flanks, with their cleft sticks in their hands and muskets on their shoulders; pikemen at the center, with their fourteen-foot lances: they all marched gaily toward the transports, which would ferry them to the troop ships. Next came the regiments of Picardy, Navarre, and Royal-Vessel. The Duke de Beaufort had made an excellent choice. He could be seen in the distance, closing off the parade with his general staff. It would take him a good hour to reach the sea.

Raoul and Athos slowly trudged toward the shore, where the son would take his place when the duke arrived. Grimaud, seething with youthful ardor, had Raoul's baggage carried to the flagship. Athos, his arm slipping into that of his son, whom he was about to lose, was absorbed in the most painful meditation, drowning his sorrow in the noise and movement.

All at once, an officer of the duke came over and informed them that the duke wished to have Raoul at his side.

"Monsieur," cried the young man, "please tell the duke that I beg him to let me enjoy this final hour in the count's presence."

"No, no!" Athos broke in. "An aide-de-camp cannot leave his general. Please tell the duke that the viscount will be joining him."

The officer galloped off.

"We can part here, we can part there," added the count. "Either way, it's a separation." While striding, he carefully dusted Raoul's suit and ran his hand over his hair.

"Listen, Raoul," said Athos, "you need money. The duke lives on a grand scale, and I'm certain that you'll indulge in buying horses and weapons, which are precious commodities in Gigelli. Now, since you serve neither the king nor the duke, and since you're acting solely upon your own free will, you cannot count on pay or largesse. I don't want you to be lacking anything. So here is two hundred pistoles. Spend it if you want to give me pleasure, Raoul."

The son shook his father's hand.

At a bend in the road, they spotted the duke riding a magnificent white jennet, which gracefully curvetted in response to the women's applause. The duke called Raoul over and held out his hand to the father. He spoke to him for a long time, and with such a sweet expression, that the poor father was somewhat comforted.

Yet both father and son felt they were being led to an execution. There was a dreadful moment when, leaving the sand of the beach, the soldiers and sailors exchanged their final kisses with their friends and families. It was a supreme moment: despite the purity of the sky, despite the heat of the sun, despite the fragrances of the air and the fine life circulating in veins, everything seemed black, everything seemed bitter, everything made you doubt God even, while speaking with His very lips.

It was customary for the admiral and his retinue to bring up the rear. The cannon was waiting to roar with its formidable voice the instant the admiral set foot on the deck of his ship.

Athos, oblivious of the duke, the fleet, and his own image as a strong man, opened his arms to his son and embraced him convulsively.

"Accompany us abroad," said the deeply moved admiral. "You'll save a good half hour."

"No," said Athos. "No. I've said my good-bye. I don't want to say it again."

"Well, Viscount, then get on board, get on board quickly!"

said the duke, trying to spare the tears of the two men, whose hearts were bursting. Tender, paternal, and as strong as Porthos would have been, the duke took Raoul into his arms and placed him in the skiff; its oars promptly started dipping at a signal. Forgetting protocol, the duke then jumped on the gunnel and with a vigorous kick he pushed the boat out.

"Good-bye!" cried Raoul.

Athos could only wave, but he felt something burning on his hand. It was Grimaud's respectful kiss, the final farewell of the loyal dog. Grimaud then leaped upon the bow of a two-oar yawl, which had just been tugged by a barge using twelve galley oars.

Athos sat down on the pier, dull, abandoned, grief-stricken. Each second carried off a feature, a nuance, of his son's pale complexion. His arms dangling, his eyes fixed, Athos remained fused with Raoul in the same gaze, the same thought, the same stupor. The sea gradually drew away vessels and figures, until the men were nothing but dots, and love was nothing but a memory.

Athos watched his son climb up to the flagship, watched him lean on the rail and place himself within his father's sight. The cannon may have boomed, the ships may have emitted a long cacophony eliciting loud cheers from the shore, the hubbub may have deadened the father's ears, and the smoke may have clouded the beloved goal of all he strove for, but Raoul was visible to him until the very last moment. And the imperceptible atom, fading from black to pale, from pale to white, from white to nothingness, disappeared for Athos, disappeared long after powerful ships and bellying sails had vanished for the other spectators.

Toward noon, when the sun was devouring space and the tops of the masts barely dominated the incandescent line of the ocean, Athos saw a gentle, airborne shadow rising and instantly melting: it was the smoke from a cannon that the Duke de Beaufort had just had fired to salute the French coast one last time.

The dot was buried in turn under the sky, and Athos painfully struggled back to his lodgings.

34
Among Women

D'Artagnan had failed to hide his emotions from his friends as much as he would have liked. For several minutes, the stoic warrior, the impassive man of arms, vanquished by fear and foreboding, had succumbed to his human weakness. Thus, quieting his heart and calming his shaken nerves, he turned to his lackey, a silent domestic servant, who always kept his ears open in order to obey more swiftly. "Look, Rabaud," said d'Artagnan, "I have to lay back thirty leagues a day."

"Fine, sir," replied Rabaud.

From then on, d'Artagnan, virtually forming a centaur with his horse, concerned himself with nothing—that is, with everything. He wondered why the king had summoned him, and why the Iron Mask had thrown a silver plate at Raoul's feet.

In regard to the king, d'Artagnan was at a loss. He knew all too well that the king would summon him only if necessary. He also knew that Louis XIV must have felt the imperious need for a private conversation with a man whose knowledge of such a dreadful secret placed him on one of the highest levels of power in the kingdom. However, d'Artagnan was incapable of pinpointing the king's wishes.

Nor did the musketeer have any doubts as to why the unfortunate Philip had revealed his identity and his birth. Buried forever under his iron mask, exiled in a country where men appeared enslaved by the elements, Philip was deprived of even the company of d'Artagnan, who had showered him with honors and delicate attention. All that the prisoner could see was ghosts and sorrows in this world; and despair was starting to gnaw at him, forcing him to lament, compelling him to believe that his revelations would find him an avenger.

The way in which d'Artagnan had nearly killed his two best friends, the fate that had so bizarrely led Athos to share the state secret, his farewell to Raoul, the obscurity of that future which would end in a sad death—all these things incessantly aroused d'Artagnan's dire forebodings, which were not dissipated, as in the past, by his mount's breakneck gallop.

Next, d'Artagnan pictured Porthos and Aramis as outcasts, as ruined and tracked fugitives, the laborious architects of a fortune they were bound to lose. And, since the king was calling for his man of deeds in a moment of rancor and revenge, d'Artagnan trembled, thinking he might receive an order that would make his heart bleed.

When charging uphill on his winded horse, its nostrils flaring, its flanks heaving, the captain, more free to ponder, would sometimes think about Aramis, that prodigious genius—a genius of acumen and intrigue, two qualities that had been produced by the Fronde and the Civil War. A soldier, a priest, and a diplomat, gallant, greedy, and cunning, Aramis had used the good things of life purely as stepping-stones to the bad things. With a generous spirit if not a noble heart, he never did wrong except to shine a bit more brightly. Toward the end of his career, within reach of his goal, he had—like that patrician Fieschi—virtually taken a false step on a plank and tumbled into the sea.

But Porthos! That good and naïve Porthos! To see Porthos starving; to see Mousqueton without gold trimming, incarcerated, perhaps; to see Pierrefonds, Bracieux razed to the very stones, dishonored to the very woods—all these things brought such agonizing heartache to d'Artagnan. And whenever he was struck by his grief, he rebounded like a horse at the sting of the gadfly under the vaults of foliage.

The man of the mind is never bored if his body is exhausted. And never has the healthy man of the body failed to find the lightness of life if something has captivated his mind. D'Artagnan, still racing, still mulling, reached Paris with fresh and tender muscles, like the athlete who's been warming up for the gymnasium.

The king, not expecting him this soon, had just gone out hunting toward Meudon. Instead of chasing after the king as he would have done in the past, d'Artagnan removed his boots and his clothes and enjoyed a bath while waiting for His Majesty to return dusty and drained. The captain spent the interval of five hours, as people phrase it, "taking the pulse of the house" and steeling himself against all bad luck.

He learned that the king had been gloomy for the past two weeks; that the queen mother was ill, indeed prostrate; that the king's younger brother was devoting himself to prayers; that his wife had the vapors; and the Monsieur de Guiche had left for one of his estates. D'Artagnan also learned that Monsieur Colbert was radiant; that Monsieur Fouquet was consulting a different physician every day, that he wasn't healing, and that his chief illness wasn't the kind that is cured by physicians—except for political physicians.

The king, d'Artagnan was told, was showing Fouquet the tenderest face, and never letting him out of his sight. But the superintendent, touched to the core, like those beautiful trees that are pierced by a worm, was fading despite the royal smile, that sun among trees at court.

D'Artagnan found out that Mademoiselle de la Vallière had become indispensable to the king, that if he didn't take her hunting, he would write her several times: not poems but, far worse, prose, and many pages to boot. Meanwhile, the deer and the pheasants were frolicking about, pursued so gently that, d'Artagnan was told, the art of venery risked degenerating at the French court.

The captain then thought about that poor Raoul's wishes, that desperate letter written to a woman who spent her days hoping. And since d'Artagnan loved to philosophize, he resolved to profit from the king's absence by conversing for a moment with Mademoiselle de la Vallière.

It was easy to arrange. During the royal hunt, Louise was strolling with some ladies in a gallery of the Palais-Royal, where the captain happened to have some guards to inspect. D'Artagnan had no doubts that if he could just bring up Raoul, Louise might give him grounds for penning a good letter to the poor exile. Now Raoul's hope, or at least his consolation in the emotional state in which we have seen him, was the son—was the lives of two men who were quite dear to our captain. He therefore headed toward the place where he knew he'd find Mademoiselle de la Vallière.

When he arrived, she was surrounded by people. In his apparent solitude, the king's favorite received like a queen—more than the queen, perhaps—an homage of which the king's sister-in-law had been so proud when the king had looked exclusively at her and commanded the courtiers' eyes as well.

D'Artagnan, albeit no ladies' man, received nothing but flattery and attention from the ladies. He was as courteous as a gallant man should be, and his incredible reputation had won him as much friendship among the men as admiration among the women. Thus, upon seeing him enter, the maids of honor addressed him, plying him with questions: Where had he been keeping himself? What had become of him? Why hadn't his lovely horse performed all those volt-faces that astonished curious spectators on the king's balcony?

He replied that he had returned from the land of oranges.

The ladies burst out laughing. In those days, everyone was traveling, and yet a trip of one hundred leagues was a problem that could often be solved by death.

"The land of oranges?" cried Mademoiselle de Tonnay-Charente. "You mean Spain?"

"No, no!" said the musketeer.

"Malta?" Mademoiselle Montalais guessed.

"Goodness! You're getting close, ladies."

"Is it an island?" asked Mademoiselle de la Vallière.

"Mademoiselle," said d'Artagnan, "I don't want to keep you on tenterhooks. I've been in the land where the Duke de Beaufort is now embarking for Algiers."

"Did you see the army?" several bellicose ladies asked.

"As plainly as I see you now," replied d'Artagnan.

"What about the fleet?"

"I saw everything."

"Do we have *friends* there?" Mademoiselle de Tonnay-Charente asked nonchalantly, yet in such a way as to draw attention to that word, focusing on it with a calculated aim.

"Why, there's Monsieur de La Gulliotière," said d'Artagnan, "Monsieur de Mouchy, Monsieur de Bragelonne."

Mademoiselle de la Vallière turned pale.

"Monsieur de Bragelonne?" exclaimed the perfidious Athénaïs. "What? He's gone off to war? . . . Him?"

Mademoiselle de Montalais stepped on her foot, but it was no use.

"Would you like to hear my theory?" the lady pitilessly asked d'Artagnan.

"Yes, mademoiselle, I'd love to hear it."

"My theory is that all the men fighting this war are desperate creatures who've been mistreated by love and who are seeking black women who are less cruel than white women."

Several ladies began to laugh. Mademoiselle de la Vallière was bewildered. Mademoiselle de Montalais coughed loudly enough to wake the dead.

"Mademoiselle," d'Artagnan broke in, "you're wrong about the women of Gigelli. Those women aren't black. It's true that they're not white—they're more yellow."

"Yellow!"

"Oh, don't put it down. I've never seen a color that blended more nicely with black eyes and coral lips."

"All the better for Monsieur de Bragelonne!" Mademoiselle de Tonnay-Charente retorted. "It will speed his recovery, the poor boy!"

Her words were followed by a profound hush. D'Artagnan had time to reflect that women—those gentle doves—treat one another more cruelly than bears and tigers.

It wasn't enough for the mademoiselle to have made Louise blanch; she wanted to make her turn red. Continuing without a pause, she said, "Louise, do you realize you've got a great sin on your conscience?"

"What sin, mademoiselle?" stammered the unfortunate Louise, casting about for support but finding none.

"Why, you were engaged to that boy. He loved you. You rejected him."

"That's the privilege of an honest woman," Mademoiselle de Montalais said in a pretentious tone of voice. "If you know you can't make a man happy, then it's better to reject him."

Louise was unable to decide whether to chide or thank the person defending her.

"Reject! Reject! That's all well and good!" said Athénaïs. "But that's not the sin that Mademoiselle de la Vallière should reproach herself for. Her real sin is to send that poor Bragelonne to war, a war in which he'll find death."

Louise ran her hand across her icy forehead.

"And if he dies," the ruthless woman went on, "you'll have killed him. That is your sin."

Louise, half dead herself, reeled as she grabbed the arm of the musketeer captain, whose face showed an unfamiliar agitation.

"You wished to speak with me, Monsieur d'Artagnan," she said in a voice altered by anger and sorrow. "What did you want to tell me?"

Holding Louise's arm, d'Artagnan took a few steps in the gallery. Once they were at a safe distance from the others, he said, "What I have to tell you, mademoiselle, was expressed by Mademoiselle de Tonnay-Charente, brutally but thoroughly."

Louise uttered a soft cry, and, deeply lacerated by this new wound, she went her way like the poor, mortally injured bird that seeks out the shadow of the thicket to die. She disappeared behind a door just as the king entered by another door. The first thing he did was look at his mistress's empty chair. Unable to find her, he frowned. But then he promptly spotted d'Artagnan, who bowed to him.

"Ah, monsieur!" said the king. "You've been very prompt, and that pleases me." It was the superlative expression of royal satisfaction. Countless men would have sacrificed their lives to obtain that response from the king.

The maids of honor and the courtiers, who had formed a respectful circle around the monarch, moved aside upon seeing him look for a private conversation with his captain of the musketeers. After peering about once more for Mademoiselle de la Vallière, the king, mystified by her absence, led the way, conducting d'Artagnan outside the room.

Once they were beyond curious ears, the monarch said, "Well, Monsieur d'Artagnan! What about the prisoner?"

"He's in his prison, sire."

"What did he say en route?"

"Nothing, sire."

"What did he do?"

"There was a point at which the fisherman who was transporting us to Sainte-Marguerite rebelled and tried to kill me. The . . . prisoner defended me instead of attempting to flee."

The king blanched. "That's enough!"

D'Artagnan bowed. Louis paced up and down his study. "Were you in Antibes when the Duke de Beaufort arrived there?"

"No, sire. I was just leaving when the duke arrived."

"Aha!" A new silence. Then: "What did you see?"

"Lots of men," d'Artagnan replied coldly.

The king saw that d'Artagnan didn't want to speak. "I sent for you, Captain, in order to tell you to prepare my lodgings in Nantes."

"Nantes?" exclaimed d'Artagnan.

"In Brittany."

"Yes, sire, in Brittany. Will Your Majesty be undertaking the long journey to Nantes?"

"The Estates are assembling there," replied the king. "I have two requests to make them; I want to be there."

"When should I leave?" asked the captain.

"Tonight . . . Tomorrow . . . Tomorrow evening—you'll need to rest."

"I'm rested, sire."

"Wonderful. Then leave between tonight and tomorrow, whenever you wish."

D'Artagnan bowed by way of leaving. But then he realized that the king was very embarrassed. "Is the king—" D'Artagnan took two steps forward. "Is the king taking along the court?"

"Certainly."

"Then the king will need the musketeers, no doubt?" And the captain's penetrating eyes compelled the king to lower his.

"Take a whole brigade," Louis responded.

"Is that all? The king has no further orders for me?"

"No . . . Ah! . . . Yes I do."

"I'm listening."

"I'm told that the castle of Nantes is poorly laid out. So you'll make sure to post musketeers at the door of each of the principal dignitaries whom I'll be taking."

"Principal dignitaries?"

"Yes."

"For instance, at Monsieur de Lyonne's door?"

"Yes."

"Monsieur Le Tellier's?"

"Yes."

"Monsieur de Brienne's?"

"Yes."

"And Monsieur the Superintendent?"

"Exactly."

"Very well, sire. I'll leave by tomorrow."

"Oh! One more thing, Monsieur d'Artagnan. In Nantes, you'll meet with the Duke de Gesvres, the captain of the guards. Make sure that your musketeers are in place before his guards arrive. 'The early bird catches the worm'!"

"Yes, sire."

"And if the Duke de Gesvres questions you?"

"Come now, sire! Will he really question me?"

And the musketeer cavalierly turned on his heel and vanished. Nantes! he mused, descending the stairs. Why didn't he dare have me go straight to Belle-Île?

As he reached the front gates, a clerk sent by Monsieur de Brienne came dashing after him: "Monsieur d'Artagnan! Forgive me! . . ."

"What is it, Monsieur Ariste?"

"It's a voucher that the king ordered me to give you."

"On your account?"

"No, monsieur, on Monsieur Fouquet's account."

A surprised d'Artagnan read the voucher, which, handwritten by the king, was made out for two hundred pistoles. What? thought the captain after graciously thanking the clerk. Monsieur Fouquet will be paying for this trip?! Damn it! That's pure Louis XIV. Why didn't he make it Monsieur Colbert's account? Colbert would have been ecstatic!

And d'Artagnan, faithful to his principle of never letting a sight draft grow cold, went to Monsieur Fouquet to pick up his two hundred pistoles.

35
The Last Supper

Fouquet, who must have gotten wind of the king's imminent departure for Nantes, threw his friends a farewell banquet. From the top of his home to the bottom, the bustling of the servants carrying plates and the diligence of the clerks closing accounts heralded an approaching upheaval in both office and kitchen.

D'Artagnan, voucher in hand, presented himself in the office, where he was told that it was after hours: the office was closed. The captain tersely responded, "The king's service."

The clerk, slightly unnerved by d'Artagnan's grave mien, replied that it was a respectable reason, but that the practices of the house were also respectable, and that the bearer of the voucher should therefore return the next day.

D'Artagnan asked to see Monsieur Fouquet. The clerk, replying that the superintendent never got involved in such minor matters, brusquely slammed the last door in d'Artagnan's face. Having foreseen this reaction, the captain thrust his boot between the door and the jamb, so that the lock didn't catch, and the clerk was still nose to nose with his interlocutor. Showing terrified politeness, the clerk sang a new tune: "If Monsieur wishes to speak to Monsieur Fouquet, he can go to the antechambers—Monsieur Fouquet never comes to the offices."

"Fine!" retorted d'Artagnan. "Just say so!"

"They're on the other side of the court," said the clerk, delighted to be free.

D'Artagnan crossed the court and landed in the very midst of the servants. "Monseigneur is not receiving at this time," said a rapscallion carrying three pheasants and twelve quail on a silver-gilt platter.

"Tell Monsieur Fouquet," said the captain, grabbing the end of the platter, "that I am Monsieur d'Artagnan, captain-lieutenant of His Majesty's musketeers."

The valet emitted a cry of surprise and disappeared. D'Artagnan followed him slowly. He arrived at the antechamber just in time to find Monsieur Pellisson, who, a bit pale, was coming from the dining hall to find out what was wrong.

D'Artagnan smiled. "There's no problem, Monsieur Pellisson. I'm just cashing a small voucher."

"Ah!" said Fouquet's friend, breathing more easily. He took d'Artagnan by the hand and led him into the dining hall; there, a good number of Fouquet's close friends surrounded the superintendent, who was buried in the cushions of an armchair. The guests included all the Epicurean poets, who, when in Vaux, had reveled in Monsieur Fouquet's home, his wit, and his money. Joyful friends, mostly loyal, they hadn't abandoned their protector before the gathering storm; and despite the threatening sky, despite the shuddering earth, they remained, smiling, considerate, and as devoted to misfortune as they had been to prosperity.

At Fouquet's left sat Madame de Bellière; at his right, his wife: as if, braving the laws of the world and silencing all vulgar reasons for propriety, these two guardian angels were joining together in a moment of crisis to lend him the support of their entwined arms.

Madame de Bellière was pale, trembling, and full of respectful attention for Madame Fouquet, who, with one hand on her husband's hand, anxiously peered at the doorway through which Pellisson conducted d'Artagnan. The captain entered, full of courtesy, then admiration, when, with his infallible glance, he had guessed, and taken in, the significance of every physiognomy.

Fouquet rose slightly in his chair. "Please forgive me, Monsieur d'Artagnan, for not receiving you as someone coming in the name of the king." And he accentuated those last few words with something like a melancholy firmness that inspired fear in the hearts of his friends.

"Monseigneur," replied d'Artagnan, "I am here in the name of the king only to cash a voucher for two hundred pistoles."

All faces cheered up; only Fouquet's remained gloomy. "Ah! monsieur, are you also leaving for Nantes?" he asked.

"I don't know where I'm heading, monseigneur."

"But, monsieur," said Madame Fouquet, once more serene,

"you are not leaving so hastily that you cannot do us the honor of joining us."

"Madame, it would be a truly great honor for me. But I am so pressed for time that, as you can see, I've taken the liberty of interrupting your banquet in order to cash my note."

"Which will be paid in gold," said Fouquet, signaling his intendant, who promptly took the voucher and left.

"Oh!" said d'Artagnan. "I wasn't worried about the payment. Your house is solid."

A painful smile passed over Fouquet's pale features.

"Are you all right?" asked Madame de Bellière.

"Do you feel an attack coming on?" asked Madame Fouquet.

"I'm fine, thank you," the superintendent responded.

"An attack?" said d'Artagnan. "Are you ill, monseigneur?"

"I've got a tertian ague, which I caught after the celebration in Vaux."

"The cool night air in the grottoes?"

"No, no. Some agitation, that's all."

"You showed too much heart when you received the king," said La Fontaine tranquilly without suspecting that he had voiced a sacrilege.

"One cannot show too much heart when receiving the king," Fouquet softly murmured to his poet.

"Monsieur meant that you displayed too much ardor," d'Artagnan broke in, perfectly candid and charming. "The fact is, monseigneur, that hospitality has never been practiced as marvelously as in Vaux."

Madame Fouquet's face clearly expressed the notion that while Fouquet had behaved well for the king, the king would not do the same for the minister. However, d'Artagnan knew the terrible secret. Only he and Fouquet knew it. D'Artagnan didn't have the courage to pity Fouquet, and the latter didn't have the right to accuse.

Upon being handed his two hundred pistoles, the captain was about to take his leave when Fouquet got to his feet, picked up a glass of wine, and ordered a servant to bring d'Artagnan a glass of wine.

"Monsieur," said Fouquet, "to the king's health, *no matter what may occur.*"

"And to your health, monseigneur," said d'Artagnan, drinking, "*no matter what may occur.*"

With those ominous words, the captain bowed to the entire company, who stood up in response; and they then heard his boots and spurs all the way from the depths of the staircase.

"For a moment, I thought it was I he was after and not my money," said Fouquet, forcing a laugh.

"You?" his friends exclaimed. "And why, for goodness' sake?"

"Oh!" said Fouquet. "Let's not fool ourselves, my dear brothers in Epicure. I don't want to draw a comparison between the humblest sinner on earth and God, Whom we adore. But look! God once gave His friends a meal that we call the Last Supper and that was simply a farewell dinner like the one we're enjoying here."

A cry of painful denial came from all the guests.

"Close the doors," said Fouquet. And the servants disappeared. "My friends," Fouquet went on, lowering his voice, "what did I used to be? What am I today? Consult one another and answer me. A man like myself automatically begins to sink once he stops rising. And what will people say if he sinks truly? I've got no money, I've got no credit. All I've got is powerful foes and powerless friends."

"Quick!" exclaimed Pellisson, standing up. "Since you're being so frank, we should be equally frank! Yes, you're doomed. Yes, you're racing to your ruin, then stop! First of all, how much cash do we have left?"

"Seven hundred thousand pounds," said the intendant.

"Bread," murmured Madame Fouquet.

"Relays," said Pellisson, "relays—and flee!"

"To where?"

"Switzerland, Savoy—just flee!"

"If Monseigneur flees," explained Madame de Bellière, "people will say that he's guilty and that he got scared."

"They'll say even more. They'll say that I've absconded with twenty million!"

"We'll draw up accounts to prove your innocence," said La Fontaine. "Flee!"

"I'm staying," said Fouquet. "Besides, doesn't everything bear me out?"

"You've got Belle-Île!" cried the Abbé Fouquet.

"And I'll go there quite naturally when I go to Nantes," the superintendent replied. "Patience! Have patience!"

"It's a long way to Nantes!" exclaimed Madame Fouquet.

"I'm well aware of that," Fouquet responded. "But what can I do? The king has summoned me to the Estates. I know quite well that it spells my doom. But refusing to leave would mean showing that I'm worried."

"Well, I've hit on a way to reconcile everything," cried Pellisson. "You'll leave for Nantes."

Fouquet looked surprised.

"But you'll travel with friends and in your own coach to Orléans. There you'll take the barge to Nantes. You'll always be ready to defend yourself if you're attacked, to escape if you're threatened. You'll carry your money against all odds, and, by fleeing, you'll simply be obeying the king. You can set sail for Belle-Île whenever you please, and embark from there wherever you please—like the eagle that soars into space when it's driven from its aerie."

Pellisson's words were received with unanimous agreement.

"Yes, do that," Madame Fouquet advised her husband.

"Do that," said Madame de Bellière.

"Do that, do that!" all the friends exclaimed.

"I'll do it," Fouquet replied.

"Tonight."

"Within the hour."

"Immediately."

"With seven hundred thousand pounds you can lay the foundation for a new fortune," said the Abbé Fouquet. "Who can stop us from arming the corsairs in Belle-Île?"

"And if we have to, we'll go and discover a new world," added La Fontaine, intoxicated with plans and enthusiasm.

A knock at the door interrupted the company's joy and hope.

"A royal courier!" cried the master of ceremonies.

A profound hush filled the hall, as if the courier's message were merely a retort to all the plans hatched a moment earlier. Each person waited for a response from the host, who, his forehead dripping with sweat, was truly suffering from his ague. Fouquet stepped into his study in order to receive His Majesty's message.

The silence filling the chambers and the service rooms was so deep that Fouquet's voice reached all the way to the dining hall: "Very well, monsieur." However, his voice was broken with fatigue and stricken with agitation. An instant later, Fouquet sent for Gourville, who strode across the gallery while everyone waited in suspense. At last, Fouquet reappeared among his guests. The pale, drawn face he had left with was now livid and decomposed. A living wraith with parched lips, he held out his arms as he trudged along, like the ghost who comes to salute the friends of his lifetime. Upon seeing him, they all stood up, they all dashed over to him.

Gazing at Pellisson, who leaned on Fouquet's wife and gripped the frozen hand of the Marquise de Bellière, Fouquet said, "Well?" There was nothing human about his voice.

"My God, what's wrong?" they asked.

Fouquet opened his damp, clenched right hand, revealing a document, which a terrified Pellisson jumped on. He read the following lines written by the king:

Dear and beloved Monsieur Fouquet,

From what is left of our funds, give us a sum of seven hundred thousand pounds, which we need today for our departure.

And since we know that you are ailing, we pray to God that He may restore your health and keep you in His holy and worthy care.

LOUIS

The present letter serves as a receipt.

A horrified murmur swept through the hall.

"Well!" cried Pellisson. "You've received this letter?"

"Yes, I've received it."

"What are you going to do?"

"Nothing, since I've received it."

"But . . ."

"If I've received it, Pellisson, it means that I've paid the money," said the superintendent with heart-wrenching simplicity.

"You've paid it!" exclaimed his wife in despair. "Then we're lost!"

"C'mon, c'mon! No useless words!" Pellisson broke in. "After money, life! Mount your horse and leave, monseigneur!"

"Leave us!" the two women, intoxicated with pain, cried simultaneously.

"C'mon, monseigneur! By saving yourself you'll save all of us! Mount your horse!"

"Just look at him! He can't even stand!"

"Let's try and figure . . ." said the intrepid Pellisson.

"He's right," muttered Fouquet.

"Monseigneur, monseigneur!" shouted Gourville, taking the stairs four steps at a time. "Monseigneur!"

"Well? What is it?"

"As you know, I escorted the royal courier with the money."

"Yes?"

"Well, when I arrived at the Royal Palace, I saw . . ."

"Catch your breath, my poor friend, catch your breath. You're suffocating."

"What did you see?" cried the impatient friends.

"I saw the musketeers mount their horses," said Gourville.

"Don't you see?" cried the guests. "Don't you see? There's not a moment to lose!"

Madame Fouquet dashed down the stairs and demanded her horses. Madame de Bellière rushed after her, caught her in her arms, and said, "Madame, for the sake of his safety, don't even drop a hint, don't show any alarm."

Pellisson ran out to prepare the coaches. Meanwhile, Gourville passed around his hat, gathering whatever gold and silver the tearful and horrified friends threw in: the final offering, the final alms, that poverty donated to misfortune.

Fouquet, dragged along by some, carried by others, was placed in his coach. Gourville climbed up to the box and grabbed the reins. Pellisson supported Madame Fouquet, who had fainted. Madame de Bellière was stronger, and she was rewarded for her strength; she received Fouquet's final kiss. Pellisson easily justified this precipitous departure, explaining that the king was summoning all his ministers to Nantes.

36
Monsieur Colbert's Coach

As Gourville had seen, the king's musketeers mounted their horses and followed their captain. D'Artagnan, brooking no interference, left his brigade in the hands of a lieutenant and galloped off by himself on post-horses after recommending his men to practice utmost diligence. As rapidly as they rode, they couldn't arrive before him.

Passing Rue Croix-des-Petits-Champs, d'Artagnan glimpsed something that gave him food for thought. He spotted Monsieur Colbert leaving his house and stepping into a coach that was standing at the gates. The captain noticed two hooded females inside the coach, and, curious as he was, he wanted to know who they were. Trying to see these women, who were concealed, and whose ears were sharp, he dashed so close to the coach that his boot scraped the vehicle's apron, shaking both vehicle and passengers. One terrified lady uttered a cry in a young voice; the other lady spewed a curse that indicated the aplomb and vigor of half a century. The hoods were thrown back, revealing Madame Vanel and the Duchess de Chevreuse. D'Artagnan's eyes were swifter than theirs: he recognized them; they did not recognize him. Affectionately squeezing one another's hands, they laughed at their panic.

Goodness! d'Artagnan mused. The old duchess is not as fussy in her choice of cronies as she used to be. She's befriended Monsieur Colbert's mistress! Poor Fouquet! It's not a good sign!

D'Artagnan spurted forward. Monsieur Colbert got into the coach, and this noble trio began a rather slow pilgrimage to the forest of Vincennes. En route, Madame de Chevreuse dropped off Madame Vanel at her husband's home, then, alone with Colbert, she chatted away. The dear duchess had an inexhaustible fund of conversation. And since she generally spoke ill of others and well of herself, her conversation always amused her interlocutor and therefore always created a fine rapport.

She informed Colbert, who was unaware of it, what a great minister he was and how bleak Fouquet's future looked. She promised Colbert that once he became superintendent, she would rally the kingdom's entire ancient nobility behind him, and she asked him what role would be given to Mademoiselle de la Vallière. She praised Colbert, she scolded him, she confused him. She revealed the secret of so many secrets that for an instant Colbert thought he was dealing with the devil. She proved to him that she held today's Colbert in her hands just as she had held yesterday's Fouquet. And when he naïvely asked her why she hated the superintendent, she retorted, "Why do *you* hate him?"

"Madame, in politics, differences in method can foster dissidences between men. Monsieur Fouquet struck me as using a method that was not in the king's best interest."

The duchess broke in: "I won't speak about Monsieur Fouquet anymore. The king's trip to Nantes will show that we are right. For me, Monsieur Fouquet is finished. And for you as well."

Colbert held his tongue. The duchess continued:

"When he returns from Nantes, the king, who is only looking for an excuse, will find that the Estates have behaved badly, that they've made too few sacrifices. The Estates will reply that taxes are too burdensome and that Fouquet has ruined them. The king will heap all the blame on Fouquet, and then . . ."

"And then . . . ?" asked Colbert.

"Oh! He'll be disgraced. Don't you agree?"

Colbert peered at her, and his gaze meant: If Monsieur Fouquet is merely disgraced, it won't be because of you.

Madame de Chevreuse hastily added: "Your place must be clearly marked, Monsieur Colbert. Do you want to have anyone between the king and yourself after Fouquet's fall?"

"I don't understand."

"You will understand. What is the goal of your ambitions?"

"I have none."

"Then there's no use toppling Fouquet, Monsieur Colbert. It's an idle matter."

"I had the honor of telling you, madame—"

"Yes, yes! The king's best interest, I know. But now let's talk about *your* best interest."

"My interest is to serve His Majesty."

"Please enlighten me. Are you or are you not dooming Monsieur Fouquet? Give me a straight answer."

"Madame, I am not dooming anyone."

"Then I don't understand why you paid me so much for Monsieur Mazarin's letters about Monsieur Fouquet. Nor do I understand why you submitted those letters to the king."

Colbert gaped at the duchess uneasily. In a constrained voice he said, "And I, madame, understand even less how you, who took the money, can reproach me for my purchase."

"You see," the old duchess went on, "we must desire what we can, unless we cannot do what we desire."

"There we have it!" said Colbert, unnerved by that brutal logic.

"So you can't? Tell me."

"I can't, I confess, destroy certain influences on the king."

"Which have sided with Monsieur Fouquet? Identify them. Wait, I'll help you."

"Please do, madame."

"Mademoiselle de la Vallière?"

"Oh, she's got little influence. She's ignorant about business, and her means are sparse. Monsieur Fouquet once courted her."

"Defending him would be tantamount to accusing herself, isn't that right?"

"I think so."

"Is there another influential person? What do you say?"

"Considerably so!"

"The queen mother, perhaps?"

"Her Majesty the queen mother has a weakness for Monsieur Fouquet, much to her son's loss."

The old duchess smiled. "You mustn't believe that."

Colbert was incredulous. "I've so often witnessed it."

"In the past?"

"Just recently, madame, in Vaux. It was she who prevented the king from arresting Monsieur Fouquet."

"One doesn't have the same feelings every day, my dear monsieur. The queen may have desired something recently that she no longer desires today."

Colbert was amazed. "Why?"

"The reason doesn't matter."

"On the contrary, it matters a great deal. If I were sure I wasn't displeasing Her Majesty the queen mother, all my scruples would be gone."

"Well, haven't you heard about a certain secret?"

"A secret?"

"Call it what you like. In short, the queen mother is horrified at all those people who in one way or another have helped to expose this secret. And I do believe that Monsieur Fouquet is one of those people."

"Then," Colbert said, "we can count on the queen mother?"

"I've just left Her Majesty, and she assured me that we can."

"So be it, madame!"

"There's more! Do you perhaps know a man who was Monsieur Fouquet's intimate friend: Monsieur d'Herblay—a bishop, I believe?"

"The Bishop of Vannes."

"Well, this Monsieur d'Herblay, who was also in on the secret—the queen mother is having him pursued relentlessly."

"Really?"

"Pursued so thoroughly that if he were dead, she would demand his head to make sure it will never speak again."

"Are those the wishes of the queen mother?"

"Her orders!"

"Then Monsieur d'Herblay will be tracked down."

"Oh, we know his whereabouts."

Colbert looked at the duchess. "Tell me, madame."

"He's in Belle-Île."

"At Monsieur Fouquet's estate?"

"Exactly!"

"We'll catch him!"

It was the duchess's turn to smile. "Don't jump to conclusions, and don't promise so lightly."

"Why not, madame?"

"Because Monsieur d'Herblay is not the sort of man who is caught at will."

"So he's a rebel, then?"

"Oh, Monsieur Colbert! We've spent our lives being rebels, and, as you can see, far from being captured we capture others."

Colbert glared at the old duchess with indescribable ferocity and with a firmness that was not lacking in grandeur. "The times are past when commoners gained duchies by waging war against the king of France. If Monsieur d'Herblay has plotted against the throne, he will perish on the scaffold. His death may or may not please his enemies, but that scarcely concerns us."

And that "us," so foreign to Colbert's lips, made the duchess reflect for an instant. She caught herself reckoning mentally with this man. Colbert had regained the upper hand in their conversation and he wanted to keep it. "Are you asking me, madame, to have Monsieur d'Herblay arrested?"

"I? I am asking nothing of you."

"I thought you were, madame. But since I'm mistaken, let it be. So far the king has said nothing."

The duchess chewed her nails.

"Besides," Colbert went on, "what a poor capture that would be. The king's prey a bishop! Oh, no, no! I won't get involved in this matter."

The duchess's hatred was as clear as day. "A woman's game, and the queen mother is a woman. If she wants to have Monsieur d'Herblay arrested, she must have her reasons. And, besides, isn't Monsieur d'Herblay friends with the man who is about to be disgraced?"

"Oh, never mind that!" said Colbert. "They will spare him if he is not the king's enemy. Does that displease you?"

"I'll hold my tongue."

"Yes, you'd love to see him in prison—say, in the Bastille?"

"I believe that a secret is better hidden behind the walls of the Bastille than behind those of Belle-Île."

"I'll discuss it with the king. He'll clear the point up."

"By the time the point is cleared up, monsieur, the Bishop of Vannes will have fled. I would flee in his place."

"Fled? He? And where would he flee? Europe is ours, in will if not in fact."

"He'll manage to find asylum, monsieur. It's obvious that you don't realize whom you're dealing with. You do not know Monsieur d'Herblay, you didn't know Aramis. He was one of those four musketeers who, under the late king, made Cardinal de Richelieu tremble. And during the Regency they caused so much trouble for Monseigneur de Mazarin."

"But, madame, how will he pull it off without the backing of his own kingdom?"

"He's got it, monsieur."

"His own kingdom? Monsieur d'Herblay?"

"I repeat, monsieur. If he needs a kingdom, he has one or he will have one."

"Well, as you set so much store by preventing his escape, madame, I can assure you that this rebel will not escape."

"Belle-Île is fortified, Monsieur Colbert, and fortified by him."

"No matter how well he defends Belle-Île, it is not impregnable. And if the Bishop of Vannes is tucked away in Belle-Île, madame, the king's forces will lay siege to it and take it."

"You may rest assured, monsieur, that the zeal you show for the interests of the queen mother will touch Her Majesty's heart and that your reward will be magnificent. But what should I tell her about your plans for this man?"

"Once he's captured, he'll be locked away in a fortress from which his secret shall never see the light of day again."

"Very good, Monsieur Colbert. And we can say that, as of this instant, you and I have formed a solid alliance, and that I am completely in your service."

"It is I, madame, who am in your service. That Chevalier d'Herblay—he's a Spanish spy, isn't he?"

"More than that."

"A secret ambassador?"

"You're getting warm."

"Wait . . . King Philip of Spain is devout. D'Herblay is . . . his confessor?"

"You're getting even warmer."

"Damn it!" cried Colbert, forgetting himself to the point of cursing in front of that grand lady, that old friend of the queen mother, that Duchess de Chevreuse. "So he's the general of the Jesuits?"

"I do believe you've guessed it," replied the duchess.

"Ah, madame! Then he will ruin us all if we don't head him off! We've got to hurry!"

"That's my opinion, monsieur, but I didn't dare tell you."

"And it's lucky for us that he attacked the throne instead of attacking us."

"Listen carefully, Monsieur Colbert. Monsieur d'Herblay is never discouraged, and, if he misses the mark, he simply starts over. If he has failed to create his own king, then sooner or later he'll create another, and you definitely won't be prime minister."

Colbert scowled ominously. "Madame, I am relying on prison to settle this matter in a way that is satisfactory for both of us."

The duchess smiled. "If you knew how often Aramis has left prison!"

"Oh, we'll make sure that he won't get out this time."

"Didn't you hear what I've just said? Are you forgetting that Aramis was one of the four invincibles who terrified Richelieu? And back then, the four musketeers didn't have what they've got today: money and experience."

Colbert chewed his lips. "We'll avoid prison," he muttered in a lower tone. "We'll find a retreat that the invincible musketeer cannot leave."

"Excellent, my ally," the duchess responded. "But it's getting late. Shouldn't we go home?"

"All the more gladly, madame, since I have to make my preparations for my departure with the king."

"To Paris!" the duchess shouted at the coachman.

And the coach drove back to Faubourg Saint-Antoine after the conclusion of this treaty, which spelled the death of Fouquet's last friend, the last defender of Belle-Île, the former friend of the duchess, the new enemy of the duchess.

. . .

37
The Two Lighters

D'Artagnan had left, and so had Fouquet, the latter with a rapidity intensified by the fond interest of his friends. The first few moments of this trip—or, rather, this escape—were disturbed by an incessant fear triggered by all horses, all vehicles that they spotted behind the fugitive. It didn't actually make sense for Louis XIV to let this prey escape if he was determined to catch him. By now, the young lion was an experienced hunter, and his bloodhounds were ardent enough for him to be able to count on them.

However, by slow degrees, all fear evaporated. Swift as he was, the superintendent managed to get so far ahead of his pursuers that none could be reasonably expected to catch up with him. As for his state of mind, it was excellent due to his friends. Wasn't he hastening to join the king in Nantes, and didn't the traveler's speed testify to his zeal?

Weary but reassured, he arrived in Orléans, where, thanks to a courier who had preceded him, Fouquet found an excellent eight-oared lighter. These slightly wide, slightly heavy vessels, which looked like gondolas, had a small covered chamber shaped like a deck and a poop chamber shaped like a tent. Plying the Loire, they carried passengers from Orléans to Nantes; and this route, a long one even today, appeared more charming and more comfortable than the highway with its worn-out post-horses and its broken-down coaches. Fouquet boarded the lighter, which set sail immediately. The rowers, aware they had the honor of ferrying the superintendent of finances, pulled like mad. And that magic word, "finances," promised them a generous gratuity, of which they wanted to be worthy.

The lighter sped over the waves of the Loire. The weather

was magnificent, and one of those sunrises that color a landscape purple left the river in all its limpid serenity. The current and the oarsmen conveyed Fouquet just as wings carry a bird, so that he reached Beaugency without a single incident. He hoped to be the first to arrive in Nantes. There he would see the notables and find support among the principal members of the Estates. He would make himself necessary, which was easy enough for a man of his merit; in this way, he would stave off the catastrophe, if not succeed in avoiding it altogether.

"Besides," said Gourville, "in Nantes you or we will figure out your enemies' intentions. We'll have the horses ready to take you to the inextricable Poitou and a boat to carry you out to sea. Once you're at sea, Belle-Île is the inviolable port. Moreover, you can see that nobody is watching you and nobody is following you."

No sooner was he done than they spotted the distant masts of a huge lighter emerging from around a bend in the river and heading downstream. Fouquet's oarsmen uttered a cry of surprise at the sight of that vessel.

"What's the matter?" asked Fouquet.

"It's really extraordinary, monseigneur," replied the skipper. "That lighter is moving like a hurricane."

Gourville shivered and then went up on deck to have a better view. Fouquet didn't join him. Bottling up his mistrust, Fouquet said, "Go and see what it is, my friend."

The lighter had just steered around the bend. It moved so quickly that they could spot the white trail of its wake illuminated by the fiery daylight.

"What speed!" said the skipper. "What speed! The pay must be great! I'd never have believed that wooden oars could outdo our oars. But there they are, proving me wrong!"

"I believe it!" cried one of the rowers. "There are twelve of them and only eight of us."

"Twelve!" exclaimed Gourville. "Twelve rowers! Impossible!"

There had never been more than eight oarsmen, even for the king. Fouquet had been honored with twelve rowers, more for speed than out of respect.

"What does that mean?" asked Gourville. They had already spotted the tent, and now he was trying to make out the travelers, whom the sharpest eyes hadn't yet managed to identify.

"They must be in a hurry," said the skipper. "That's not the king."

Fouquet shivered.

"How can you tell it's not the king?" said Gourville.

"First of all, because the vessel isn't flying the white flag with the fleurs-de-lys, which the royal lighter always sports. Besides, it can't possibly be the king, Gourville, given that he was still in Paris yesterday."

Gourville responded with a look that signified, But you were there yourself. To gain time, he asked out loud, "And how can you tell they're in a hurry?"

"Because, monsieur," said the skipper, "they must have set sail a long time after us and they've almost caught up with us."

"Huh!" said Gourville. "How can you tell they didn't start in Beaugency or even Niort?"

"We didn't see any lighter of that strength except in Orléans. She's coming from Orléans, monsieur, and she's in a big hurry!"

Fouquet and Gourville exchanged winks. The skipper noticed their anxiety, and, to put him off the trail, Gourville said, "It's a friend who's wagered he can overtake us. Let's win the bet and not allow him to catch up."

The skipper opened his mouth to express his disbelief, but Fouquet haughtily snapped, "If it's someone who wants to overtake us, let him try!"

"One can try, monseigneur," the skipper murmured timidly. "C'mon, men! Give it your all! Row, damn it, row!"

"No!" exclaimed Fouquet. "Stop short!"

"That's crazy, monseigneur!" Gourville whispered into Fouquet's ear.

"Stop short!" Fouquet repeated. The eight oars stopped, and, resisting the water, they caused the lighter to move back. It stopped.

At first, the twelve oarsmen of the other vessel didn't spot this maneuver, for they kept rowing so hard that they arrived within gunshot of Fouquet's lighter. Fouquet was shortsighted;

Gourville was bothered by the sun, which glared directly into his eyes. Only the skipper, with the habit and clarity induced by struggles with the elements, distinctly made out the voyagers on the other lighter.

"I see them!" he shouted. "There are two of them!"

"I don't see anything!" said Gourville.

"You'll see them soon enough. They'll be twenty feet away from us within twenty more strokes of their oars."

But the skipper's prediction failed to materialize. The lighter imitated the movement commanded by Fouquet; and, instead of joining its supposed friends, it halted in the middle of the river.

"I don't understand!" said the skipper.

"Neither do I!" said Gourville.

"Since you can see the passengers on that lighter so clearly," Fouquet told the skipper, "try to describe them before we steer too far away."

"I think I saw two passengers," the skipper replied. "But now I can see only one in the tent."

"What's he look like?"

"He's got dark hair, broad shoulders, and a short neck."

A cloudlet drifted across the azure sky, masking the sun.

Gourville, cupping his eyes as he gazed at the other vessel, could now see what he was looking for; and suddenly he dashed from the deck to the room where Fouquet was waiting. In a voice altered by emotion, Gourville exclaimed, "Colbert!"

"Colbert!" Fouquet repeated. "Why, that's odd! No! It's impossible!"

"I tell you I recognized him. And he himself recognized me so clearly that he went to the poop chamber. Maybe the king has sent him to make us turn back."

"In that case, he'd join us instead of heaving to. What's he doing?"

"He must be watching us, monseigneur!"

"I don't like uncertainties," cried Fouquet. "Let's steer over to him."

"Oh, monseigneur! Don't do that! His lighter is full of armed men!"

"So you think he's going to arrest me, Gourville? Then why doesn't he come?"

"Monseigneur, it is inconsistent with your dignity to rush toward your doom."

"So then I should endure being scrutinized like a common criminal?"

"Nothing indicates that you're being scrutinized, monseigneur. Be patient."

"What should we do?"

"Don't stop the boat. You were going this fast only to be zealous in obeying the king's orders. Double our speed. Time will tell!"

"You're right! Let's go!" cried Fouquet. "Since they're pausing, let's get on with it!"

The skipper signaled, and Fouquet's oarsmen resumed their rowing with all the success that could be expected of well-rested men. No sooner had Fouquet's vessel covered a hundred fathoms than the twelve oarsmen of the other lighter started rowing again.

The race lasted all day, but the distance between the two vessels neither grew nor shrank. Toward evening, Fouquet wanted to test his pursuers' intentions. He ordered his oarsmen to head for shore, as if he meant to get off the lighter. Colbert's lighter imitated the maneuver, veering toward land. There, by the greatest coincidence, a stableman of the Castle of Langeais happened to be walking along the flowery riverbank, leading three horses by their halters. The passengers on the other lighter must have figured that Fouquet was planning his escape with those horses, for Colbert's men saw four or five musket bearers jump ashore and stride along the bank as if to catch up with the horses and the horsemen.

Pleased that he'd forced the enemy to show his hand, Fouquet reboarded his lighter and took off. Colbert's men promptly reboarded their lighter, and the race between the two vessels resumed with new perseverance.

Seeing this, Fouquet felt the other lighter was too close for comfort and he muttered in a prophetic tone, "Well, Gourville?! What did I say at our last supper? Am I or am I not heading for my doom?"

"Oh! Monseigneur!"

"We're speeding along the Loire as if Monsieur Colbert and

I were competing for a prize—and don't our two boats represent our two fates? Don't you think, Gourville, that one boat will be wrecked in Nantes?"

"At least nothing is certain now," Gourville objected. "You're going to appear at the Estates, you're going to show the kind of man you are. Your eloquence and your business acumen are the shield and the sword that will help you to defend yourself and even to emerge as the victor. The Bretons don't know you. And once they know you, your cause will be won. Monsieur Colbert had better watch out! For his lighter can capsize just as easily as yours. Both vessels are zooming along, his faster than yours, that's true. We'll see which one is wrecked first."

Fouquet took Gourville's hand: "My friend, everything considered, remember the proverb: 'First come, first served!' Well, Monsieur Colbert is taking care not to pass me. He's a prudent man, that Colbert."

Fouquet was right. The two lighters rowed all the way to Nantes, with the passengers on one scrutinizing the passengers on the other. When Fouquet landed, Gourville hoped he'd seek his lodgings immediately and have relays prepared. But at the disembarkment, the second vessel joined the first, and Colbert, approaching Fouquet on the pier, bowed in the most profound respect. His courtesy was so meaningful, so overt, that a huge crowd gathered.

Fouquet was utterly self-possessed. In those final moments of grandeur, he felt he had obligations toward himself. He wanted to plunge from such a great height that his fall would crush a few of his foes. Colbert was there—too bad for Colbert.

Fouquet, going up to him, responded with the arrogant blinking that was peculiar to him. "What? Is that you, Monsieur Colbert?"

"I'm paying you my homage, monseigneur."

"You were on that lighter?" He pointed to the famous vessel with its twelve oarsmen.

"Yes, monseigneur."

"Twelve oarsmen! What luxury, Monsieur Colbert! For an instant, I believed it must be the queen mother or the king."

Colbert reddened. "Monseigneur . . ."

"That trip must be expensive for the people footing the bill, monsieur," said Fouquet. "But at last you've arrived." A moment later he added: "You can see that even though I've got only eight rowers, I arrived before you." And he turned his back on Colbert, leaving him to wonder whether all the vacillations of the second lighter had escaped the notice of the first. At least, Fouquet was not giving Colbert the satisfaction of showing any fear.

Colbert, so annoyingly assaulted, did not lose heart. "I did not go fast, monseigneur, because I stopped whenever you stopped."

"And why did you do so, Monsieur Colbert?" cried Fouquet, irritated by that vile audacity. "After all, your crew was superior to mine, so why didn't you join me or outrun me?"

"Out of respect," said Colbert, bowing to the ground.

Mounting into a carriage supplied by the city (who could say why or how?), Fouquet drove to the town hall. He was escorted by a large throng, which, for several days now, had been ardently looking forward to the convocation of the Estates.

No sooner was he settled than Gourville went to order horses for the road to Poitiers and Vannes and a boat for the voyage to Paimboeuf. He accomplished these various tasks so thoroughly, generously, and mysteriously that Fouquet, laid low by a fit of ague, had never been closer to salvation—except for the cooperation of that immense disrupter of human plans: chance.

That night, it was rumored throughout the city that the king was coming swiftly on post-horses and would be reaching Nantes within ten or twelve hours.

While waiting for the king, the population was delighted to see the musketeers, freshly arrived with their captain, Monsieur d'Artagnan, and already installed at the castle, where they occupied all the posts as guards of honor. Around ten o'clock, Monsieur d'Artagnan, who was extremely polite, presented himself to Fouquet in order to pay him his respectful homage. And even though the minister was ill, even though he was suffering and drenched with sweat, he wanted to receive Monsieur d'Artagnan, who was charmed by this honor, as we shall see in their conversation.

38
Friendly Advice

Fouquet was in bed, like a man who clings to life, husbanding as much as possible that flimsy tissue of existence, whose irreparable frailty is worn out by the shocks and keen edges of this world.

D'Artagnan, appearing at the threshold, was welcomed by an affably happy Fouquet.

"Good day, monseigneur," replied the musketeer. "How do you feel after your voyage?"

"Quite well, thank you."

"And your ague?"

"Quite bad. No sooner did I arrive in Nantes than I levied a contribution of herb tea."

"You've got to have a good night's sleep, monseigneur."

"Damn it! I'd be glad to sleep in Monsieur d'Artagnan's quarters."

"What's preventing you?"

"You, for one."

"I? Aha, monseigneur! . . ."

"Certainly. Haven't you come, in Nantes as in Paris, in the name of the king?"

"For heaven's sake, monseigneur," the captain retorted, "leave the king in peace! On the day that I come on behalf of the king for what you wish to tell me, I promise not to keep you on tenterhooks. You'll see me clutch my sword according to rules, and you'll immediately hear me say in my official voice: 'Monseigneur, I arrest you in the name of the king!' "

The Gascon's lively intonation was so natural and vigorous that Fouquet trembled in spite of himself. The depiction of the event was almost as terrifying as the event itself.

"You promise to be that forthright?" said Fouquet.

"On my honor. But things haven't gone that far, believe me."

"What makes you think that, Monsieur d'Artagnan? I believe they have."

"I've heard nothing of the kind," replied d'Artagnan.

"I see," said Fouquet.

"No, no. You've got nothing to worry about despite your ague. The king cannot, he must not help loving you from the bottom of his heart."

Fouquet made a face. "What about Monsieur Colbert? Does he love me as much as you say?"

"I'm not talking about Monsieur Colbert. He's an exceptional man, that Monsieur Colbert! He may not like you—that's possible! But, damn it! The squirrel can stave off the adder without much effort."

"Do you realize that you're speaking to me like a friend," Fouquet responded, "that in all my life I've never found a man with your heart and your intelligence?"

"So you say," d'Artagnan answered. "And you've waited until now to pay me such a compliment!"

"Blind as we are!" Fouquet murmured.

"You're getting hoarse," said d'Artagnan. "Drink, monseigneur, drink." And he offered Fouquet a cup of tea with the most cordial friendliness. Fouquet took it and thanked him with a genial smile.

"These things only happen to me," said the musketeer. "I've spent ten years under your very nose while you've been rolling barrels of gold. You've been earning four million a year. You've never noticed me before, and now you notice my existence at the very moment—"

"That I'm about to fall!" Fouquet interrupted. "That's true, my dear Monsieur d'Artagnan."

"That's not what I'm saying."

"You're thinking it—that amounts to the same thing. Well, if I fall, you can take my word that I won't let a single day go by without my smacking my forehead and saying: 'Fool! Fool! Stupid man! You had Monsieur d'Artagnan under your hand and you never used him! You never enriched him!' "

"I'm overwhelmed," said the captain. "You have my undying esteem."

"One more man who doesn't think like Monsieur Colbert," said Fouquet.

"You're obsessed with that Colbert! It's worse than your ague!"

"Ah, I've got my reasons," said Fouquet. "You can judge them for yourself." And he described the details of the race of the lighters and Colbert's hypocritical pursuit. "Isn't that the most obvious sign of my ruin?"

D'Artagnan looked grim. "You're right. 'It bodes ill,' as Monsieur de Tréville put it." And he gazed at Fouquet with intelligent and meaningful eyes.

"Haven't I been singled out, Captain? Hasn't the king brought me here in order to isolate me from all my friends in Paris and to grab hold of Belle-Île?"

"Where is Monsieur d'Herblay?" d'Artagnan asked.

Fouquet lifted his head.

"As for me, monseigneur," d'Artagnan went on, "I can assure you the king has said nothing against you to me."

"Really?"

"The king ordered me to leave for Nantes, that's true, and to say nothing to Monsieur de Gesvres."

"My friend."

"To say nothing to Monsieur de Gesvres, your friend, yes, monseigneur." D'Artagnan's eyes spoke a different language than his lips. "The king also ordered me to take along a brigade of musketeers—which seems useless since the area is calm."

"A brigade?" said Fouquet, propping himself on one elbow.

"Ninety-six horsemen, yes, monseigneur. The same number they used to arrest Monsieur de Chalais, Monsieur de Cinq-Mars, and Monsieur Montmorency."

Fouquet's ears pricked up at these apparently casual words. "And what else?"

"My other orders were insignificant: I'm to guard the castle, guard each lodging, not allow any of Monsieur de Gesvres's guards to occupy a single post. . . . Monsieur de Gesvres, your friend."

"And what orders regarding me?" cried Fouquet.

"Not the slightest word regarding you, monseigneur."

"Monsieur d'Artagnan . . . My honor is at stake and possibly my life. You wouldn't be deceiving me?"

"I? For what purpose? Are you being threatened? Still, there was one order concerning the coaches and the boats . . ."

"An order?"

"Yes, but it doesn't concern you. A simple police measure."

"What is it, Captain, what is it?"

"No horse or boat can leave Nantes without a safe-conduct signed by the king."

"Good God! But . . ."

D'Artagnan burst out laughing. "This applies only after the king's arrival in Nantes. So you see, monseigneur, the order doesn't concern you in the least."

Fouquet grew pensive, and d'Artagnan pretended not to notice Fouquet's preoccupation. "Telling you about the orders I've received shows that I care for you and that I insist on proving that no order is directed against you."

"No doubt," said Fouquet absentmindedly.

"Let's recapitulate," said the captain, staring hard. "A special and rigorous guard in the castle you'll be staying in, right?"

"Do you know this castle? . . ."

"Ah, monseigneur! It's a true prison!

"Total absence of Monsieur de Gesvres, who has the honor of being your friend.

"Closure of the gates of the city and the river, unless one has a pass—but only after the king arrives.

"Do you know, Monsieur Fouquet, that if, instead of speaking to a man like you, one of the king's most beloved men, I were speaking to someone with a troubled and anxious conscience, I'd be compromising myself forever? What a perfect opportunity for a man who wants to decamp! No police, no guards, no orders! The water open and the highway free! Monsieur d'Artagnan obliged to lend his horses if asked!

"All these things ought to reassure you, Monsieur Fouquet, for the king wouldn't have left me so independent if he had nasty designs. Honestly, Monsieur Fouquet, ask me for anything you desire. I'm at your service. And you can do something for me, but only if you consent. Say hello for me to Aramis and Porthos in case you sail to Belle-Île—which you have the right to do immediately, without delay, in your robe, just as you are."

With those words, and with a deep bow, the musketeer, whose eyes had lost none of their intelligent benevolence, walked out of the room and disappeared. Before he even reached the stairway in the vestibule, Fouquet, beside himself, rang his bell and shouted, "My horses! My lighter!"

No one responded.

The superintendent dressed himself with whatever he got his hands on.

"Gourville! . . . Gourville! . . ." he shouted, pocketing his watch. And he rang again, while repeating, "Gourville! . . . Gourville! . . ."

Gourville showed up, pale and panting.

"We're leaving! We're leaving!" cried Fouquet upon seeing him.

"It's too late," said poor Fouquet's friend.

"Too late?! Why?!"

"Listen."

They heard drums and trumpets in front of the castle.

"What is it, Gourville?"

"The king is arriving, monseigneur."

"The king?"

"The king. He hasn't paused at a single stage. He's killed horses and he's reached us eight hours ahead of your calculations."

"We're doomed!" murmured Fouquet. "Good d'Artagnan! You got to me too late!"

The king was indeed arriving in the city. People soon heard the cannon booming on the rampart and the cannon responding from a vessel downstream. Fouquet scowled, called his valets, and donned ceremonial garments. From behind his window curtains, he witnessed the eagerness of the crowd and the movement of a large troop that had followed the king—though nobody knew how. The king was conducted to the castle with great pomp, and Fouquet watched him dismount at the portcullis and whisper something to d'Artagnan, who was holding his stirrup. Once the king had passed under the arch, d'Artagnan headed toward Fouquet's house, but so slowly, so slowly, frequently halting to speak to his musketeers, who lined the route. D'Artagnan seemed to be counting the seconds or the paces before delivering his message.

Fouquet opened the window in order to speak to d'Artagnan

in the courtyard. "Ah!" cried d'Artagnan upon spotting him. "So you're still here, monseigneur?" And that "still" proved to Fouquet how much useful advice and information the musketeer had supplied during his first visit.

The superintendent was content to sigh. "My goodness, yes, monsieur," he replied. "The king's arrival has interrupted my plans."

"Ah, so you know the king has just arrived?"

"Yes, monsieur, I saw him, and this time you've come on his behalf."

"To find out if you've got any news, monseigneur, and, if your health is not too bad, to ask you to please come to the castle."

"Immediately, Monsieur d'Artagnan, immediately."

"Ah, damn it!" said the captain. "Now that the king is here, there will be no more promenades for anyone, no more free choice. At present, strict orders govern all of us, you and me, me and you."

Fouquet heaved a final sigh. He felt so weak that he stepped into the coach and headed toward the castle, escorted by d'Artagnan, whose politeness was no less terrifying than it had been cheerful and consoling a little while ago.

39
How King Louis XIV Played His Little Part

As Fouquet stepped out from the carriage in order to enter the Castle of Nantes, a man who emerged from the crowd approached the superintendent with all the marks of the greatest respect and handed him a letter. D'Artagnan tried to prevent this man from speaking to Fouquet, but the message was already delivered. Fouquet unsealed the letter and read it. A vague terror, which d'Artagnan easily caught, whipped across Fouquet's face. He slipped the letter into the portfolio under his arm and continued walking toward the king's apartments.

Through the small windows on each landing, d'Artagnan,

following Fouquet up the dungeon stairs, spotted the man who had brought the letter. Standing in the square, the messenger looked around and signaled various people, who disappeared in the adjacent streets after signaling back.

For a moment, Fouquet had to wait on the terrace that we have mentioned—a terrace running into a small corridor that led to the king's cabinet. D'Artagnan, having respectfully escorted the superintendent, now stepped in front of him and entered the royal cabinet.

"Well?" asked Louis XIV, who, upon perceiving his visitor, tossed a large green cloth over the table, which was covered with documents.

"Your order is executed, sire."

"And Fouquet?"

"Monsieur Superintendent is behind me," replied d'Artagnan.

"He'll be brought to me in ten minutes," said the king, dismissing d'Artagnan with a gesture.

D'Artagnan walked out; but scarcely had he reached the corridor, where Fouquet was awaiting him at the other end, than the musketeer was summoned back by the king's bell.

"He didn't seem astonished?" asked the king.

"Who, sire?"

"Fouquet," said the king without saying "Monsieur"—a detail that confirmed d'Artagnan's suspicions.

"No, sire," he replied.

"Fine." And Louis sent him away a second time.

Fouquet hadn't retreated from the terrace, where he'd been left by his guide. Instead, he was rereading the letter:

> People are plotting against you. Perhaps they won't dare at the castle, they'll wait till you're home again. Your lodging is already surrounded by the musketeers. Don't go back there, a white horse is waiting for you behind the esplanade.

Fouquet had recognized Gourville's zeal and handwriting. In case of misfortune, Fouquet didn't want the letter to compromise a loyal friend; so he ripped it up into thousands of shreds, which the wind scattered across the terrace balustrade.

D'Artagnan caught him watching the final bits flutter into space. "Sir," said the musketeer, "the king awaits you."

Fouquet strode resolutely along the small corridor, where Monsieur de Brienne and Monsieur Rose were at work; the Duke de Saint-Aignan, who, sitting on a small chair with his sword between his legs, seemed to be waiting for orders, yawned with feverish impatience.

It struck Fouquet as odd that Messieurs de Brienne, Rose, and de Saint-Aignan, normally so attentive and obsequious, barely glanced at the superintendent as he passed them. But how could the man whom the king now addressed merely as Monsieur Fouquet expect anything else from the courtiers? He lifted his head and, determined to confront everything bravely, he entered the king's cabinet after the bell had announced him to His Majesty.

Without rising, the king nodded and asked with genuine interest, "Well, how do you feel, Monsieur Fouquet?"

"I'm suffering from a fit of ague, but I'm entirely at the king's service."

"Fine. The Estates are convening tomorrow. Have you prepared a speech?"

Fouquet gaped at the king. "I haven't, sire, but I'll improvise. I'm acquainted with the whole business too thoroughly to remain at a loss. I've got only one question: Will Your Majesty permit me?"

"Yes."

"Why did His Majesty not do his prime minister the honor of informing him in Paris?"

"You were sick, I didn't want to tire you."

"No work, no explanation ever tires me, sire, and since the time has come for me to ask my king for an explanation—"

"Oh, Monsieur Fouquet! What sort of explanation?"

"An explanation of His Majesty's intentions regarding myself."

The king reddened.

"I've been slandered," Fouquet vividly exclaimed, "and I've got to challenge royal justice to investigate."

"There's no use in your saying that, Monsieur Fouquet. I know what I know."

"His Majesty can know things only if he's been told, and I've told him nothing, while other people have told him any number of things—"

"What do you mean?" asked the king, eager to end this embarrassing conversation.

"I'll get straight to the point, sire. I accuse a man of defaming me to Your Majesty."

"No one is defaming you, Monsieur Fouquet."

"Your response, sire, proves that I'm right."

"Monsieur Fouquet, I don't like anyone to accuse—"

"When a man is accused! . . ."

"We've discussed this issue too often."

"Your Majesty does not want me to defend myself?"

"I repeat: I am not accusing you."

Fouquet stepped back with a half bow. I'm certain, he thought to himself, that he's made up his mind. Only the man who can't back up will be that obstinate. I'd be blind if I didn't see the danger at this moment, and I'd be stupid if I didn't avoid it. Then he said aloud, "Does Your Majesty want me for some kind of work?"

"No, Monsieur Fouquet. I need to give you some advice."

"I wait respectfully, sire."

"Get some rest, Monsieur Fouquet. Don't waste your strength. The Estates will be meeting only briefly. And when my secretaries close the session, I don't want any business discussed in France for the next two weeks."

"Does the king have nothing to tell me about the assembly of the Estates?"

"No, Monsieur Fouquet."

"Even though I'm the superintendent of finances?"

"Please rest. That's all I have to tell you."

Fouquet bit his lip and lowered his head. He was obviously brooding and worrying.

His anxiety was contagious. The king asked him, "Are you angry that you have to rest, Monsieur Fouquet?"

"Yes, sire. I'm not used to resting."

"But you're sick. You have to take care of yourself."

"Your Majesty asked me about a speech I'm to give tomorrow."

The king didn't answer. That sudden question made him feel awkward. Fouquet felt the weight of that hesitation. He believed that he saw danger in the king's eyes—a danger precipitated by Fouquet's defiance. If I show fear, he thought to himself, then I'm doomed.

The king, for his part, was nervous only because of Fouquet's defiance. "Has he gotten wind of something?" Louis muttered to himself.

If his first word is harsh, Fouquet mused, if he's irritated or feigns irritation in order to have a pretext, how will I get out of it? Let's find a gentler slope. Gourville was right.

"Sire," Fouquet suddenly exclaimed, "since the king in his goodness watches so closely over my health as to free me from all work, might I not be exempt from attending the session tomorrow? I would spend the day in bed and ask the king to allow his physician to try a remedy for that accursed ague."

"As you wish, Monsieur Fouquet. You'll be excused from the meeting, you'll have the physician, you'll have your health."

"Thank you," said Fouquet with a bow. Then he went on: "Won't I have the happiness of conducting the king to Belle-Île, my home?" And he peered into Louis's face to gauge the effect of his question.

The king reddened again. He tried to smile. "Do you realize you've just said: 'To Belle-Île, my home'?"

"That's true, sire."

"Well, don't you remember," the king continued in the same cheerful tone, "that you've given me Belle-Île?"

"That's true also, sire. Only, since you haven't taken it, you will come and take possession."

"I certainly want to."

"Besides, that was both Your Majesty's intention and mine, and I cannot tell Your Majesty how proud and happy I was to see the king's military household come from Paris for that occasion."

The king stammered that this was not his only reason for bringing his musketeers.

"Oh, I'm sure of that!" Fouquet vividly cried. "Your Majesty knows only too well that all he need do is come alone, holding a cane, and all the fortifications of Belle-Île will come tumbling down."

"Damn it!" shouted the king. "I don't want them to come tumbling down! Those beautiful fortifications cost a fortune! No! Let them stand against the Dutch and the British. You'll never guess what I'd like to see at Belle-Île, Monsieur Fouquet. I want to see those lovely peasant girls and women of the soil or the strand—they dance so charmingly and are so seductive in their scarlet petticoats. I've heard such wonderful things about them, Monsieur Superintendent. Come on, let me see them."

"Whenever Your Majesty cares to."

"Do you have some means of transportation? We could do it tomorrow, if you like."

The superintendent felt the anything but subtle blow. "No, sire. I was unaware of Your Majesty's wishes. Above all, I was unaware that Your Majesty wanted to go so urgently, and so I haven't taken any precautions."

"But you do have a boat of your own, don't you?"

"I've got five. But they're either in the harbor or in Paimboeuf, and it would take me at least twenty-four hours to go there or have them brought here. Should I send a courier? Do you want me to?"

"No, wait. Let the fever run its course. Wait till tomorrow."

"Fine. Who can say if we won't have a thousand other ideas by then?" Fouquet answered. His doubts were gone, and he was very pale.

The king shuddered and reached for his bell, but Fouquet stopped him. "Sire, I'm running a fever, I'm trembling with cold. If I stay here for even one more instant, I may faint. I request Your Majesty's permission to go and hide under my blankets."

"Goodness, you *are* shivering. It looks awful. Go to bed, Monsieur Fouquet, go to bed. I'll send someone to inquire after you."

"Your Majesty, I'm overwhelmed. An hour from now, I'll be much better."

"I'll have somebody escort you."

"As you please, sire. I'd gladly lean on someone."

"Monsieur d'Artagnan!" cried the king, shaking his bell.

"Oh! Sire!" Fouquet broke in with a laugh that chilled the king. "You're having a musketeer captain escort me to my lodgings? An ambiguous honor, sire! A simple footman would be enough."

"Oh, why, Monsieur Fouquet? Monsieur d'Artagnan often accompanies me!"

"Yes, but when he accompanies you, sire, he is obeying you, whereas with me . . ."

"Well?"

"Well, if I have to be escorted by the head of your musketeers, everyone will say that you're having me arrested."

"Arrested!" the king repeated, turning paler than Fouquet himself. "Arrested! Oh!"

"Really! Why wouldn't they say so!" Fouquet continued mirthfully. "And I bet there'll be no end of people who'll be nasty enough to laugh."

This sally disconcerted the monarch. Fouquet was skillful enough, or fortunate enough, to make Louis XIV recoil at the thought of what he was planning. When Monsieur d'Artagnan appeared, the king ordered him to designate a musketeer to escort the superintendent.

"It's unnecessary," said Fouquet. "Sword for sword, I'd just as soon have Gourville, who's waiting for me down below. But that won't prevent me from enjoying Monsieur d'Artagnan's company. I'm glad that he'll get to see Belle-Île, since he's an expert on fortifications."

D'Artagnan bowed, utterly at a loss. Fouquet bowed likewise and left, affecting the slow gait of a stroller. Once outside the castle, he cried: "I'm saved! Yes, indeed, disloyal king, you'll see Belle-Île all right, but only when I'm no longer there." And he disappeared.

D'Artagnan remained with the king. "Captain," said His Majesty, "you'll walk a hundred paces behind Monsieur Fouquet."

"Yes, sire."

"He's going to his lodgings. You will go there too."

"Yes, sire."

"You will arrest him in my name and you will lock him up in a coach."

"In a coach? Fine."

"In such a way that he can't converse with anyone en route or toss notes to passersby."

"Oh, that would be difficult, sire."

"Not at all."

"Forgive me, sire. I cannot suffocate Monsieur Fouquet, and, if he asks me to let him breathe some fresh air, I won't stop him by shutting the windows and the carriage aprons. He'll shout through the doors and toss out notes as much as he can."

"We've taken that into account, Monsieur d'Artagnan. A coach with a lattice will prevent both possibilities."

"A coach with an iron lattice!" exclaimed d'Artagnan. "But we can't conjure up an iron lattice in half an hour, and Your Majesty has told me to go to Monsieur Fouquet's lodgings immediately."

"That's why such a coach has already been made."

"Ah! That's different!" said the captain. "If the coach has already been made, that's fine. All we have to do is get it going."

"The horses have already been harnessed."

"Ah!"

"And the coachman, with the outriders, is waiting in the lower courtyard of the castle."

D'Artagnan bowed. "Then all that's left is for me to ask the king where I should conduct Monsieur Fouquet."

"First, to the Castle of Angers."

"Very good."

"Then we'll see."

"Yes, sire."

"Monsieur d'Artagnan, one last word: You notice that I'm not using my own guards to apprehend Fouquet, which will infuriate Monsieur de Gesvres."

"Your Majesty is not using his guards," said the slightly humiliated captain, "because Your Majesty distrusts Monsieur de Gesvres. That's all."

"It's to tell you, monsieur, that I trust you."

"I know that, sire! And there's no need to dwell on it."

"It's simply to point out, monsieur, that as of this moment, if by chance, any chance whatsoever, Monsieur Fouquet happened to escape . . . Such things have occurred, monsieur . . ."

"Oh, sire, very often. But only with others, not with me."

"Why not with you?"

"Because, sire, there was an instant when I wanted to save Monsieur Fouquet."

The king shivered.

"Because," the captain went on, "I had the right to do so upon guessing Your Majesty's plan without your revealing it to me, and because I found Monsieur Fouquet interesting. At that juncture, I was still free to show my interest in him."

"Honestly, monsieur, you're not very reassuring about your service to me!"

"If I had saved him back then, I'd be perfectly innocent. In fact, I would have done a good thing, for Monsieur Fouquet is not a wicked man. But he refused, his destiny won out. He missed the moment of his freedom. Too bad! Now I've got my orders. I will obey my orders, and you can regard Monsieur Fouquet as under arrest. Monsieur Fouquet is at the Castle of Angers."

"Oh, but you don't have him yet, Captain."

"That's my concern. To each his own trade, sire. Only, once again, think it over. Do you really want me to arrest Monsieur Fouquet, sire?"

"Yes! A thousand times yes!"

"Then write the letter."

"Here it is."

D'Artagnan read it, saluted the king, and left.

From the height of the terrace he spotted Gourville, who was cheerily heading toward Monsieur Fouquet's lodgings.

40
The White Horse and the Black Horse

That's a surprise, the captain mused. Gourville so cheerful and hurrying through the streets when he's pretty certain that Monsieur Fouquet is in danger; and it's likewise fairly certain that it was Gourville who warned him in that note—the note that Fouquet tore into a thousand pieces on the terrace and scattered in the wind. Gourville is rubbing his hands—he must have done something clever. Where is Gourville coming from? Gourville is coming from the rue aux Herbes. Where does the rue aux Herbes go?

And scanning the housetops, which were dominated by the castle, d'Artagnan followed the line traced by the streets as if he were studying a map. But instead of flat and lifeless, empty and deserted paper, the living chart stood out in relief with the cries, shadows, and movements of men and objects. Beyond the enceinte of the town, the vast, green plains swept along the Loire and seemed to be stretching toward the purple horizon, which was cut by the azure bodies of water and the dark green of the marshes. Immediately outside the gates of Nantes, two white roads branched apart like the splaying fingers of a gigantic hand.

By crossing the terrace, d'Artagnan took in the entire panorama at a mere glance. The line of the rue aux Herbes led him to one of those roads that began at the gates of Nantes. One more step and he was about to go down the stairs in order to reenter the dungeon, get his latticed coach, and head for Fouquet's house. But as chance would have it, his eyes were attracted by a moving dot that was gaining ground on that very road.

What's that? the musketeer wondered. A galloping horse, a runaway horse, no doubt! What speed!

The moving dot left the road and charged into the alfalfa fields. "A white horse," said the captain upon seeing the color shine out against the dark background. "And someone's riding him. It must be a boy veering off and leading the horse to water." These reflections, as swift as lightning and parallel with his visual perception, were already forgotten by the time d'Artagnan began descending the stairs.

Bits of paper were scattered over the steps, sparkling against the blackened stone. Huh! the captain mused. Those are some of the pieces of the letter that Fouquet ripped up. Poor man! He gave his secret to the wind. But the wind doesn't want it, so it's bringing it to the king. Poor Fouquet! You're really out of luck! The playing field isn't even. Fortune is against you. The king's star is eclipsing yours. The adder is stronger or more cunning than the squirrel.

As he descended, d'Artagnan picked up one of the scraps and examined it. Gourville's delicate handwriting! I wasn't wrong. And he read the word "horse." The next scrap was blank. "Hey!" On a third scrap he read the word "white." "White horse," he repeated, like a child spelling out a sentence. "Oh my God!" cried the distrustful captain. "White horse!" And like the grain of gunpowder that, when burning, expands a hundredfold, d'Artagnan, swollen with thoughts and suspicions, hurried back up the stairs.

The white horse was still dashing, dashing toward the Loire, where, at the far end of the river, a small sail, blurring into the watery vapors, seemed to balance like an atom. "Oh! Oh!" exclaimed the musketeer. "There's only one man who would escape so rapidly across farmlands. It could only be a financier, a Fouquet, who would flee on a white horse in broad daylight. It could only be the lord of Belle-Île who would gallop toward the sea rather than through dense forests on land. And d'Artagnan is the only man able to catch up with Fouquet, who's got thirty minutes' head start and who'll reach his boat within an hour."

Having spoken, the musketeer ordered his men to take the latticed coach to a small grove located outside the town. He chose his best steed, jumped on its back, and raced along the rue aux Herbes. But instead of following Fouquet's course, d'Artagnan skirted the banks of the Loire, certain he'd gain an extra ten minutes, thereby heading off the fugitive, who wouldn't suspect that he was being pursued from that route. The speed, the pursuer's impatience, the excitement as in hunting or warring, altered d'Artagnan's mood; normally so kind and gentle toward Fouquet, the musketeer was surprised by how ferocious and almost bloodthirsty he became.

For a long time he galloped without sighting the white horse. His intensity bordered on rage. He was assailed by doubts. He figured that Fouquet had vanished on some underground road, where he had swapped the white horse for one of those famous black horses that were as swift as the wind. Back in Saint-Mandé, d'Artagnan had so often admired them, had envied their vigorous agility.

At those moments, when the wind was lacerating his eyes, producing tears, when his saddle was burning beneath him, when the galled and gashed horse was bellowing with pain and its hooves were kicking up a rain of fine sand and pebbles, d'Artagnan raised himself up on his stirrups. Seeing nothing out on the river, nothing under the trees, he scanned the air like a madman—he felt he was losing his mind. In his frantic obsession, he dreamed of aerial roads (not discovered until the next century), he recalled Daedalus and his vast pinions, which carried him from the Cretan prisons.

A hoarse sigh broke from d'Artagnan's lips. Devoured by the fear of looking ridiculous, he kept repeating: "Me! Me! Hoodwinked by a Gourville! Me! . . . They'll say I'm growing old! They'll say I've been paid a million to let Fouquet escape!"

And the musketeer dug both spurs into the horse's belly. He had just covered a league in two minutes. Suddenly, beyond a hedge at the far end of a pasture, he spotted a white shape, which first appeared, then vanished, and finally emerged on higher terrain. D'Artagnan trembled with joy and instantly recovered his serenity. He wiped his sweaty forehead and relaxed his knees, thereby letting his horse breathe more freely. Then, pulling in his reins, d'Artagnan slowed the gait of his vigorous animal, his accomplice in this manhunt. He could now study the lay of the road, and his position with regard to the superintendent.

By now, after crossing softer ground, Fouquet's mount was thoroughly winded. The superintendent, wanting to reach firmer soil, was taking the shortest cut to the highway. Meanwhile, all that d'Artagnan had to do was ride straight under a cliff, which concealed him from his enemy's eyes. The musketeer would then catch up with him on the highway. That was where the real race would begin, that was where the struggle would get serious.

D'Artagnan let his horse breathe its fill. He noticed that Fouquet was now trotting—that is, he was likewise letting his horse get its wind. But both riders were in too much of a hurry. Upon entering more resistant terrain, the white horse whizzed off like an arrow. D'Artagnan gave his black horse full rein and it galloped away. Both men were taking the same route. The quadruple echoes of the hooves mingled together. Fouquet had not yet sighted d'Artagnan. But upon his charging out from under a cliff, a single echo struck the air: it was d'Artagnan's horse, which was rumbling like thunder. Fouquet looked back. A hundred paces behind him he spotted his enemy hunched over his courser's neck. There could be no doubt: the shiny shoulder belt, the red cloak—it had to be a musketeer. Fouquet likewise gave his white horse full rein, and it put another twenty paces between him and his adversary.

Hey! d'Artagnan nervously mused. That's no ordinary horse. Pay attention! And with his infallible eyes, he attentively examined the courser's pacing and bearing. A round croup; a long, thin tail; legs as dry and slender as steel wires; hooves as hard as marble. He dug in his spurs, but the gap between the two riders remained the same. D'Artagnan listened closely: no breath reached him from the white horse, which, however, seemed to rend the wind, while the black horse, on the contrary, was starting to gasp as if overwhelmed by a fit of coughing. I've got to catch Fouquet even if I kill my horse! And he sawed the poor creature's mouth and buried his spurs in its bloody skin.

The desperate horse racked up a hundred paces, arriving within a pistol shot of Fouquet. "Courage!" murmured the musketeer. "Courage! His horse may weaken, and, if it doesn't collapse, its master will!"

But horse and rider remained upright and together, gaining the advantage little by little.

D'Artagnan uttered a savage shriek, which made Fouquet

look back and his horse speed up. "A great horse! An insane horseman!" snarled the captain. "Hey! Damn it, Monsieur Fouquet! Hey! In the name of the king!"

Fouquet didn't answer.

"Do you hear me?!" yelled d'Artagnan, whose horse had just stumbled.

"Damn it!" Fouquet retorted laconically.

And on he dashed.

D'Artagnan nearly lost his mind. His boiling blood rushed to his temples, to his eyes. "In the name of the king!" he repeated. "Stop or I'll shoot you down with my pistol!"

"Go ahead!" cried Fouquet, racing as fast ever.

D'Artagnan grabbed a pistol and cocked it, hoping that the click would make his enemy halt. "You've got pistols too. Defend yourself."

And when he heard that sound, Fouquet did turn his head and he looked his pursuer square in the face. With his right hand, he opened the coat he was wrapped in, but he didn't touch his saddle holsters. Only twenty paces were left between the two horses.

"Damn it!" exclaimed d'Artagnan. "I'm not going to kill you. If you refuse to fire at me, surrender! What is a prison, after all?"

"I'd rather die!" retorted Fouquet. "That way, I'd suffer less!"

D'Artagnan, crazy with despair, threw away his pistol. "I'm taking you alive!" And by a miraculous feat of which only this incomparable horseman was capable, he came within ten paces of the white horse—he was already holding out his hand to seize his prey.

"Fine! Kill me! It's more humane!" shouted Fouquet.

"No!" muttered the captain. "Alive! Alive!"

His horse stumbled again. And Fouquet's horse widened the gap.

It was an amazing spectacle—that race between two horses that were kept alive purely by the will of their masters. It might be said, however, that d'Artagnan was carrying his horse between his knees. The furious gallop was replaced by a brisk trot, then a slow trot. And the chase appeared equally intense in the two frazzled riders. D'Artagnan, losing patience, grabbed another pistol and aimed at the white horse.

"Your horse! Not you!" he shouted at Fouquet. And he fired. The animal was hit in the croup. It sprang furiously and reared up. At that very instant, d'Artagnan's horse collapsed and died. I'm dishonored! the musketeer thought to himself. I'm a miserable man! For pity's sake, Monsieur Fouquet! Toss me one of your pistols so I can blow my brains out!

But Fouquet lunged on.

"For mercy's sake! For mercy's sake!" cried d'Artagnan. "What you refuse to do now I'll be doing as an honor. But here on this road, I'll die bravely, I'll die esteemed. Do me this favor, Monsieur Fouquet!"

Monsieur Fouquet didn't respond. He kept trotting. D'Artagnan dashed after his foe. Hampered by his hat and his cloak, he threw them on the ground. He also tossed away his sheath, which was banging between his legs. His sword got too heavy in his hand, so he likewise hurled it off.

The white horse began to rattle in its throat. D'Artagnan was gaining on it. The exhausted creature slowed down, began toddling, its head shaken by dizziness. Its foam was bloody.

D'Artagnan made a desperate effort. He jumped toward Fouquet and grabbed his leg. Panting, gasping, the captain croaked, "I arrest you in the name of the king! Crack my skull! We'll both have done our duty."

D'Artagnan might have snatched his enemy's two pistols, so Fouquet hurled them into the river. He then dismounted. "I am your prisoner, monsieur. Please take my arm, you're about to faint."

"Thank you," murmured d'Artagnan, feeling the ground giving way and the sky collapsing on him. Winded and drained, he rolled on the sand.

Fouquet climbed down the riverbank and filled his hat with water. He moistened the musketeer's temples and poured a few cool drops between his lips. D'Artagnan stood up, scanning the area with his distraught eyes. He saw Fouquet kneeling, clutching his wet hat, and smiling with ineffable sweetness. "You didn't try to escape!" said d'Artagnan. "Oh, monsieur! The true king in loyalty, in heart, in soul, is not Louis, is not Philip at

Sainte-Marguerite. The true king is you, the outlaw, the fugitive!"

"I'm doomed today because of a single fault, Monsieur d'Artagnan."

"My God! Namely?"

"For not having you as a friend. But how are we supposed to return to Nantes? It's quite a distance."

"That's true," said d'Artagnan, pensive and gloomy.

"The white horse may recover. It's a fine animal! Mount it, Monsieur d'Artagnan. I'll walk until you've rested."

"The poor creature's injured!" said the musketeer.

"It can walk, I tell you. I know the horse. But we can do better. Both of us can ride it."

"Let's try," said the captain.

But no sooner had they loaded their double weight than the horse began to reel. It managed to straighten up and walk for a few minutes. Then it reeled again, collapsed, and died next to the black horse.

"We'll walk. It's the will of destiny," said Fouquet, slipping his arm into d'Artagnan's. "The stroll will be superb."

"Damn it!" cried the captain, his eyes gaping, his brow furrowed, his heart heavy. "An ugly day!"

They slowly trudged the four leagues to the forest, where the coach was waiting with an escort. When Fouquet sighted that sinister tableau, he said to d'Artagnan (who lowered his eyes, as if ashamed of Louis XIV), "This wasn't thought up by a decent man, Captain d'Artagnan. The idea isn't yours. Why those trellises?"

"To keep you from sneaking out letters."

"Ingenious!"

"But you can talk even if you can't write," said d'Artagnan.

"Talk to whom?"

"Well . . . If you want to."

Fouquet mused for a moment, then peered into the captain's face. "One single word. Will you remember it? . . ."

"I will remember it."

"Will you repeat it to whomever I indicate?"

"I will."

"Saint-Mandé!" Fouquet articulated very softly.

"Fine! Why?"

"For Madame de Bellière, or Pellisson."

"It's as good as done."

The coach rolled across Nantes and swerved onto the highway to Angers.

41

In Which the Squirrel Falls, in Which the Adder Flies

It was two in the afternoon. The impatient king was walking from his cabinet to the terrace. Now and then, he opened the corridor door to check up on his secretaries.

Monsieur Colbert, in the very seat that Monsieur de Saint-Aignan had occupied for a good part of the morning, was softly chatting with Monsieur de Brienne.

Suddenly, the door flew open, and the king asked them, "What are you saying?"

"We're talking about the first session of the Estates," said Monsieur de Brienne, rising to his feet.

"Very good," the king responded, and he returned to his cabinet.

Five minutes later, the king's bell recalled Rose, whose time it was. "Have you finished your copies?" asked the king.

"Not yet, sire."

"See if Monsieur d'Artagnan is back yet."

"He's not, sire."

"That's odd!" the king muttered. "Summon Monsieur Colbert."

Colbert entered. He had been waiting for this moment all morning.

"Monsieur Colbert," the king vividly exclaimed, "we've got to find out what's become of Monsieur d'Artagnan."

Colbert's voice was calm. "Where would the king wish me to search for him?"

"Oh, Monsieur!" Louis replied in a sour voice. "Don't you know where I sent him?"

"Your Majesty hasn't told me."

"Monsieur, there are things that one guesses, and you more than anyone else can guess them."

"I could assume something, sire, but I would never have presumed to guess fully."

Scarcely had Colbert spoken when a voice cruder than the king's interrupted the conversation between the monarch and his clerk.

"D'Artagnan!" cried the happy king.

Pallid and furious, d'Artagnan said to the king, "Sire, was it Your Majesty who gave orders to my musketeers?"

"What orders?" asked the king.

"In regard to Monsieur Fouquet's house."

"I gave no such orders!" Louis replied.

"Aha!" said d'Artagnan, chewing his mustache. "Then I wasn't wrong, it was Monsieur Colbert!" And the captain pointed at him.

"What order? Tell me," said the king.

"An order to turn an entire mansion upside down, to beat Monsieur Fouquet's servants and officers, to smash the drawers, to plunder a peaceful home. Damn it! That was a savage order!"

Colbert blanched. "Monsieur!"

"Monsieur!" d'Artagnan interrupted. "Only the king—do you hear me?—only the king has the right to give orders to my musketeers. As for you, I forbid you to do so, and I say so in front of His Majesty. A noblemen who carries a sword is not a good-for-nothing with a quill behind his ear!"

"D'Artagnan! D'Artagnan!" murmured the king.

"It's humiliating!" the musketeer went on. "My soldiers are dishonored! I do not command thugs or clerks from the financial department!"

"But what's wrong? Come on!" the king exclaimed autocratically.

"What's wrong, sire, is that Monsieur, who couldn't guess His Majesty's orders, didn't realize that I was arresting Monsieur Fouquet! Monsieur, who had an iron cage made for his patron of yesterday, sent Monsieur de Roncherat to Monsieur Fouquet's house, and, under pretense of carrying off

Monsieur Fouquet's documents, they carried off all his furniture! My musketeers have been stationed around the house all morning. Those were my orders. Why did somebody presume to have them go inside? Why did somebody make them accomplices by forcing them to witness the pillage? Damn it! We musketeers serve the king! We do not serve Monsieur Colbert!"

"Monsieur d'Artagnan!" the king snapped. "Watch yourself! Such explanations, and in that tone of voice to boot, are not to take place in my presence!"

"I did act for the good of the king," said Colbert, his voice faltering. "It's a harsh thing being treated like this by His Majesty's officer—and because of the respect I owe the king, I do not take vengeance."

"The respect you owe the king," cried d'Artagnan with blazing eyes, "consists, first of all, of respecting his authority and cherishing his person. Any agent of unchecked power represents that power. And when the people curse the hand that strikes them, it is the royal hand that God reproaches—do you hear? Does a soldier hardened by forty years of rain and blood have to teach this lesson, monsieur? Must mercy be on my side and ferocity on yours? You have arrested, fettered, and imprisoned innocent people!"

"Possible accomplices of Monsieur Fouquet," said Colbert.

"Who says that Monsieur Fouquet has accomplices, or even that he's guilty of anything? Only the king knows—his justice is not blind. If he says, 'Arrest, imprison so-and-so,' then he'll be obeyed. Stop talking about your respect for the king, and be careful what you say—your words may sound like threats. And the king does not allow those who serve him well to be threatened by those who serve him badly. And in case, God forbid, I had such an ungrateful master, I would make myself respected!"

Having spoken, d'Artagnan took up a haughty stance in the king's cabinet. His flashing eyes, his hand on his sword, his trembling lips expressed far more anger than he actually felt. Colbert, humiliated, devoured by rage, bowed to the king as if requesting permission to withdraw. The king, piqued both in his pride and in his curiosity, didn't know whose side to take. D'Artagnan saw him wavering. It would have been a mistake for him to remain any longer. He had to triumph over Colbert, and the only way to do so was to sting Louis to the quick—so sharply and so powerfully that His Majesty would have no choice but to support one of the two antagonists. So d'Artagnan likewise bowed.

However, the king was, above all, intent on hearing a very precise and graphic report on Fouquet's arrest as described by the man who'd made him tremble for an instant. Realizing that d'Artagnan's sulky mood would mean a fifteen-minute delay, the king, so eager to learn every last detail, forgot all about Colbert. Since the latter had nothing new to say anyhow, the king called back his captain of the musketeers.

"Come on, monsieur!" said Louis. "First, let's hear your report. Then you can rest."

D'Artagnan, about to pass through the door, was stopped by the king's voice. He came back, and Colbert was compelled to leave. Colbert's face had a purple tinge, and his nasty black eyes burned with a somber fire under their thick brows. He strode toward the king, bowed, half-drew himself up when passing d'Artagnan, and left with death in his soul.

D'Artagnan, now alone with the king, softened immediately and composed his face. "Sire, you are a young king. It's at dawn that a man ascertains whether the day will be happy or sad. How, sire, will the people whom the hand of God has placed under your law foretell what your reign will be like if you allow angry ministers, acting between and your subjects, to perpetrate their violence? However, let's talk about me, sire. Let's leave a discussion that strikes you as idle, perhaps inconvenient. Let's talk about me. I've arrested Monsieur Fouquet."

"You certainly took your time about it!" snapped the king.

D'Artagnan gazed at him. "I see that I've expressed myself badly. I announced to Your Majesty that I had arrested Monsieur Fouquet."

"Yes? Well?"

"Well, it would have been more accurate to tell Your Majesty that Monsieur Fouquet had arrested me. So let me establish the truth: I was arrested by Monsieur Fouquet."

It was Louis XIV's turn to be surprised—astonished! With

his quick glance, d'Artagnan recognized what was going on in the king's mind. The musketeer left him no time to ask questions. With the poetic and picturesque energy that made d'Artagnan virtually unique in his era, he described Fouquet's escape, the pursuit, the fierce race, and finally the superintendent's inimitable generosity. Fouquet could have fled ten times over, he could have killed his pursuer twenty times over. But he chose prison, and possibly worse, rather than humiliate the man who wanted to rob him of his freedom.

As the captain spoke, the king grew more and more agitated, devouring d'Artagnan's words and clicking his nails together.

"The bottom line, sire, at least in my eyes, is that a person who behaves so nobly must be a gallant man and cannot be an enemy of the king. That is my opinion, which I repeat for Your Majesty. I know what the king is about to tell me, and I submit to his judgment: reason of state. So be it! I find that quite respectable. But I'm a soldier, I received my orders. I executed my orders—quite reluctantly, it's true. But they were carried out. I hold my tongue."

"Where is Fouquet at this moment?" asked the king after an instant of silence.

"Sire," d'Artagnan answered, "Monsieur Fouquet is in the iron cage that Monsieur Colbert prepared for him. The coach is rolling along, drawn by four vigorous horses that are galloping toward Angers."

"Why did you leave him en route?"

"Because His Majesty did not order me to go to Angers. The proof, the best proof of what I'm saying, is that the king was looking for me a few minutes ago. . . . And then, I had another reason."

"Namely?"

"Had I been with him, that poor Monsieur Fouquet would never have tried to escape."

"And so?" cried the stupefied king.

"Your Majesty must understand, and certainly does understand, that my keenest wish is to know that Monsieur Fouquet is free. I handed him over to one of my brigadiers, the clumsiest I could find among them, so that the prisoner may flee."

"Are you crazy, Monsieur d'Artagnan?" shouted the king, crossing his arms on his chest. "Does a man articulate such shocking things if he is miserable enough to think them?!"

"Ah, sire! You can't expect me to be Monsieur Fouquet's enemy after what he's just done for me and for you. No, don't ever have me guard him if you insist that he remain locked up. No matter how close the bars of a cage, the bird will eventually fly away."

"I'm amazed," the king said gloomily, "that you didn't immediately throw in your lot with the man whom Monsieur Fouquet wanted to place on my throne. You had everything you needed: affection and gratitude. In my service, monsieur, one finds only a master."

"If Monsieur Fouquet hadn't gone to look for you in the Bastille, sire," d'Artagnan retorted, dwelling on each syllable, "then one single man would have gone there, and I am that man. You know that very well, sire."

The king paused. There was nothing he could object to in those frank and truthful words. Upon hearing them, he recalled the earlier d'Artagnan: the man who'd hidden behind the bed curtains at the Palais-Royal when the people of Paris, led by Cardinal Retz, had come to make certain of the king's presence; the man whom the king had saluted at his carriage door when going to Notre Dame after reentering Paris; the soldier who'd left the king's service in Blois; the lieutenant he'd summoned when Mazarin's death restored the king's power; the man he had always found to be loyal, courageous, devoted.

Louis strode over to the door and called Colbert.

The latter hadn't left the corridor, where the secretaries were working. Colbert appeared.

"Colbert, did you search Monsieur Fouquet's home?"

"Yes, sire."

"What did you find?"

"Monsieur de Roncherat, who was sent with Your Majesty's musketeers, handed me some documents."

"I'll look them over. . . . You're going to give me your hand."

"My hand, sire?"

"Yes, so I can put it in Monsieur d'Artagnan's hand." With a smile, the king turned toward the soldier, who'd resumed his haughty stance at the sight of the clerk. "In fact, d'Artagnan, you don't know this man. Get to know him." And he pointed at Colbert. "He is a middling servant in subaltern positions, but he'll be a great man if I raise him to the first rank."

"Sire!" Colbert stammered, overwhelmed with joy and fear.

"I understood why," d'Artagnan whispered to the king. "He was jealous."

"Precisely, and his jealousy was binding his wings."

"From now on, he'll be a winged serpent," the musketeer grumbled with a vestige of hatred toward his former adversary.

But when Colbert came over, his face was so different from the face that he normally showed. He appeared so kind, so gentle, so easygoing; his eyes expressed such a noble intelligence that d'Artagnan, a connoisseur of physiognomies, was deeply moved, almost changing his convictions about Colbert.

Colbert shook d'Artagnan's hand.

"What the king has told you, monsieur, proves how well His Majesty knows human nature. The fierce opposition I've hitherto deployed toward abuses, not toward individuals, confirms that I was intent on preparing a grand reign for my king and great well-being for my country. I've got lots of ideas, Monsieur d'Artagnan. You'll see them blossom in the sun of public peace. And if I don't have the certainty and good fortune to win the friendship of decent men, I am at least assured of gaining their esteem, monsieur. I would, monsieur, give my life to obtain their admiration."

This change of character, this sudden elevation, this mute approval by the king gave the musketeer a lot to mull over. He very civilly saluted Colbert, whose eyes were glued to d'Artagnan. Seeing them reconciled, the king dismissed them. They left together.

Once outside Louis's cabinet, the new minister stopped the captain. "Is it possible, Monsieur d'Artagnan, that with an eye like yours you didn't recognize me on the spot, upon your first inspection?"

"Monsieur Colbert,"* the captain responded, "the sunbeam in an eye prevents one from seeing the most furious flames. A man in power is radiant—you know that. And since you're in power, why do you continue persecuting the man who has fallen in disgrace and from such a height at that?"

"I, monsieur," said Colbert. "Oh, I, monsieur—I will never persecute him. I wanted to administer the finances and administer them alone, because I'm ambitious, and, above all, because I have utmost confidence in my merit. I know that all the gold in the kingdom will pass before my eyes, and I love to see the king's gold. If I live another thirty years, not one denier will remain in my hands. With this gold, I'll build granaries, edifices, cities. I'll dig harbors. I'll create a navy, I'll fit out ships that will carry the name of France to the most far-flung nations. I'll establish libraries, academies. I will make France the greatest country in the world and the richest. Those are the reasons for my animosity toward Monsieur Fouquet, who prevented me from acting. And then, when I will be great and powerful, when France will be great and powerful, it will be my turn to cry: 'Mercy!' "

" 'Mercy'? Then let's ask the king to release Monsieur Fouquet. The king is crushing him only because of you."

Colbert raised his head again. "Monsieur, you know very well that that's not so; the king bears his own grudge toward Monsieur Fouquet. It's not my job to inform you."

"The king will grow tired. He'll forget."

"The king never forgets, Monsieur d'Artagnan. . . . Listen, the king is about to call and he's going to issue an order. I haven't influenced him, have I? Just listen!"

And indeed the king summoned his secretaries. Then: "Monsieur d'Artagnan?"

"Here I am, sire."

"Give Monsieur de Saint-Aignan twenty of your musketeers to guard Monsieur Fouquet."

D'Artagnan and Colbert exchanged glances.

"From Angers," the king went on, "the prisoner will be taken to Paris, to the Bastille."

"You were right," the captain told the minister.

"Saint-Aignan," the king continued, "en route, you will shoot down anyone who tries to speak privately to Monsieur Fouquet."

"I, sire?" said the duke.

"You, monsieur. You will talk to him only in the presence of the musketeer."

The duke bowed and went off to execute his order.

D'Artagnan was also about to retire, but the king stopped him.

"Monsieur, you will go immediately to take possession of the island and the fief of Belle-Île-en-Mer."

"Yes, sire. I alone?"

"You will take along as many troops as you need in case you meet resistance."

A murmur of sycophantic disbelief was heard among the courtiers.

"It's been seen before," said d'Artagnan.

"I saw it in my childhood," the king rejoined, "and I don't wish to see it again. Do you hear? Now go, monsieur, and do not come back until you hold the keys to the fortress."

Colbert approached d'Artagnan. "If you carry this mission out properly, you may become a marshal of France."

"Why do you say if I carry it out properly?"

"Because it's a difficult assignment."

"In what way?"

"You've got friends in Belle-Île, Monsieur d'Artagnan, and it's not easy for a man like you to find success by climbing over a friend's corpse."

D'Artagnan hung his head while Colbert walked back to the king.

Fifteen minutes later, the captain received a written order to blow up Belle-Île in case of resistance, with all civil and criminal justice applied to the inhabitants and refugees. Not a single one was to escape.

Colbert was right, d'Artagnan mused. If I'm made a marshal of France, it will cost me the lives of two friends. Only people forget that my friends are no more stupid than birds and that they're not waiting for the fowler's hand in order to spread their wings. I'll show them this hand so effectively that they'll have time to see it. Poor Porthos! Poor Aramis! No! My good fortune won't cost you a feather from your wings.

Having reached this conclusion, d'Artagnan gathered the royal army, embarked at Paimboeuf, and sailed off without wasting a moment.

42
Belle-Île-en-Mer

At the far end of the pier, on the promenade, which is lashed by the furious evening tide, two men holding each other by the arm were engaged in an animated and effusive conversation. No one could make out their words, each of which was blasted off by the gusts of wind and the white foam of the wave crests. The sun had just set in the vast expanse of reddened ocean, which looked like a gigantic crucible.

Every so often, one of the two men halted, turned toward the east, and scrutinized it with gloomy anxiety. The other, probing his companion's features, appeared to be trying to read his mind. Then, both of them wordless, both teeming with somber thoughts, they resumed their stroll. These two men, recognized by everyone, were our outlaws, Porthos and Aramis; they had sought refuge at Belle-Île since the dashing of their hopes, since the failure of Monsieur d'Herblay's extensive plan.

"You can say what you like, my dear Aramis," said Porthos, as he vigorously inhaled the salt air into his powerful, swelling lungs. "You can say what you like, Aramis. But there's nothing common about the fact that all the fishing boats vanished two days ago. There's been no storm; the weather's been consistently calm, not even the slightest gale. And if there had been a tempest, it wouldn't have claimed our every last boat. I repeat: it's odd, and I'm amazed by that total disappearance."

"It's true," Aramis murmured. "You're right, my friend. It's true. There's more here than meets the eye."

Aramis's assent seemed to inspire Porthos to augment his ideas. "Furthermore," the latter added, "if the boats were wrecked, how come not a single piece of jetsam has been washed ashore?"

"I've noticed that too."

"Have you also noticed that the only two boats that remained here and that I sent out to find the others—"

Aramis broke in with a shout and a movement so brusque that Porthos halted, stupefied.

"What are you saying, Porthos?! What? You sent out the two remaining boats . . . ?"

"Of course," Porthos replied simply, "to search for the others."

"That's horrendous! What have you done?" cried the bishop. "We're doomed!"

"Doomed? What did you say?" Porthos was terrified. "Why doomed, Aramis? Why are we doomed?"

Aramis bit his lip. "Never mind! Never mind! Forgive me! I meant—"

"What?"

"I meant that if we felt like taking a boat ride, we couldn't do it."

"Fine! So that's what's eating you. A great pleasure, damn it! As for me, I don't miss it. What I do miss is certainly not the enjoyment that can more or less be found in Belle-Île. No, Aramis. I miss Pierrefonds and Bracieux and Le Vallon—I miss my beautiful France! This isn't France, old friend. I don't know where we are. Oh, I can tell you with all the sincerity of my soul, and your affection will excuse my frankness. I tell you, I'm not happy in Belle-Île. No, really, I'm not happy here!"

Aramis sighed very softly. "My dear friend, that's why you shouldn't have sent out the two remaining boats to find the others. If you hadn't expedited them, we could have left."

"Left?! And what about our mission, Aramis?"

"What mission?"

"Why, the mission that you keep repeating to me on any and all occasions. We're guarding Belle-Île against the usurper. You know it very well!"

"That's true!" Aramis murmured.

"You can readily see, my friend, that we can't leave. Sending out the two boats to hunt for the others doesn't harm us in any way!"

Aramis held his tongue, and his eyes, as luminous as those of a gull, swept across the sea for a long time, questioning the vast space and trying to peer beyond the horizon.

"With all that, Aramis," said Porthos, who clung to his idea all the more strongly because the bishop agreed with him, "with all that, you haven't provided any explanation for what's happened to those unfortunate boats. I'm assailed by shouts and laments wherever I go. The children cry because the women are so desperate—as if I could bring back their sons and fathers. What do you speculate, my friend, and what should I tell them?"

"Let's speculate, my good Porthos, but let's say nothing."

The response did not satisfy Porthos. He turned around, grouching and grumbling.

Aramis stopped the valiant soldier. "Do you remember," he said mournfully, squeezing the giant's hands with affectionate cordiality, "do you remember that in the wonderful days of our youth—do you remember that when we were strong and fearless, the two others and you and I—that if we had felt an urge to return to France, this sheet of salt water wouldn't have stopped us?"

"Oh!" exclaimed Porthos. "Six leagues!"

"If you had seen me climb a plank, would you have stayed on dry land, Porthos?"

"No, Aramis, by God! But what a plank we'd need today, dear friend, especially me!"

And laughing with pride, the Seigneur de Bracieux glanced at his own colossal rotundity.

"Seriously, aren't you also a bit bored in Belle-Île, and wouldn't you prefer the charms of your home, your episcopal palace in Vannes? Come on, admit it."

"No," replied Aramis without daring to look at Porthos.

"Then let's stay," said Porthos with a sigh that, despite his efforts to repress it, noisily escaped his chest. "Let's stay! Let's stay! And yet, and yet, if someone were determined, very determined, to go back to France, but had no boats . . ."

"Did you notice something else, my friend? Ever since the disappearance of our boats and our fishermen two days ago, not even a dinghy has reached these shores?"

"You're very right! I noticed it too—I did, and it was easy to observe, because, prior to those two fateful days, dozens of boats and launches arrived here."

"We have to get to the bottom of this," an excited Aramis suddenly exclaimed. "If I could have a raft built . . ."

"But we have canoes, dear friend. Do you want me to ride one?"

"A canoe? A canoe? . . . What are you thinking, Porthos? A canoe that will capsize? No, no! It's not like us to skim across the waves. Let's wait, let's wait."

And Aramis continued strolling with all the signs of a growing agitation.

Porthos, tired of following his friend's hectic movements; Porthos, who, in his calm faith, understood nothing of that convulsive exasperation—Porthos halted. "Let's sit down on this rock, Aramis. Sit right next to me, and I beg you one last time: explain it in terms that I can understand, explain to me what we are doing here."

"Porthos . . . ," said Aramis awkwardly.

"I know that the false king wanted to dethrone the real king. That's a fact, I understand it. Well?"

"Yes," said Aramis.

"I know that the false king planned to sell Belle-Île to the British. I understand that too."

"Yes."

"I know that we engineers and captains plunged head-on into the Belle-Île project. We took charge of the work and the ten companies that were raised, paid, and commanded by Monsieur Fouquet, or rather the ten companies headed by his son-in-law. I understand all that too."

Aramis, out of patience, stood up. He was like a lion pestered by a gadfly. Porthos grabbed his arm.

"But what I don't understand, despite all my mental efforts, all my reflections—what I don't understand, and will never understand, is why, instead of sending us troops, instead of sending us more men, food, and ammunition, they've left us without boats, they've left Belle-Île without consignments, without help. Instead of contacting us through signals or by written or verbal correspondence, they intercept all communications with us. Listen, Aramis, answer me—or, rather, before answering me, do you want to hear what I think? Do you want to know what I believe, what I imagine?"

The bishop raised his head.

"Well, Aramis," Porthos continued, "I think, I believe, I imagine, that something has happened in France. . . . I dreamed about Monsieur Fouquet all night. I dreamed about dead fish, broken eggs, shabby, ugly rooms. Nightmares, my dear d'Herblay, unlucky nightmares."

"Porthos! What's that?" Aramis interrupted, jumping to his feet and pointing to a black dot on the purple line of the water.

"A boat," said Porthos. "Yes! It's a boat! Ah! So we'll finally have some news!"

"Two boats!" cried the bishop, spotting another set of masts. "Two! Three! Four!"

"Five!" Porthos added in turn. "Six! Seven! Oh my God! It's a whole fleet! My God! My God!"

"It's probably our boats coming back," said Aramis. He was nervous despite the self-assurance he displayed.

"They're too big for fishing boats," Porthos observed. "And haven't you noticed, old friend, that they're coming from the Loire?"

"They're coming from the Loire, that's right. . . ."

"And look, everyone else has seen them. The women and children are thronging the jetties."

An old fisherman trudged by.

"Are those our boats?" Aramis asked him.

The old man peered into the depths of the horizon. "No, monseigneur, those are lighters in the king's service."

"Royal service?" Aramis shuddered. "How can you tell?"

"By the colors."

"But those vessels are barely visible," said Porthos. "How the hell can you make out the colors?"

"I can see there's a flag," replied the old man. "Neither our boats nor the commercial barges fly any colors. Those boats heading our way, monsieur, are normally used for carrying troops."

"Ah!" said Aramis.

"Hurray!" cried Porthos. "They're sending us reinforcements—isn't that so, Aramis?"

"Probably!"

"Unless the British are arriving!"

"Via the Loire? That would be a calamity for them, Porthos. They'd have to sail through Paris."

"You're right. Those are definitely reinforcements or supplies."

Instead of answering, Aramis buried his head in his hands. Then he suddenly exclaimed, "Porthos, sound the alarm!"

"The alarm? . . . Are you sure?"

"Yes. Tell the cannoneers to mount to their batteries; tell the gunners to get to their guns. And be especially watchful with the coastal batteries."

Porthos gaped and gawked. He scrutinized his friend as if to convince himself that Aramis hadn't lost his mind.

"I'm going over there, my good Porthos," Aramis murmured in the gentlest of voices. "I'll carry out these orders if you don't go, my dear friend."

"Why, I'm going this very instant!" Porthos took off while looking back to see if the bishop had changed his mind, regained his sanity, and was calling Porthos back.

The alarm resounded, the drums rolled, the trumpets blared, the huge bell in the belfry swung to and fro. The dikes and piers filled up with soldiers and curiosity seekers. The fuses sparkled in the hands of the artillerists behind the enormous cannon perching on their stone carriages.

When every man was at his post, when all the defense preparations were done, Porthos timidly whispered, "Allow me to try to understand, Aramis."

"Come on, old friend, you'll understand all too soon," Monsieur d'Herblay muttered to his lieutenant.

"That fleet over there, with its sails unfurled, that fleet heading toward the harbor of Belle-Île—it's a royal fleet, isn't it?"

"There are two kings in France, Porthos. To which of the two kings does this fleet belong?"

The giant was crushed by that argument. "Oh! You're opening my eyes!" And Porthos, whose eyes had been opened by his friend's rejoinder—or, rather, whose blindfold had become thinner—ran to the batteries in order to supervise his men and exhort each one to do his duty.

However, Aramis, his eyes still glued to the horizon, watched the ships approaching. The soldiers and the civilians, who had all climbed to the summit of the rocks or the caves in them, could distinguish the masts, then the lower sails, and finally the hulls of the lighters flying the royal colors of France.

It was after nightfall when one of the boats that had so deeply stirred up the whole of Belle-Île was moored within cannon-shot of the fort. Despite the darkness, the onlookers saw a kind of agitation aboard this vessel. The sailors lowered a skiff, in which three oarsmen, hunched over their oars, raced toward the harbor. Within moments, the skiff had landed at the foot of the fort.

The skipper of that yawl jumped on the pier. Clutching a letter, which he waved in the air, he apparently wanted to communicate with someone. A few soldiers promptly recognized him as one of the pilots of the island. He was the skipper of one of the two boats that had been kept by Aramis and that Porthos, worried about the two fishermen who had been missing for two days, had sent out in search of the lost boats.

The seaman asked to be taken to Monsieur d'Herblay. At a sergeant's gesture, two soldiers flanked the newcomer and escorted him. Aramis was on the dock. The envoy presented himself to the Bishop of Vannes. The night was almost pitch-black despite the torches carried at a certain distance by the soldiers who followed Aramis as he did his rounds.

"Hey, Jonathas, on whose behalf are you coming here?"

"Monseigneur, on behalf of the men who captured me."

"Who captured you?"

"Monseigneur, you know that we'd gone out to look for our comrades?"

"Yes, and then?"

"Well, monseigneur, after barely covering a league, we were taken prisoner by a coastal lugger belonging to the king."

"Ah!" said Aramis.

"Which king?" asked Porthos.

Jonathas gaped.

"Keep talking," the bishop continued.

"Well, we were captured, monseigneur, and reunited with the men who'd been captured yesterday morning."

"Who was crazy enough to capture all of you?" Porthos broke in.

"Monsieur, they wanted to prevent us from telling you," Jonathas replied.

Porthos was totally confused. "And you were released today?" he asked.

"To tell you, monsieur, that we've been captured."

Worse and worse, thought our decent Porthos.

Meanwhile, Aramis was reflecting. "Hey!" he exclaimed. "So a royal fleet is blockading the coasts?"

"Yes, monseigneur."

"Who's in command?"

"The captain of the king's musketeers."

"D'Artagnan?"

"D'Artagnan!" said Porthos.

"I think that's his name."

"And he's the one who gave you this letter?"

"Yes, monseigneur."

"Bring over the torches."

"It's his handwriting," said Porthos.

Aramis ardently read the following lines:

> Order of the King to take Belle-Île;
> Order of the King to put the garrison to sword if it resists;
> Order to take all the garrison men prisoner.
> Signed, D'ARTAGNAN, who arrested MONSIEUR FOUQUET two days ago to send him to the Bastille.

Aramis blanched and crumpled up the letter.

"What is it?" asked Porthos.

"Nothing, my friend! Nothing!"

"Jonathas, tell me?"

"Monseigneur?"

"Did you talk to Monsieur d'Artagnan?"

"Yes, monseigneur."

"What did he tell you?"

"That for more ample information he would chat with Monseigneur."

"Where?"

"Aboard his vessel."

"Aboard his vessel?!"

Porthos repeated: "Aboard his vessel."

"Monsieur Musketeer," Jonathas went on, "told me to take you and Monsieur the engineer, to ferry you to him in my boat."

"Let's go," said Porthos. "That dear d'Artagnan!"

Aramis stopped him. "Are you crazy? How do you know it's not a trap?"

"Set by the other king?" Porthos retorted with an air of mystery.

"Simply a trap! That says everything, my friend!"

"It's possible. So what should we do? But if d'Artagnan is summoning us . . ."

"How do you know it's d'Artagnan?"

"Oh! Well . . . But his handwriting . . ."

"Handwriting can be forged. This handwriting is forged; it's shaky."

"You're always right. But, meanwhile, we know nothing."

Aramis was silent.

"It's true," said our good Porthos, "that we don't need to know anything."

"What should I do?" asked Jonathas.

"You'll return to this captain's vessel."

"Yes, monseigneur."

"And you'll tell him that we'd like him to come to this island."

"Yes, monseigneur. But what if he refuses to come to Belle-Île?"

"If he refuses, we've got cannon and we'll use them!"

"Against d'Artagnan?"

"If it's d'Artagnan, Porthos, he'll come. Go back, Jonathas, go back."

"Goodness," murmured Porthos, "I don't understand a thing."

"You'll understand everything now, dear friend. The time has come. Sit down on this gun carriage, listen carefully, and heed everything I say."

"I'm listening, damn it! You can bet on it!"

"Can I leave, monseigneur?" cried Jonathas.

"Leave and bring back an answer. Let the boat through, men!"

The boat headed back toward the ship.

Aramis took Porthos's hand and launched into an explanation.

43
Aramis's Explanation

"What I'm about to tell you, my friend, will probably surprise you—but also instruct you."

"I like surprises," Porthos said benevolently. "Please don't spare my feelings. I'm hardened against emotions—so don't be afraid. Out with it!"

"It's difficult, Porthos, it's . . . difficult. You see—let me warn you again—I've got very strange things to tell you, very extraordinary things."

"Why, you're speaking so well, dear friend, that I could listen to you for days on end. Out with it, please. Hey! I've got an idea. To make it easier on you to tell me those strange things, I'll ask you questions."

"Fine."

"What are we going to fight for, dear Aramis?"

"If you ask me a lot of questions like that, if that's how you want to make my job easier, my need to reveal things, Porthos, then your questions will make nothing easier on me. Quite the opposite. That's precisely the Gordian knot. Listen, my friend, with a good, generous, and devoted man like you, I must—for both his sake and mine—start my confession by screwing up my courage. I've deceived you, my worthy friend."

"You've deceived me?!"

"Yes, by God!"

"Was it for my own good, Aramis?"

"I thought so, Porthos. I sincerely thought so, my friend."

"Then," said the honest Lord de Bracieux, "you did me a favor, and I'm grateful to you. For if you hadn't deceived me, I might have deceived myself. In what way have you deceived me? Tell me."

"I served the usurper on whom Louis XIV is focusing all his efforts."

"The usurper?" said Porthos, scratching his forehead. "It's . . . I don't really understand . . ."

"He's one of the two kings who are struggling over the French throne."

"Fine! So you were serving the man who isn't Louis XIV?"

"You've hit the nail on the head!"

"The result being . . ."

"The result being that we are rebels, my poor friend."

"Damn it! Damn it!" cried Porthos, disappointed.

"Oh, my dear Porthos, stay calm! We'll find some way to save ourselves—trust me!"

"That's not what worries me," Porthos replied. "The only thing that bothers me is that ugly word 'rebel.' "

"Aha!"

"And so the duchy I've been promised . . ."

"It was the usurper who gave it."

"That's not the same thing, Aramis," said Porthos majestically.

"My friend, if it had been up to me, you'd have become a prince."

Porthos started chewing his nails mournfully. "That's what you shouldn't have deceived me about. I was seriously counting on that duchy, for I know that you're a man of your word, my dear Aramis."

"Poor Porthos! Forgive me, I beg you."

"And so," Porthos persisted, ignoring the bishop's pleas, "and so I've had quite a falling-out with the king, right?"

"I'll take care of that, my good friend, I'll take care of that. I'll take everything upon my own shoulders."

"Aramis! . . ."

"No, no, Porthos, I beg you, let me do it. No false generosity! No inopportune devotion! You knew nothing about my plans. You did nothing on your own. With me, it's different. I'm the sole architect of the plot. I needed my inseparable companion. I summoned you, and you came to me, recalling our old pledge: 'All for one and one for all!' My crime, dear Porthos, was my egotism."

"That's a word that I like," said Porthos. "And since you acted purely for yourself, I can't possibly blame you for anything. It's so natural!"

And with that sublime word, Porthos warmly shook his friend's hand. Aramis felt small in the presence of that simple spiritual grandeur. It was the second time that he was compelled to bow before that true superiority of the heart—something far more powerful than splendor of the mind. Aramis mutely responded to his friend's warm generosity with an energetic squeeze of his hand.

"Now that everything's been fully explained," said Porthos, "now that I understand your situation in regard to the king, I believe, dear friend, that it's time for me to understand the political intrigue that has victimized us—for I clearly see that a political intrigue is behind it all."

"D'Artagnan, my good Porthos, d'Artagnan is coming and he'll give you a detailed account of the intrigue. But forgive me, I'm overwhelmed with pain and grief, and I need my full presence of mind, my complete lucidity, to steer you out of the mess in which I've imprudently entangled you. However, from now on, nothing can be clearer, nothing can be plainer, than the position. The king has only one enemy now—and that enemy is myself, myself alone. I made you my prisoner, you followed me. Today, I set you free; you will return to your ruler. You can see, Porthos, that this doesn't involve any difficulty."

"Do you believe that?"

"I'm sure of it."

"Then why," asked Porthos, relying on his admirable common sense, "why, if we're in such an easy position, why, my good friend, are we preparing cannon, muskets, and all sorts of war engines? I figure it would be simpler to tell Captain d'Artagnan: 'Dear friend, we made a mistake, it can be rectified. Open the door, allow us to pass—and good-bye!' "

"Oh my!" said Aramis, shaking his head.

"What do you mean 'Oh my,' dear friend? Don't you approve of my plan?"

"I see a snag."

"Namely?"

"The possibility that d'Artagnan might receive orders that would force us to defend ourselves."

"Cut it out! Defend ourselves against d'Artagnan? That's crazy! Our good d'Artagnan! . . ."

Aramis shook his head again. "Porthos, if I've had the fuses lit and the cannon pointed, if I've had the alarm sounded, and ordered every single man to his post on the ramparts—those wonderful Belle-Île ramparts that you've fortified so marvelously!—if I've done all these things, I must have my good reasons. Just wait and judge for yourself—or, better still, don't judge. . . ."

"What should we do?"

"If I knew, my friend, I'd have told you."

"Well, there's something much easier than defending ourselves. A boat en route to France in which—"

"Dear friend," rejoined Aramis with a sad smile, "don't let's argue like children. Let's be adults in both counsel and execution. Hey! I hear the men in the harbor hailing some kind of vessel. Pay attention, Porthos, serious attention!"

"It must be d'Artagnan!" Porthos thundered as he approached the parapet.

"You're right!" replied the captain of the musketeers, lightly bounding up the steps of the pier. And he swiftly reached the small esplanade where his two friends were waiting.

Once they got under way, Porthos and Aramis made out an officer who was following on d'Artagnan's heels. The captain stopped halfway up the pier steps. His companion did likewise.

"Withdraw your men!" d'Artagnan shouted at his friends. "Tell them to wait out of earshot."

The order, given by Porthos, was instantly carried out.

D'Artagnan turned toward his companion. "Monsieur, we are no longer in the royal fleet, where you talked to me so arrogantly by virtue of your orders."

"Monsieur," the officer responded, "I wasn't being arrogant! I was simply but rigorously obeying my orders. I was told to follow you, so I'm following you. I was told not to let you communicate with anyone whomsoever without my observing you. I'm therefore involved in your communications."

D'Artagnan shook with anger. Porthos and Aramis, listening to this exchange, also shook—but with fear and anxiety. Chewing his mustache with an exasperation that usually verged on a dreadful explosion, d'Artagnan strode over to the officer. "Monsieur," he said in a softer, calmer, clearer voice that concealed a tempest. "Monsieur, when I sent a dinghy here, you wanted to know what I was writing to the defenders of Belle-Île. You showed me an order. I immediately showed you my letter. When the skipper I had dispatched returned, when I received an answer from these two gentlemen, you heard the complete message. All those things were based on your orders—they were carefully listened to and executed to the letter! Isn't that so?"

"Yes, monsieur," the officer stammered. "No doubt about it, monsieur. . . . But—"

"Monsieur," d'Artagnan continued more angrily, "when I revealed, when I announced out loud, my intention to go ashore on Belle-Île, you insisted on accompanying me. I did not hesitate, I took you along. You are now in Belle-Île, aren't you?"

"Yes, monsieur, but—"

"But we are no longer subject to instructions from Monsieur Colbert or from anyone else who commands you! We are dealing here with a man who is bothering Monsieur d'Artagnan and who is alone with Monsieur d'Artagnan on the steps of a stairway washed by thirty feet of salt water. A bad position for that man, a bad position, monsieur! I have to warn you."

"But, monsieur," said the officer timidly, almost blanching, "if I'm troubling you, it's because my service—"

"Monsieur! You, or whomever you've been sent by, have had the misfortune to offend me. It's done! I can't confront your superiors! I don't know them, or else they're too far away! But you're within my striking distance, and I swear to God that if you take a single step behind me when I raise my foot to reach these gentlemen . . . I swear upon my good name that I will split your skull with my sword and dump you in the water. Oh, it will happen—count on it! I've lost my temper only six times in my entire life, monsieur, and I've killed all five men the preceding five times."

The officer didn't budge. He blanched at that dreadful threat and said in all simplicity, "Monsieur, you are wrong to go against my orders."

Porthos and Aramis, wordlessly shuddering on the parapet, now shouted: "Dear d'Artagnan, watch out!"

D'Artagnan motioned for them to be silent. He raised his foot with a terrifying calm and turned around, clutching his sword, to see if the officer was following him. The officer made a sign of the cross and followed him. Porthos and Aramis, who knew their friend, shrieked and dashed down the steps to prevent the blow that they thought they heard coming. But d'Artagnan switched the sword to his left hand.

"Monsieur," he said, deeply moved, "you are a brave man. You ought to grasp more easily what I'm about to tell you than what I said before."

"Speak, Monsieur d'Artagnan, speak," the brave officer replied.

"These gentlemen whom you see here and against whom you've got orders—they are my friends."

"I know that, monsieur."

"You can understand that I cannot follow your instructions in regard to them."

"I understand your reluctance."

"Well, allow me to confer with them without a witness."

"Monsieur d'Artagnan, if I gave in to your request, if I did what you're asking me to do, I would be flouting my oath. And if I don't do as you ask, I'd be offending you. I prefer the former. Converse with your friends and don't despise me for doing out of love for you, a man I esteem and honor—don't despise me for performing an unworthy action for you and for you alone."

D'Artagnan, again deeply moved, threw his arms around the young man and strode up to his friends. The officer, enveloped in his cloak, sat down on the steps, which were covered with wet seaweed.

"Well," d'Artagnan said to his friends, "this is the position. Judge for yourselves."

All three embraced one another. All three were locked in one another's arms as in the glorious days of their youth.

"What do all these severe measures mean?" asked Porthos.

"You must suspect something, dear friends," replied d'Artagnan.

"Not really, my dear captain, I assure you." The fine man added: "Neither I nor Aramis have done anything."

D'Artagnan eyed the prelate reproachfully, penetrating his firm heart.

"Dear Porthos!" cried the Bishop of Vannes.

"You can see what they've done," said d'Artagnan. "They're intercepting everything coming from or going to Belle-Île. All your boats have been seized. If you had tried to escape, you'd have fallen into their hands—their cruisers are plowing the water and watching for you. The king wants you and he's going to have you!" And d'Artagnan furiously tore out a few hairs from his gray mustache.

Aramis turned somber, and Porthos was furious.

"This was my plan," said d'Artagnan. "Bring both of you on board, keep you near me, and then set you free. But how do I know that when I return to my ship, I won't find a superior officer, that I won't find secret orders transferring my command to someone else, who'll dispose of you and me with no hope of rescue?"

"We've got to remain on Belle-Île," Aramis said resolutely, "and I can guarantee that I won't be captured without a fight!"

Porthos held his tongue. D'Artagnan noticed his silence. "I've got to test this officer once again, this brave man who's accompanying me. His loyal and courageous resistance makes me happy. For it signifies an honorable man, and, even though he's our enemy, he's worth a thousand times more than an obliging coward. Let's try to find out what he's got the right to do, what his orders permit or prohibit."

"Let's give it a try!" said Aramis.

D'Artagnan reached the parapet, turned toward the steps, and summoned the officer, who came instantly.

"Monsieur," said d'Artagnan after the exchange of the most

cordial courtesies, which are natural between gentlemen who know and appreciate one another in a worthy manner. "Monsieur, if I were to conduct these gentlemen from here, what would you do?"

"I wouldn't oppose you, monsieur. But having strict and direct orders to guard them, I would guard them."

"Ah!" said d'Artagnan.

"It's over," murmured Aramis.

Porthos didn't budge.

"Take Porthos away!" said the bishop. "With my help, and yours too, Monsieur d'Artagnan, Porthos can prove to the king that he had nothing to do with this matter."

"Hmm!" murmured d'Artagnan. "Do you want to come, Porthos? Do you want to follow me? The king is a clement man."

"Let me think about it," Porthos replied nobly.

"Then you'd rather stay here?" d'Artagnan asked Aramis.

"Until new orders are issued!" Aramis exclaimed sharply.

"Until we have a plan," d'Artagnan resumed. "And I think we'll have one soon enough, I've already got one."

"Then let's say good-bye," said Aramis. "But, dear Porthos, you really ought to leave."

"No," said Porthos laconically.

"As you like," said Aramis, who, nervous and susceptible, was slightly wounded by his companion's morose tone. "However, I'm reassured by d'Artagnan's promise of an idea—an idea that I think I've guessed."

"Let's see!" The musketeer listened to Aramis's whisper. Aramis murmured several swift words, to which d'Artagnan replied: "You've hit the nail on the head!"

"So it's inevitable!" cried Aramis joyfully.

"When you first feel the emotions sparked by this resolution, keep your head, Aramis."

"Don't worry!"

"And now, monsieur," d'Artagnan said to the officer, "thank you a thousand times! You've just made three friends for life!"

"Yes," Aramis seconded him.

Porthos, the only man holding his tongue, acquiesced by nodding.

After tenderly hugging his two old friends, d'Artagnan left

with the inseparable companion supplied by Monsieur Colbert.

Thus, apart from the makeshift explanation that was enough for our worthy Porthos, nothing appeared to have changed the fate of either man.

"Only," said Aramis, "there's d'Artagnan's plan."

D'Artagnan did not return to his dinghy without carefully examining his plan. And we know that when d'Artagnan examined anything, he usually saw the light at the end of the tunnel. As for the wordless officer, d'Artagnan respectfully gave him time to think. Thus, setting foot on his vessel, which was within the firing range of the cannon of Belle-Île, the musketeer captain had mentally marshaled all his offensive and defensive possibilities. He immediately gathered his council.

This council was made up of the officers who served under him—eight in all: a leader of the maritime forces, a major in charge of artillery, an engineer, the young officer whom we've met, and four lieutenants.

Assembling them in his poop chamber, d'Artagnan stood up, removed his felt hat, and began: "Gentlemen, I've reconnoitered Belle-Île and I've found a good and solid garrison as well as preparations for a defense that could prove troublesome. I therefore intend for us to meet with two senior officers of the island and to converse with them. If they're separated from their troops and their cannon, we can parley more easily, especially if we offer good arguments. Do you agree, gentlemen?"

The artillery major rose to his feet. "Monsieur," he said respectfully but firmly, "I've just heard you say that the fortress is preparing a troublesome defense. So it's determined to rebel?"

D'Artagnan was visibly chagrined by this response, but he wasn't a man to be upset by a trifle: "Monsieur, your assumption is fair. But you know that Belle-Île is Monsieur Fouquet's fief, and the earlier kings granted the lords of Belle-Île the right to arm themselves."

The major tried to speak, but d'Artagnan went on. "Oh, don't interrupt me. You're about to say that this right to arm themselves against the British is not a right to arm themselves against their king. But it's not Monsieur Fouquet who's holding Belle-Île now. You see, I arrested him two days ago. However, the inhabitants and defenders of Belle-Île know nothing about that arrest. You can announce it all you like—the arrest is so extraordinary, so unexpected, that they won't believe you! A Breton serves his master but not his masters. He serves him until he sees him dead. Now, as far as I can tell, the Bretons have not seen Monsieur Fouquet's corpse. So it's not surprising that they hold out against everything that is not Monsieur Fouquet or his signature."

The major bowed as a sign of assent.

"That," d'Artagnan continued, "is why I propose inviting two senior officers from the garrison to come here, aboard my vessel. They will see you, gentlemen, they will see the power we've got at our disposal. They will thereupon see the fate that awaits them in case they rebel. We will swear on our honor that Monsieur Fouquet is incarcerated and that any resistance on their part will only be harmful to him. We will tell them that the instant a cannon goes off, they can no longer expect any mercy from the king. So I at least hope that they won't resist. They will surrender without a fight, and we will amiably acquire a fortress that would be costly to conquer."

The officer who had followed d'Artagnan to Belle-Île, was about to take the floor—but d'Artagnan interrupted him. "I know what you're going to say, monsieur. I know that the king has ordered us to prevent any secret communication with the defenders of Belle-Île, and that's precisely why I suggest that we communicate only in the presence of my complete general staff." And d'Artagnan nodded at his officers to indicate this compliance.

The officers exchanged glances, trying to read each other's minds and obviously intending to agree with d'Artagnan and act on his instructions. D'Artagnan was delighted to see that his officers were ready to send a boat to Porthos and Aramis—but then the king's officer produced a sealed letter from his chest and handed it to d'Artagnan. The letter bore the number 1 in its address.

The captain was surprised. "What is this?" he murmured.

"Read it, monsieur," said the officer, bowing with a slightly woeful courtesy.

D'Artagnan, filled with distrust, unfolded the document and read it:

> Monsieur d'Artagnan is prohibited from assembling any kind of council or deliberating in any fashion before Belle-Île surrenders and the prisoners are shot.
>
> Signed: LOUIS

D'Artagnan repressed the impatience sweeping through his entire body and said with a gracious smile: "That's fine, monsieur. We will adhere to the king's orders."

44
The Results of the King's Plans and d'Artagnan's Plans

The blow was direct. It was harsh and mortal. Although furious that the king had anticipated his plan, d'Artagnan nevertheless did not despair. Thinking about the plan he had brought back from Belle-Île, he hit on a new way of helping his friends.

"Gentlemen," he said abruptly, "since the king has charged someone else and not me with his secret orders, then I obviously no longer enjoy his trust, and I would be truly unworthy of that trust if I had the courage to keep a command subject to so many insulting suspicions. I will therefore go to the king immediately and tender my resignation. I resign before all of you, and I call upon you to sail back to the French coast so as to avoid compromising the armed forces that His Majesty has entrusted me with. Get to your posts and order the return. The tide will ebb within the hour. To your posts, gentlemen!" Seeing everyone obeying him except for that surveillant officer, d'Artagnan added: "I assume that you have no order to object to this action?"

And d'Artagnan was almost triumphant in uttering those words. His plan would save his friends. With the lifting of the blockade, they could embark instantly and sail to Spain or England without fear of trouble. While they fled, d'Artagnan would appear before the king and justify his return with his indignation at the distrust provoked by Colbert. The king would then send d'Artagnan back to Belle-Île with full honors, and old d'Artagnan would capture it—that is, capture the cage but not the departed birds.

However, the officer opposed this plan with a second royal order:

> The instant Monsieur d'Artagnan manifests the desire to tender his resignation, he will no longer be the leader of the expedition, and any officer placed under his orders will not be allowed to obey him any further. Moreover, Monsieur d'Artagnan, having forfeited his position as head of the army sent against Belle-Île, will leave immediately for France, accompanied by the officer who will have given him this message and who will regard him as a prisoner, for whom he will be answerable.

D'Artagnan, normally so brave and carefree, now blanched. Everything had been calculated with a depth that, for the first time in thirty years, reminded him of the solid foresight and inflexible logic of Cardinal Richelieu. D'Artagnan propped his head on his hand, musing, barely breathing. If I put this order in my pocket, he thought to himself, who would know and who would stop me? By the time the king finds out, I'll have saved those poor people on Belle-Île. Let's be daring! My head's not the kind that an executioner chops off for disobedience. So let's disobey! But at that very instant, he saw the officers around him reading similar orders distributed by that infernal agent of Colbert's thought. Disobedience was anticipated as much as any other action.

"Monsieur," said the officer, "I am waiting to leave at your convenience."

"I am ready, monsieur," replied d'Artagnan, gritting his teeth.

The officer promptly ordered a dinghy for d'Artagnan, who turned almost insane with fury. "How," he stammered, "will the different corps be directed?"

"Once you've gone, monsieur," replied the commander of the ships, "the king has entrusted me with his fleet."

"If that's the case, monsieur," Colbert's man addressed the new leader, "then this last order is meant for you. Let us see what your powers are."

"Here they are," the officer answered, displaying a royal signature.

"Here are your instructions," replied the other officer, handing him the document. Then he faced d'Artagnan. "Well, monsieur," he said, deeply moved by the despair of that man of iron, "do me a favor—let's leave."

"Right away," d'Artagnan murmured feebly, vanquished, shattered by the implacable possibility. And he let himself slide down into the small vessel, which headed toward France, aided by the favorable wind and the rising tide. The king's guards had embarked with the musketeer captain. But he hoped to arrive in Nantes very quickly and to move the king to mercy by eloquently pleading his friends' cause.

The boat flew like a swallow. D'Artagnan distinctly saw the French mainland jutting out black against the white clouds of the night. "Ah, monsieur!" he murmured to the officer, with whom he hadn't spoken for the last hour. "I'd give anything to know the instructions of the new commander. They're all peaceful, aren't they? . . ."

He couldn't finish. A distant cannonball boomed across the waves, then another, then two or three louder ones. D'Artagnan shivered.

"They're firing at Belle-Île," replied the officer.

The dinghy reached French soil.

45
Porthos's Forebears

When d'Artagnan left them, Aramis and Porthos returned to the main fort in order to converse privately. Porthos, still brooding, annoyed Aramis, whose mind had never been freer.

"Dear Porthos," Aramis suddenly said, "I'm going to explain d'Artagnan's plan to you."

"What plan, Aramis?"

"A plan we'll owe our freedom to within twelve hours."

"Really?" Porthos was astonished. "Let's see."

"You noticed—didn't you?—that through the scene our friend had with that officer, he was annoyed by certain orders regarding us?"

"I noticed."

"Well, d'Artagnan is going to give the king his resignation, and during the confusion caused by his absence, we'll sail out to sea—or, rather, you'll sail out. Only one man can escape."

Shaking his head, Porthos replied, "We'll escape together, Aramis, or we'll stay here together!"

"You have a big heart," said Aramis. "But I'm distressed by your gloomy anxiety."

"I'm not anxious," said Porthos.

"Then you must be angry with me?"

"I'm not angry."

"Well, old friend, why that somber face?"

"I'll tell you: I'm drawing up my will." Our good Porthos gazed sadly at Aramis.

"Your will?!" cried the bishop. "Come on! Do you think you're doomed?"

"I feel tired. It's the first time, and there's a tradition in our family."

"Namely?"

"My grandfather was twice as strong as me."

"Aha!" said Aramis. "Then he must have been Samson?"

"No, his name was Antoine. Well, he was the same age as I am now when he rode out to hunt one day and his legs grew feeble—something he had never experienced."

"What did his fatigue signify, old friend?"

"Nothing good, as you're about to hear. After starting off again, and still complaining about the weakness in his legs, he ran into a wild boar. The animal confronted him; he aimed his harquebus at the boar and missed it. The beast gored him. My grandfather died instantly."

"That's no reason for you to be alarmed, dear Porthos."

"Oh, just listen! My father also had twice my strength. He was a tough soldier, and he served both Henry III and Henry IV. His name wasn't Antoine, it was Gaspard, like Monsieur de Coligny. He was always on horseback, and he didn't know the meaning of fatigue. One evening, when he was getting up from dinner, his legs failed him."

"Maybe he'd overeaten," said Aramis, "and that's why he reeled."

"Bah! A friend of Monsieur de Bassompierre, come on! No, I tell you. He was surprised by his weakness, and when my mother scoffed at him, he said, 'Doesn't it look as if I'm facing a wild boar, like my late father, Monsieur Duvallon?' "

"Well?" said Aramis.

"Well, my father tried to ignore his buckling legs and go down to the garden rather than going to bed. His foot slipped on the very first step. The stairs were steep. My father fell on a stone angle containing an iron hinge. The hinge tore open his temple. He died on the spot."

Aramis peered at his friend. "Those were two extraordinary circumstances. Don't automatically assume there'll be a third one. It doesn't suit a man of your strength to be superstitious, my good Porthos. Besides, when have your legs ever buckled? You've never been this sturdy and this proud. You could carry a house on your shoulders."

"At this point," said Porthos, "I feel great. But just a moment ago I staggered and collapsed. And since then, this circumstance, as you put it, occurred four times. I'm not saying I'm scared, but it would bother me. Life is wonderful. I've got money, I've got beautiful estates, I've got horses I love. I've also got friends I love: d'Artagnan, Athos, Raoul, and you." Our admirable Porthos didn't even take the trouble to conceal Aramis's rank in that hierarchy.

Aramis shook his hand. "We've still got a lot of years left to preserve examples of unusual men for the world. Trust me, dear friend, we've had no response from d'Artagnan—that's a good sign. He must have given orders to mass the ships and clear out. A short while ago, I myself ordered the men to roll a boat to the mouth of the huge cavern of Locmaria—you know, where we've waited so often to catch foxes."

"Yes. The cavern opens into the small cove that we discovered the time that magnificent fox escaped that way."

"Precisely. In an emergency, a boat will be hidden for us in that cavern. It must be there by now. We'll wait for the right moment and set sail at night!"

"That's a great idea. What'll we gain?"

"We'll gain time. Aside from us and two or three hunters on the island, nobody knows this grotto, or, rather, nobody knows its outlet. If the island is occupied, the scouts won't see any boat on the shore, they won't suspect the possibility of escape. And so they'll stop their surveillance."

"I get it."

"Fine. And how are your legs?"

"Oh, they're excellent for now."

"So you see, everything is helping us to relax and hope. D'Artagnan is clearing the sea and liberating us. We no longer have to worry about the royal fleet or an occupation. By God, Porthos! We've still got fifty years of fabulous adventures ahead of us. And if I reach Spanish soil," the bishop added with dreadful intensity, "I swear that your ducal title won't be a mere figment!"

"Let's hope it won't," said Porthos, a bit cheered up by his friend's sudden warmth.

All at once, they heard a shout: "To arms! To arms!" This shout, repeated by a hundred voices, surprised one of the two friends and unnerved the other. Aramis opened the window. He saw a mob of people carrying torches. The women were trying to find safety, the armed men were taking up their posts.

"The fleet! The fleet!" cried a soldier who recognized Aramis.

"The fleet!" Aramis repeated.

"Halfway within cannon range!"

"To arms!" cried Aramis.

"To arms!" Porthos repeated formidably.

And the two friends dashed toward the pier, seeking shelter behind the batteries.

Boats filled with soldiers were approaching the island. They took three different directions so the men could go ashore in three different places.

"What should we do?" a guard officer asked.

"Capture them!" said Aramis. "And if they pursue you, shoot them!"

Five minutes later, the cannonade started. That was the booming that d'Artagnan had heard when reaching the mainland. However, the boats were too close to the pier for the cannon to aim with precision. The men landed, the hand-to-hand combat began.

"What's wrong, Porthos?" asked Aramis.

"Nothing . . . My legs . . . It's incomprehensible! . . . They'll recover when we charge!"

And Porthos and Aramis charged so vigorously, they roused their men so thoroughly that the invaders dashed back to their vessels with nothing but their wounded.

"Hurry, Porthos!" cried Aramis. "We need a prisoner! Hurry! Hurry!"

Porthos leaned over the stairs of the pier and grabbed one of the officers by the back of his neck. He'd been waiting for all the men to fill up the boat. Porthos's gigantic hand caught the prey, which served him as a shield, so that not a single shot was fired at him. "Here's a prisoner," Porthos said to Aramis.

"Great!" shouted Aramis, laughing. "You've slandered your legs!"

"I caught him with my arm, not my legs!" Porthos answered ruefully.

46
Biscarrat's Son

The Bretons of the island were quite proud of that victory; Aramis did not encourage them. When everyone had gone home, Aramis told Porthos: "The king will be furious when he hears about the resistance. These brave men will be decimated or burned alive when the island is taken, which is bound to happen."

"So the result," said Porthos, "is that we've done nothing useful."

"For the moment it may be a bit useful. We've got a prisoner, and he can tell us what our enemies are up to."

"Right! Let's interrogate him," said Porthos. "It'll be easy getting him to talk. We'll invite him to supper. Once he drinks, he'll talk!"

And so it went. The officer, a bit nervous at first, was reassured by the sight of the men he was dealing with. Having no fear of compromising himself, he supplied every last detail concerning d'Artagnan's resignation and departure. After d'Artagnan had left, according to the officer, the new leader of the expedition had ordered a surprise attack on Belle-Île. That was where the prisoner stopped. Aramis and Porthos exchanged a glance that testified to their despair. They could no longer bank on d'Artagnan's brave imagination, and so they had no resources in case of defeat.

Aramis, continuing his interrogation, asked the prisoner what the invaders had in store for the leaders of Belle-Île. "They are to be killed during the fighting or hanged afterward."

Aramis and Porthos exchanged another glance. Their faces were crimson. "I'm too light for the gibbet," Aramis responded. "Men like me don't get hung."

"And I'm too heavy," said Porthos. "For men like me, the rope always snaps."

"I'm certain," said the prisoner gallantly, "that they'll do you the favor of letting you choose the manner of your death."

"Thanks loads," said Aramis grimly.

Porthos bowed. "Another glass of wine to your health," he said, drinking.

The supper drifted from subject to subject. The officer, a nobleman with a lively mind, gradually yielded to Aramis's wit and Porthos's warmth.

"Forgive me for asking you a question," said the officer, "but a man who's up to his sixth bottle has the right to forget himself a little."

"Ask away," said Porthos, "ask away."

"Go ahead," said Aramis.

"Gentlemen," said the officer, "weren't the two of you musketeers of the late king?"

"Yes, monsieur," replied Porthos, "and two of the best, if you please."

"That's true. And I'd even say the two best of all soldiers if I weren't afraid to offend my father's memory."

"Your father?!" exclaimed Aramis.

"Don't you know my name?"

"Damn it, no, monsieur. But you'll tell me, and—"

"I am Georges de Biscarrat."

"Oh!" cried Porthos in his turn. "Biscarrat! Have you ever heard that name, Aramis?"

"Biscarrat . . . ," the bishop reflected. "I think so."

"Rack your memory, monsieur," said the officer.

"By God!" said Porthos. "It won't take long. Biscarrat, called 'Cardinal' . . . One of the four men who interrupted us the day we became friends with d'Artagnan, our swords in our hands. . . ."

"Precisely, gentlemen."

"The only man," said Aramis enthusiastically, "whom we didn't wound!"

"He must have been quite a swordsman!" said the prisoner.

"That's true. Oh, very true," the two friends said in unison. "By God, Monsieur de Biscarrat, we're delighted to make the acquaintance of such a fine man."

Biscarrat shook hands with the two former musketeers. Aramis glanced at Porthos as if to say: This is a man who'll help us. And on the spot. The bishop then said aloud: "Admit it, monsieur, it's good to have been a man of honor."

"My father always said so, monsieur."

"Also admit that these are dismal circumstances—meeting doomed men and realizing that they are old acquaintances, old hereditary acquaintances."

"Oh, you won't be suffering that awful fate, my friends!" the young man exclaimed.

"Bah! You said so yourself!"

"I said so a little while ago when I didn't know you. But now that I do know you, I tell you: you can avoid that horrible fate if you like."

"What do you mean if we like?" cried Aramis, his intelligent eyes darting between his prisoner and Porthos.

"So long as we're not required to be cowards," said Porthos, gazing with noble fearlessness at the prisoner and the bishop.

"Nothing whatsoever will be required of you, gentlemen," said the officer of the royal army. "What do you want us to ask of you? If they find you, they'll kill you—that's certain. So try to keep them from finding you, gentlemen."

"I don't believe I'm mistaken," said Porthos with dignity, "but it seems to me that if they want to find us, they have to come looking for us here."

"You're perfectly right, my worthy friend," said Aramis, his eyes still studying the face of the tense and silent prisoner. "Monsieur de Biscarrat, you'd like to tell us something, make overtures to us, but you don't dare—isn't that so?"

"Ah, my friends! If I speak, I'll be flouting my orders. Hey, listen! I hear a voice that's much louder than mine!"

"The cannon!" cried Porthos.

"The cannon and the muskets!" cried the bishop.

They heard the noise coming from the distant rocks, the sinister hubbub of a brief struggle.

"What's that?" asked Porthos.

"Damn it!" shouted Aramis. "It's what I suspected!"

"What?"

"Your attack was nothing but a feint! Isn't that so, monsieur? And while your companies let themselves be driven back, the others easily landed on the opposite side of the island."

"Oh, on various parts, monsieur."

"Then we're doomed," the bishop said peacefully.

"Doomed," Porthos echoed. "That's possible. But they haven't caught us or hanged us yet." Uttering those words, he rose from the table, strode over to the wall, and coolly took down his sword and his pistols. He examined them as carefully as an old soldier who is preparing for combat and who feels that his life depends largely on the excellence and good condition of his weapons.

At the booming of the cannon, with the news of the surprise attack that could deliver the island into the hands of the royal troops, a terrified throng dashed to the fort, imploring the leaders for help and advice.

Flanked by two torches, Aramis, pale and vanquished, appeared at the window facing the large courtyard, which was filled with soldiers waiting for orders and bewildered civilians begging for assistance.

"My friends," said d'Herblay in a grave and sonorous voice, "Monsieur Fouquet, your protector, your friend, your father, has been arrested by orders of the king and thrown into the Bastille."

A long cry of fury and menace swept up to the bishop and enveloped him in an aura of resonance.

"Vengeance for Monsieur Fouquet!" shouted the most exalted voices. "Death to the royal troops!"

"No, my friends!" Aramis solemnly replied. "No, my friends! No resistance! The king is the master of his domain! The king is God's agent. Louis and God have struck Monsieur Fouquet. Humble yourselves before the hand of God. But do not avenge your lord, Monsieur Fouquet; do not try to avenge him. You'll be sacrificing yourselves for nothing—and your wives and your children, and your property and your freedom. Put down your weapons, my friends! Put down your weapons, because those are the king's orders, and go peacefully to your homes. I, Aramis, am asking you to do so, begging you to do so—if need be, commanding you to do so in the name of Monsieur Fouquet."

A huge tremor of rage and dread smashed through the crowd.

Aramis went on. "The king's soldiers have set foot on the island. It won't be a fight between you and them, it'll be a massacre. Go home, go home and forget about it. This time I order you in the name of God."

The mutineers slowly dispersed, wordless, submissive.

"Ah, my friend!" said Porthos. "What were you just saying?"

"Monsieur," Biscarrat said to the bishop, "you're saving all these inhabitants, but you won't save yourself or your friend."

"Monsieur de Biscarrat," the bishop said with a strange tone of nobility and courtesy. "Monsieur de Biscarrat, please be so good as to take your freedom."

"I'd like to, monsieur, but—"

"You'd be doing us a favor. By informing the king's lieutenant about the surrender of the islanders, you might obtain some mercy for us if you explain how this surrender occurred."

"Mercy!" replied Porthos, his eyes blazing. "Mercy! What are you saying?"

Aramis smacked Porthos's elbow as he had done in the halcyon days of their youth when he had wanted to warn Porthos that he had committed a blunder, or was about to commit one. Porthos caught his drift and held his tongue.

"I'll go, gentlemen," Biscarrat responded, a bit surprised by the word "mercy" used by the proud musketeer. And yet several moments ago, the prisoner had so exuberantly praised Aramis's heroic exploits, which Biscarrat had heard about from his father.

"Please leave, Monsieur de Biscarrat," said Aramis with a bow, "and please accept our full gratitude."

"But you, gentlemen, you whom I am honored to call my friends since you wished me to receive this title—what's to become of you in the meantime?" The officer was deeply moved as he said good-bye to those two former adversaries of his father.

"We're going to wait here."

"But, my God! . . . The order is categorical!"

"I'm the Bishop of Vannes, Monsieur de Biscarrat, and they don't kill a bishop any more than they hang an aristocrat."

"Ah, yes, monsieur! Yes, monseigneur!" said Biscarrat. "Yes, that's true, you're right. You still have that chance. Well, then,

I'll leave. I'll join the expedition commander, the king's lieutenant. Farewell, gentlemen! Or, rather, see you soon!"

And, indeed, the worthy officer, jumping on the horse that Aramis had given him, galloped off toward the gunfire that they had heard and that had interrupted their conversation with the prisoner because the shooting had drawn the crowd to the fort.

Aramis, watching his departure, remained alone with Porthos. "Well," said the bishop, "do you understand?"

"No, by God!"

"Weren't you bothered by Biscarrat here?"

"No, he's a fine fellow."

"Yes, but the Grotto of Locmaria—does the whole world have to know about it?"

"Ah, that's true, that's true! I get it. We'll escape underground."

"Please," Aramis joyfully replied. "En route, my friend, our boat is waiting for us. And the king hasn't caught us yet."

47
The Grotto of Locmaria

The Grotto of Locmaria was so far from the pier that the two friends had to husband their strength to reach it. Furthermore, the night was setting in. Midnight had already struck at the fort. Porthos and Aramis were loaded down with money and weapons. As they cut across the heath separating the pier from the grotto, they listened to every single sound and tried to avoid any ambush. From time to time, while carefully staying to the right of their road, they passed refugees who were fleeing from the interior after hearing that the royal troops had landed.

Aramis and Porthos, hidden behind some crag, managed to catch a word or two uttered by trembling refugees, who were lugging their most precious belongings. Listening to their groans, the two friends tried to glean something that could be useful for them. Finally, after a swift advance with many prudent halts, they reached the deep grottoes; this was where the farsighted bishop had rolled in a sturdy boat that was seaworthy during this lovely season.

"My good friend," said Porthos after breathing noisily, "I think we've arrived. But I believe you told me about three men, three servants, who were supposed to accompany us. I don't see them—where are they?"

"Why would you see them, my dear Porthos?" said Aramis. "They must be waiting for us in the cavern. I'm sure they're resting for a moment after completing this harsh and difficult task."

Aramis stopped Porthos, who was about to enter the grotto. "Would you let me go in first, my good friend? I know the signal I gave our men, and, if they don't hear it, they'll shoot you down or hurl their knives at you in the darkness."

"Go ahead, dear Aramis, go in first. You're the wisest and most prudent of men. Ah! I feel that fatigue I told you about—it's gotten hold of me again."

While Porthos sat down at the entrance to the cavern, Aramis lowered his head and, mimicking the hooting of an owl, he strode into the interior. A plaintive response, barely audible, came from the depths of the cavern. The bishop kept moving, and soon the hooting came from only ten paces away.

"Is that you, Yves?" asked Aramis.

"Yes, monseigneur, and Goennec is here too. His son is accompanying us."

"Fine! Is everything ready?"

"Yes, monseigneur."

"Go to the entrance, my good Yves, and you'll find Monsieur de Pierrefonds relaxing after our exhausting march. If by chance he can't walk, lift him up and carry him to me."

The three Bretons obeyed. But Aramis's order concerning Porthos was unnecessary. The refreshed giant had started off on his own, and his heavy plodding resounded amidst the cavities shaped and supported by the columns of silex and granite. When Monsieur de Bracieux joined the bishop, the Bretons lit a lantern, and Porthos assured his friend that he felt as strong as ever.

"Let's check the dinghy," said Aramis, "and first make sure it's got the stuff we need."

"Don't bring the light too close," said Yves, the skipper. "Because, as you told me, monseigneur, I put the explosives in the chest under the poop bench—you know, the powder kegs and the musket charges you sent me from the fort."

"Fine," said Aramis. And taking the lantern, he scrutinized every nook and cranny. He was as cautious as a man who is neither timid nor ignorant in the face of danger. The dinghy was long, light, drawing little water, and with a thin keel and slightly high sides—the kind of dinghy that has always been so well constructed in Belle-Île. It is solid on water, very easy to handle, and furnished with planks that, in unsettled weather, form a sort of bridge which can protect the rowers from the waves that slide over it.

In two tightly shut chests under the benches fore and aft, Aramis found bread, biscuits, dried fruit, a flitch of bacon, and countless bottles of water. These rations were sufficient for men who never had to leave the coast and who could therefore replenish their supplies when necessary. The weapons, eight muskets and eight horse pistols, were loaded and in good condition. There were extra oars in case of an emergency, plus a storm jib, which is useful in a breeze, because it helps the rowers to keep a dinghy moving without loading it down. All in all, Aramis was satisfied with the results of his inspection.

"Dear Porthos, let's try to figure out our route. Should we leave through the unknown extremity of the grotto by following the slope and the darkness? Or should we go out into the open air and slide the dinghy over the rollers, through the bushes? We can level the road along the small cliff—it's only twenty feet high, and, when the tide's in, the water at the foot of the cliff runs three or four fathoms deep over a solid bottom."

"Begging your pardon, monseigneur," said Yves respectfully. "But if we take the underground passage along the slope, we'll have a lot more trouble maneuvering through the darkness. I believe that the open-air route is more feasible. I know that cliff, and I can assure you that it's as smooth as a lawn, while the floor of the grotto is bumpy. Besides, monseigneur, when we get to the far end and we find the trench leading to the sea, the dinghy may not be able to squeeze through."

"I've made my calculations, and I'm certain the boat will pass."

"Fine, I'm all for it, monseigneur," the skipper persisted. "But Your Grace knows that if the dinghy reaches the end of the trench, we'll have to heave up an enormous rock, which a fox can always manage to slip under. The rock closes the trench like a door."

"We'll heave it up," said Porthos. "It's nothing."

"Oh, I know that Monseigneur has the strength of ten men, but it's quite a burden!"

"I think the skipper may be right," said Aramis. "Let's try the open air."

"All the more so, monseigneur, because we can't embark before daylight, there's too much work to be done. At the crack of dawn, we'll need to place a good vedette on the upper part of the grotto. It's indispensable for watching the maneuvers of the lighters or the cruisers that are looking to catch us."

"Yes, Yves. Your reasoning is sound. We'll go by way of the cliff."

The three robust Bretons were about to start putting the rollers in place when the distant baying of dogs swept through the countryside. Aramis dashed out of the grotto; Porthos followed him. The waves and the plain were tinged purple and white by the dawn. In the dim light, the two friends saw the stubby, mournful pines twisting above the stones, and the black wings of long flocks of crows grazed the meager fields of buckwheat. Another quarter hour and the day would be bright. The awakened birds, singing joyfully, announced the new day to all nature. The baying, which had stopped the three fishermen in their tracks and caused Aramis and Porthos to dash outdoors, resounded through a deep gorge about one league from the grotto.

"It's a pack of hounds," said Porthos. "They've whiffed a scent."

What is it? Aramis thought to himself. Who'd go hunting at such a time?

And especially around here, where people are scared of the arrival of the royals.

The barking's getting closer. Yes, you're right, Porthos, the dogs are hot on a trail.

"Damn it!" Aramis suddenly cried. "Yves, Yves, get over here!"

Yves dashed up, abandoning the cylinder he was clutching. He'd been about to slide it under the boat when he heard the bishop shout.

"What's this hunt all about?" asked Porthos.

"Monseigneur, I don't understand it at all! Monsieur de Locmaria wouldn't go hunting at a time like this! And yet the hounds . . ."

"Unless they've escaped the kennel!"

"No," said Goennec, "those aren't Monsieur de Locmaria's dogs."

"For prudence's sake," said Porthos, "let's get back into the grotto. The noise is obviously getting closer, and we'll soon find out what's going on."

They reentered the cavern, but no sooner had they walked one hundred paces in the dark than a noise like the hoarse sigh of a terrified creature echoed through the grotto. A frightened, panting fox raced past the fugitives, jumped over the dinghy, and vanished. It left behind an acrid smell, which hovered for several moments under the low vaults.

"The fox!" shouted the Bretons with the joyful surprise of hunters.

"We're caught, damn it!" cried the bishop. "They've discovered our lair!"

"What do you mean?" said Porthos. "Are we afraid of a fox?"

"What are you saying, my friend, and why are you worried about a fox? The fox isn't the issue, by God! Don't you know, Porthos, that dogs come behind a fox, and men behind the dogs?"

Porthos lowered his head. As if to confirm Aramis's words, they heard the tumultuous pack arriving with dreadful speed on the animal's trail. Six hounds reached the small heath at the same moment, and their barking sounded like the fanfare of a victory.

"Those are hounds, all right," said Aramis, hiding behind a crevice between two rocks. "Now, then, who are the hunters?"

"If it's Monsieur de Locmaria," replied Yves, "he'll let the dogs scour the grotto—he knows them, and he personally won't enter it. He's certain the fox will emerge at the other end. That's where he'll go to wait for the animal."

"It's not Monsieur de Locmaria who's hunting," said Aramis, blanching despite himself.

"Then who's hunting?" asked Porthos.

"Take a look!"

Porthos pressed his eye against the chink and saw them on the peak of a hillock: a dozen riders yelling "Talleyho" and urging their horses to follow the dogs.

"The guards!" said Porthos.

"Yes, my friend. The king's guards!"

"The king's guards, monseigneur?" cried the Bretons, likewise turning pale.

"With Biscarrat at their head, mounted on my gray horse," said Aramis.

That same moment, the hounds plunged into the grotto like an avalanche, and the depths of the cavern rang with their deafening roars.

"Damn it all!" said Aramis, regaining his sangfroid at the sight of this certain and inevitable danger. "I know we're practically doomed, but we do have a very slim chance. If the guards who are going to follow their hounds find that there's a way out of the grotto, then it's hopeless. Because if they enter here, they'll discover us and the boat. We mustn't let the dogs leave. We mustn't let the masters enter."

"You're right," said Porthos.

"You understand," Aramis added with the swift precision of an order, "there are six hounds that'll be forced to stop at the huge rock. The fox can squeeze through the aperture but not the hounds—and the hounds will be stopped and killed."

The Bretons rushed out, clutching their knives. Several minutes later, there was a horrible concert of mortal whimpering and howling, then silence.

"Fine!" said Aramis coldly. "And now for the masters!"

"What should we do?" asked Porthos.

"Wait for them to arrive. Then hide out and kill them."

"Kill them!" Porthos repeated.

"There are sixteen of them," said Aramis. "At least for now."

"And they're well armed," added Porthos with a smile of consolation.

"It will take ten minutes," said Aramis. "Let's go!" And he resolutely grabbed a musket and inserted his hunting knife between his teeth. "Yves, Goennec, and his son will pass us the muskets. You, Porthos, will shoot point-blank. We'll have killed eight of them before the others suspect a thing—count on it! Then all five of us will dispatch the last eight with our knives."

"What about poor Biscarrat?" said Porthos.

Aramis reflected for a moment. Then: "Biscarrat will be the first to go," he answered coldly. "He knows us."

48
The Grotto

Despite the reasonable intuition that constituted the remarkable side of Aramis's character, the event, subject to the happenstance of uncertainty, did not occur precisely as foreseen by the Bishop of Vannes. Biscarrat, better mounted than his cohorts, was the first to reach the grotto; he realized that everything—fox and hounds—was engulfed in the interior. Stricken with the superstitious terror aroused by any dark underground trail, Biscarrat halted at the entrance and waited for the others to gather round him.

"Well?" said the breathless young men, confused by his inaction.

"Well, we don't hear the hounds. Both the pack and the fox must be swallowed up in the cavern."

"The hounds were too sure of themselves," said one of the guards, "to have lost the scent. Besides, we'd hear them from one side or the other. Biscarrat is right, they must be in this grotto."

"Then why," said one of the young men, "aren't they barking?"

"It's odd," said another.

"Well, then, let's go inside," said a fourth guard. "Is there any law against it?"

"No," replied Biscarrat. "But the interior is pitch-black, a man can break his neck."

"The hounds can testify to that!" cried a guard. "They seem to have broken their necks all right!"

"What the hell's become of them?" the young men asked in unison. And each master called his hound by name, whistled, or sounded its favorite fanfare. But not a single hound responded to a call, whistle, or fanfare.

"Maybe it's an enchanted grotto," said Biscarrat. "Let's go see." And dismounting, he stepped inside.

"Wait, wait, I'll go with you," said one of the guards at the sight of Biscarrat about to melt into the penumbra.

"No!" Biscarrat retorted. "Something extraordinary is afoot. Let's not risk all our lives. If I don't show up within ten minutes, then go inside—all of you together."

"Done!" said the young men, who didn't feel that Biscarrat was in any great danger. "We'll wait!" And without dismounting their horses, they formed a circle around the entrance. Biscarrat walked in alone and advanced all the way to Porthos's musket. Biscarrat was astonished by this resistance; he reached out and grabbed the icy barrel. That same instant, Yves raised a knife and was about to plunge it into the young man with all the strength of a Breton arm when Porthos's iron wrist stopped him. Then, like a dull rebuke, Porthos's voice could be heard in the darkness: "I don't want him dead!"

Biscarrat was trapped between a protection and a threat, each almost as terrible as the other. Brave as he was, he uttered a cry, which Aramis promptly muffled with a handkerchief over the young man's mouth. "Monsieur de Biscarrat," Aramis whispered, "we mean no harm, and you must realize that if you've recognized us. But if you so much as sigh, or even breathe, we'll be forced to kill you just as we killed your dogs."

"Yes, I do recognize you, gentlemen," the young man murmured. "But why are you here? What are you doing here? Damn you! Damn you! I thought you were in the fort!"

"And what about you, monsieur? I believe that you were supposed to obtain conditions for us?"

"I did what I could, gentlemen, but . . ."

"But . . . ?"

"There are strict orders."

"To kill us?"

Biscarrat didn't respond. It was too painful for him to discuss the noose with noblemen. Aramis understood his silence. "Monsieur de Biscarrat, you'd be dead by now if we didn't respect your youth and our old link with your father. But you can still escape this cavern if you swear that you won't tell your companions what you've seen."

"Not only do I swear that I won't breathe a word, but I swear that I'll do anything I can to prevent my companions from setting foot in this grotto."

"Biscarrat! Biscarrat!" The shouts came from several men who were engulfed in the cavern as if in a whirlwind.

"Answer them!" said Aramis.

"Here I am!" cried Biscarrat.

"Go ahead. We'll rely on your word." And Aramis released him. The young man walked toward the light.

"Biscarrat! Biscarrat!" The voices were nearer. And the shadows of several human shapes emerged in the grotto. Biscarrat dashed toward his friends to stop them from venturing into the depths.

Aramis and Porthos listened carefully, as if their lives depended on a puff of air. Biscarrat, followed by his friends, had reached the entrance of the grotto. "Damn it!" exclaimed a guard, reaching the daylight. "You're so pale!"

"Pale?" shouted someone else. "You mean livid!"

"Me?" said Biscarrat, trying to pull himself together.

"In the name of God," all the voices cried, "what happened to you?"

"My poor friend," a guard laughed, "you haven't got a drop of blood in your veins."

"Gentlemen," said another guard, "it's serious. He's about to faint—have you got smelling salts?" And they burst out laughing.

Biscarrat was caught in the cross fire of all this probing, all this mocking. He regained his strength under the deluge of interrogation. "What do you expect me to have seen?" he asked. "I was very hot when I entered the grotto, and I was overwhelmed by the cold. That's all."

"What about the hounds? Did you see them? Did you hear anything? Do you have any news about them?"

"They must have taken a different road," said Biscarrat.

"Gentlemen," said one of the guards, "all this pallor and all this silence conceal a mystery that Biscarrat doesn't wish to reveal or maybe can't reveal. But you can bet your lives that Biscarrat saw something in the grotto. Well, I'm very curious to see what it is, even if it's the devil himself! To the grotto, gentlemen, to the grotto!"

"To the grotto!" all voices repeated.

And the underground echo menaced Porthos and Aramis with those words: "To the grotto!"

Biscarrat threw himself in front of his companions. "Gentlemen! Gentlemen! For God's sake, don't go in!"

"What's so terrible inside?" several voices asked.

"Come on! Talk, Biscarrat!"

"He really must have seen the devil!" said a man who had already expressed that hypothesis.

"Well, if he did see the devil," cried another man, "he shouldn't be so selfish! He should let us see him too!"

"Gentlemen, gentlemen, please!" Biscarrat persisted.

"Come on, let us pass!"

"Gentlemen, I beg you! Don't go in!"

"Well, but you went in!"

One of the officers, a bit older and more mature than the others, had stayed in the background, holding his tongue. But now he came to the front. "Gentlemen," he said, his tranquillity contrasting with the excitement of the younger men, "there's someone or something in there that's not the devil. Whoever or whatever it is, it was strong enough to silence our dogs. We have to find who or what it was."

Biscarrat made a final effort to stop his friends, but it was no use. He vainly threw himself in front of the boldest men; he vainly clung to the rocks, trying to block the way. The mob of young men burst into the cavern, following the older officer; he'd been the last to speak, and, sword in hand, he was the first to confront the unknown danger.

Biscarrat, shoved aside by his friends, was unable to accompany them since Porthos and Aramis would regard him as a liar and a traitor. Listening hard and wringing his hands, he leaned against the rough side of a rock, which he figured would be exposed to the musketeers' gunfire.

As for the guards, more and more of them charged into the cavern, their shouts growing fainter and fainter in the distance. All at once, the thunder of musketry boomed under the vaults. Two or three bullets smashed against the rock on which Biscarrat was leaning. At the same time, he heard moans, howls, and curses as the guards reappeared; some were pale, some bloody, and all of them were enveloped in a cloud of smoke that the outside air seemed to breathe from the depths of the cavern.

"Biscarrat! Biscarrat!" cried the fleeing men. "You knew there was an ambush in the grotto and you didn't tell us!"

"Biscarrat! Biscarrat! You've caused the deaths of four of our men! Damn you, Biscarrat!"

"It's your fault that I'm mortally wounded," said one of the young men. He scooped up some blood and threw it into Biscarrat's face. "May my blood be on your head!" And he rolled agonizingly at Biscarrat's feet.

"At least tell us who's in there!" several voices yelled furiously.

Biscarrat held his tongue.

"Tell us or die!" shouted the wounded man as he rose, leaning on one knee and aiming a useless sword at Biscarrat.

The latter dashed toward him, offering his chest, but the wounded man collapsed, never to get up again, and heaved a sigh, his last.

Biscarrat, his hair bristling, his eyes haggard, his head reeling, hurried into the cavern. "You're right! Let me die. I've let my own companions be killed. I'm a coward!" And flinging away his sword because he wanted to die without defending himself, he lowered his head as he dashed into the cavern. The other men did likewise. The eleven survivors of the original group of sixteen joined him as they plunged into the darkness.

However, they got no farther than the earlier guards. A second burst of musket fire left five on the icy sand. And since they couldn't see where the volley was coming from, the surviving guards pulled back with a terror that is easier to imagine than to express. However, rather than fleeing like the others, Biscarrat remained on a rock, safe and sane, and waited.

Only six men were left. "Honestly," said one of them, "is it the devil?"

"Damn it, it's much worse!"

"Ask Biscarrat! He knows!"

"Where is he?"

The young men peered around and realized that Biscarrat wasn't responding. "He's dead!" said two or three of them.

"Not at all," replied another. "I saw him in the middle of the smoke, he was sitting on a rock nonchalantly. He's in the cavern, he's waiting for us."

"He must know whoever's inside there."

"And how would he know them?"

"He was captured by the rebels."

"That's right. Well! Let's call him so he can tell us whom we're dealing with." And all voices shouted: "Biscarrat! Biscarrat!" But Biscarrat didn't answer.

"Fine!" said the officer who had shown so much sangfroid. "We don't need him! Look, we've got reinforcements!" And, indeed a guard company, some seventy-five or eighty men left behind by their officers, who'd been carried away by the hunting fever, arrived in fine fettle. They were guided by the captain and the first lieutenant. The five officers dashed over to their men and, with an eloquence that is easy to imagine, they explained what was happening and asked for help.

The captain interrupted them. "Where are your companions?"

"Dead!"

"But there were sixteen of you!"

"Ten are dead. Biscarrat is in the cavern, and there are five of us here."

"So Biscarrat is a prisoner?"

"Probably!"

"No! There he is! Look!"

And indeed, Biscarrat appeared at the entrance to the grotto.

"He's signaling us to go over!" said the officers. "Let's go!"

"Let's go!" they all repeated. And they moved toward him.

"Monsieur," said the captain to Biscarrat, "I've been assured that you know who the men in the grotto are—the men who are mounting a desperate defense. In the name of the king, I order you to tell us what you know."

"Captain," said Biscarrat, "you don't need to order me. My tongue has been restored to me this very instant, and I am coming in the name of those men!"

"To tell me that they're surrendering?"

"To tell you that they're resolved to defend themselves to the death unless they're granted a decent compromise."

"Just how many are there?"

"Two," said Biscarrat.

"Two, and they want to impose conditions on us?"

"Two, and they've already killed ten of our men," said Biscarrat.

"What are they?! Giants?!"

"Worse than that. Captain, do you recall the story of the bastion of Saint-Gervais?"

"Yes! Four of the king's musketeers held out against an entire army!"

"Well, these men are two of those musketeers!"

"What are their names?"

"Back then, their names were Porthos and Aramis. Today they're called Monsieur d'Herblay and Monsieur du Vallon."

A murmur spread through the soldiers at the mention of Porthos and Aramis. "The musketeers!" repeated the men, "The musketeers!"

"And why are they defending the cavern?"

"They're the men who held Belle-Île for Monsieur Fouquet."

And the thought that these brave young men were about to fight against two of the oldest heroes of the army made them shiver, half in enthusiasm, half in terror. For those four names—d'Artagnan, Athos, Porthos, and Aramis—were truly venerated by any sword bearer, just as Antiquity venerated the names of Hercules, Theseus, and Castor and Pollux.

"Two men!" cried the captain. "And they've killed ten officers in two volleys?! That's impossible, Monsieur Biscarrat!"

"Well, Captain, I'm not saying that they haven't got two or three men as the musketeers had three or four servants at the bastion of Saint-Gervais. But believe me, Captain, I've seen those men! I was captured by them! I know them! The two of them alone could destroy an entire corps!"

"We'll see!" said the captain. "In a moment. Attention, gentlemen!"

No one stirred and everyone prepared to obey. Biscarrat alone made a last effort. "Monsieur," he murmured, "take my word for it. Let it go. Those two men, those two lions that you want to attack, will defend themselves to the death. They've already killed ten men. They'll kill twice that number, and they'll kill themselves rather than surrender. What will we gain by fighting them?"

"Monsieur, we will gain the realization that eighty royal guards won't take to their heels before two rebels. If I followed your advice, monsieur, I would be dishonored, and by dishonoring myself I would dishonor the army! Forward charge, men!"

And the captain was the first to enter the grotto. Upon getting inside, he halted. He wanted to give Biscarrat and his companions a chance to describe the interior of the cavern. Then, when he felt he knew the area well enough, he divided the company into three corps, who were to enter in succession and blaze away in all directions. They would most probably lose five, perhaps ten, men, but they would eventually capture the rebels, since there was no other exit; and, at any rate, two men couldn't wipe out eighty.

"Captain," said Biscarrat, "I would like permission to march at the head of the first corps."

"Permission granted!" replied the captain. "The honor is all yours. It's my gift to you."

"Thank you!" said the young man with all the firmness of his breed.

"Then take your sword!" said the captain.

"I'll go as I am, Captain. I'm not going there to kill; I'm going in order to be killed." And placing himself at the head of the first squad, with his forehead uncovered and his arms crossed, he exclaimed, "Forward march, gentlemen."

49
A Homeric Chant

We now must switch to the other camp and describe both the combatants and the battlefield there.

Aramis and Porthos had entered the Grotto of Locmaria in search of the fully armed boat and their three Breton helpers. Initially, they hoped to move the boat through the small underground exit, thereby concealing their work and their escape. But the arrival of the fox and the hounds had forced them to remain hidden.

The grotto measured several hundred feet, reaching a small slope over a creek. Formerly a temple for Celtic deities, it had witnessed any number of human sacrifices in its mysterious depths.

Visitors entered the first part of the cavern along a gentle slope with piles of rocks forming a low arcade. The interior, with its uneven ground and the dangerous bumpiness of the vault, was subdivided into several compartments. These dominated one another by means of broken, rugged steps that were affixed left and right to enormous natural pillars.

In the third compartment, the vault was so low, the corridor so narrow, that the boat would have barely squeezed through. Nevertheless, in a moment of despair, wood softens and rock submits under the breath of human willpower.

Those were Aramis's thoughts, when, after battling, he decided to flee—certainly a perilous fight, since not all the assailants were dead. Indeed, if the boat reached the sea, the fugitives would be escaping in broad daylight, exposed to the defeated guards, who, recognizing the small number of victors, would pursue them.

After killing ten men with two volleys, Aramis, familiar with the underground twists and turns, went to reconnoiter, counting the dead one by one, since he couldn't see outside. He immediately ordered his crew to roll the boat up to the huge rock that blocked the gateway to freedom. Porthos gathered all his strength and grabbed the boat with both hands while the Bretons slid it rapidly over the rollers.

They reached the third compartment, they reached the stone blockade. Porthos, putting his robust shoulder to the stone, struck it so hard that it cracked. A cloud of dust came plunging down from the vault, including the ashes of ten thousand generations of seagulls whose nests were glued to the rock like cement. He struck the stone again. Then, with the third strike, it yielded, then oscillated for a moment. Porthos, shoving his back against adjacent rock, kicked the stone away from the limestone heaps that served as its hinges and frame.

When the blockade collapsed, the fugitives saw daylight—brilliant, radiant daylight—which burst through the opening of the cavern, revealing the blue sea to the delighted Bretons. They started lifting the boat over the fallen stone. A few dozen yards more and the boat would slip into the ocean. But now the soldiers arrived, and the captain set up his men, who were ready either for a climb or an assault. Aramis helped his friends by keeping his eyes peeled. He spotted this reinforcement, counted the guards, and, with a single glance, he grasped the insurmountable peril of a new battle. Escaping by water when the cavern was about to be invaded was impossible!

Indeed, the daylight, which had just illuminated the cavern's final two compartments, would have exposed the boat and the two rebels to musket fire, and a single volley would riddle the boat if not kill its five passengers.

Furthermore, assuming all those things, if the boat escaped with its passengers, wouldn't the guards sound the alarm? Wouldn't they notify the royal lighters? Wouldn't the rebels' tiny boat, pursued on land and sea, succumb before the end of the day? Aramis, furiously raking his salt-and-pepper hair, invoked God's help, and the devil's help as well. Calling to Porthos, who was laboring harder than the rollers and his helpers, Aramis muttered, "My friend, a reinforcement has just arrived for our adversaries!"

"Ah!" said Porthos calmly. "What should we do?"

"A new fight would be very risky."

"Yes," said Porthos, "it's hard to imagine that you or I won't be killed, and, if either of us *were* killed, the others would likewise die." Porthos spoke with the heroism that grew out of his full size and strength.

Aramis virtually felt a spur dig into his heart. "Porthos, my friend, none of us will be killed if you do exactly as I say."

"Namely?"

"Those men are about to charge into the grotto."

"Right."

"We'll kill about fifteen—at most."

"How many are there altogether?" asked Porthos.

"They've gotten a reinforcement of seventy-five men."

"Seventy-five plus five makes eighty. Aha!"

"If they fire in unison, they'll riddle us to bits."

"Definitely."

"Not to mention that the detonations could provoke landslides in the cavern."

"Just now," said Porthos, "a chip of rock grazed my shoulder."

"There you are!"

"Oh, it's nothing!"

"We have to make up our minds on the spot. Our Bretons are going to keep rolling the boat toward the sea."

"That's very good!"

"We two will guard the powder here, the bullets, and the muskets."

"But dear Aramis," said Porthos naïvely, "the two of us will never fire three shots together. Using muskets is a difficult approach."

"Then find another way."

"I've found it!" the giant suddenly exclaimed. "I'm going to lie in ambush behind the pillar with that metal bar. I'll be invisible and invincible. And when they enter in waves, I'll smash their heads with the bar thirty times a minute! So what do you say to my plan?" Porthos smiled.

"It's excellent, dear friend, it's perfect. I approve wholeheartedly. Except that you'd terrify them, and half the men will wait outside and let us starve. What we need, my good friend, is the destruction of the entire corps. Even a single survivor would spell our doom."

"You're right, my friend. But how can we draw them in?"

"By not stirring. Then, once they're all inside here . . ."

"Let me try—I've got an idea."

"If your idea is good—and it must be good—my mind will be tranquil."

"You'll lie in wait, and you'll count all the men who come in here."

"But what are you going to do?"

"Don't worry about me. I've got my task."

"I think I hear voices."

"They're here. To your post. . . . Stay within earshot of me, and within reach of my hands."

Porthos retreated into the second compartment, which was pitch-black. Aramis slipped into the third compartment. Porthos was clutching a fifty-pound iron bar that had helped to move the boat. He was manipulating this lever with marvelous dexterity. Meanwhile, the Bretons were pushing the boat all the way out to the cliff. Inside the illuminated compartment, Aramis, who kept down and out of sight, was doing something mysterious.

They heard a loud command. It was the captain's last order. Twenty-five men jumped from the high rocks into the first compartment of the grotto. Upon landing, they opened fire. The echoes boomed, the bullets whistled, the space was filled with an opaque smoke. "To the left! To the left!" shouted Biscarrat. During his first assault, he had spotted the passage to the second chamber; and now, animated by the smell of powder, he wanted to lead his men in that direction. The soldiers dashed to the left, through the narrowing passage. Biscarrat, holding out his arms, dedicated to his death, marched ahead of the muskets. "Come on! Come on! I can see daylight!"

"Strike, Porthos!" cried Aramis's sepulchral voice.

Porthos sighed, but he obeyed. The iron bar smashed down into Biscarrat's head, killing him before he could finish his order! The terrible lever rose and dropped ten times in ten seconds, leaving ten corpses. The soldiers saw nothing. They heard shouts and sighs. They trampled bodies. But they were still at a loss, and they kept tripping over one another. The implacable bar, still dropping, wiped out the first squad, and not a single sound warned the quietly advancing second squad. However, the latter, commanded by the captain, had shattered a thin pine tree growing on the cliff, and the captain made a torch by twisting its resinous branches together.

Upon reaching the compartment where Porthos, like the angel of death, had struck down everyone he touched, the first rank retreated in terror. No fusillade had responded to the fusillade of the guards. And yet, their way was blocked by a heap of corpses; they were literally walking in blood. Porthos was still behind his pillar. The captain, brandishing his quivering torch, and, unable to grasp this horrible carnage, fell all the way back to Porthos's pillar. Then a gigantic hand emerged from the darkness and stuck to the captain's throat, which emitted a muffled rattle. His arms flailed the air, his torch dropped, and the fire was doused by the blood. A second later, the captain's dead body fell next to the extinguished torch, adding one more corpse to the pile that was blocking the way.

All this occurred magically, mysteriously. The captain's rattle had caused his men to turn their heads. They saw his open arms, his protruding eyes. And when the torch dropped, they were plunged into darkness.

In an instinctive, mechanical, and unreflected movement, the captain shouted: "Fire!"

A volley of musket-shot burst and boomed in the cavern, tearing huge fragments from the vaults. For an instant, the fusillade lit up the cavern, which then fell back into darkness that was thickened by the smoke. Now the cavern was filled with a vast hush disturbed only by the footsteps of the third brigade, which was pouring into the underground space.

50
The Death of a Titan

More accustomed to the darkness than all these men emerging from daylight, Porthos looked for a signal from Aramis. The giant's arm was then touched gently, and a feeble voice whispered, "Come on."

"Oh!" said Porthos.

"Shh!" whispered Aramis even more softly.

And amid the noise made by the advancing third brigade, amid the curses uttered by the guards left standing, and amid the final moans of the dying men, the two rebels imperceptibly hugged the granite walls of the cavern. Aramis led his friend to the second-to-last compartment and showed him a barrel of powder in a hollow. Aramis had attached a fuse to the barrel, which weighed seventy or eighty pounds.

"My friend," said Aramis, "I'm going to light the fuse, and you're going to hurl the barrel into the throng of our enemies. Can you do that?"

"Damn it!" replied Porthos, lifting the small keg with one hand. "Light the fuse!"

"Wait," said Aramis, "till they're all together, and then, my Jupiter, hurl your bolts into their midst."

"Light the fuse," Porthos repeated.

"As for me," Aramis went on, "I'm going to join our Bretons and help them put the boat to sea. I'll wait for you on the beach. Send your firm lightning and then hurry out to us."

"Light the fuse," said Porthos for the last time.

"Did you understand everything?"

"Damn it!" said Porthos, laughing and making no effort to suppress his laughter. "When someone explains something to me, I always understand. Go ahead and give me the fire."

Aramis gave the burning tinder to Porthos, who, because his right hand was full, let Aramis shake his arm. Aramis shook it with both hands and hurried to the rear outlet of the cavern, where the three oarsmen were expecting him.

Porthos, now alone, bravely applied the tinder. A feeble spark, the start of an immense blaze, the tinder shone in the darkness like a firebug, then stuck to the fuse and made it burn. Porthos blew on the flame, activating it. The smoke had slightly dispersed, and, in the light of the sparkling fuse, Porthos could make out objects for a second or two. This was a brief but wonderful spectacle for this pale and bleeding giant, his face lit up by the fuse that was burning in the darkness.

The invaders spotted him. They spotted the barrel in his hand. They realized what was about to happen.

These agonized men, terrified by what had already occurred, horrified by what was about to occur, bellowed in unison. Some tried to flee, but the third brigade blocked their way. Others automatically aimed and tried to fire their empty muskets. And still others fell to their knees. Two or three officers shouted at Porthos, promising him his freedom if he spared their lives. The lieutenant of the third brigade yelled at his men to shoot, but the terrified companions of the guards formed a living rampart for Porthos.

As I have said, the light produced when Porthos puffed on the tinder and the fuse lasted for only two seconds. But during those two seconds, it illuminated a number of things: first, the giant looming in the darkness; then, six paces away from him, a tangle of crushed, shattered, bloody corpses. In their midst, a final quiver of agony lifted the mass the way a final gasp raises the flanks of a shapeless monster succumbing in the night. Each puff of the giant, while fanning the fuse, sent the mound of bodies a sulfurous hue with purple streaks.

Besides this main group, which had been randomly scattered by death or surprise, a few isolated cadavers looked ominous because of their gaping wounds.

Above this blood-soaked ground, the squat pillars, mournful and glittering, rose in the cavern, their sharply accentuated nuances displaying their luminous touches.

And all these things were seen in the flicker of the glimmering fuse that led to a barrel of powder—virtually a torch that, while illuminating past death, also showed future death.

As I have said, this spectacle lasted only a couple of seconds. During that brief time, an officer of the third brigade gathered eight musket bearers and ordered them to shoot Porthos through an opening. However, these men were shaking so hard that three of them fell at this volley, while the five other bullets whistled through the air, grazing the vault, plowing the ground, or notching the walls.

This thundering was met by a burst of laughter. Then the giant's arm whipped around. Then they saw a trail of airborne fire like a shooting star. The barrel, hurled thirty paces, scooted across the barricade of corpses and crashed into a group of howling soldiers, who threw themselves on the ground. The officer had watched the dazzling flight. He wanted to pounce on the barrel and yank out the fuse before the flame reached the powder. A useless sacrifice. The air had activated the flame. The fuse, which would have burned for five minutes on the ground, was devoured in thirty seconds, and the infernal barrel exploded.

Furious whirlwinds; hissing sulfur and saltpeter; ravaging, devouring, shattering fire; dreadful thundering of the explosion—that was what happened during the second that followed the initial two seconds. In this grotto, equal in horrors to a cavern of demons, the rocks split like pinewood hacked by an ax. A jet of fire, smoke, and debris churned up from the middle of the cavern, growing bigger as it soared. The large silex walls collapsed on the sand, and the sand itself, an implement of pain, its hardened layers thrashing up, riddled all faces with its myriad wounding atoms.

Shouts, howls, curses, lives: everything was extinguished in an immense fracas. The first three sections of the cavern turned into a gulf, and each shred—animal, vegetable, or mineral—plunged back into it at a speed determined by weight. Next, the lighter sand and ashes floated down in their turn, spreading and fuming across this lugubrious entombment like a grayish winding-sheet. And now, just look. Look through this burning sepulcher. Look through this subterranean volcano. Look for the king's guards in their blue, silver-laced uniforms. Look for the golden officers, look for the weapons they had counted on to defend themselves, look for the rocks that killed them, look for the ground that had carried them. A single man had turned all this into a more confusing, more turbulent, more horrifying chaos than the chaos that had existed one hour before God had come up with the idea of creating the world. Nothing remained of the three compartments, nothing that God Himself could have recognized as His own work.

As for Porthos, after pitching the barrel of powder into the midst of his enemies, he had followed Aramis's advice and dashed to the grotto's last compartment, which had an aperture that let in air, daylight, and sunshine. No sooner had he turned the corner separating the third compartment from the fourth then he spotted, a hundred paces ahead, the boat bobbing up and down on the waves. That was where his friends were. That was where freedom was. That was where life after victory was. Another six of his formidable strides and he'd be outside. And once he got outside, three bursts of vigor and he'd reach the boat.

All at once, his knees buckled—they felt empty—and his legs softened under him! "Uh-oh!" he muttered in surprise. "My fatigue is tripping me up. I can't walk. What's wrong?"

Aramis, on the other side of the exit, spotted Porthos, and he couldn't understand why his friend had halted. "Hurry, Porthos!" yelled Aramis. "Hurry! Hurry!"

"Oh!" replied the giant, making a supreme effort, uselessly tensing all the muscles in his body. "I can't!" And uttering those words, he fell to his knees. However, his robust hands clung to the rocks, lifting him up.

"Hurry! Hurry!" Aramis repeated, bending toward the shore as if to pull Porthos along.

"Here I am!" Porthos stammered, mustering his full strength to take another step.

"For God's sake, Porthos! Hurry! Hurry! The second barrel's about to explode!"

"Hurry, monseigneur!" shouted the Bretons while Porthos floundered as if in a nightmare.

But time had run out. The explosion boomed. The ground cracked apart. The smoke bursting through the wide fissures darkened the sky. The sea recoiled, virtually driven by the fiery breath that spurted from the grotto as though from the maw of a giant gargoyle. The water swept the boat away. All the rocks cracked down to their bases and separated as if wedges had been driven into their crevices. Part of the vault zoomed to the sky. The green and rosy fire of the sulfur, the black lava of clayey liquefactions, clashed and fought under a majestic dome of smoke. Then the sharp ridges that had not been uprooted from their age-old substratum swayed one by one, then leaned, then fell, greeting one another like grave and earnest old men as they collapsed forever into their dusty tomb.

This dreadful shock appeared to restore Porthos's lost strength. He stood up, a giant among these giants. But as he fled between the double rows of granite phantoms, the latter, unsupported by lintels, began to crash down around this titan, who looked as if he had been flung from the sky amid the rocks that he had just blown up. Underneath him the ground was shaken by this long split, and he stretched his enormous arms right and left, trying to shove back the crumbling rocks. A gigantic block drove against each of his extended palms. He lowered his head, and a third granite mass weighed down between his shoulders.

For an instant, Porthos's arms had yielded, but this Hercules gathered all his strength, and the two walls of this prison, in which he was buried, slowly moved apart, giving him a little space. For an instant, he remained in that granite frame like the ancient angel of chaos. But as he pushed away the lateral rocks, he lost his point of support for the monolith crushing his powerful shoulders. Leaning on him with all its force, the monolith shoved the giant to his knees. The side rocks, wedged apart for a moment, closed ranks again, adding their load to the weight that would have smashed ten men.

The giant collapsed without calling for help. As he fell, he yelled words of hope and encouragement to Aramis, because for an instant he believed that the arch formed by his vigorous arms would shake off that triple weight, like Enceladus, the giant who had rebelled against Zeus. But little by little, Aramis saw the block settle. The hands tightened for a moment, the elbows bent, and, stiffened by a final effort, the tensed and torn shoulders gave way, and the rock kept sinking bit by bit.

"Porthos! Porthos!" shouted Aramis, tearing out his hair. "Porthos! Where are you? Say something!"

"Here! Here!" murmured Porthos in a fading voice. "Patience! Patience!" Barely had he whispered that last word when the enormous rock grew heavier, squeezed down by the two other rocks, and enclosed Porthos in a coffin of broken stones.

Upon hearing his friend's dying voice, Aramis had leaped ashore. He was followed by two of the Bretons, who were clutching levers; one Breton sufficed to guard the boat. The men were guided through the rubble by the final death rattle of the valiant warrior.

Aramis, marvelous, sparkling, and as young as a twenty-year-old, rushed toward the triple mass. With his hands, which were as delicate as a woman's, he miraculously succeeded in lifting a corner of the immense granite sepulcher. Then, in the darkness of that grave, he spotted the still-shining eyes of his friend, who could breathe temporarily because the crushing mass was lifted for an instant. The two other men rushed over, clutching the iron levers, concentrating their triple effort not to raise the levers but to maintain them. However, it was all futile. Shouting with pain, the three men slowly yielded. And in his crass, jeering voice, Porthos, seeing their strength waning in a useless battle, muttered these supreme words, which reached his lips with his final breath: "Too heavy!"

After which his eyes darkened and closed. His face turned pale. His hand was white. And the reclining titan emitted a final sigh. As he settled, so did the rock, which he had been propping up despite his agony!

The three men dropped the levers, which rolled across the tombstone. Then, pallid, breathless, with a tight chest and a sweaty forehead, his heart ready to burst, Aramis listened. "There's nothing!"

The giant was sleeping his eternal sleep in the grave that God had fitted to Porthos's measure.

51
Porthos's Epitaph

Aramis, icy, silent, rose from the tomb, shivering like a fearful child. A Christian doesn't walk over graves. However, capable of standing, he was unable to walk. It was as if something inside him had died along with Porthos. He was surrounded by his Bretons. Aramis submitted to their embraces, and the two mariners heaved him up and carried him to the boat. Then, placing him on the bench near the rudder, they rowed full force: they preferred the oars since a sail might give them away.

Amid that entire leveled surface of the ancient Grotto of Locmaria, amid that flattened beach, their gazes were drawn to a single hillock. Aramis's eyes were glued to that spot. And as the boat gained the open sea, the proud and threatening rock seemed to loom as Porthos used to loom. And the rock lifted a smiling face, an invincible head like that of the honest and valiant friend, the toughest of the four musketeers and yet the first to die.

A strange destiny for these men with their iron constitutions! The one with the simplest heart and the craftiest heart; his physical strength guided by his mental subtlety! And at that decisive moment, when vigor alone could save both mind and body, a rock—a vile, material load—had won out over vigor, driving away the mind as the stones crumbled on the body.

Worthy Porthos! Born to help others, always ready to sacrifice himself for the weak, as if God had given him strength for that sole purpose! When dying, he had thought only to fulfill the conditions of his pact with Aramis—a one-sided pact, however, that Aramis had drawn up and that Porthos had known only in terms of its terrible solidarity.

Noble Porthos! What good were the castles stuffed with furniture, the forests crowded with game, the lakes teeming with fish, the cellars crammed with riches? What good were the lackeys in dazzling livery, with Mousqueton in their midst, so proud of serving as your delegate? Oh, noble Porthos! Meticulous accumulator of treasures! Why did you labor so arduously to gild and sweeten your life only to reach a forsaken shore, the cries of ocean birds, and have your bones crushed under a cold stone? Noble Porthos! Did you have to gather so much gold and not have even a poor poet's distich on your monument?

Valiant Porthos! He must still be sleeping, lost, forgotten, under the rock that the shepherds on the heath mistake for the gigantic roof of a dolmen.

And so much chilly heather, so much moss caressed by the bitter ocean wind, so much hardy lichen have fused the coffin with the earth, that no passerby could imagine that this huge granite block could have been lifted by a mortal's shoulder.

Aramis, still pale, still frozen, his heart on his lips, watched the beach fading into the horizon until the final ray of the sun. No word escaped his lips, no sigh raised his deep chest. The superstitious Bretons trembled as they gazed at him. His silence was that of a statue and not a human being. Nevertheless, amid the first gray streaks in the sky, the boat had hoisted its small sail. With the canvas bellying in the breeze, the boat rapidly left the coast, crossed the dreadful tempest-ridden Gulf of Gascony, and bravely headed toward Spain.

But scarcely half an hour after the hoisting of the sail, the now inactive rowers leaned over their benches. Cupping their eyes with one hand, they made one another aware of a white dot that, hovering on the horizon, was as motionless as a gull cradled by the imperceptible respiration of the waves. However, what might have seemed immobile to ordinary eyes kept grazing the ocean, scudding rapidly for the trained eyes of a sailor.

For a while, the oarsmen, noting Aramis's profound torpor, didn't dare awaken him; they contented themselves with exchanging their conjectures in low, nervous voices. Aramis, normally so vigilant, so active; Aramis, whose eyes, like those of a lynx, were usually peering nonstop, seeing better at night than during the day—Aramis slept in the despair of his soul.

An hour wore by, during which the sun was gradually setting, and during which the dot, a boat, gained so swiftly on the dinghy that Goennec, one of the three mariners, ventured to say out loud, "Monseigneur, we're being followed."

Aramis failed to respond, and the other boat continued gaining on them. Then, of their own accord, the two sailors, on the skipper's orders, lowered the sail so that it wouldn't serve to guide the enemy pursuing them. However, the enemy boat increased its speed by running up two more small sails to the tops of the masts. Unfortunately, these days were the longest of the year, and the nefarious day was succeeded by the moon in all its brightness. Therefore, the balancelle chasing the dinghy, dashing before the wind, could rely on another half hour of twilight and an entire semi-illuminated night.

"Monseigneur! Monseigneur! We're done for!" cried the skipper. "Look! They spotted us even though we brailed up our sails!"

"It's not so amazing," muttered one of the sailors. "They say that with the devil's help the city dwellers have devised instruments with which they can see both near and far, day or night."

From the bottom of the dinghy, Aramis grabbed a telescope, silently adjusted it, and handed it to the sailor. "Here! Have a look!"

The sailor hesitated.

"Calm down," said the bishop. "It's no sin. And if there's any sin, I'll take it upon myself."

The sailor held the telescope to one eye and emitted a shout. By some miracle, the balancelle, which had seemed to be a cannonball away, had suddenly leaped across the gap between the two vessels. However, upon withdrawing the telescope from his eye, the sailor realized that, aside from the brief distance the pursuer had covered during that moment, he was still far away.

"So," muttered the sailor, "they can see us just as we can see them."

"They see us," said Aramis, and he sank back into his impassive torpor.

"What do you mean they see us?" said the skipper. "Impossible!"

"Here, Captain," said the sailor. "Look for yourself." And he handed him the telescope.

"Does Monseigneur assure me that the devil is not involved in this?" said the skipper.

Aramis shrugged.

The skipper held the instrument to his eye. "Yes, monseigneur, it's a miracle. There they are! I think I can touch them. At least twenty-five men! Ah! I can see the captain in front of them. He's holding a telescope like this one and he's looking at us. Ah! He's turning, he's giving an order. They're rolling a cannon, they're loading it, they're aiming it. . . . Damn it! They're firing at us!" And the skipper automatically removed the telescope from his eye, so that the distant objects, pulled back to the horizon, reappeared in their natural aspect. The vessel was still about a league away, but the maneuver announced by the skipper was no less real.

A wisp of smoke floated under the sails, whiter than the canvas and fanning out like a blossoming flower. Then, roughly a mile from the dinghy, the cannonball shattered the crowns of two or three waves, left a white furrow in the sea, and disappeared at the end of the furrow. This ball was still as harmless as a schoolboy's stone ricocheting across a watery surface. It was both a threat and a warning.

"What should we do?" asked the skipper.

"They're going to sink us," said Goennec. "Grant us absolution, monseigneur!" And the sailors genuflected before the bishop.

"You're forgetting that they're watching us," said Aramis.

"You're right!" said the sailors, ashamed of their weakness. "Give us your orders, monseigneur! We're ready to die for you!"

"Let's wait!" said Aramis.

"Wait?"

"Yes. As you just said, if we try to flee, they'll sink us."

"But maybe," the skipper ventured to say, "maybe we can escape them under cover of night?"

"Oh!" said Aramis. "They must have Greek fire to light up their course and ours."

At the same time, as if the small pursuer wanted to respond to Aramis, a second cloud of smoke slowly drifted skyward, ejecting a fiery arrow. Describing a parabola like that of a rainbow, the arrow plunged into the sea, where it continued to burn, lighting up an enormous space. The Bretons exchanged terrified glances.

"You can see," Aramis said, "that it's better to wait for them."

The oars slipped out of the rowers' hands, and their small dinghy drifted to a halt and rocked on the whitecaps. Night was coming, but the pursuer kept advancing. Its speed seemed to be doubling with the darkness. From time to time, like a bloody-throated vulture lifting its head out of its nest, the formidable Greek fire darted forth, hurling its flame in the middle of the ocean like incandescent snow. Finally, the pursuer drew within musket-shot. All the men were on deck, clutching their weapons; the gunners were at their cannon, their tinders ignited. It was as if they had to confront a frigate and battle a much larger crew rather than capturing a dinghy with four men.

"Surrender!" cried the captain of the balancelle through a megaphone. The Bretons looked at Aramis. Aramis nodded. Yves, the dinghy skipper, waved a white cloth at the end of a boat hook. It was the equivalent of running up a flag. The balancelle advanced like a racehorse. It hurled another Greek fire, which plummeted some twenty paces from the dinghy, illuminating it more fully than a ray of the brightest sunshine.

"At the first sign of resistance," shouted the skipper of the balancelle, "fire!"

The soldiers aimed their muskets.

"We said we're surrendering!" cried Yves.

"Alive! Alive! Captain!" cried several exalted soldiers. "We have to take them alive!"

"Fine! Yes! Alive!" the captain agreed. Then he turned toward the Bretons: "You are all safe, my friends! But not Monsieur d'Herblay!"

Aramis shivered imperceptibly. For an instant his eyes focused on the depths of the ocean, its surface lit by the final glimmers of the Greek fire. Those glimmers flashed alongside the waves, playing on their crests like plumes and making the watery gulfs more somber, more mysterious, and more terrible.

"Did you hear that, monseigneur?" said the sailors.

"Yes."

"What are your orders?"

"Accept."

"What about you, monseigneur?"

Aramis bent farther, the tips of his white, slender fingers toying with the greenish water, and he smiled at the sea as if it were his friend. "Accept," he repeated.

"We accept," the sailors repeated. "But what security can you offer us?"

"My word as a gentleman," said the officer. "I swear, on my rank and on my name, that everyone except for Monsieur d'Herblay will be safe. I am the lieutenant of the royal frigate *La Pomone*, and my name is Louis-Constant de Pressigny."

With a quick motion, Aramis, already leaning halfway toward the sea, raised his head, got to his feet, and smiled with ardent eyes. "Throw out the ladder, gentlemen," he said as if he were the commander.

The men obeyed.

Next, seizing the rope railing, Aramis was the first to board the balancelle. But, to the great surprise of its sailors, instead of being filled with fear, Aramis walked firmly toward the lieutenant, gazing at him, and making an enigmatic and unfamiliar gesture—at the sight of which the officer blanched, trembled, and bowed his head.

Without uttering a word, Aramis then raised his hand to the officer's eye level and showed him the bezel of a ring that he wore on his left ring finger. And, in making that sign, Aramis, draped in cold, silent, haughty majesty, looked like an emperor holding out his hand to be kissed. The officer, after raising his head for an instant, bowed again with the deepest respect. Then, pointing at the poop—his room, that is—he stepped aside, letting Aramis pass. The three Bretons, who had climbed up after their bishop, traded stupefied glances. The entire crew of the balancelle was speechless.

Five minutes later, the officer summoned his second in command, who immediately returned and ordered the pilot to steer toward Corunna. While this order was carried out, Aramis reappeared on deck and sat down by the railing. Night had arrived, the moon hadn't yet emerged, and yet Aramis kept stubbornly gazing at Belle-Île. Yves, approaching the officer, who had taken up his post in the stern, asked very softly and humbly, "What course are we sailing, Captain?"

"Our course is the one that Monseigneur likes," replied the officer.

Aramis spent the night leaning on the railing. In the morning, Yves, coming over to him, remarked that the night must have been very damp, because the wood on which the bishop's head was leaning was as wet as dew.

Who knows? Perhaps the moisture may have been the first tears that Aramis had ever shed.

What epitaph would have been worth that? Good Porthos!

52
The Duke de Gesvres's Rounds

D'Artagnan was unaccustomed to the kind of resistance he had just faced. He returned from Nantes profoundly irritated. The irritation in that vigorous man was translated into an impetuous attack that few men, be they kings or giants, could have managed to resist. Shuddering furiously, d'Artagnan headed straight for the castle and asked to speak to the king. It might have been seven A.M., and the king had been rising early ever since his return from Nantes. But upon reaching the small corridor that we are familiar with, d'Artagnan found Monsieur de Gesvres, who stopped him very politely and recommended that he speak softly so as not to wake up the king.

"The king is asleep?" said d'Artagnan. "Then I'll let him sleep. Around what time do you suppose he'll get up?"

"Oh, in two hours, more or less. The king was up all night."

D'Artagnan took back his hat, bowed, and left. He returned at nine-thirty. He was told that the king was breakfasting.

"That's just my cup of tea. I'll talk to the king while he's eating."

Monsieur de Brienne observed that the king refused to receive anybody during his meals.

"But," said d'Artagnan, eying Brienne askance, "you may not realize, Monsieur Secretary, that I am received anywhere and at any time."

Brienne gently took the captain's hand: "Not in Nantes, dear Monsieur d'Artagnan. For this journey the king has restructured his entire household."

D'Artagnan, a bit softened, asked toward what time the king would be done eating.

"Nobody knows," said Brienne.

"What do you mean nobody knows? What are you saying? Nobody knows how long the king eats? It usually takes him an hour, and, if the air of the Loire whets his appetite, we can say an hour and a half. That's enough, I think. I'll wait for him here."

"Oh! Dear Monsieur d'Artagnan. Our orders are to let nobody into this corridor. I'm guarding it to make sure of that."

D'Artagnan felt his anger rushing to his head again. He hurried out, fearing that his awful mood could complicate the matter. Once he was outside, he started reflecting: The king refuses to see me—it's obvious. That young man is annoyed. He's afraid of what I might tell him. Yes, but during this time, they're laying siege to Belle-Île, and they may be capturing or killing my two friends. Poor Porthos! As for Master Aramis, he's very resourceful, and I'm not worried about him. But no, no! Porthos is not yet an invalid, and Aramis is not a senile idiot. Both of them—one with his hands and the other with his imagination—will provide hard work for His Majesty's soldiers. Who knows if these two brave men are going to redo a small Bastion Saint-Gervais for the edification of His Very Christian Majesty? I'm not giving them up for lost. They've got cannon and a garrison. However, d'Artagnan shook his head, I think it would be better to stop the combat. For me alone, I wouldn't endure the king's arrogance or betrayal, but for my friends I must suffer anything—rebuffs, insults. . . . What if I went to Monsieur Colbert? Now, there's a man whom I have to get in the habit of scaring. Let's go to Monsieur Colbert!

And d'Artagnan bravely started out. He learned that Monsieur Colbert was working with the king at the Castle of Nantes. "Fine!" d'Artagnan cried. "I'm back in the days when I went from Monsieur de Tréville to the cardinal, from the cardinal to the queen, from the queen to King Louis XIII. People are right when they say that old men revert to childhood. To the castle!"

He returned there. Monsieur de Lyonne was leaving. He gave d'Artagnan both hands and told him that the king would be working all evening, and perhaps all night, and that he would be receiving no one.

"Not even the captain who takes the order?" cried d'Artagnan. "That's a bit much!"

"Not even!" said Monsieur de Lyonne.

"If that's the case," d'Artagnan retorted, wounded to the quick, "if the captain of the musketeers, who has always entered the royal bedroom, can no longer enter the cabinet or the dining room, then either the king is dead or his captain is in disgrace. Either way, the king no longer needs him. Please be so good, Monsieur de Lyonne, since you are in favor—please be so good as to plainly inform the king that I am sending him my resignation."

"D'Artagnan, be careful!" cried de Lyonne.

"Please go and tell him, out of friendship for me." And he gently pushed him toward the cabinet.

"I'm going," said Monsieur de Lyonne.

D'Artagnan waited, pacing up and down the corridor. De Lyonne came back.

"Well?" asked the captain. "What did the king say?"

"The king said that it was fine," de Lyonne answered.

"That it was fine!" D'Artagnan exploded. "You mean he accepts? Fine! I'm free! I'm a civilian, Monsieur de Lyonne! Till I have the pleasure of meeting you again. Farewell, castle, corridor, antechamber! As a civilian who will finally breathe again, I salute you!"

And waiting no longer, the captain leaped down the stairs where he had found the scraps of Gourville's letter. Five minutes later, d'Artagnan returned to the hostelry, where, observing the custom of all the high-ranking officers who lodge at the castle, he had taken what was known as his "city chamber." However, instead of throwing down his sword and his cloak, he grabbed his pistols, put his money in a big leather pouch, sent for his horses from the stables, and ordered his men to reach Vannes that same night.

His wishes were carried out. At eight in the evening, as

d'Artagnan was slipping his foot into his stirrup, Monsieur de Gesvres drew up with a dozen men at the hostelry. D'Artagnan caught everything from the corner of his eye; he couldn't fail to see those thirteen men and thirteen horses. But he pretended not to notice them and he continued mounting his steed.

De Gesvres galloped up. "Monsieur d'Artagnan!" he cried out.

"Ah! Monsieur de Gesvres, good evening!"

"You seem to be mounting a horse, don't you?"

"More than that! I've already mounted, as you can see!"

"It's a good thing I've found you."

"You're looking for me?"

"Goodness, yes!"

"On behalf of the king, I bet?"

"Of course."

"Just as I was looking for Monsieur Fouquet two or three days ago?"

"Oh!"

"Come on! You're not going to play games! It's a waste of time! Tell me that you're arresting me!"

"Arrest you! Good God, no!"

"Well, then, why are you accosting me with twelve horsemen?"

"I'm making the rounds."

"Not bad! And you're picking me up in your rounds?"

"I'm not picking you up. I've found you and I'm asking you to come with me."

"Where to?"

"The king!"

"Fine!" said d'Artagnan facetiously. "The king has nothing better to do?"

"Good God, Captain!" Monsieur de Gesvres murmured. "Don't compromise yourself—these men can hear you!"

D'Artagnan laughed and retorted, "Let's go! A person who's arrested is placed between the first six and the last six men."

"Since I'm not arresting you, you'll ride in back with me, if you please. . . ."

"Well," said d'Artagnan, "that's a good procedure, Duke. And you're right. Because if I ever had to make the rounds near your city chamber, I'd be as courteous as you, I can assure you on my word as a gentleman. Now, one more favor! What does the king want of me?"

"Oh, the king is furious!"

"Fine! The king, who's gone to the trouble of being furious, will take the trouble to calm down—that's all! I won't die, I swear to you."

"No, but—"

"But I'll be keeping company with that poor Monsieur Fouquet, damn it! He's a gallant man! We'll live together, and very pleasantly at that, I swear!"

"Here we are!" said the duke. "Captain, please keep calm in front of the king."

"Oh, definitely! You're such a decent man with me, Duke. I've been told that you'd like to merge your guards with my musketeers. Here's a golden opportunity!"

"I won't take it. God help me, Captain."

"Why not?"

"For lots of reasons, first of all. And for this reason: If I succeeded you as musketeer captain after arresting you—"

"Aha! You admit you're arresting me?"

"No, no!"

"Then let's call it an encounter. If, as you say, you succeeded me after encountering me . . ."

"At their first drill with live ammunition, the musketeers would shoot me by mistake."

"Ah, I won't deny it! Those men love me deeply."

The Duke de Gesvres gave d'Artagnan the right-of-way as he conducted him to the cabinet, where the king was waiting for his musketeer captain. Once there, the duke stood behind his colleague in the antechamber. They very distinctly heard the king speaking with Colbert in the same cabinet where, several days earlier, the king had spoken with Monsieur d'Artagnan. The mounted guards picketed outside the main gate while the rumor spread that the captain of the musketeers had been arrested at the king's orders.

Then those men started moving as in the good old days of Louis XIII and Monsieur de Tréville. Groups formed, stairways filled up, vague murmurs drifting from the courtyards wafted toward the upper floors like the hoarse lamentations of waves at high tide.

The Duke de Gesvres was worried. He looked at his guards, who, when questioned by the musketeers who were mingling with them, were starting to draw away; and the guards too were a bit worried.

D'Artagnan was certainly far less worried than the duke. Upon entering, d'Artagnan settled on a window ledge, where he watched everything with his eagle eyes, never batting an eye. None of the agitation triggered by the news of his arrest escaped him. He foresaw the moment when the explosion would occur; and we know how certain his predictions were.

It would be quite bizarre, he mused, if my pretorians made me king of France tonight. How I'd laugh!

But all at once everything stopped. Guards, musketeers, officers, soldiers, mutterings and worries dissipated, disappeared, faded away; gone was the tempest, gone the threat, gone the sedition.

One word had calmed the waves.

The king had just ordered Brienne to cry, "Shush, gentlemen! You're disturbing the king."

D'Artagnan sighed. "It's over! Today's musketeers aren't those of His Majesty Louis XIII. It's over!"

"Monsieur d'Artagnan to see the king!" shouted an usher.

53
King Louis XIV

The king was in his cabinet with his back to the door. Facing him was a mirror, in which, while shuffling papers, he could spot anyone entering the room. Ignoring d'Artagnan's arrival, the king took the large green silk cloth which served to hide his secrets from snoopers, and he drew it across his letters and his plans.

D'Artagnan understood the game and remained in the background so that, after a moment, the king, who heard nothing and saw only from the corner of his eye, was obliged to shout, "Isn't that Monsieur d'Artagnan?"

"Here I am," replied the musketeer, drawing closer.

"Well, monsieur," said the king, focusing his clear eyes on d'Artagnan, "what do you have to say to me?"

"I, sire?" D'Artagnan was waiting for his adversary's first blow in order to make a good retort. "I have nothing to say to Your Majesty except that I've been arrested—and here I am."

The king was about to respond that he hadn't had d'Artagnan arrested, but those words struck him as an excuse, and so he held his tongue. D'Artagnan likewise maintained an obstinate silence.

"Monsieur," the king went on, "what did I charge you with doing at Belle-Île? Please tell me." And he stared at his captain.

D'Artagnan was too fortunate; the king was playing into his hands. "I believe," said the captain, "that Your Majesty is paying me the honor of asking me what I went to do at Belle-Île."

"Yes, monsieur."

"Well, sire, I have no idea. It's not I you should ask, it's that endless number of all kinds of officers who were given an endless number of all sorts of orders, while I, the head of the expedition, was not given any precise orders."

The king was wounded; and he showed it in his response. "Monsieur, orders were given only to men who were judged to be loyal."

"Then I'm astonished, sire, that a captain like myself, who ranks with a field marshal of France, should be under the orders of five or six lieutenants or majors. They might make good spies, that's possible. But they're useless for leading military expeditions. I came to ask Your Majesty for an explanation, but the door was slammed in my face, which was the ultimate outrage for a decent man. That is why I want to leave Your Majesty's service."

"Monsieur," replied the king, "you still believe that you are living in an age in which kings—as you yourself actually complain—are under the orders and at the discretion of their inferiors. You seem to forget that a king is accountable for his actions to God alone."

"I don't forget that at all, sire," said the musketeer, offended in his turn by the lesson. "Besides, I don't see how a man of honor is offending the king by asking him in what way he has served him badly."

"You served me badly, monsieur, by siding with my enemies."

"Who are your enemies, sire?"

"The people I sent you to fight."

"Two men! Enemies of Your Majesty's army! It's unbelievable, sire!"

"You are not to judge my wishes."

"I have to judge my friendships, sire."

"The man who serves his friends is not serving his master."

"I understood that so well, sire, that I respectfully offered Your Majesty my resignation."

"And I accepted it, monsieur. But prior to a parting of the ways, I wanted to prove to you that I can keep my word."

"Your Majesty did more than keep his word, for Your Majesty had me arrested," d'Artagnan coolly bantered. "He never promised me that."

The king ignored the joke and remained serious. "You can see, monsieur, what your disobedience has forced me to do."

"My disobedience!" cried d'Artagnan, crimson with rage.

"That's the gentlest word I could find. My idea was to capture and punish the rebels. Was I supposed to be worried if those rebels were your friends?"

"I was to be worried, I?" replied d'Artagnan. "It was cruel of Your Majesty to send me to capture my friends and bring them to your gallows."

"It was, monsieur, my way of testing my alleged servants, who eat my bread and ought to protect me. You failed the test, Monsieur d'Artagnan."

"For a bad servant that Your Majesty is losing," said the musketeer bitterly, "there are ten servants who've passed the test this very day. Listen to me, sire. I am not accustomed to this service. I am a rebellious swordsman when I am told to do wrong. It was wrong of me to pursue to their deaths two men whose lives had been requested by Monsieur Fouquet, Your Majesty's savior. Furthermore, those two men were my friends. They didn't attack Your Majesty, they succumbed under the weight of a blind anger. And why not let them escape? What crime did they commit? I accept your challenging my right to judge their conduct. But why suspect me before the action? Why surround me with spies? Why dishonor me in front of the army? In the thirty years that I've been attached to your person, you've always shown me your full confidence, and I've given you a thousand proofs of my devotion—for I must say this now that I've been accused. Why reduce me to watching three thousand of the king's soldiers go to war against two men?"

"You seem to forget what those two men have done to me!" said the king in a hollow voice. "And that it was no merit of theirs that I wasn't doomed."

"Sire, you seem to forget that I was there."

"Enough, Monsieur d'Artagnan, enough of those overbearing interests that darken the sun of my interests. I am establishing a state that will have only a single master—I once promised you that. And the time has come for me to keep my promise. In line with your taste and your friendships, you want to be free to thwart my plans and save my enemies? I will destroy you or have nothing further to do with you. Find a more accommodating master. I realize that another king would not act as I do and that he would let himself be overruled by you—at the risk of someday sending you to keep company with Monsieur Fouquet and the others. But I've got an excellent memory, and for me a man's service is a sacred title to gratitude, to impunity.

"Monsieur d'Artagnan, you will have only this one lesson to punish your lack of discipline, and I will not imitate my predecessors in their anger since I have not imitated them in their favor. And there are other reasons why I am behaving mildly toward you. First of all, you are a man of good sense, a man of great sense, a man of heart, and you will be a good servant to the man who will master you. Second, you will lose any motives for insubordination: your friends are destroyed or ruined by me. I've done away with those supports on which your capricious mind instinctively rested. By now, my soldiers have captured or killed the rebels of Belle-Île."

D'Artagnan blanched. "Captured or killed! Oh, sire! If you really meant what you've said! If you were sure that you were telling me the truth! I would forget all that is just, all that is magnanimous in your words—and I would call you a barbarous king, a debased man. But I forgive you for those words." D'Artagnan smiled proudly. "I forgive the young ruler, who doesn't know, who can't comprehend what men like us are—men like Monsieur d'Herblay, like Monsieur du Vallon, like me. Captured or killed! Ah! Ah! Sire, tell me: If the news is true, how many men, how much money it has cost you! We will determine afterward if the gain is greater than the loss."

As d'Artagnan was speaking, the king angrily approached him: "Monsieur d'Artagnan, those are the responses of a rebel! Tell me, if you please, who is the king of France, and do you know of any other?"

"Sire," the musketeer captain coldly retorted, "I recall that you asked that question one morning in Vaux—you asked many men, who were unable to answer. But I answered. If I recognized the king that day, when the matter was not an easy one, then I believe that it would be useless to ask me today when Your Majesty is alone with me."

At those words, Louis lowered his eyes. He felt as if the shadow of the unhappy Philip had passed between d'Artagnan and himself, evoking the memory of that dreadful adventure.

Almost that same moment, an officer entered, delivering a dispatch that the king read, his face changing color. D'Artagnan noticed it. After rereading the dispatch, the king remained silent and motionless. Then he suddenly pulled himself together. "Monsieur, you'll eventually learn what I've just been told. It's better if I tell you and you find out from your king. A battle has been fought in Belle-Île."

"Aha!" said d'Artagnan calmly while his pounding heart almost burst from his chest. "Well, sire?"

"Well, monsieur. I've lost a hundred and six men."

D'Artagnan's eyes shone with joy and pride. "What about the rebels?"

"The rebels have fled."

D'Artagnan uttered a cry of triumph.

"Except," the king added, "that I've got a fleet blocking Belle-Île tightly and I'm certain that not a single boat will escape."

"So that," said the musketeer more somberly, "if those two gentlemen are caught . . ."

"They will be hanged," said the king tranquilly.

"And do they know that?" asked d'Artagnan, repressing a shiver.

"They know it because you must have told them, and because the entire country knows it."

"Well, then, sire, they won't be taken alive, I can assure you."

"Ah!" said the king casually as he picked up the dispatch again. "Well, then, we'll take them dead, Monsieur d'Artagnan. It all boils down to the same thing, because I'd capture them only to hang them."

D'Artagnan wiped the sweat pouring from his forehead.

"I've told you," Louis XIV went on, "that someday I'd be an affectionate, generous, and constant master. Today you are the only man of earlier times who is worthy of both my wrath and my friendship. I won't hold back with either, depending on your conduct. Would you, Monsieur d'Artagnan, understand serving a king who had a hundred other kings, his equals, in the kingdom? Tell me, could I then, despite that weakness, accomplish the great things that I am planning? Have you ever heard of an artist producing solid works with a rebellious instrument? Monsieur, let's purge out those old leavens of feudal abuses! The Fronde, which was to doom the monarchy, emancipated it. I am the master in my palace, Captain d'Artagnan, and I would have servants who, lacking your genius perhaps, would push their devotion and obedience to the point of heroism. What does it matter, I ask you—what does it matter if God hasn't given genius to arms and legs? He gives it to the head, and everything else, you know, obeys the head. I am the head, monsieur!"

D'Artagnan shuddered.

Louis continued as if he'd seen nothing even though that shudder had not escaped his notice. "And now, let the two of us conclude the bargain that I promised I'd conclude with you. I was still a little boy, in Blois. Be grateful to me, monsieur, for not forcing anyone to pay for the tears of shame that I shed.

Look around you; the great heads have bowed. Bow like them or choose the exile that suits you best.

"Perhaps, on reflection, you will find that this king has a generous heart and that he counts enough on your loyalty to leave you with a state secret, yet know that you are dissatisfied. You're a decent man, I realize that. Why did you judge me in advance? Instead, you should judge me as of today, d'Artagnan, and you may be as severe as you like."

D'Artagnan was stunned, wordless, irresolute for the first time in his life. He had just found a worthy adversary. This was no ruse now, this was calculation; this was no violence now, this was strength; this was no anger now, this was willpower; this was no bragging now, this was advice. This young man, who had brought down Fouquet, and who could do without d'Artagnan, was shaking up the musketeer's slightly obstinate reckonings.

"Come on, what's holding you back?" the king said gently. "You've handed in your resignation—do you want me to refuse to accept it? I admit that it may be a bit difficult for an old captain to overcome his bad mood."

"Oh!" d'Artagnan replied mournfully. "That's not my worst problem. I hesitate to take back my resignation because I'm old compared with you and because I've got habits that are hard to break. You need courtiers who know how to amuse you, lunatics who know how to sacrifice their lives for what you call your 'great works.' Your works will be great—I can sense it. But if I don't find them great? I've witnessed war, sire, I've witnessed peace. I've served Richelieu and Mazarin. I've been scorched with your father by the fire of La Rochelle, I've been riddled with shots like a sieve—and I've grown over ten new skins, like a snake.

"After the affronts and injustices, I gained a command that used to be something, because it gave me the right to speak to the king however I wished. But now your musketeer captain will be an officer guarding the lower doors. Truly, sire, if that must become my position, then let's take advantage of our being on good terms and let's cancel that possibility. Don't think that I hold a grudge. Not at all. You've tamed me, as you've said. But we must admit that by dominating me, you've lessened me. By bending me, you've convicted me of weakness. If you only knew how well it suits me to hold my head high—and I'll cut such a poor figure if I sniff the dust of your carpets! Oh, sire! I honestly miss—and you will miss too—the time when the king of France saw all those insolent noblemen in his vestibules: those skinny and insolent aristocrats, those cursing, swearing mastiffs who bit mortally on battle days. Those men are the best courtiers for the hand that feeds them—the hand that they lick. But for the hand that hits them—oh, what a bite! A little gold on the lace of their cloaks, a little paunch in their breeches, a little gray in their stringy hair, and you will see the fine dukes and peers, the proud field marshals of France!

"But why say all this? The king is my master, he wants me to write poems, he wants me to polish the mosaics in his antechambers with silk slippers. Damn it! That's hard! But I've done harder things. I'll do it. And why will I do it? Because I love money? I've got enough money. Because I'm ambitious? My career has gone as far as it can. Because I love the royal court? No. I'll stay on because for thirty years now, I've been in the habit of getting my cue from the king and hearing him say, 'Good evening, d'Artagnan,' with a smile that I haven't begged for. I will now beg for this smile. Are you content, sire?"

D'Artagnan slowly bowed his silvery head, and the smiling king haughtily placed his white hand upon it.

"Thank you, my old servant, my loyal friend," said the monarch. "Since, as of today, I have no enemies left in France, it remains for me to dispatch you to a foreign field to obtain your field marshal's baton. You can rely on me to find the occasion. Meanwhile, eat my best bread and sleep peacefully."

"Wonderful!" said d'Artagnan, deeply moved. "But what about those poor souls in Belle-Île? Especially one so good and so brave!"

"Are you asking for mercy on their behalf?"

"On my knees, sire."

"Well, then, inform them of my mercy if there's still time. But will you answer for them?"

"I will answer for them with my life!"

"Go. Tomorrow I'm heading for Paris. Come back by then, for I never want you to leave me again."

"You may count on it, sire!" cried d'Artagnan, kissing the king's hand. And, his heart bursting with joy, he dashed out of the castle and took the road to Belle-Île.

54

Monsieur Fouquet's Friends

The king had returned to Paris, accompanied by d'Artagnan. Within twenty-four hours, the captain had most carefully gathered all his information in Belle-Île, but he was still unaware of the secret guarded by the heavy rock of Locmaria, Porthos's heroic tomb.

D'Artagnan knew only one thing about those two valiant men, those two friends, whose lives he had so nobly defended and tried to save: he knew that, with the help of three faithful Bretons, they had held out against an entire army. The captain, visiting the neighboring heath, had viewed the human remains, the bloodstained flints scattered in the heather. He also knew that a dinghy had been spotted far out to sea, and that, like a bird of prey, a royal vessel had pursued, caught up with, and devoured that poor little bird, which had been racing away.

Those were d'Artagnan's only certainties. Beyond that, all he had were conjectures. What should he think now? The vessel had not returned. True, a brisk wind had blown for three days. But the corvette was a fine windjammer with a solid frame. It didn't fear the blasts of the wind. And in d'Artagnan's opinion, the vessel carrying Aramis should have returned to Brest or regained the mouth of the Loire.

That was the news—ambiguous but somewhat reassuring for the captain himself—that d'Artagnan reported to Louis XIV, when the king returned to Paris, followed by the entire court.

Louis, content with his success—Louis, gentler and more affable now that he felt more powerful—Louis hadn't, for even an instant, stopped riding near Mademoiselle de la Vallière's carriage door.

Everyone was eager to distract the two queens and make them forget their abandonment by the son and the husband. Everything smacked of the future; the past meant nothing to anyone. But then that past came like a painful and bleeding wound in the hearts of a few tender and devoted souls. And no sooner had the king settled in than he received a touching proof of this.

Louis XIV had just risen and breakfasted when his captain of the musketeers presented himself. The visitor was a bit pale and seemed ill at ease. The king instantly noticed the change in the usually so even features. "What's wrong, d'Artagnan?"

"Sire, something awful has happened to me."

"Good God! What?"

"Sire, I lost one of my friends, Monsieur du Vallon, in the Belle-Île expedition." And d'Artagnan focused his eagle eyes on the king, to capture his first emotion.

"I know about it," replied the monarch.

"You know about it and you haven't told me?" exclaimed the musketeer.

"What good would it do? Your pain, my friend, is so worthy of respect. I had to treat it with kid gloves. If I'd told you about your misfortune, d'Artagnan, you'd have regarded me as triumphing. Yes, I knew that Monsieur du Vallon was buried under the rocks of Locmaria. I knew that Monsieur d'Herblay had taken one of my vessels and its crew to sail to Bayonne. But I wanted you to learn about these events directly so you'd be convinced that my friends are sacred to me and worthy of my respect. In me, the man will always sacrifice himself to men, because the king is so often compelled to sacrifice men to his majesty, his power."

"But, sire, how do you know . . ."

"How did you find out, d'Artagnan?"

"Through Aramis's letter from Bayonne—he's free and out of danger."

"Look," said the king, drawing a letter from a box placed on a chest near the chair against which d'Artagnan was leaning; the letter was an exact copy of the one written by Aramis.

"This is the very letter that Colbert passed on to me eight hours before you received yours. I'm well served, as you can see."

"Yes, sire," murmured the musketeer. "You were the only man whose fortune was capable of dominating the fortune of my two friends. You've used it, sire, but you won't abuse it, will you?"

"D'Artagnan," said the king with a benevolent smile, "I could have Monsieur d'Herblay banished from Spanish soil and brought back here alive to make him face justice. But, believe me, I won't yield to that first, very natural urge. He's free. Let him stay free."

"Oh, sire! You won't always be as merciful, as noble, as generous as you've just been to me and Monsieur d'Herblay. You'll be flanked by advisers who'll cure you of that weakness."

"No, d'Artagnan, it's wrong of you to accuse my advisers of wanting me to take extreme measures. It was Monsieur Colbert himself who suggested that I treat Monsieur d'Herblay gently."

"Ah, sire!" said d'Artagnan, stupefied.

"As for you," the king went on with unusual kindness, "I've got lots of good news for you, and you'll hear it, my dear captain, as soon as I've completed my accounts. I've said that I wanted to make and would make your fortune. Those words will now become a reality."

"Thank you a thousand times, sire. I can wait. And while I go and practice patience, I beg Your Majesty to take care of those poor supplicants who've been besieging your antechamber for a long time now, waiting to humbly place a request at the king's feet."

"Who are they?"

"Enemies of Your Majesty."

The king raised his head.

"Friends of Monsieur Fouquet," d'Artagnan added.

"Their names?"

"Monsieur Gourville, Monsieur Pellisson, and a poet, Monsieur Jean de La Fontaine."

The king reflected for a moment. Then: "What do they want?"

"I don't know."

"How do they seem to be?"

"In mourning."

"What are they saying?"

"Nothing."

"What are they doing?"

"They're weeping."

"Have them enter," said the king, frowning.

D'Artagnan whirled around, lifted the tapestry closing off the royal chamber, and shouted into the adjacent room: "Let them enter!"

The three men named by d'Artagnan soon appeared at the door of the cabinet, where the king and his captain were waiting. The petitioners came in amid a profound hush. As the friends of the unfortunate superintendent of finances approached them, the courtiers drew away as if to avoid any contagion of disgrace and affliction.

D'Artagnan strode over and led those unhappy men, who were trembling and hesitating in the doorway. He guided them to the chair of the king, who, taking refuge in a window embrasure, waited for the supplicants and prepared to receive them with diplomatic rigor.

The first to come forward was Pellisson. He had stopped weeping, but only so that the king could more clearly hear his voice and his prayer. Out of respect for the king, Gourville bit his lip to halt his tears. La Fontaine buried his face in his handkerchief, and his only signs of life were the convulsive heaving of his shoulders, which rolled under his sobs.

The king maintained his full dignity. His face was impassive. He even kept the frown that had appeared when d'Artagnan had announced the king's enemies. Louis gestured as if saying: Speak. And he remained standing, scouring the faces of these three desperate men.

Pellisson bowed almost to the floor, and La Fontaine genuflected as if in church. The obstinate silence, disturbed only by doleful sighs and moans, began to move the king—not out of compassion, but out of impatience.

"Monsieur Pellisson," he said, his tone curt and dry, "Monsieur Gourville, and you, monsieur . . . [he did not mention La Fontaine's name]. I see with sharp displeasure that you have come to petition me on behalf of one of the worst criminals that my justice must punish. A king allows himself to be swayed purely by tears or by remorse: tears of the innocent, remorse of the guilty. I will not believe in either Monsieur Fouquet's remorse, or the tears of his friends, because he is rotten to the core, and because his friends should fear offending me in my chambers. That is why, Monsieur Pellisson, Monsieur Gourville, and you, monsieur, I ask you to say nothing that doesn't testify to your profound respect for my wishes."

"Sire," replied Pellisson, trembling at those terrible words, "we have come to Your Majesty purely to express the deepest and most sincere respect and love that are due to a king from all his subjects. Your Majesty's justice is formidable; everyone must yield to its verdicts. We bow to it respectfully. We are far from even thinking of defending the man who has had the misfortune of offending Your Majesty. The man who is disgraced in your eyes may be a friend of ours, but he is a foe of the state. We will abandon him, while weeping at the king's severity."

"In any event," the king broke in, calmed by that pleading voice and those persuasive words, "my parliament will judge him. I never strike without first weighing the crime. My justice wields no sword without first using its scales."

"We therefore have full confidence in the king's impartiality and we can hope to have the king hear our weak voices when the time has come for us to defend an accused friend."

"Well, gentlemen, then what are you asking for?" said the king with his imposing air.

"Sire," Pellisson continued, "the defendant has a wife and a family. His few assets barely sufficed to pay off his debts. And since her husband's imprisonment, Madame Fouquet has been abandoned by everyone. Your Majesty's hand strikes as powerfully as the hand of God. When the Good Lord sends a family the curse of leprosy or pestilence, other people flee and steer clear of the patient's home. Now and then, though very seldom, a generous physician dares to approach the accursed threshold alone, to cross it undauntedly, and risk his life in the battle against death. The physician is the final resource of the dying man; he is the instrument of celestial mercy. Sire, we beg you, kneeling with our hands joined as one pleads with God! Madame Fouquet has no friends left, no support. She weeps in her poor, deserted house, forsaken by all the people who thronged their door when her husband was in favor. She has no credit, no hope. The unhappy target of your anger, guilty as he is, receives your bread, which is moistened daily by his tears. But Madame Fouquet, as afflicted as her husband and more destitute; Madame Fouquet, who had the honor of receiving Your Majesty at her table; Madame Fouquet, the spouse of Your Majesty's former superintendent of finances—Madame Fouquet has no bread!"

Here the deathly hush curbing the breath of Pellisson's two friends was disrupted by a burst of moans; and d'Artagnan, his chest crumpling as he listened to that humble plea, turned toward the corner of the room to freely chew his mustache and repress his sighs.

The king had preserved his dry eyes, his severe face; but his cheeks had flushed, and his self-assurance diminished visibly. "What do you wish?" he asked, deeply moved.

"We have come to humbly ask Your Majesty," said Pellisson, gradually overwhelmed by his emotions, "to permit us, without our incurring his displeasure, to lend Madame Fouquet two thousand pistoles that we have gathered among all her husband's former friends so that the widow may not lack the barest necessities of life."

At the word "widow," uttered by Pellisson though Fouquet was alive, the king blanched as white as a ghost. His pride fell, heartfelt pity reached his lips. He gazed tenderly at all these men sobbing at his feet.

"God forbid," he replied, "that I confuse the innocent with the guilty! People do not know me if they doubt my mercy toward the weak. I will never strike anyone but the arrogant. Go ahead, gentlemen, do whatever your hearts advise to relieve Madame Fouquet's misery. Go ahead, gentlemen, go!"

The three men rose silently, their eyes arid. Their tears had dried in the burning contact with eyelids and cheeks. The supplicants didn't even have the strength to thank the king, who, however, cut short their solemn reverence by suddenly retrenching behind his armchair.

D'Artagnan remained alone with the king. "Fine," he said, approaching the young ruler, who peered at him quizzically. "Fine, my master! If you didn't have the watchword that adorns your sun, I would offer one that would be rendered into Latin by Monsieur Conrart: 'Gentle to the meek, harsh to the strong'!"

The king smiled and stepped into the next room, after saying to d'Artagnan, "I grant you the furlough you probably need to put the affairs of your friend, the late Monsieur du Vallon, into order."

55
Porthos's Will

Mourning ruled Pierrefonds. The courtyards were deserted, the stables closed, the flower beds neglected. In the fountains, the jets, once so bright, bubbly, and glistening, petered out on their own. Around the castle, several grave people on mules or nags trotted along the roads. They were country neighbors, priests, bailiffs of neighboring estates.

They all silently entered the castle, handing their mounts to a mournful groom, and, conducted by a footman in black, they stepped into the great hall, where Mousqueton greeted them at the threshold. Mousqueton had lost so much weight in the past few days that his clothes dangled like an oversized sheath in which a sword bobs around. His face, a blotch of red and white like Van Dyck's Madonna, was furrowed by two silvery streams digging into his cheeks, which had once been full, but were now flabby with grief.

With each new visitor, Mousqueton found fresh tears, and it was pitiful seeing him squeeze his throat with his big hand to keep from blubbering. These people were gathering to attend the reading of Porthos's last will and testament. Inspired by greed or friendship, they wanted to be present since the deceased had left no relative. They took their seats as they came in, and the door of the great hall was shut just before the clock struck noon, the time scheduled for the reading.

Porthos's attorney, quite naturally Monsieur Coquenard's successor, began by slowly unrolling the vast parchment on which Porthos's powerful hand had inscribed his supreme wishes. The seal was broken, the glasses were put on, the preliminary coughing was heard—and everyone lent an ear. Mousqueton was huddling in a corner the better to weep, the lesser to hear.

All at once, the two-winged door, which had been closed, was opened as if by some miracle, and a male figure appeared on the threshold, resplendent in the dazzling sunshine.

It was d'Artagnan. Arriving alone and finding no one to hold his stirrup, he had tied up his horse and was announcing himself.

The splendid daylight bursting into the hall, the murmuring of the visitors, and, more than that, the instinct of a faithful dog wrenched Mousqueton out of his reverie. He raised his head, recognized his employer's old friend, and, howling with grief and watering the floor with his tears, he embraced d'Artagnan's knees. The captain lifted up the poor steward and hugged him like a brother. Then, after nobly greeting the visitors, who all bowed while whispering his name, he sat down at the far end of the sculpted-oak hall. He still held the hand of Mousqueton, who, suffocating, settled on the steps.

Now the attorney, who was as deeply moved as the others, began to read the will.

After a thoroughly Christian avowal of his faith, Porthos asked his enemies to forgive him for any wrong he may have caused them.

During the reading of this paragraph, a ray of inexpressible pride shone in d'Artagnan's eyes. He remembered the old soldier. He then counted up the number of foes struck down by that valiant hand, and he mused that Porthos had been wise enough not to go into detail about his enemies or the wrongs he had done them: the chore would have been too harsh for the reader.

Now came the following enumeration:

> At present I possess by the grace of God:
>
> 1. The domain of Pierrefonds—lands, woods, meadows, bodies of water, forests—surrounded by strong walls.
>
> 2. The domain of Bracieux—castle, forests, tillable lands, forming three farms.
>
> 3. The small estate of Vallon [valley], so named because it lies in the valley.
>
> Decent Porthos!
>
> 4. Fifty farms in Touraine, covering a total of five hundred acres.
>
> 5. Three mills on the Cher, each yielding six hundred pounds.
>
> 6. Three ponds in Berry, each yielding two hundred pounds.
>
> As for my movable goods, so named because they can move, as so well explained by my knowledgeable friend, the Bishop of Vannes . . .

D'Artagnan shuddered upon gloomily recalling that name. The attorney continued imperturbably:

> They consist of:
>
> 1. Furnishings that I will not itemize for lack of space and that fill all my castles and houses; however, my steward has drawn up a complete list.

All eyes turned toward Mousqueton, who was still overwhelmed with grief.

> 2. Twenty saddle and draft horses, especially in my castle in Pierrefonds; their names are: Bayard, Roland, Charlemagne, Pépin, Dunois, La Hire, Ogier, Samson, Milon, Nemrod, Urgande, Armide, Faistrade, Dalila, Rebecca, Yolande, Finette, Grisette, Lisette, and Musette.

3. Sixty dogs, forming six packs, divided as follows: the first for stags, the second for wolves, the third for boars, the fourth for rabbits, and two others for arresting and guarding.

4. War and hunting weapons locked up in my weapons gallery.

5. My Anjou wines, chosen for Athos, who loved them; my Burgundies, Champagnes, Bordeaux, and my Spanish wines, filling eight storerooms and twelve cellars in my various homes.

6. My paintings and statues, which are supposedly very valuable and which are numerous enough to cause eyestrain.

7. My library of six thousand brand-new volumes that have never been opened.

8. My silverware, which may be slightly worn, but which must weigh one thousand or twelve hundred pounds, for I could scarcely lift the coffer containing it, and I could not manage to carry it around the room more than six times.

9. All those objects, plus my house linen and table linen, are distributed throughout the homes that I loved best.

Here the reader halted to catch his breath. Everyone sighed, coughed, and refocused. The attorney resumed:

I lived without having children, and I most likely will never have any, which pains me deeply. I am mistaken, however, for I do have a son in common with my friends; that son is Monsieur Raoul-Auguste-Jules de Bragelonne, the true son of Monsieur the Count de La Fère.

This young lord strikes me as worthy of succeeding my friends, the three valiant noblemen, whose very humble servant I remain.

At this moment, there was a sharp clatter. It was d'Artagnan's sword, which, slipping from his belt, had banged on the resonant floor. All eyes turned in that direction, and the viewers saw that a huge tear had rolled from d'Artagnan's thick eyelash to his aquiline nose, its luminous bridge shining like a crescent in blazing sunlight.

That is why I have left all my worldly goods, movables and immovables, as included in the above tally, to Monsieur the Viscount

Raoul-Auguste-Jules de Bragelonne, the son of Monsieur the Count de La Fère, to console him for the grief that he appears to suffer and to enable him to gloriously bear his name.

A long murmur passed through the audience.

The attorney went on, supported by d'Artagnan's flaming eyes, which, subduing the listeners, restored the disrupted silence.

On condition that Monsieur the Viscount de Bragelonne give Monsieur the Chevalier d'Artagnan, captain of the king's musketeers, whatever the Chevalier d'Artagnan asks him of my property.

On condition that Monsieur the Viscount de Bragelonne render a good pension to my friend, Monsieur d'Herblay, if the latter needs to live in exile.

On condition that Monsieur the Viscount de Bragelonne support all my servants who have been in my employ for at least ten years and that he pay five hundred pounds to each of the others.

I bequeath to my steward Mousqueton my entire wardrobe of town, war, and hunting garments, a total of forty-seven suits, which I am certain he will wear out for the love and memory of myself.

Furthermore, I bequeath to Monsieur the Viscount de Bragelonne my old retainer and loyal friend Mousqueton, already named, on condition that the above-named Viscount de Bragelonne will treat him in such a way that, when Mousqueton dies, he will never have stopped being happy.

Upon hearing those words, Mousqueton bowed, pale and trembling. His broad shoulders heaved convulsively; his face, marked by terrifying sorrow, emerged from his frozen hands; and the visitors saw him flounder and hesitate as if he wanted to get out but didn't know the way.

"Mousqueton, my good friend," said d'Artagnan, "leave this hall and go and make your preparations. I'll take you to Athos, whom I'll visit after leaving Pierrefonds."

Mousqueton didn't respond. He was barely breathing, as if from now on everything in this hall was to be alien to him. He opened the door and slowly vanished.

The attorney finished reading, after which most of the disappointed but respectful visitors, who had come to hear Porthos's final wishes, scattered to the four winds.

As for d'Artagnan, who remained alone after receiving the attorney's ceremonial reverence, the captain admired the profound wisdom of the deceased: Porthos had so judiciously distributed his possessions among the worthiest and most needful; and no one among the finest courtiers and noblest hearts could have revealed such perfect delicacy.

In asking Raoul de Bragelonne to give d'Artagnan anything he'd request, our worthy Porthos knew that d'Artagnan would request nothing. And even if he did ask for something, nobody but himself could say what. Porthos bequeathed a pension to Aramis, who, if inclined to demand too much, would be held back by d'Artagnan's example. And as for the word "exile," tossed out so casually, wasn't it the gentlest and most exquisite critique of Aramis's conduct, which had caused Porthos's death?

Finally, the testament didn't mention Athos at all. Could Porthos have assumed that the son wouldn't offer his father the lion's share? With his rough mind, Porthos had judged all these matters, grasped all these nuances—better than law, better than custom, better than taste.

Porthos had a heart, mused d'Artagnan with a sigh. And he seemed to hear a groan from the ceiling. He instantly thought of that poor Mousqueton, who needed to forget his pain. D'Artagnan therefore hurried in search of the worthy steward, who didn't return to the hall. The captain mounted the stairs leading to the next floor. Upon reaching Porthos's chamber, d'Artagnan saw a mound of suits in all colors and materials, where Mousqueton had lain down after piling them up. It was the legacy for the loyal friend. Those garments were certainly his, they had been given to the steward. His hand stretched out over these relics, which he showered with kisses, burying his entire face in them and covering them with his entire body.

D'Artagnan went over to console the poor man. "My God! He's not budging. He's fainted!"

D'Artagnan was wrong: Mousqueton was dead.

Dead like a dog who, after losing his master, goes and dies on his garments.

56
Athos's Old Age

While all these events forever separated the four musketeers, who had once been tied with seemingly indissoluble bonds, Athos, remaining alone after Raoul's departure, starting paying his tribute to the anticipated death that is called the absence of the people we love. Returning to his home in Blois, Athos didn't even have Grimaud to offer him a meager smile when Athos passed across the flower beds. And from day to day he witnessed the growing feebleness of his constitution, which had always struck him as invincible.

Old age, which had been kept at bay by the presence of the beloved object, was arriving with its convoy of afflictions and inconveniences, which goes on growing the more it waits. Athos no longer had his son, who had compelled him to hold his body straight and his head erect, to provide a good example. Athos no longer had a young man's shining eyes, an ever-burning hearth in which his eyes could keep regenerating their fire. And then, it must be said, his nature, exquisite in its reserve and tenderness, found nothing to hold back its emotional outbursts; and so it yielded to grief with the full impetus of a vulgar character giving itself up to joy.

The Count de La Fère, still youthful at the age of seventy, the warrior who had preserved his strength despite his bouts of fatigue, his mind still fresh despite his misfortunes, his body and soul still gentle and serene despite Milady, despite Mazarin, despite Mademoiselle de la Vallière—within a week, Athos, upon losing the support of his latter-day youth, had become an old man.

Still handsome but bent, noble but sad, mild and tottering under his white hair, he kept looking, despite his solitude, for the clearings where the sun penetrated the foliage along the garden paths. When Raoul was gone, Athos stopped doing the powerful exercises he had practiced all his life. The servants, accustomed to seeing him rise at the crack of dawn in all seasons, were amazed to hear the clock strike seven on a summer morning and their master was still in bed. Athos lay there, with a book under his bolster, but he neither slept nor read. Reclining to avoid carrying his body, he let his soul and his mind escape his flesh and focus on his son or on God.

At times the servants were horrified to see him spending long hours absorbed in mute and insensible reveries. He no longer heard the footsteps of the frightened valet, who appeared at the threshold to watch his master sleep or wake up. Athos might forget that the day was half over, that it was past his two first meals. So the valet woke him up. His master then rose, went down to his shaded path, and briefly emerged in the sunlight as if to share a minute of its warmth with his absent son. The lugubrious stroll recommenced until the worn-out father regained his bedroom, his bed—his favorite domicile.

For several days, the count had not uttered a single word. He refused to meet with visitors, and, at night, the servants saw him rekindle his lamp and devote many hours to writing or to leafing through parchments.

Athos wrote a letter to Vannes, another to Fontainebleau; there was no response to either. It was obvious why not. Aramis had left France; d'Artagnan was en route from Nantes to Paris, from Paris to Pierrefonds. Athos's valet noticed that his master's strolls were getting shorter day by day. The grand avenue of lindens might now be too long for his legs, which, in the past, had walked the entire length a thousand times a day. They saw the count struggling to reach the central trees, where he settled on a mossy bank that cut into a lateral path. There he waited for the renewal of his strength, or, rather, the arrival of night.

Soon, a hundred paces drained him fully. Eventually, he no longer wished to rise. He refused all food, and his servants were horrified. Although he never complained, although he usually had a smile on his lips, although he continued speaking in his soft voice, the servants went to Blois to find the physician of the late king's younger brother and bring him back. In this way, the physician could see the count without being seen by him. They placed him next door to the patient and begged the doctor not to reveal his presence; they were scared of displeasing their master, who hadn't asked for a healer.

The doctor obeyed. Athos was something like a paragon for

the local aristocrats. The residents of the province boasted of possessing this sacred survivor of the old French glories. Athos was quite a grand lord compared with these nobles whom the king had created by letting his young and fertile scepter touch the dried-out trunks of the heraldic trees of the area.

As we have said, people loved and respected Athos. And the doctor couldn't bear to watch the servants crying and the canton's paupers flocking around the count, whose alms and kind words had always sustained their lives and consoled them. The doctor, from his hiding place, therefore examined the symptoms of this mysterious illness, which, from day to day, buckled and devoured more and more lethally a man who had always been full of life and joie de vivre. In his scrutiny, the doctor noticed that Athos's cheeks were purple with a fever that kindled itself and nourished itself, a slow, pitiless fever born in some fold in the heart, hiding behind that rampart, growing from the agony it triggers, and both cause and effect of a perilous situation.

As we have said, the count spoke to no one, not even himself. His mind feared noise, and it reached that degree of overexcitement that borders on ecstasy. When a man is that deeply absorbed, he may not yet belong to God, but he certainly no longer belongs to the earth.

The doctor spent a few hours studying that painful battle between willpower and a superior force. He was frightened by those gaping eyes that were always attached to an invisible goal. He was frightened by the even beating of the heart, which never released a sigh. Sometimes a sharpness of pain is the physician's hope.

Half a day dragged by. The doctor bravely and firmly made up his mind. He suddenly emerged from his retreat and went straight to Athos, who saw him without showing more surprise than if he had understood nothing about the doctor's visit.

"Forgive me, Count," said the doctor, approaching the patient with outspread arms, "but I have something to reproach you for. Please hear me out." And he sat down by Athos's pillow, while the patient struggled to overcome his preoccupation.

"What is it, Doctor?" asked the count after a brief hush.

"You're sick, monsieur, and yet you refuse treatment."

"Me? Sick?" Athos smiled.

"Fever, consumption, feebleness—you're wasting away, Count!"

"Feebleness? Is that possible? I don't get up."

"Come on, come on, Count! Don't play games with me—you're a good Christian."

"I think so."

"Are you trying to kill yourself?"

"Never, Doctor."

"Well, monsieur, you're going to die. If you won't do anything about it, you'll be committing suicide. Recover, monsieur, recover!"

"From what? I've never felt better in my life, the sky has never looked so beautiful, I've never taken care of my flowers more tenderly."

"Something is secretly gnawing at you."

"Secretly? . . . By no means. . . . I miss my son. That's my whole illness, Doctor, and it's no secret."

"Monsieur, your son is alive, he's strong, he's facing the future of men of his merit, his breed. Live for him. . . ."

"I *am* living! Oh, don't worry," Athos added with a melancholy smile. "As long as Raoul lives, everyone will know that I'm alive, for as long as he lives I will live."

"What are you saying?"

"It's very simple. At this moment, Doctor, my life is suspended within me. A dissipated, forgetful, indifferent life would go beyond my strength, now that Raoul has left. You don't ask a lamp to burn when the spark hasn't ignited the flame. And don't ask me to live amid noise and light. I'm vegetating, I'm preparing, I'm waiting. Listen, Doctor, do you remember those soldiers whom we've seen so often at the gates when they were waiting to set sail? They were lying down, indifferent, half in one element, half in the other. They were neither in the place where the sea would carry them nor in the place where the land would doom them. Their bags were packed, their minds tense, their eyes fixed—those men were waiting. I repeat that last word, it sums up my present life. I'm lying down like those soldiers, my ears are alert for those noises that reach me; I want to be ready to leave at the first call. What will call me? Life or death? God or Raoul? My bags are packed, my soul is prepared, I am waiting for the signal. . . . I am waiting, Doctor, waiting!"

The physician was familiar with the cast of Athos's mind. He appreciated the solidity of that body. After reflecting for a moment, he saw that words were useless, remedies absurd, and he departed after exhorting the servants not to leave Athos alone for even a second. When the doctor was gone, the count was neither angry nor resentful about the disturbance. He didn't even ask his servants to promptly bring him any letters that arrived. He knew perfectly well that any distraction was a joy, a hope that his servants would have given their life's blood to procure for him.

Athos now got little sleep. Lost in thought, he forgot himself for a few hours, at most, in an obscure and profound reverie that other people would have called a dream. This momentary repose made him forget his body and fatigued his soul. For he lived a twofold life during those spiritual wanderings. One night, he dreamed that Raoul was dressing in a tent, preparing to go on an expedition led by the Duke of Beaufort himself. The young man was sad; he slowly fastened his cuirass, he slowly put on his sword.

"What's wrong?" his father inquired tenderly.

"I'm haunted by our good friend Porthos's death. I suffer here from the grief that you will feel over there."

And the vision disappeared with Athos's slumber.

At daybreak, a footman entered his master's bedroom and handed him a letter from Spain.

Aramis's handwriting, the count mused. And he read.

"Porthos is dead!" he cried after the first few lines. "Oh, Raoul! Raoul! Thank you! You've kept your promise: you've warned me!"

And seized with a deadly sweat, Athos fainted in his bed, felled purely by his weakness.

57
Athos's Vision

Upon coming to again, the count, almost ashamed of being stricken by that supernatural event, threw on his clothes and asked for a horse. He was determined to reach Blois and correspond more soundly with Africa, with d'Artagnan, and with Aramis.

Indeed, Aramis's letter apprised the count of the failure of the Belle-Île expedition. It also supplied enough details of Porthos's death to move our tender and devoted Athos to the very core of his being. Athos therefore wanted to pay a first visit to Porthos's grave site. In order to pay that honor to his former comrade-in-arms, Athos planned to notify d'Artagnan and get him to repeat the painful trip to Belle-Île. The two friends would go on the sad pilgrimage to the tomb of the giant whom they had loved so deeply; and Athos would then return home to obey the secret influence that was leading him to eternity along mysterious roads.

The joyful servants dressing their master were delighted to see him prepare for a voyage that would dissipate his melancholy. But no sooner was the count ready, and no sooner was the gentlest horse in his stable saddled and led to the perron than Athos's mind swam, his legs buckled, and he realized he couldn't possibly walk another step. He asked to be taken to the sunlight and he stretched out on a mossy bank, where he spent a good hour recovering his spirits.

Nothing was more natural than his feebleness after his inert rest of the past few days. He sipped a cup of bouillon to gather his energy and he wet his parched lips with his favorite wine, that old Anjou wine that Porthos had mentioned in his admirable will. Next, with his mind free and comforted, Athos called for his horse; but he needed help in his painful effort to mount.

He didn't ride even a hundred paces: he began shuddering at the turning of the road.

"That's odd," he said to his valet, who was accompanying him.

"Let's stop, monsieur, I beg you," replied the faithful servant. "You're white as a sheet!"

"That won't prevent me from taking my trip now that I've set out!" And he slackened the reins.

Suddenly, however, the animal, instead of obeying his master, halted. A gesture that Athos failed to notice had checked the bit. "Something doesn't want me to advance. Support me," he added, stretching out his arms. "Hurry! Come back! I feel all my muscles relaxing, I'm about to tumble off my horse."

The servant had seen his master's gesture just as he received the order. He dashed over and caught the count in his arms. They hadn't gone far enough for the other servants, who were at the threshold, not to perceive the confusion in the count's normally regular gait. The valet appealed to his comrades with his voice and his gestures, and the onlookers came rushing over.

Scarcely had Athos gone several paces toward the house than he felt better. His vigor seemed reborn, and he again wanted to forge ahead to Blois. Remounting his horse, he made it turn around. But at its first movement, he relapsed into that state of torpor and anguish.

"Well, it's obvious that I'm supposed to remain at home," he murmured.

His servants approached him, they helped him down, and they swiftly carried him to the house. Everything was soon prepared in his chamber, and they put him to bed.

"Be sure to remember," he told them as he was about to nod off, "that I'm expecting some letters from Africa to arrive today."

"Monsieur will no doubt be happy to learn that Blaisois's son has ridden out to gain an hour over the Blois courier," the valet answered.

"Thank you," said Athos, smiling kindly.

He drifted off; his anxious sleep resembled suffering. The servant watching over him noticed several expressions of mental torture. Perhaps the count was dreaming.

The day dragged on. Blaisois's son returned; the courier had brought no news. The count desperately calculated the minutes. He shuddered when those minutes formed an hour. At one point, he felt as if he'd been forgotten, and an atrocious pain cut through his heart.

No one in the house expected the courier to arrive. His hour had passed long ago. The express messenger was dispatched to Blois four times but returned empty-handed. Athos knew that the courier arrived only once a week. So he would have to endure seven agonizing days. He began the night with that tormenting thought. During the first few hours of that horrible night, Athos heaped up all the gloomy suppositions that a patient, irritated by suffering, can add to his dismal assumptions.

His fever rose. It invaded his chest, where the fire soon caught, as diagnosed by the physician who'd been brought back from Blois by Blaisois's son on his last trip. Soon the fever reached the count's head. The doctor performed two successive bleedings, which relieved the fever but weakened the patient and left him with the strength of action only in his brain. Nevertheless, the dreadful fever had dropped. Its final throbbings besieged his rigid extremities. By the stroke of midnight, it stopped altogether.

Noting the obvious improvement, the doctor left for Blois after ordering some prescriptions and declaring that the count was saved.

Now a bizarre, indefinable mental state began for Athos. His mind, set free, focused on his beloved son. The count's imagination showed him the fields of Africa around Gigelli, where the Duke de Beaufort must have landed with his army. There were gray rocks, parts of them stained green by the sea when its gales and tempests whipped the beach. Beyond the shores, with their scattered tomblike rocks, something like a townlet, filled with smoke, hectic noise, and frightened tumult, rose like an amphitheater among the cactuses and mastic trees.

All at once, the smoke released a flame, which, creeping along the ground, enveloped the whole townlet. Growing little by little, its red whirlwinds devoured cries, tears, arms stretching toward the sky. For a moment, there was a dreadful hurly-burly of crumbling beams, twisted blades, scorched rocks, charred and vanished trees.

It was odd: in this chaos, where Athos managed to distinguish arms, shouts, moans, sighs, he couldn't discern a single human figure.

The cannon boomed in the distance, the muskets crackled, the sea bellowed, the herds bounded across the slopes, fleeing the batteries of cannon: no mariner helped the maneuver of this fleet, no shepherd helped the flocks.

After the ruin of the village and the destruction wrought, magically, with no human involvement whatsoever, the flame went out, the smoke swept upward, then thinned out, grew pale, and evaporated completely. The night set in—a night that was opaque on the earth and brilliant in the firmament. The huge, blazing stars, scintillating in the African sky, shone without illuminating anything around them.

A long hush ensued, allowing Athos's troubled imagination to relax for a moment. And sensing that what he was seeing was not yet terminated, he focused most intently on the strange spectacle produced by his imagination.

The spectacle soon continued for him.

A soft, pale moon rose behind the coastal slopes, streaking the wavy folds of the sea, which now seemed calm after bellowing throughout Athos's vision. The moon attached its opals and diamonds to the bushes and brambles of the hills. The gray rocks, like so many silent and attentive phantoms, seemed to lift their greenish heads to examine the battlefield in the moonlight. And Athos realized that this field, entirely empty during the combat, was now bristling with corpses.

An inexpressible shudder of dread and terror overwhelmed his soul when he recognized the blue-and-white uniforms of the troops of Picardy, their long pikes with blue handles and their musket butts with the fleur-de-lys.

He saw all the cold wounds gaping at the azure sky as if to demand the return of the souls that they had sent to heaven. He saw the morbid, disemboweled horses, their tongues dangling out, their bodies sleeping in the frozen blood around them, the blood that soiled their manes and their cloth coverings. He saw the duke's white horse stretched out, its head shattered, at the front rank on the field of corpses.

When Athos saw all those things, he passed his cold hand

across his forehead and he was amazed to find that it wasn't burning. He was trying to convince himself that for an onlooker without fever, this was the day after a battle fought on the shores of Gigelli by the French expedition. He had seen the army leave the French coast and disappear over the horizon, and, in mind and in gesture, he had saluted the final gleam of the cannon-shot that the duke had sent as a farewell to his country.

Who could depict the mortal agony with which the count's soul, like a vigilant eye, peered at the corpses one by one, trying to learn whether Raoul might be sleeping among them? Who could repress the divine and intoxicating joy with which Athos bowed to God and thanked Him because the father did not find his son, whom he had been seeking so fearfully among the dead?

And, indeed, fallen in their ranks, frozen stiff, all these corpses, easy to recognize, seemed to turn to the count, complaisantly and respectfully, the better to be viewed during his funereal inspection.

Nevertheless, seeing all these corpses, he was astonished that he couldn't spot any survivors. He was so deeply absorbed in his vision that it became a real journey for him, undertaken by the father to obtain more precise information about the son. Worn out from having crossed so many oceans and continents, he tried to rest in one of the tents sheltered behind a rock and topped by the white fleur-de-lys pennant. He looked for a soldier who could take him to the duke's tent. Then, gazing across the plain in all directions, he saw a white shape appear behind the resinous myrtles.

This figure was dressed in an officer's uniform and was clutching a broken sword. It slowly advanced toward Athos, who, suddenly halting and staring at the figure, did not speak and did not stir. The count wanted to open his arms because he recognized that pale and silent officer: it was Raoul. The father tried to cry out, but his cry was stifled in his throat. Putting his finger to his lips and slowly withdrawing, though Athos could not see his legs moving, Raoul indicated that the count should remain silent.

More pallid than his son and trembling harder, the count followed his son, painfully trudging through bushes and heather, rocks and ditches. Raoul didn't seem to touch the ground, and no obstacle interfered with the lightness of his gait.

The count, worn out by the rugged terrain, soon stopped short; he was drained. Raoul continued to signal him that he should follow. The tender father, reactivated by love, made one final effort: he climbed the hill, following the young man, who drew him along with his gesture and his smile. Finally, he reached the top, and there he saw Raoul's airy, poetic figure, which stood out black against the lunar whiteness of the horizon. On that plateau, Athos held out his hand toward his beloved son, who likewise extended his. Suddenly, however, as if the young man had been swept away, retreating despite himself, he wafted upward, and the clear sky shone between his feet and the peak of the hill. He rose imperceptibly in the void, drifting toward the heavens, still smiling, still gesturing.

Athos cried out, tender and frightened. Looking down, he spotted a destroyed camp and, like motionless atoms, all those white corpses of the royal army. And then, raising his head, he saw Raoul, who was still gesturing, inviting his father to rise with him.

58
The Angel of Death

Athos was fully absorbed in his marvelous vision when the spell was abruptly broken by a loud noise from outside the gates of the house. A horse was galloping over the hardened sand of the main garden avenue, and the sounds of the most clamorous and most animated conversations rose all the way to the chamber of the dreaming count.

The count didn't budge. He barely glanced at the door in order to identify those sounds. Heavy footsteps came up the perron. The horse, which had been racing so swiftly, now slowly headed toward the stable. Shivers accompanied the steps, which gradually approached Athos's chamber. Then a door opened, and Athos, turning toward the noise, exclaimed feebly, "It's a courier from Africa, isn't it?"

"No, monsieur." The voice made Raoul's father tremble on his bed.

"Grimaud!" he murmured. And the sweat began to slide down his emaciated cheeks.

Grimaud appeared at the threshold. But he was no longer the Grimaud whom we have seen—once kept youthful by his courage and devotion, when he had been the first to jump into the boat that carried Raoul de Bragelonne to the vessels of the royal fleet. Now Grimaud was an old man, stern and pale, his clothes dusty, his meager hair whitened by the years. He trembled as he leaned against the door frame, and he nearly collapsed upon seeing his master's face in the distant lamplight.

Those two men had coexisted on and on, in a profound rapport, and their eyes, accustomed to terseness, had always conversed silently about so many things. These two old friends, equally noble in their hearts, albeit unequal in birth and fortune, now gazed at each other wordlessly. At a single glance, they had plumbed the depths of each other's hearts.

Grimaud's face was marked by a grief that already looked old and grimly familiar. His mind seemed to be filled with a single thought. As in former days, he refrained from speaking, he refrained from smiling.

With one glimpse, Athos read all the details on his loyal servant's face. And in the tone he had used when dreaming about his son, he said, "Grimaud, Raoul is dead, isn't he?"

Behind Grimaud, the other servants listened all atremble, their eyes glued to their master's bed. They heard the terrible question, which was followed by a dreadful hush.

"Yes," replied the old man with a hoarse sigh, tearing that monosyllable from his chest.

Lamentable voices arose, groaning immeasurably and filling the room with regrets and prayers, while the agonized father cast about for the portrait of his son. For the count, this was virtually the transition that returned him to his dream.

Without a cry, without a tear, patient, gentle, and resigned like a martyr, he peered upward again in order to see the sky above the mountain of Gigelli, to spot the dear shadow that had been floating away from him just as Grimaud had arrived.

Gazing at the sky as he resumed his wonderful dream, he must have followed the same paths he had taken in his both awful and lovely vision. For after half-shutting his eyes, he reopened them and smiled: he had just seen Raoul, who had smiled back at him.

With his arms crossed on his chest, his face turning toward the window, his body basking in the cool night air, which brought him the scents of flowers and forests, Athos, never to come back, lapsed into the contemplation of the paradise that the living never see.

God, no doubt, wanted to open the treasures of everlasting bliss for this chosen man, at a time when other men fear the severity of the Lord and cling to the life they know, dreading the other life that they glimpse in the grim and harsh torches of death.

Athos was guided by Raoul's pure and tranquil soul, which was carrying away his father's soul. For this just man, everything was perfume and melody on the rough path that is taken by souls returning to their celestial country. After an hour of this ecstasy, Athos softly raised his hands, which were as white as wax. The smile didn't leave his lips, and, almost inaudibly, he whispered three words to God, or to Raoul: "Here I am!" And his hands slowly dropped as if he himself had placed them on his bed.

For this noble person, death had been gentle and comfortable. It had spared him anguish and agony, the convulsions of the supreme departure. With a favorable hand, death had opened the gateway to eternity for this great soul, which merited all respect. God must have arranged this, so that the pious memory of this sweet death might linger in the hearts of its witnesses and in the minds of other men—a demise that would make the passage from this life to the next a lovable crossing for people whose existence on this earth creates no fear of the Last Judgment.

Even in his everlasting slumber, Athos retained that sincere and placid smile, an ornament that had to accompany him to his grave. Because of his peaceful features, his calm presence, the servants for a long while doubted that he was gone. They wanted to send away Grimaud, who, from a distance, was devouring that blanching face; Grimaud failed to approach the count because he piously feared that he might bring him the breath of final doom. But Grimaud, exhausted though he was, refused to leave. He sat down at the threshold and guarded his master with a sentinel's vigilance, intent on receiving the count's first look upon awakening or his last sigh upon succumbing.

The noises faded throughout the mansion, and each person respected the count's slumber. Grimaud, however, listening hard, realized that the count was no longer breathing. Propping his hands on the floor, Grimaud peered at his master, trying to ascertain even a quiver in the count's body.

Nothing! He was seized with dread. He got to his feet. And at that same instant, he heard someone rushing up the stairs. Spurs jingling against a sword—a familiar warlike sound—made him stop as he was approaching Athos's bed. A voice more vibrant than steel and copper resounded three paces away.

"Athos! Athos! My friend!" cried that tearful voice.

"Monsieur d'Artagnan," Grimaud stammered.

"Where is he?" asked the musketeer.

Grimaud grabbed d'Artagnan's arm with his bony fingers and pointed to the bed, its sheets already tinged by the corpse's livid hue. D'Artagnan's throat was filled with panting, the opposite of a sharp cry. Trembling, he tiptoed over, terrified by the sounds of his steps, his heart torn by a nameless anguish. He placed his ear on Athos's chest, facing the count's mouth. No sound, no breath. D'Artagnan backed away.

Grimaud, who had been watching him and for whom each movement had been a revelation, timidly settled at the foot of the bed and put his lips on the sheet that was raised by his master's stiff feet. And now large tears escaped his bloodshot eyes.

This despairing old man, bent, weeping, and speechless, presented the most moving sight that d'Artagnan had ever witnessed in his life, which had always been filled with emotions. The captain stood there, meditating in front of that smiling dead man, who seemed to have kept his final thought for the man he had loved the most after Raoul. The count appeared to be graciously welcoming d'Artagnan from the afterlife. And as if responding to this supreme flattery of hospitality, d'Artagnan kissed Athos's forehead and, with trembling fingers, he closed the count's eyes. Then he sat down by the count's pillow without fearing the corpse of this man who had been so tender and benevolent to him for thirty-five years. He avidly indulged in throngs of memories evoked by the count's noble face: some of these memories were charming and flowery, some bleak, gloomy, and icy like that face, whose eyes were shut for all eternity.

Suddenly, the bitter flood, which was rising minute by minute, burst into d'Artagnan's heart and shattered his chest. Incapable of mastering his emotions, he stood up, violently tearing himself from this chamber after finding his dead comrade, to whom he had wanted to bring the news of Porthos's death. The visitor's sobs were so heartrending that the servants, who seemed to be waiting only for an explosion of pain, responded with their lugubrious clamors; and the dogs likewise reacted with their lamentable howls.

Grimaud was the only person who didn't raise his voice. Even in his paroxysm of grief, he wouldn't have dared profane death or disturb his master's sleep. Athos, incidentally, had accustomed him never to speak.

At the crack of dawn, d'Artagnan, after wandering about in the low hall and biting his fists to squelch his sighs, ran back up the stairs. Waiting until Grimaud turned his head, d'Artagnan motioned him to come over, and the faithful servant obeyed, making no more noise than a shadow. D'Artagnan went down, followed by Grimaud.

In the vestibule, d'Artagnan took the old man's hands. "Grimaud, I saw how the father died, now tell me how the son died."

Reaching in his shirt, Grimaud produced a large letter bearing Athos's address. D'Artagnan, recognizing the Duke de Beaufort's handwriting, broke the seal and began to read. In the first rays of bluish daylight, d'Artagnan strode along the gloomy rows of ancient chestnut trees, which were marked by the still visible footsteps of the recently deceased count.

59
Bulletin

The Duke de Beaufort had written to Athos. The letter, meant for a living man, reached a corpse. The duke had the broad penmanship of an inept schoolboy:

My dear Count,

A great misfortune has struck us in the midst of a grand triumph. The king has lost one of his bravest soldiers. I have lost a friend. You have lost Monsieur de Bragelonne.

His death was glorious—so glorious that I do not have the strength to weep as I would like.

Please receive my sad compliments, my dear count. Heaven distributes our trials according to the greatness of our hearts. This greatness was immense, but not above your courage.

Your good friend,
THE DUKE DE BEAUFORT

This letter was accompanied by a report written by one of the duke's secretaries. It was the most touching and most truthful account of the lugubrious episode that had undone two lives. Although D'Artagnan's heart, accustomed to the emotions of battles, was armored against tenderness, he couldn't help shivering when reading Raoul's name, the name of that beloved child who had become a shadow like his father.

In the morning, Monseigneur the Duke commanded the attack. Normandy and Picardy had taken their positions among the gray rocks dominated by the mountain, with the bastions of Gigelli rising on the other side.

The cannon started to boom, opening the action; the regiments marched resolutely; the pikemen held up their pikes; the musket bearers clutched their weapons. The duke attentively watched the marches and movements of his troops, which he was ready to support with a powerful reserve.

Monseigneur was flanked by the oldest captains and his aides.

The Viscount de Bragelonne had been ordered not to leave His Grace's side.

However, the enemy cannon, which had at first thundered unsuccessfully against the masses, regulated its fire, and the most carefully aimed balls killed several men around the duke. The regiments, formed into columns and advancing toward the ramparts, were a bit maltreated. Our troops hesitated since they were poorly seconded by our artillery. Indeed, because of their positions, the batteries, which had been set up the previous day, fired weakly and uncertainly. The bottom-to-top direction interfered with their range and accuracy.

Monseigneur, grasping the harmfulness of the artillery's position in the siege, ordered the frigates moored broadside in the small roadstead to initiate a regular firing against the cannon. Monsieur de Bragelonne was the first to volunteer to convey this order. But Monseigneur refused to acquiesce.

And Monseigneur was right, for he loved this young aristocrat and wanted to spare him. It was a sound decision: the outcome justified the duke's foresight. No sooner had the sergeant, whom the duke had sent with his answer, reached the seashore than he was felled by two shots from the enemy's long blunderbusses. The sergeant collapsed on the sand, staining it with his blood.

Upon seeing this, Monsieur de Bragelonne smiled at Monseigneur, who said: "Well, Viscount, I've saved your life. Later on, you may report that to your father so that he may be grateful to me."

The young man smiled sadly and replied: "It's true, monseigneur, that without your benevolence I would have been killed on the spot where the poor sergeant fell, and I'd now be fast asleep."

His retort was so sharp that Monseigneur vividly replied: "Good God, young man! You seem to be yearning for death. But, by the soul of Henry IV, I promised your father that I'd bring you back alive, and, if it pleases the Lord, I'll keep my word."

Monsieur de Bragelonne reddened, and he murmured: "Monseigneur, forgive me, I beg you. I've always longed to take advantage of opportunities, and it's wonderful for a man to distinguish himself in front of his general, especially when that general is Monsieur the Duke de Beaufort."

Monseigneur calmed down a little, and, turning toward his officers, who were crowding around him, he issues various orders.

The grenadiers of the two regiments got close enough to the ditches and trenches to hurl their grenades, which, however, had little effect. Meanwhile, Monsieur d'Estrées, the commander of the fleet, having witnessed the sergeant's attempt to reach the vessels, realized that they had to fire without orders. The Arabs, struck by the fleet's cannonballs, and by the ruins and explosions of their rickety walls, cried out fearfully. Their horsemen, bent over their saddles, galloped down the mountain and dashed full tilt into the infantry columns, which crossed their pikes and checked their insane charge. Shoved back by the solid battalion, the furious Arabs threw themselves against our headquarters, which were unguarded at that moment.

The danger was immense. Monseigneur drew his sword. His secretaries and his men followed suit. The officers in his retinue launched into a battle with those raging enemies. Now Monsieur de Bragelonne could satisfy the urge he had shown since the start of this action. He fought near the duke with a Roman vigor and killed three Arabs with his small sword.

But it was obvious that his bravery was not rooted in the pride of all warriors. His courage was impetuous, affected, even forced. He was seeking the intoxication of mayhem and slaughter. He got so excited that Monseigneur ordered him to stop. He must have heard His Grace, for we heard him, we were at his sides. Nevertheless, Monsieur did not stop, he kept lunging toward the retrenchments.

Since Monsieur de Bragelonne was a thoroughly disciplined officer, everyone was shocked by his disobedience, and Monsieur de Beaufort shouted, twice as intensely: "Stop, Bragelonne! Where are you going? Stop! I order you to stop!"

All of us, imitating the duke, gave free rein. We expected the viscount to turn back. But he kept racing toward the palisades.

"Stop, Bragelonne," the duke repeated very loudly. "Halt, in your father's name!"

At those words, Monsieur de Bragelonne spun around, his

face expressing a keen grief. But he didn't stop. We figured that his horse had bolted.

When the duke realized that the viscount no longer controlled his mount, and that he had sped past the frontmost grenadiers, His Grace cried out: "Musketeers, kill his horse! A hundred pistoles to the man who kills his horse!"

But who could have shot the animal without hitting the horseman? No one dared to try. At last someone volunteered, a sharpshooter from the Picardy regiment. His name was Luzerne. He aimed, shot, and he must have hit the croup, for blood reddened the horse's white coat. But instead of collapsing, the accursed jennet galloped more frantically than ever.

Watching that unfortunate young man racing toward his death, the entire Picardy regiment yelled at the top of their lungs: "Jump off, monsieur! Jump off! Jump off!" (Monsieur de Bragelonne was extremely popular throughout the army.)

He had already come within firing range of the rampart. A volley wrapped him in fire and smoke. We lost sight of him. When the smoke dispersed, we saw him standing. His horse had just been killed. The Arabs shouted at the viscount to surrender. But he shook his head and kept striding toward the palisades. It was a fatal imprudence. Nevertheless, the entire French army was grateful to him for not backing away, for his misfortune had brought him so close to the enemy. He walked a few more paces, and both regiments applauded.

It was at this moment that a second discharge shook the walls, and the Viscount de Bragelonne vanished once more in the whirling smoke. But when it cleared this time, he was no longer on his feet. He lay there in the bushes, his head lower than his legs, and the Arabs were about to leave their entrenchments and cut off the viscount's head or carry off his corpse, as is customary among the infidels.

But the Duke de Beaufort had been watching all the time, and this dismal spectacle had torn deep and painful sighs from his heart. Seeing the Arabs running like phantoms among the mastic trees, he shouted: "Grenadiers, pikemen—are you going to let them grab that noble body?" Shouting those words and waving his sword, he dashed toward the foe. The regiments came rushing behind him, their hollering as dreadful as the Arabs' hollering was savage.

The combat began over Monsieur de Bragelonne's body, and it was so ferocious that one hundred sixty Arabs were killed next to at least some fifty of our own men. It was a Norman lieutenant who heaved the body over his shoulder and carried it back to our lines.

Meanwhile, our side was gaining. Our regiments took along the reserve and they devastated the enemy palisades. The Arabs stopped firing at three o'clock. The hand-to-hand fighting lasted two hours. It was a massacre. At five o'clock, we were victorious on all counts. The Arabs had abandoned their positions, and the duke planted the white flag on the top of the hill.

Now we could think about Monsieur de Bragelonne. His body had eight large wounds, and he had lost most of his blood. Nevertheless, he was still breathing, which brought ineffable joy to Monseigneur, who wanted to be present at the first dressing and the consultation with the surgeons. Two of the surgeons declared that Monsieur de Bragelonne would survive. The duke threw his arms around them and promised each doctor a thousand louis if they saved the viscount's life.

The viscount heard these joyful exclamations; and whether he felt desperate or was suffering from his injuries, his face revealed annoyance. This was surprising, especially for one of the secretaries when he heard the following.

The third surgeon was Brother Sylvain de Saint-Cosme, the most knowledgeable of our men. He examined the wounds but said nothing. Monsieur de Bragelonne opened his eyes and seemed to be interrogating the expert's every movement, his every thought. When questioned by Monseigneur, this surgeon replied that there were three fatal wounds among the eight. However, the viscount's constitution was so strong, his youth so powerful, and the Lord's goodness so endless, that the patient would recover—so long as he remained absolutely motionless.

Turning toward his assistants, the brother added: "Don't move him, not even a finger, or you'll kill him."

And we all left the tent with a smidgen of hope. The secretary thought he spotted a pale, sad smile flit across the viscount's lips when the duke told him in an affectionate voice: "Oh, Viscount! We're going to save you!"

But that evening, when we believed that the patient must have rested, one of the aides entered his tent and reemerged, yelling loudly. We rushed over with the duke, helter-skelter, and the aide showed us the viscount's body on the ground. He was bathing in the remainder of his own blood. He looked as if he had endured a convulsion, some feverish movement, and had tumbled off the bed. This fall had accelerated his end, according to Brother Sylvain's diagnosis.

They lifted up the viscount. He was cold and dead. His right hand, clutching a blond curl, was clenched over his heart.

Next came the details of the expedition and the victory over the Arabs. D'Artagnan halted at the account of poor Raoul. "Oh!" he murmured. "The unfortunate child! A suicide!" And turning his eyes toward the chamber where Athos was sleeping an eternal sleep, d'Artagnan murmured very softly: "They kept their promises to one another. And now they must be happy and they must be reunited." And he slowly trudged along the flower beds.

The entire road, the entire surroundings, were already filling up with grief-stricken neighbors, who were telling each other about the twofold catstrophe and preparing for the funeral.

60
The Final Canto of the Epic

The next day, all the nearby aristocrats, all those who resided in the province, or wherever the messengers had managed to bring the news, began arriving. D'Artagnan had remained in his room, unwilling to speak to anyone. Two overwhelming deaths after the demise of Porthos had struck down that usually indefatigable spirit. Aside from Grimaud, who entered the room just once, the musketeer received neither servants nor fellow diners. Given the hubbub in the house, the endless comings and goings, he figured that preparations were under way for the count's funeral. He wrote to the king asking for an extension of his furlough.

Grimaud, as we have said, had entered d'Artagnan's room once. He had settled on a stool near the door, like a man engrossed in meditation. Then, upon rising, he had signaled to d'Artagnan to follow him. D'Artagnan obeyed in silence. Grimaud went down to the count's bedroom, pointed to the empty bed, and eloquently raised his eyes toward the heavens.

"Yes," d'Artagnan responded, "yes, my good Grimaud. Near the son he loved so deeply."

Grimaud went to the hall, where, as was customary in the province, the body was laid out prior to being buried forever.

D'Artagnan was struck by the sight of the two open coffins. At Grimaud's mute invitation, the musketeer came over. In one coffin, he saw Athos, handsome even in death; and, in the other, he saw Raoul, his eyes closed, his cheeks pearly white like Pallas in Virgil's *Aeneid*, and a smile on his violet lips.

The musketeer shivered at seeing father and son, who, with their souls gone, were represented on earth by two bleak cadavers, unable to approach one another even though they were so close together.

"Raoul here!" d'Artagnan murmured. "Oh, Grimaud! You didn't tell me!"

Grimaud shook his head and didn't answer. However, taking d'Artagnan by the hand, he led him to the coffin and showed him, under the thin shroud, the black wounds that had slain him. The captain turned away, and, judging it useless to question Grimaud, who wouldn't respond, d'Artagnan recalled that the Duke de Beaufort's secretary had written more than he, d'Artagnan, had had the courage to read. Picking up once more the account of the engagement that had cost Raoul his life, d'Artagnan found the last paragraph of the letter:

> The duke ordered that the viscount's body be embalmed, as is the practice among the Arabs when they wish their bodies to be carried to their native soil. The duke then ordered the establishment of relays so that a confidential servant, who had raised the young man, might convey his coffin to the Count de La Fère.

And so, d'Artagnan mused, I will follow your funeral, my dear child—I, an old man; I, worthless on this earth. And I will spread dust on your forehead, which I kissed just two months ago. God wished it. You wished for it yourself. I don't have the right to weep any longer. You chose death. You felt it was preferable to life.

It finally arrived, the moment when those two noblemen were to be restored to the earth. There were so many soldiers and civilians that the town road was mobbed with black-clad riders and pedestrians heading toward the grave site in the plain. Athos had chosen as his final resting-place the small enclosure of a chapel that he had erected on the edge of his property. He had brought the stones, cut during 1550, of an old Gothic manor house in Berry that had sheltered him in his early youth.

The chapel, transported and reconstructed, stood out delightfully in a clump of poplars and sycamores. Mass was said there each Sunday by the priest from the next townlet, whom Athos had paid an annual sum of two hundred pounds. And all the roughly forty vassals of his domain, plus the plowmen and farmers with their families, attended mass there instead of having to go to the city.

Behind the chapel lay the enclosure, which was flanked by two big hedges of hazel, elder, and hawthorn and encircled by a deep ditch. Although uncultivated, this enclosure was joyful in its barrenness—because the moss grew high; because the wild heliotrope and ravenala mingled their perfumes; because a profuse wellspring, imprisoned in a marble cistern, flowed under the chestnut trees; and because the thyme all around was visited by thousands of bees from the neighboring plains, while the finches and robins sang wildly among the blossoms.

That was where the two coffins were brought amid a hushed and contemplative throng. The Office of the Dead was celebrated; the final farewells to the dead nobles were spoken; the visitors scattered along the roads, talking about the father's virtues and gentle death, and the hopes of the son and his sad demise on the African shores.

Little by little, the noise faded as did the lamps in the humble nave. The priest bowed one last time at the altar and the fresh graves. Then, followed by his assistant, who rang a rasping bell, the priest slowly trudged back to his rectory.

D'Artagnan, who remained alone, noticed the onset of night; lost in thought about the dead, he had failed to notice the time. He stood up from the oak bench, and, like the priest, he wanted to say his final farewell to his friends in the double grave.

A woman was praying, kneeling on that damp ground. D'Artagnan halted on the chapel threshold to avoid disturbing her, and also to identify the pious friend, who was fulfilling her sacred duty with so much zeal and perseverance. The unknown visitor was hiding her face in her hands, which were as white as alabaster. The noble simplicity of her clothes revealed a woman of distinction. Outside the chapel, a stagecoach and a few servants on horseback were waiting for her. D'Artagnan tried to figure out what was causing her delay.

She was still praying, and she often passed her handkerchief across her face. D'Artagnan understood that she was crying. She struck her chest with the pitiless compunction of a Christian. Several times he heard the cry of a shattered heart: "Forgive me! Forgive me!" She seemed totally absorbed in her grief as she threw herself down, almost fainting amid her prayers and laments.

Touched by her love for his friends, whom she mourned so deeply, d'Artagnan took several steps toward the grave, trying to interrupt the penitent's eerie dialogue with the dead. But no sooner had his foot crunched on the sand then the unknown visitor raised her head, revealing a tearstained face—a friend's face.

It was Mademoiselle de la Vallière.

"Monsieur d'Artagnan!" she whispered.

"You?" replied the captain in a somber voice. "You here? Oh, madame. I would much rather have seen you adorned with flowers in the count's manor house. You would have wept less, so would they, and so would I."

"Monsieur!" she sobbed.

"For it was you," said the pitiless friend of the dead, "it was you who sent those two men to their graves."

"Oh! Spare me!"

"God forbid that I should offend a woman or make her weep in vain. But I must tell you that the murderer has no place on the graves of his victims."

She tried to respond.

He spoke icily. "What I am saying to you here, I said to the king."

She clasped her hands. "I know that I have caused the death of the Viscount of Bragelonne."

"Ah, you know it?"

"The news reached the court yesterday. I set out at two A.M., covering forty leagues, to ask forgiveness from the count, who, I thought, was still alive, and to beg God, on Raoul's tomb, to send me all the inflictions I deserve—but one. Now, monsieur, I know that the son's death killed the father. I have two crimes to reproach myself for. I have two punishments to expect from God."

"Mademoiselle, I will repeat to you what Monsieur de Bragelonne told me in Antibes when he was already contemplating his death: 'If she was led astray by pride and flirtation, I forgive her while scorning her. But if she succumbed to love, I forgive her while swearing to her that no one else would ever have loved her as I do.' "

"You know," Louise broke in, "I was about to sacrifice myself for my love. You know that I was suffering so deeply when you found me lost, dying, abandoned. Well, I have never suffered as much as I'm suffering today, because previously I was hoping, I was wishing—but today I've got nothing left to wish for. This death has taken all my joy to the grave, and I dare not love now without remorse. I sense that the man I love—oh, it's the law—will torture me the way I've tortured others."

D'Artagnan didn't respond. He felt all too well that she wasn't mistaken.

"Well, dear Monsieur d'Artagnan! Do not strike me down today—I beg you. I am like a branch torn from a trunk. I no longer cling to anything in this world, and a torrent is sweeping me I don't know where. I'm madly in love, so madly that I have come to say it—impious as I am—on the remains of this man. And I'm not ashamed, I'm not remorseful. This love is a religion. Later on you will see me alone, forgotten, disdained.

You will see me punished. Therefore, spare me my ephemeral happiness. Let me have it for several days, for several minutes. It may no longer exist by now. My God! Perhaps this double murder is already expiated."

She was still speaking. The sounds of human voices made the captain prick up his ears. Monsieur de Saint-Aignan, an officer of the king, was coming for Mademoiselle de la Vallière. He'd been sent by the monarch, who, said the officer, was being devoured by jealousy and anxiety. Saint-Aignan didn't see d'Artagnan, who was half-concealed by a chestnut tree that was casting its shadow across the two graves. Louise thanked the officer and dismissed him with a gesture. He left the enclosure.

"You see, madame," the captain said bitterly, "that your happiness still endures."

The young woman stood up solemnly. "Someday you will repent your poor judgment. And on that day, monsieur, I will be the one to ask God to forget your injustice toward me. Furthermore, I will suffer so deeply that you will be the first to lament my suffering. Do not reproach me for this happiness, monsieur. It is costing me dearly, and I have not yet paid my full debt."

Saying those words, she knelt down gently and tenderly. "My fiancé, Raoul, forgive me one last time. I broke our chain. Both of us are doomed to die of love. You are the first to leave. Fear nothing, I will follow you. Only see that I haven't been a coward and that I have come to say my supreme good-bye. God is my witness, Raoul, that if my life could have redeemed yours, I would have given my life without hesitating. I could not give you my love. Once again, forgive me!"

She picked up a twig and thrust it into the earth. Then she wiped her tear-filled eyes, curtsied to d'Artagnan, and disappeared.

The captain watched them leave—the horses, the riders, and the coach. Then he crossed his arms on his swelling chest. "When will it be my turn to leave?" he said, deeply moved. "What is left for a man after youth, after love, after glory, after friendship, after strength, after wealth? . . . The rock under which Porthos is sleeping—Porthos, who possessed all those things; the moss under which Athos and Raoul are resting—

they who possessed even more." He hesitated for a moment, his eyes blank. Then he got to his feet. "Keep marching. When my time comes, God will tell me as He told the others."

His fingertips touched the earth, which was wet with evening dew. He crossed himself as if he'd been at a church font, and he headed in the direction of Paris. He was alone—alone forever.

Epilogue

Early one morning, four years after the scene we have just described, two well-mounted riders galloped across Blois. They were arranging everything for a fowling party that the king wanted to enjoy in that uneven and beautiful plain, which, divided by the Loire, borders on Meung on one side and Amboise on the other side. These two horsemen were the captain of the king's greyhounds and the governor of the falcons—two officers who were deeply respected during the reign of Louis XIII but were slightly neglected by his successor.

After reconnoitering the terrain and making their observations, they spotted tiny and scattered groups of soldiers whom the sergeants, at long intervals, were placing at the openings of enceintes. These soldiers were the king's musketeers.

Behind them the captain, riding a good horse, was recognizable because of his gold embroideries. He had gray hair and a salt-and-pepper beard. He seemed slightly bent even though he was handling his mount easily and peering all around, surveying the countryside.

"Monsieur d'Artagnan isn't growing old," said the captain of the greyhounds to his falconer. "He's ten years older than us, but he looks like a cadet on horseback."

"That's true," replied the captain of the falcons. "He hasn't changed in twenty years."

The captain was wrong. During the past four years, d'Artagnan had aged twelve years. Old age was imprinting its pitiless claws at each corner of his eyes. His forehead was bald. His hands, once brown and sinewy, were whitening as if the blood in them was starting to cool off.

D'Artagnan rode up to the two officers with the touch of affability that distinguishes superior men. In exchange for his courtesy, he received two respectful bows.

"Ah! How lucky to see you here, Monsieur d'Artagnan!" cried the falconer.

"It's really my pleasure to tell you that, gentlemen. For nowadays the king uses his musketeers more often than his birds."

"It's not like the good old days," sighed the falconer. "Do you remember, Monsieur d'Artagnan, when the late king flew his magpie in the vineyards beyond Beaugency? Damn it! Back then, you weren't the captain of the musketeers, Monsieur d'Artagnan."

"And you were only a junior officer for the tiercelets," d'Artagnan retorted playfully. "No matter. But those were the good old days, given that it's always the good old days when you're young.

"Good day, Captain of the Greyhounds."

"You honor me, Count."

D'Artagnan didn't respond. He wasn't struck by the title of count, which had been conferred on him four years ago.

"Aren't you worn out from your long trip, Captain?" the falconer went on. "It's two hundred leagues, isn't it, from here to Pignerol?"

"Two hundred sixty to go there, and the same to return," d'Artagnan said calmly.

"And is he all right?" the falconer whispered.

"Who?" asked d'Artagnan.

"Why, that poor Monsieur Fouquet," the falconer continued.

The captain of the greyhounds had prudently moved away.

"No," replied d'Artagnan. "The poor man is seriously afflicted. He doesn't understand that prison is a boon for him. He says that Parliament absolved him by banishing him, and that banishment is freedom. He fails to see that they had sworn to execute him, and that saving him from the clutches of Parliament was too much of an obligation to God."

"Ah, yes! The poor man narrowly escaped the scaffold," the falconer responded. "I hear that Monsieur Colbert had given the orders to the warden of the Bastille and that the execution was commanded."

"Enough!" said d'Artagnan pensively, cutting short the conversation.

"Enough!" repeated the captain of the greyhounds, coming back. "So Monsieur Fouquet is in Pignerol. He certainly deserves it. He was lucky to be conducted there by you—he stole enough from the king."

D'Artagnan glared at the captain. "If I'd been told that you'd eaten the meat of your dogs, not only wouldn't I believe it; but if you'd been condemned to the whip or to jail, I'd feel sorry for you, and I wouldn't permit anyone to bad-mouth you. However, monsieur, as honest as you may be, I assure you that you are no more honest than that poor Monsieur Fouquet."

After that harsh reprimand, the captain of His Majesty's greyhounds hung his head and let the falconer walk ahead with d'Artagnan.

"He's content," the falconer whispered to the musketeer. "It's obvious that greyhounds are in fashion nowadays. If he were a falconer, he wouldn't talk like that."

D'Artagnan smiled mournfully upon seeing that grand political issue resolved by the discontent of such a humble person. He mused for another moment about the superintendent's earlier good fortune, its collapse, and the grim death that awaited him. Then, by way of conclusion, he said, "Did Monsieur Fouquet like falconry?"

"Oh, passionately, monsieur," the falconer replied with a touch of bitter regret, and with a sigh that constituted the funeral oration for Fouquet.

D'Artagnan, ignoring one man's bad mood and the other man's sadness, continued his advance across the plain. Far in the distance, they saw the hunters at the entrances of the forest, the plumes of the equerries like shooting stars in the clearings, and the white horses, their luminous appearance cutting through the gloomy thickets of the copses.

"Are we in for a long hunt?" asked d'Artagnan. "Please give us a fast bird—I'm exhausted. Is it a heron or a swan?"

"Both, Monsieur d'Artagnan," said the falconer. "But don't

worry, the king isn't much of a hunter. He doesn't hunt for himself; he simply wants to entertain the ladies."

Those two words, "the ladies," were pronounced so strangely that d'Artagnan pricked up his ears. "Ah!" he said, eyeing the falconer with surprise.

The captain of the greyhounds smiled, no doubt to make up with the musketeer.

"Oh, go ahead, laugh!" said d'Artagnan. "I'm not up on the latest bulletins. I've just been gone for a month. When I left, the court was still mourning the queen mother's death. The king refused to enjoy himself after witnessing Anne of Austria breathe her last. But everything ends in this world. Well, he's no longer sad. So much the better!"

"And everything also begins," said the captain, guffawing broadly.

"Ah!" d'Artagnan repeated, eager to hear the news. But his dignity prevented him from questioning someone of a lower station. "So something is beginning, it seems?"

The captain of the greyhounds winked significantly. But d'Artagnan didn't want to find out anything from that man.

"Will we see the king at an early hour?" d'Artagnan asked the falconer.

"Why, at seven A.M., monsieur, I'll be releasing the birds."

"Who's coming with the king? How is his sister-in-law? How is the queen?"

"Better, monsieur."

"So she was ill?"

"Monsieur, Her Majesty has been unwell since her most recent grief."

"What grief? Don't be afraid to clue me in, my dear monsieur. I'm all ears."

"It appears that the queen, who's been slightly neglected since her mother-in-law's death, complained to the king. And he supposedly said: 'Don't I spend each night with you, madame? What more do you want?' "

"Ah!" said d'Artagnan. "Poor thing! She must hate Mademoiselle de la Vallière."

"Oh, no! Not Mademoiselle de la Vallière."

"Then who?"

The hunting horn interrupted them. It summoned the hounds and the birds. The falconer and his companion took off immediately, leaving d'Artagnan dangling. In the distance, the king appeared, surrounded by ladies and riders. The group ambled along in a leisurely and orderly way, with the various kinds of horns animating the hounds and the horses. It was a movement, a noise, a mirage of light, of which nothing now could give an idea except for the false majesty and meretricious opulence of a theatrical production. With slightly weakened eyes, d'Artagnan made out three carriages beyond the group; the first carriage was the queen's carriage—it was empty.

Since Mademoiselle de la Vallière was not at the king's side, d'Artagnan peered hard and found her in the second carriage. She was alone with two women, who seemed as bored as their mistress.

To the king's left, on a spirited mount reined in by a skillful hand, sat a startlingly beautiful woman. The king was smiling at her, and she was smiling at the king. People burst out laughing at anything she said.

I know that woman, the musketeer mused. Just who is she? And he leaned toward his friend, the falconer, and asked him.

The falconer was about to answer when the king noticed d'Artagnan: "Ah, Count! You're back! Why haven't I seen you?"

"Sire, Your Majesty was sleeping when I arrived, and you weren't yet awake when I began my service this morning."

"Always the same," the satisfied king exclaimed. "Have a good rest, Count, that's an order. You'll dine with me tonight."

A murmur of admiration enveloped d'Artagnan like an immense caress. Dining with the king was an honor that he did not lavish as Henry IV had done. The king took a few steps forward, and d'Artagnan was stopped by a new group, in the middle of which Colbert was shining.

"Good day, Monsieur d'Artagnan," said the minister with affable courtesy. "Did you have a good trip?"

"Yes, monsieur," said d'Artagnan, bowing over the neck of his horse.

"I heard the king invite you to dinner tonight. You'll find an old friend of yours."

"An old friend of mine?" D'Artagnan painfully dove into the gloomy waves of the past, which had swallowed so many friendships and hatreds.

"The Duke of Alameda, who arrived from Spain this morning," Colbert went on.

"The Duke of Alameda?" said d'Artagnan, cudgeling his brain.

"That's me!" cried an old, white-haired man. He sat bent in his carriage, which he ordered his servant to open so that he might go meet the musketeer.

"Aramis!" cried d'Artagnan, stupefied.

And, inert as it was, he let the old aristocrat's thin, trembling arm hang around the count's neck.

After a moment of silent observation, Colbert pushed his horse forward and left the two old friends to their private conversation.

"Well," said the musketeer, taking Aramis's hand, "you here—you, the exile, the rebel, in France?"

"And I'll be dining with you and the king." Aramis smiled. "Yes, you're wondering what use loyalty is in this world, aren't you? Listen, that's our poor Mademoiselle de la Vallière. Let her carriage roll by. Look how nervous she is. She's tearfully watching the king riding his horse over there!"

"With whom?"

"With Mademoiselle de Tonnay-Charente, who's become Madame de Montespan."

"So Mademoiselle de la Vallière is jealous—she's been cheated on?"

"Not yet, d'Artagnan, but she soon will be."

They chatted while following the hunt, and Aramis's coachman drove so skillfully that they arrived just as the falcon, swooping on the prey, forced it down and pounced on it. The king dismounted. So did Madame de Montespan. They had arrived at an isolated chapel concealed by large trees whose leaves had been stripped by the first autumn winds. In back of this chapel there was an enclosure with a latticed gate. The falcon had forced its prey to fall into that enclosure, and the king wanted to go there and pluck the first feather, according to custom.

The entire hunting party circled the chapel and the hedges, which were too small to admit all of them. D'Artagnan, holding back his friend, who wanted to step down and join the others, said tersely, "Aramis, do you know where chance has led us?"

"No."

"This is the resting-place for people whom I knew," said d'Artagnan, deeply moved by a sad memory.

Aramis had no idea who was meant. With quivering legs, he stepped into the chapel through a small door opened by d'Artagnan.

"Where are they buried?" asked Aramis.

"Out there, in the enclosure. There's a cross, you see, under that small cypress. The tree was planted on their tomb—don't go there. The king is heading there; that's where the heron dropped."

Aramis halted and hid in the shadows. Without being seen, he saw the pallid face of Mademoiselle de la Vallière, who, forgotten in her carriage, had at first been watching mournfully. But then, overwhelmed by jealousy, she had likewise entered the chapel. There, leaning on a pillar, she peered at the enclosure, where the smiling monarch signaled to Madame de Montespan to come and not be afraid. She approached him and took the hand offered by the king, who plucked the first feather of the heron that had been strangled by the falcon. The king attached the feather to his beautiful companion's hat. And she, smiling in turn, tenderly kissed the hand that had proffered this gift. The king turned crimson with pleasure and he gazed at Madame de Montespan with the flames of love and desire.

"What will you give me in exchange?" he asked her.

She broke off a tuft from the cypress and presented it to the king, who was intoxicated with hope.

"It's a dismal gift," Aramis whispered to d'Artagnan, "this cypress is shading a grave."

"Yes, and this is the grave of Raoul de Bragelonne," said d'Artagnan aloud. "Raoul, who is sleeping next to his father under that cross."

A groan resounded behind them. They saw a woman faint. Mademoiselle de la Vallière had seen everything, and now she had heard everything.

"Poor thing!" murmured d'Artagnan, helping the women to place Mademoiselle de la Vallière inside her carriage. "From now on, it's her turn to suffer!"

That evening, d'Artagnan sat at the king's table, next to Messieurs Colbert and Aramis. The king was merry. He showed endless courtesy to his wife, and endless affection to his sister-in-law, who sat at his left and was very melancholy. It was like those calm lulls when the king read his mother's eyes to determine if she approved or disapproved of whatever he had just said. There was no question of including his mistress at this dinner. The king addressed Aramis two or three times, calling him "Monsieur Ambassador." This increased d'Artagnan's surprise at seeing his rebellious friend treated so wonderfully at court.

Standing up, the king offered the queen his hand and signaled to Colbert, whose eyes were glued to his master. Colbert took d'Artagnan and Aramis aside. The king started chatting with his sister, while his nervous brother, his mind elsewhere, talked to the queen but kept glimpsing his wife and his brother from the corner of his eye.

The conversation among Aramis, d'Artagnan, and Colbert dealt with indifferent topics. They spoke about earlier ministers; Colbert described Mazarin's deeds and heard about Richelieu's actions.

D'Artagnan was astonished at seeing this man, with his thick eyebrows and low forehead, reveal so much knowledge and joyful humor. Aramis was amazed at that mental lightness, which enabled a serious man to put off a more serious topic, to which no one alluded even though all three interlocutors sensed its imminence.

One could tell by the embarrassed mien of the king's brother how troubled he was by the king's conversation with Henriette, his brother's wife. Her eyes were almost red. Was she about to lament? Was she about to cause a scandal in the very midst of the court?

The king took her aside, and, in a tone so gentle that it must have reminded her of the days when she was loved for herself, he said, "My sister, why have those beautiful eyes been weeping?"

"But, sire . . ."

"My brother is jealous, isn't he, my sister?"

She looked askance at her husband—an unerring sign that they were talking about him. "Yes," she said.

"Listen," said the king, "if your friends are compromising you, it isn't your husband's fault." He spoke so tenderly, encouraging her; and she, who had been suffering so much grief for a long time and whose heart was breaking, she nearly burst into tears.

"Come on, come on, my dear little sister," said the king. "Describe your sorrows. As your brother, I sympathize with them. As your king, I will end them."

Raising her lovely eyes, she mournfully answered, "It's not my friends who compromise me. They're absent or hidden. They've been disgraced in Your Majesty's eyes—yet they are so good, so loyal, so devoted."

"Are you referring to Guiche, whom I exiled at your husband's plea?"

"During this unjust exile, he keeps trying to get himself killed once a day!"

" 'Unjust,' my sister?"

"So unjust that if I didn't feel both the respect and the friendship that I've always felt toward you. . . ."

"Well?"

"Well, I would have asked my brother Charles, upon whom I can . . ."

The king shivered. "Go on."

"I would have asked him to make it clear to you that my husband and his favorite, Monsieur the Chevalier de Lorraine, must not destroy my honor and my happiness—destroy them with impunity."

"The Chevalier de Lorraine?" asked the king. "That somber figure?"

"And my mortal enemy. So long as that man lives in my house, where my husband lodges him and grants him full power, I will be the last woman in this kingdom."

"Then," the king said slowly, "you call your brother in England a better friend than I?"

"The facts speak for themselves, sire."

"And you would rather request help from . . ."

"From my country!" she exclaimed proudly. "Yes, sire!"

"You are the grandchild of Henry IV, my dear. Cousin and brother-in-law. Doesn't that make us full siblings?"

"Then act," said Henriette.

"Let's form an alliance!"

"Start."

"You say I've exiled Guiche unjustly."

"Oh, yes!" she replied, blushing.

"Guiche will come back."

"Excellent."

"And you also say that I'm wrong to keep the Chevalier de Lorraine in your home, where he poisons your husband's mind against you."

"Please retain what I'm saying, sire. The Chevalier de Lorraine, one day . . . Listen, if ever I have an awful end, remember that I've accused the Chevalier de Lorraine in advance. . . . He's capable of any crime!"

"The Chevalier de Lorraine will no longer bother you—you have my personal guarantee."

"That will be a true preliminary of our alliance, sire. I sign the preamble. . . . And now that you've done your part, tell me what my part should be."

"Instead of causing me friction with your brother Charles, you have to make me his friend—more intimate than ever."

"That's easy."

"Oh, not as easy as you think. In a normal friendship, people hug, they entertain—that's easy enough. And all it costs is a kiss or a reception. But in a political friendship—"

"Oh? It's a 'political friendship'?"

"Yes, my sister. And so, instead of embraces and banquets, we have to serve our friends live and well-equipped soldiers, vessels fully armed with cannon and provisions. The result is that our coffers are not always ready for such friendships."

"Ah, you're right," said Henriette. "For some time now the coffers of the king of England have been sounding a bit hollow."

"But you, my sister, you, who've got so much influence over

your brother, you might bring about something that no ambassador can ever achieve."

"For that, I would have to go to London, my dear brother."

"I've mulled it over," the king vividly retorted, "and I feel that such a trip would provide you with a bit of distraction—"

"Except," Henriette broke in, "that I might possibly fail. The king of England has dangerous advisers."

"You mean *female* advisers, don't you?"

"Precisely. If, by chance, Your Majesty had the intention—it's a mere hypothesis—had the intention of asking Charles II for a military alliance . . ."

"Military?"

"Yes. Well, Charles has seven female advisers: Mademoiselle Stewart, Mademoiselle Wells, Mademoiselle Gwyn, Miss Orchay, Mademoiselle Zunga, Miss Daws, and the Countess of Castelmaine. And this septet will tell the king that a war is very costly, and that it's better to give balls and suppers at Hampton Court than to equip ships of the line in Portsmouth and Greenwich."

"So your negotiation will miscarry?"

"Oh, those ladies destroy any negotiations that aren't theirs."

"Would you like to hear my idea, my sister?"

"Yes, go ahead."

"By searching all around you, you might have found a female adviser to take to the king—a woman whose eloquence would paralyze the ill will of that septet."

"A good idea, sire. I'll look for her."

"You'll find her."

"I hope so."

"She would have to be very pretty—a pleasant face is better than an ugly face, isn't it?"

"Definitely."

"A woman with a quick, playful, audacious mind?"

"Certainly."

"An aristocrat—enough of one, that is, to approach the king without awkwardness. And as minor a one as not to worry about the dignity of her breeding."

"Exactly."

"And she should know a little English." Henriette then cried out: "My goodness! Someone like Mademoiselle de Kéroualle, for instance."

"Yes!" said Louis XIV. "You've found her. . . . It's you who've found her, my sister."

"I'll take her along. I assume she won't mind."

"Not at all. First, I'll name her plenipotentiary seductress, and then I'll add jointures to her title."

"Fine."

"I can already picture you en route, dear little sister, and you've been consoled for all your grief."

"I'll sail on two conditions. First of all, I have to know what I'm negotiating."

"This is it. The Dutch, as you know, insult me daily in their gazettes and with their republican stance. I dislike republics."

"I can imagine, sire."

"It pains me to see those 'kings of the sea'—that's what they dub themselves—prevent France from trading in the Indies. Their vessels will soon occupy all the European ports—and that's too close for comfort, my sister."

"But they're your allies."

"That's why they were wrong to strike that medal—you know the one I mean. It depicts Holland making the sun stop, like Joshua, and it says: 'The sun has stopped before me.' That's not very fraternal, is it?"

"I thought you'd forgotten that awful business."

"I never forget anything, my sister. And if my true friends, such as your brother Charles, are willing to support me . . ."

Henriette was pensive.

"Listen," the king went on, "we can share the empire of the oceans. For this division, which England submitted to, couldn't I constitute the second half as ably as the Dutch?"

"We've got Mademoiselle de Kéroualle to deal with that issue," said Henriette.

"Your second condition, if you please, my sister?"

"My husband's consent."

"You'll have it."

"Then I'm on my way, my brother."

Upon hearing those words, Louis XIV turned toward the corner where Colbert was conversing with Aramis and d'Artagnan. The king nodded at his minister. Colbert broke off his chitchat with Aramis. "Monsieur, would you like to talk business now?"

D'Artagnan discreetly withdrew. He headed toward the fireplace, where he remained within earshot of the king. Louis's brother nervously walked toward the monarch, whose face was animated. His brow expressed a redoubtable will that brooked no contradiction in France and would soon brook none in Europe. "Monsieur," the king addressed his brother, "I am unhappy with the Chevalier de Lorraine. Since you do him the honor of protecting him, advise him to go traveling for a few months."

These words collapsed like an avalanche on the younger brother, who adored his favorite and focused all his affection on him. "In what way has the chevalier displeased Your Majesty?" He glared furiously at his wife.

"I will tell you once he's gone," replied the impassive monarch. "And once Henriette has sailed to England."

"England!" her stupefied husband muttered.

"Within a week, my brother, while we two will go where I say." And the king spun around after smiling at his brother to mellow the bitterness of those two bits of news.

Meanwhile, Colbert was still chatting with Aramis: "Monsieur, now is the time for us to reach an understanding. I've reconciled you with the king, which I owed anyway to a man of your merit. But since you've shown me friendship a few times, you now have the opportunity to offer me proof. Besides, you're more French than Spanish. Please be frank: can we rely on Spain's neutrality if we undertake anything against the Netherlands?"

"Monsieur," replied Aramis, "Spain's interest is quite clear. Our policy is to promote friction between the rest of Europe and Holland, a country that is still resented for the freedom it has achieved. However, the king of France has an alliance with Holland. And you are not unaware of the fact that such a war would be a maritime war, something that I believe France is in no position to wage."

Turning at that moment, Colbert spotted d'Artagnan, who was seeking an interlocutor during the king's private dialogue with his brother. Colbert summoned d'Artagnan. Then he whispered to Aramis, "We can talk to d'Artagnan, can't we?"

"Oh, certainly!" replied the ambassador.

"We were saying, Monsieur d'Alameda and I, that a war with the Netherlands would be a maritime war."

"That's obvious," the musketeer responded.

"And how do you feel about it, Monsieur d'Artagnan?"

"I think we would need a huge land army in order to wage that maritime war."

"Excuse me?" said Colbert, who thought he'd heard wrong.

"Why a land army?" asked Aramis.

"Because if the king doesn't have the British with him, he'll be defeated at sea, and if he's defeated at sea, he'll soon be invaded, either by the Dutch in the ports or by the Spaniards on land."

"What if Spain remains neutral?" said Aramis.

"Neutral so long as the king is the strongest," retorted d'Artagnan.

Colbert admired that sagacity, which never focused on an issue without a thorough examination. Aramis smiled. He knew that when it came to diplomats, d'Artagnan acknowledged no master. Colbert, who like all haughty men cherished his fantasy with a certainty of success, recommenced: "Who says, Monsieur d'Artagnan, that the king has no navy?"

"Oh, I'm not concerned with those details. I'm a mediocre mariner. Like all nervous people, I hate the sea. Nevertheless, I assume that since France has a port with two hundred heads, we would have sailors."

From his pocket, Colbert produced a small oblong notebook whose pages were divided into two columns. The first column listed the names of ships, the second column listed the number of cannon and men who would equip those vessels. "I had the same idea as you," Colbert said to d'Artagnan, "and I've had a list made of all the vessels we've added up. Thirty-five vessels."

"Thirty-five vessels?! That's impossible!" cried d'Artagnan.

"Something like two thousand cannon," added Colbert.

"That's what the king possesses at this moment. Thirty-five vessels make three squadrons, but I want five."

"Five!" cried Aramis.

"They will be afloat by the end of this year, gentlemen. The king will have fifty vessels of the line. We can wage war with that number, can't we?"

"Building ships," said d'Artagnan, "is difficult but possible. But how will we arm them? France has no foundries or military shipyards."

"Listen!" Colbert retorted, beaming. "I've been installing them for the past eighteen months—don't you know? Are you acquainted with Monsieur d'Infreville?"

"D'Infreville?" d'Artagnan rejoined. "No."

"He's my discovery. And his specialty is making workers work. He was the man who cast the cannon in Toulon and cut down the forest of Burgundy. Now, you may not believe what I'm about to tell you, Monsieur Ambassador: I've had another idea."

"Oh, Monsieur?" said Aramis courteously. "I believe you."

"Relying on the character of our Dutch allies, I thought to myself, They are merchants, they are friends with the king, they will be happy to sell His Majesty whatever they manufacture for themselves. And so, the more we buy . . . Oh, I have to add something: I've got Forant. . . . Do you know Forant, d'Artagnan?" Colbert was forgetting himself. He had addressed the captain purely as d'Artagnan, like the king.

But the captain smiled. "No," he replied, "I don't know him."

"He's another discovery of mine. His specialty is purchasing. He's bought 330,000 pounds of cannonballs for me, 200,000 pounds of gunpowder, 12 shiploads of northern lumber, plus tinder, grenades, pitch, tar, and whatnot. And for seven percent less than if all those items had been manufactured in France."

"That's quite an idea," replied d'Artagnan, "casting Dutch cannonballs that will return to the Dutch!"

"Isn't that so? With a loss too." And Colbert burst into guffaws. He was delighted with his joke. "Furthermore," he added, "those same Dutchmen are making something for our king: six vessels identical with the best ships in their navy. Destouches . . . Ah! You may not know Destouches?"

"No, monsieur."

"His eyes are so discerning that when a new boat is launched, he can instantly spot its defects and its merits. That's invaluable, you know! Nature is really bizarre. Well, this Destouches struck me as being useful in a port, and now he's supervising the construction of six vessels with seventy-eight cannon, which the Dutch are building for His Majesty. As a result, my dear Monsieur d'Artagnan, if the king wanted to fight the Dutch, he'd have a very nice fleet. And you know better than anyone else if our land army is good."

D'Artagnan and Aramis exchanged glances, admiring the secret work that this man had been doing in a few brief years. Colbert understood them and he was touched by this flattery, the best of its kind.

"If we in France don't know whether our land army is good, then foreigners are even less informed."

"That is why," said Colbert, "I was telling Monsieur Ambassador that if Spain promises its neutrality and England helps us—"

"If England helps you," said Aramis, "then I'll vouch for Spain's neutrality."

"We can shake on it," Colbert promptly said with his brusque bonhomie. "And apropos Spain, Monsieur d'Alameda, you don't have the Golden Fleece. Just the other day, I heard the king state that he would rather you wore the Grand Ribbon of Saint Michael."

Aramis bowed.

Oh! d'Artagnan thought to himself. Too bad Porthos isn't here! How many yards of ribbon it would take to circle his girth! Good Porthos!

"Monsieur d'Artagnan," replied Colbert, "this is *entre nous*. I'd bet that you'd be inclined to lead the musketeers to Holland, wouldn't you? Can you swim?" And he burst out laughing like a man in an excellent mood.

"I can swim like a fish," d'Artagnan retorted.

"Ah! But Holland has rough passages through canals and

marshes, Monsieur d'Artagnan, and the best swimmers drown there."

"That's my job," the musketeer responded, "to die for His Majesty. Still, in wartime one seldom finds a lot of water without a little fire. And so I declare in advance that I will do my best to choose fire. I'm getting long in the tooth, and water makes me freeze. Fire warms us, Monsieur Colbert." And in making that statement, d'Artagnan was so attractive with his vigor and his youthful pride that Colbert, in his turn, couldn't help admiring him. D'Artagnan noticed the effect of his words and he remembered that a good businessman sets a high price on his valuable merchandise. He therefore fixed the price ahead of time.

"So we're going to the Netherlands," said Colbert.

"Yes," replied d'Artagnan. "Only . . ."

"Only . . . ?"

"Only we have to deal with the issues of interest and pride. The captain of the musketeers receives a handsome salary. But you have to realize that we now have the king's guards and the king's military household. A musketeer captain should either command all those forces, in which case he'd require a hundred thousand pounds a year for his goods and entertainment expenses . . ."

"Do you honestly believe that the king would dicker with you?" asked Colbert.

"Ah, monsieur! You don't understand!" d'Artagnan retorted, certain he had carried the day in regard to the issue of interest. "I'm an old captain; I used to be head of the king's guard and I had precedence over the field marshals of France. Now, once I was in the trenches together with two men who were my equals in rank: the captain of the guards and the colonel in charge of the Swiss mercenaries. I myself would never put up with that. Old habits are hard to break."

Colbert felt the blow. However, he had prepared for it. "I've been thinking about what you just said."

"Namely, monsieur?"

"We were talking about canals and marshes where men can drown."

"And so?"

"Well, if a man drowns it's for lack of a boat, a plank, a stick."

"No matter how small a stick," said d'Artagnan.

"Precisely," said Colbert. "And I've never heard of a French field marshal drowning."

D'Artagnan, turning pale with delight, went on in a firm tone. "The French would be very proud of me if I were a field marshal. But a man would have to have led an expedition in order to be given a field marshal's baton."

"Monsieur," said Colbert, "here is my notebook, which I'd like you to study. It contains a campaign plan for an army corps, whom the king will place under your command for the campaign next spring."

Shivering, d'Artagnan took the notebook. And, with their fingers touching, the minister loyally shook hands with the musketeer. Colbert then said, "Monsieur, both of us have been seeking revenge over one another. I've begun. Now it's your turn!"

"I will make amends for you, monsieur, and I beg you to tell the king that I will win a victory at my very first opportunity or I will die."

"Then," said Colbert, "I'll have them immediately embroider the golden fleur-de-lys for your field marshal's baton."

The next day, Aramis, who was heading for Madrid in order to negotiate Spain's neutrality, came to embrace d'Artagnan in his mansion. The two friends hugged for a long time. "We have to love each other for four," said d'Artagnan. "There are only two of us left."

"And you may never see me again, dear d'Artagnan," said Aramis. "If you only knew how much I care for you! I'm old, I'm faded. I'm dead."

"My friend," said d'Artagnan, "you'll outlive me. Diplomacy orders you to live—whereas honor condemns me to die."

"Bah, Monsieur Field Marshal! Men like us die only when we're satiated with joy and glory."

"Ah!" replied d'Artagnan with a sad smile. "At present, Your Grace, I have no craving for either."

They embraced again, and two hours later they went their separate ways.

Monsieur d'Artagnan's Death

Contrary to what usually occurs in politics and morals, each man kept his promises and honored his obligations.

The king recalled Monsieur de Guiche and drove out the Chevalier de Lorraine, which sickened the king's brother.

Henriette sailed to London, where she was so good at getting her brother, Charles II to listen to political advice from Mademoiselle de Kéroualle, that the alliance between France and England was signed; and the British vessels, carrying French gold worth millions, conducted a dreadful campaign against the Dutch navy. The British king had promised Mademoiselle de Kéroualle a bit of gratitude for her good advice: he made her Duchess of Portsmouth.

Colbert had promised the king vessels, ammunition, and victories. He kept his word, as we know.

Finally, Aramis, who could be least relied on, wrote to Colbert about the negotiations in Madrid:

Monsieur Colbert,

I have the honor of sending you Reverend Father d'Oliva, the general ad interim of the Society of Jesus, my provisional successor.

The Reverend Father will explain to you that I direct all the order's affairs concerning France and Spain, but that I do not wish to retain the title of general: it would shed too much light on the progress of the negotiations with which His Catholic Majesty is willing to charge me. I will reassume this title by order of His Majesty when the assignment that I have undertaken with you, for the greater glory of God and His Church, will be carried out to a good end.

Reverend Father d'Oliva will also instruct you, monsieur, about the consent granted by His Catholic Majesty to the signing of a treaty that assures the neutrality of Spain in case of a war between France and the Netherlands.

This consent would be valid even if England were to be satisfied with remaining neutral instead of being active.

As for Portugal, about which you and I have spoken, monsieur, I can assure you that Portugal will contribute all its resources to aid the Very Christian King in his war.

I beg you, Monsieur Colbert, to maintain your friendship with me and also to believe in my profound devotion and to place my respect at the feet of His Very Christian Majesty.

Signed: THE DUKE OF ALAMEDA

Aramis had thus achieved more than he had promised. They now had to find out if the king, Monsieur Colbert, and Monsieur d'Artagnan would be loyal to one another.

In the spring, as Colbert had predicted, the land army entered the campaign. It preceded, in a magnificent order, the court of Louis XIV; the latter, taking off on horseback amid carriages carrying ladies and courtiers, brought the kingdom's elite to that bloody celebration. The army officers, it is true, had no music other than the artillery of the Dutch forts; but that was enough for a huge number of men, who found honor, advancement, fortune, or death in that war. Monsieur d'Artagnan, who commanded a corps of twelve thousand men—cavalry and infantry—was ordered to capture the different strongholds that constitute the vital centers of the strategic network known as Friesland.

Never had a military expedition been led more gallantly. The officers knew that their master, as cunning and prudent as he was brave, would never sacrifice a man or an inch of ground unless it were necessary. He had the old habits of war: live off the countryside, and keep the soldiers singing and the enemy weeping. The captain of the musketeers placed all his pride in showing that he knew what he was doing. No opportunities had ever been chosen more carefully, no surprise raids had ever been supported more powerfully, no mistakes of the enemy had ever been profited from more thoroughly. Within a single month, d'Artagnan's army had conquered a dozen small forts.

For five days now, they had been besieging the thirteenth. D'Artagnan had his men open the trenches although he didn't seem to think that these men would ever surrender. In d'Artagnan's army, the pioneers and the laborers were filled with zeal, ideas, and rivalries because he treated them like soldiers, he knew how to make their task glorious, and he never let them be killed unless he couldn't prevent it. One should therefore have seen them churning up the marshy Dutch soil. According to the soldiers, these clay bogs and these peat bogs melted like butter in the vast skillets of Friesian housewives.

Monsieur d'Artagnan dispatched a courier to the king, informing him of the latest French successes. And this news intensified His Majesty's excellent mood and his inclination to entertain the ladies. Monsieur d'Artagnan's victories lent the king so much majesty that Madame de Montespan now referred to him as Louis the Invincible. As a result, Mademoiselle de la Vallière, who nicknamed him Louis the Victorious, went way down in his favor. Furthermore, her eyes were often red, and for an invincible man nothing is as unpleasant as a mistress who keeps weeping while everyone else around him is smiling. Mademoiselle de la Vallière's star was fading in the clouds and tears on the horizon! In contrast, Madame de Montespan's gaiety increased with the king's triumph, consoling him for any disasters.

Since he owed his good fortune to Monsieur d'Artagnan, the monarch wanted to acknowledge these services; and so he wrote to Monsieur Colbert:

> We have to keep a promise that we made to Monsieur d'Artagnan, who keeps his promises. I hereby notify you that it is time for me to keep my word. You will be apprised of all details in due course.
>
> LOUIS

Next, Colbert, who was retaining d'Artagnan's envoy, handed him a letter to d'Artagnan as well as a small, gold-encrusted ebony coffer, which didn't look big but was probably very heavy, for the messenger was provided with five guards to help him carry it. At daybreak, those men arrived in front of the fortress that Monsieur d'Artagnan was besieging, and they presented themselves at the general's lodgings. They were told that Monsieur d'Artagnan had been held back by a sortie that the crafty commander of the stronghold had attempted on the previous evening. The fortress had been destroyed and seventy-seven men had been killed. The repairs had begun, and d'Artagnan had just left with a dozen grenadier companies to continue the reconstruction.

Ordered to seek Monsieur d'Artagnan wherever he might be, and at any time day or night, the messenger and his escorts galloped toward the trenches. They spotted Monsieur d'Artagnan out in the open, with his long cane, his gold-laced hat, and his large gilded sleeves. He was biting his white mustache while his left hand was shaking off the dust thrown on him by the cannonballs as they thrashed the soil.

In this terrible hail of fire, which whistled through the air, the men saw officers shoveling, soldiers trundling wheelbarrows, and vast, rising fascines, dragged or lugged by ten or twenty men, covering the front of the trench. The trench was shielded to its very heart by the general's furious effort, which animated his soldiers.

Within three hours, everything had been restored. D'Artagnan began talking more gently. He was entirely calm when the captain of the pioneers, clutching his hat, informed him that the trench was inhabitable. Scarcely had this man spoken than a cannonball sliced through one leg, and he collapsed in d'Artagnan's arms. D'Artagnan lifted him up and, with soothing, tranquil words, he carried him down into the trench amid the enthusiastic applause of the regiments.

The ardor was now gone—this was delirium. Two companies sneaked off and dashed toward the outposts, which they immediately wiped out. When their comrades, whom d'Artagnan had a hard time restraining, saw them lodged on the bastions, they likewise raced forward. And soon a furious charge assaulted the counterscarp on which the safety of the stronghold depended. D'Artagnan realized that there was only one way to stop his army: he had to lodge it in the fort. He pushed all his men to two breaches, which the enemies were busy repairing. The shock was dreadful. Eighteen companies participated in it, while d'Artagnan and the rest of the soldiers got to within half a cannon-shot of the stronghold in order to support the assault by echelons.

The French distinctly heard the cries of the Dutchmen skewered by d'Artagnan's grenadiers. The fighting grew more and more ferocious, the Dutch commander more and more desperate as he disputed his position foot by foot. In order to finish the battle and squelch the endless booming of the cannon, d'Artagnan sent out a fresh column, which drilled through the still solid posts. Then, amid the shooting, he saw the the terrified retreat of the besieged as they were chased over the ramparts.

It was at this moment that the general, breathing freely and cheerfully, heard a voice at his side: "Monsieur, from Monsieur Colbert, if you please."

D'Artagnan broke the seal of the letter, which read:

> Monsieur d'Artagnan,
>
> The king has charged me with informing you that he has named you Field Marshal of France, as a reward for your fine services and the honor that you bring to his weapons.
>
> The king, monsieur, is delighted with the victories you have won; and he commands you, above all, to finish the siege that you have begun and to complete it with good fortune for you and success for him.

D'Artagnan stood there, his face flushed, his eyes sparkling. He looked up in order to see the progress of his troops on those walls, which were enveloped in red and black whirlwinds.

"I've finished," he told the messenger. "The city will surrender within fifteen minutes."

He continued reading:

> This coffer, Monsieur d'Artagnan, is my personal present. You will not regret seeing that, while you warriors draw your swords to defend the king, I promote the peaceful arts to create tributes that are worthy of you.
>
> I recommend myself to your friendship, Monsieur Field Marshal, and I beg you to believe in my full friendship for you.
>
> COLBERT

D'Artagnan, intoxicated with joy, signaled to the messenger, who came over holding the coffer. But just as the field marshal was about to look at it, a powerful explosion rocked the ramparts, making him focus on the city. "That's odd," he said. "I don't see the king's flag on the walls and I don't hear the drums indicating the surrender."

He sent out three hundred fresh soldiers under an eager officer and he commanded him to beat another breach. Then, more tranquil, he turned back to the coffer, which the envoy was holding out to him. It belonged to d'Artagnan—he had earned it.

D'Artagnan was just reaching out to open the coffer when a cannonball fired from the city smashed the coffer and struck him squarely in the chest. He fell back on a sloping pile of soil, while the field marshal's baton, slipping from the mangled sides of the coffer, rolled under his failing hand. D'Artagnan tried to get up. The others assumed he had been felled but not wounded. But then the terrified officers let out a dreadful shriek: the marshal was covered with blood, and the pallor of death rose gradually to his noble face.

Leaning on the arms extended to him from all directions, d'Artagnan peered once more at the fortress, trying to make out the white flag on the crest of the main bastion. His ears, already deaf to the noises of life, feebly caught the booming of the drums announcing victory. Then, clutching the baton with its fleur-de-lys embroideries on velvet, he gazed down at it. His eyes no longer had the strength to glimpse the sky. He collapsed, muttering those strange words that, to his surprised men, sounded like cabalistic spells. Those words had once represented so many things in this world, but were understood only by this dying man:

"Athos, Porthos, good-bye! Aramis, good-bye forever!"

Of the four valiant men whose history we have told, there remained only a single body. God had taken their souls.